# SYLVIA

## By Upton Sinclair

SYLVIA

LOVE'S PILGRIMAGE

PLAYS OF PROTEST

THE FASTING CURE

THE JUNGLE

THE INDUSTRIAL REPUBLIC

THE METROPOLIS

THE MONEYCHANGERS

SAMUEL THE SEEKER

KING MIDAS

PRINCE HAGEN

THE JOURNAL OF ARTHUR STIRLING

MANASSAS

THE OVERMAN

# SYLVIA

*A NOVEL*

—— BY ——

UPTON SINCLAIR

THE JOHN C. WINSTON COMPANY
PHILADELPHIA                    CHICAGO

Republished 1976
Scholarly Press, Inc., 22929 Industrial Drive East
St. Clair Shores, Michigan 48080

Copyright, 1913, by
THE JOHN C. WINSTON CO.

Library of Congress Catalog Card Number:  79-115276
Standard Book Number 403-00291-5

To

THE PEOPLE AT HOME

# CONTENTS

### Book I
Sylvia Loves . . . . . . . . . . . . . . . . . . . . . . . . 11

### Book II
Sylvia Lingers . . . . . . . . . . . . . . . . . . . . . . . 147

### Book III
Sylvia Loses . . . . . . . . . . . . . . . . . . . . . . . 277

# SYLVIA

## BOOK I

*Sylvia Loves*

## § 1

THIS is the story of Sylvia Castleman, of her
love and her marriage. The story goes back to
the days of her golden youth; but it has to be
told by an old woman who had no youth at all,
and who never dreamed of having a story to
tell. It begins with scenes of luxury among the
proudest aristocracy of the South; it is told by
one who for the first thirty years of her life was
a farmer's wife in a lonely pioneer homestead in
Manitoba, and who, but for the pictures and stories
in magazines, would never have known that such
a world as Sylvia Castleman's existed.

Yet I believe that I can tell her story. Eight
years of it I lived with her, so intensely that it
became as my own existence to me. And the
rest I gathered from her lips, even to the tiniest
details. For years I went about my daily tasks
with Sylvia's memories as a kind of radiance
about me, like a rainbow that shimmers over the
head of a plodding traveler. In the time that
I knew her, I never came to the end of her
picturesque adventures, nor did I ever know
what it was to be bored by them. The incident
might be commonplace—a bit of a flirtation,
the ordering of a costume, the blunder of a negro
servant; but it was always Sylvia who was telling
it—there was always the sparkle of her eyes, the

mischievous smile, the swift glow of her countenance. And as the story progressed, suddenly
would come some incident so wild that it would
make you catch your breath; some fantastic,
incredible extravagance, some strange, quixotic
trait of character. You would find yourself face
to face with an attitude to life out of the Middle
Ages, with some fierce, vivid passion that carried
you back even farther.

What a world it is! I know that it exists—
for Sylvia took me home with her twice. I saw
the Major wearing his faded gray uniform (it
was "Reunion Day") and discoursing upon the
therapeutic qualities of "hot toddies." I watched
the negro boy folding and unfolding the newspaper, because Mrs. Castleman was obeying her
physician and avoiding unnecessary exertion.
I shook hands with Master Castleman Lysle,
whose names were reversed by special decree of
the state legislature, so that the memory of his
distinguished ancestress might be preserved to
posterity. And yet it will always seem like a
fairy-story world to me. I can no more believe
in the courtly Bishop, praying over my unre-
pentant head, than I can believe in Don Quixote.
As for "Uncle Mandeville"—I could more easily
persuade myself that I once talked with Pan
Zagloba in the flesh.

I have Sylvia's picture on my desk—the youth-
ful picture that means so much to me, with its
strange mixture of coquetry and wistfulness, of
mischief and tenderness. Downstairs in the

dining-room is the portrait of Lady Lysle, which is so much like her that strangers always mistook it. And if that be not enough, now and then Elaine steals into my room, and, silent as a shadow, takes her seat upon the little stool beside me, watching me with her sightless eyes. Her fingers fly swiftly at her knitting, and for hours, if need be, she moves nothing else. She knows by the sound of my pen that I am busy; with the wonderful acuteness of the blind she knows whether I am successful or not, whether what I write be joyous or painful.

How much she knows—much more than I dream, perhaps! I wonder about it, but I never ask her. Both Frank and I have tried to talk to her, but we cannot; it is cowardly, pitiful, perhaps—but we cannot! She used to ask questions in the beginning, but she must have felt our pain, for she asks no more; she simply haunts our home, the incarnation of the tragedy. So much of her mother she has—the wonderful red-brown eyes, the golden hair, the mobile, delicate features. But the sparkle of the eyes and the glow in the cheeks, the gaiety, the rapture—where are they? When I think of this, I clutch my hands in a sort of spasm, and go to my work again.

Or perhaps I go into Frank's den and see him sitting there, with his haggard, brooding face, his hair that turned gray in one week. He never asks the question, but I see it in his eyes: "How much have you done to-day?" A cruel task-

master is that face of Frank's! He is haunted
by the thought that I may not live to finish the
story.

The hardest thing of all will be to make you see
Sylvia as she was in that wild, wonderful youth
of hers, when she was the belle of her state, when
the suitors crowded about her like moths about
a candle-flame. How shall one who is old and
full of bitter memories bring back the magic
spirit of youth, the glamor and the glow of it,
the terrifying blindness, the torrent-like rush, the
sheer, quivering ecstasy of it?

What words shall I choose to bring before you
the joyfulness of Sylvia? When I first met her
she was twenty-six, and had known the kind of
sorrow that eats into a woman's soul as acid
might eat into her eyes; and yet you would think
she had never been touched by pain—she moved
through life, serene, unflinching, a lamp of cheer-
fulness to every soul who knew her. I met her
and proceeded to fall in love with her like the
veriest schoolgirl; I would go away and think
of her, and clasp my hands together in delight.
There was one word that kept coming to me;
I would repeat it over and over again—"Happy!
Happy! Happy!" She was the happiest soul
that I have ever known upon the earth; a veri-
table fountain of joy.

I say that much; and then I hasten to correct
it. It seems to be easy for some people to smile.
There comes to me another word that I used
to find myself repeating about Sylvia. She was

wise! She was wise! She was wise with a
strange, uncanny wisdom, the wisdom of ages
upon ages of womanhood—women who have
been mothers and counselors and homekeepers,
but above all, women who have been managers
of men! Oh, what a manager of men was Sylvia!
For the most part, she told me, she managed them
for their own good; but now and then the irresistible imp of mischievousness broke loose in her,
and then she managed them any way at all, so
long as she managed them!

Yet that, too, does her less than justice, I
think. For you might search all over the states
of the South, where she lived and visited, and
where now they mention her name only in whispers; and nowhere, I wager, could you find a
man who had ceased to love her. You might
find hundreds who would wish to God that she
were alive again, so that they might run away
with her. For that is the third thing to be noted
about Sylvia Castleman—that she was good.
She was so good that when you knew her you
went down upon your knees before her, and never
got up again. How many times I have seen the
tears start into her eyes over the memory of what
the imp of mischievousness and the genius of
management had made her do to men! How
many times have I heard her laughter, as she
told how she broke their hearts, and then used
her tears for cement to patch them up again!

### § 2

I REALIZE that I must make some effort to tell you how she looked. But when I think of words —how futile, stale and shopworn seem all the words that come to me. In my early days my one recreation was cheap paper-covered novels and historical romances, from which I got my idea of the *grand monde*. Now, when I try to think of words with which to describe Sylvia, it is their words that come to me. I know that a heroine must be slender and exquisite, must be sensitive and haughty and aristocratic. Sylvia was all this, in truth; but how shall I bring to you the thrill of wonder that came to me when I encountered her—that living joy she was to me forever after, so different from anything the books had ever brought me!

She was tall and very straight, free in her carriage; her look, her whole aspect was quick and eager. I sit and try to analyze her charm, and I think the first quality was the sense she gave you of cleanness. I lived with her much; I saw her, not merely made up for parties, but as she opened her eyes in the morning; and I cannot recall that I ever saw about her any of those things that offend us in the body. Her eyes were always clear, her skin always fair; I never saw her with a cold, or heard her speak of a headache. If she were tired, she would not tell you so—at least, not if she thought you needed her. If there was anything the matter with her, there was only one way you found it out—that she stopped eating.

She would do that at home, when someone was ill and she was under a strain. She would literally fade away before your eyes—but still just as cheerful and brave, laughing at the protests of the doctors, the outcries of her aunts and her colored "aunties." At such times she had a quite new kind of beauty, that seemed to strike men dumb; she used to make merry over it, saying that she could go out when other women had to shut themselves behind curtains. For thinness brought out every line of her exquisitely chiseled features; every quiver of her soul seemed to show—her tense, swift being was as if cut there in living marble, and she was some unearthly creature, wraith-like, wonderful, thrilling. There were poets in Castleman County; they would meet her in this depleted state, and behave after the fashion of poets in semi-tropical climates—stand with their knees knocking and the perspiration oozing out upon their foreheads; they would wander off by moonlight-haunted streams and compose enraptured verses, and come back and fall upon their knees and implore her to accept the poor, feeble tribute of their adoration.

I have seen her, too, when she was strong and happy, and then she would be well-made and shapely, with a charm of a more earthly sort. Then her color would be like the roses she always carried; and in each of her cheeks would appear the most adorable of dimples, and under her chin

2

another.   She had a nose that was very straight
and finely carved; and right in the center, under
the tip, the sculptor had put a tiny little groove.
She had also a chin that was very straight, and
right in the center of this was a corresponding
little groove.   You will laugh perhaps; but those
touches added marvelously to the expressiveness
of her countenance.   How they would shift and
change when, for instance, her nostrils quivered
with anger, or when the imp of mischievousness
took possession of her, and the network of quaint
wrinkles gathered round her eyes!

Dimples, I know, are an ultra-feminine property; but Sylvia's face was not what is ordinarily
called feminine—it was a kind of face that paint-
ers would give to a young boy singing in a church.
I used to tell her that it was the kind they gave
to angels of the higher orders; whereupon she
would put her arms about me and whisper, "You
old goose!"   She had a pair of the strangest red-
brown eyes, soft and tender; and then suddenly
lighting up—shining, shining!

I don't know if I make you see her.   I can
add only one detail more, the one that people
talked of most—her hair.   You may see her hair,
very beautifully done, in the portrait of Lady
Lysle.   The artist was shrewd and put the great
lady in a morning robe, standing by the open
window, the sunlight falling upon a cascade of
golden tresses.   The color of Sylvia's hair was
toned down when I knew her, but they told me
that in her prime it had been vivid to out-

rageousness. I sit before the painting, and the present slips away and I see her as she was in the glow of her youth—eager, impetuous, swept with gusts of merriment and tenderness, like a mountain lake in April.

So the old chroniclers report her, nine generations back, when she came over to marry the Governor of Massachusetts! They have her wedding gown preserved in a Boston Museum, and the Lysles have a copy of it, so that each generation can be married in one like it. But Sylvia was the first it became, being the first blonde since her great progenitor. How strange seems such a whim of heredity—not merely the color of the hair and eyes, the cut of the features, but a whole character, a personality hidden away somewhere in the germ-plasm, and suddenly breaking out, without warning, after a couple of hundred years!

## § 3

WHEN I think of Sylvia's childhood and all the hairbreadth escapes of which she told me, I marvel that she ever came to womanhood. It would seem to be a perilous part of the world to raise children in, with horses and dogs and guns, and so many half-tamed negroes—to say nothing of all the half-tamed white people. Sylvia had three younger sisters and whole troops of cousins —the Bishop's eleven children, and the children of Barry Chilton, his brother. I picture their existence as one long series of perilous escapes, with runaway horses, kicking mules and biting dogs, and negroes who shot and stabbed one another in sudden, ferocious brawls, or set fire to Castleman Hall in order that some other negro might be suspected and lynched.

Also there were the more subtle perils of the pantry and the green-apple orchard. I did not see any accident during my brief stay at the place, but I saw the dietetic ferocities of the family and marveled at them. It seemed to me that the life of that most precious of infants, Castleman Lysle, was one endless succession of adventures with mustard and ipecac and castor oil. I want somehow to make you realize this world of Sylvia's, and I don't know how I can do it better than by telling of my first vision of that future heir of all the might, majesty and dominion of the Lysles. It was one of the rare occasions when the Major was taking him on a journey. The old family horses were hitched to the old family carriage, and with a negro on the box, another walking at the horses' heads, a third riding on a mule behind, and a fourth sent ahead to notify the police, the procession set forth to the station. I know quite well that I shall be called a liar; yet I can only give my solemn word that I saw it with my own eyes—the chief of police, duly notified, had informed all the officers on duty, and the population of a bustling town of forty thousand inhabitants, in the United

States of America in the twentieth century, were
politely requested not to drive automobiles along
the principal avenue during the half-hour that
it took to convey Master Lysle to the train!
And of course such a "request" was a command
to all the inhabitants who were genteel enough
to own automobiles. Was not this the grandson
of the late General Castleman, the grand-nephew
of a former territorial governor? Was he not
the heir of the largest, the oldest and the most
famous plantation in the county, the future dis-
penser of favors and arbiter of social fates? Was
he not, incidentally, the brother of the loveliest
girl in the state, to whom most of the automobile
owners in the town had made violent love?

I would like to tell more about that world and
Sylvia's experiences in it—some of those amazing
tales! Of the negro boy who bit a piece out
of the baby's leg, because he had heard someone
say that the baby looked sweet enough to eat;
of the negro girl who heard a war-story about
"a train of gun-powder," and proceeded with
Sylvia's aid to lay such a train from the cellar
to the attic of the house. I would like to tell
the whole story of her girlhood, and the strange
ideas they taught her; but I have to pick and
choose, saving my space for the things that are
necessary to the understanding of her character.

Sylvia's education was a decidedly miscellaneous
one at first. "I think it is time the child had
some regular training," her great-aunt, Lady
Dee, would say to the child's mother. "Yes,

I suppose you are right," would be the answer.
But then Lady Dee would go, and Major Castleman would come in, observing, "It's marvelous
the way that child picks things up, Miss Margaret." (A habit from his courtship days, you
understand.) "We must be careful not to over-
stimulate her mind." To which his wife would
respond, agreeably, "I'm sure you know best,
Mr. Castleman."

Every morning Sylvia would go with her father
on his rounds to interview the managers of the
three plantations; the Major in his black broad-
cloth frock-coat, a wide black hat and a white
"bosom" shirt, riding horseback with an umbrella
over his head, and followed at a respectful distance by his "boy" upon a mule. On these
excursions Sylvia would recite the multiplication
table, and receive lessons in the history of her
country, from the point of view of its unrecon-
structed minority. Also she had lessons on this
subject from her great-aunt, who never paid one
of her numerous servants their small quarterly
stipend that she did not exclaim: "Oh, how I
*hate* the Yankees!"

I must not delay to introduce this great-aunt,
who was Sylvia's monitress in the arts and graces
of life, and left her on her death-bed such a curious
heritage of worldiness. Lady Dee was the last
surviving member of a younger branch of the
line of the Lysles. She was not a real countess,
like her great ancestress; the name "Lady" had
been given her in baptism. Early in the last

century she had come over the mountains in a
lumbering coach, with an escort of mounted
riders, to marry the Surveyor General of the
Territory. She still had a picture of this coach,
along with innumerable other treasures in cedar
chests in her attic: fan-sticks of carved ivory,
inlaid with gold; gold garter buckles with wonderful enameling; old seals and silver snuff-boxes;
rare jewels, such as white topazes and red
amethysts; and a whole trunkful of the curious
tiny silk parasols with which great ladies used
to protect their creamy complexions—no more
than ten inches across, and with handles of
inlaid and carven ivory. When Sylvia was a
little girl with two pigtails hanging down her
back, it was one of the joys of her life to explore
these treasures, and deck herself in faded ball
costumes and chains of jewels and gold.

Also, from Lady Dee she received contributions
to her moral training; not in set discourses, but
incidentally and by allusions. Rummaging in
the cedar chests she once came upon a miniature
which she had never seen before; a lady in whom
she recognized the eyes of the Lysles, and the
arrogance which all their portraits show. "Who
is this, Aunt Lady?" she asked; and the old
gentlewoman frowned and answered, "We never
speak of her, my dear. She is the one woman
who ever disgraced our name."

Sylvia hesitated a long time before she spoke
again. She had heard much of family skeletons
in the table-talk—but always other families.
"What did she do?" she asked, at last.

"She was married to three men," was the reply.

Again Sylvia hesitated. "You mean," she ventured—"you mean—at the same time?"

Lady Dee stared. "No, my dear," she said, gravely. "Her husbands died."

"But—but—" began the other, timidly, groping to find her way in a strange field of thought.

"If she had been a woman of delicacy," pronounced Lady Dee, "she would have been true to one love." Then, after a pause, she added, solemnly, "Remember this, my child. Think before you choose, for the women of our family are like Sterne's starling—when they have once entered their cage, they never come out."

It was Lady Dee who objected to the desultory nature of Sylvia's education, and began a campaign, as a result of which the Major sent her off to a "college" at the age of thirteen. You must not be frightened by this imposing statement, for it is easy to call yourself a "college" in the South. Sylvia was away for three years, during which she really studied, and acquired much more than the usual accomplishments of a young lady.

She had an extraordinarily capable mind; serene and efficient, like everything else about her. When I met her I was a woman of forty-five, who a few years before had broken with my whole past, having discovered the universe of knowledge. I had been like a starving person breaking into a well-filled larder, and stuffing myself greedily and promiscuously. I had taken upon myself the task of contending with other people's prejudices, and my rapture over Sylvia Castleman was partly the realization that here was a woman—actually a woman—who had no prejudices whatever. She wanted me to tell her all I knew; and it was a great delight to expound to her a new set of ideas, and see her mind go from point to point, leaping swiftly, laying hold of details, ordering, comparing—above all, applying. That you may have a picture of this mind in action, let me tell you what she did in her girlhood, all unassisted—how she broke with the religion of her forefathers.

## § 4

THAT brings me to the Bishop, Basil Chilton, who had come into the family by marriage to one of Sylvia's aunts. At the time of his marriage he had been a young Louisiana planter, handsome and fascinating. He had met Nannie Castleman at a ball, and at four o'clock in the morning had secured her promise to marry him before sunset. People said that he was half drunk at the time, and this was probably a moderate estimate, for he had been wholly drunk for a year or two afterwards. Then he had shot a man in a brawl and, despite the fact that he was a gentleman, had almost been punished for it. The peril had sobered him; a month or two later, at a Methodist revival, he was converted, made a sensational confession of his sins, and then, to the horror of his friends, became a preacher of Methodism.

To the Castlemans this was a calamity—to Lady Dee a personal affront. "Whoever heard of a gentleman who was a Methodist?" she demanded; and as the convert had no precedents to cite, she quarreled with him and for many years never spoke his name. Also it was hard upon Nannie Castleman—who had entered her cage and had to stay! They had compromised on the bargain that the children were to be brought up in her own faith, which was Very High Church. So now the unhappy preacher, later Bishop, sat in his study and wrote his sermons, while one by one his eleven children came of age, and danced and gambled and drank themselves to perdition in the very best form imaginable. When I met the family, the last of the daughters, Caroline, was just making her *début*, and her mother, nearly sixty, was the gayest dancer on the floor. It was the joke of the county, how the family automobile would first take the Bishop to prayer meeting, and then return to take the mother and the children to a ball.

Basil Chilton looked like an old-world diplomat, as I had come to conceive that personage from reading novels. He had the most charming manners—the kind of manners which cannot be cultivated, but come from nobility of soul. He was gentle and gracious even to servants; and yet imposing, with his stately figure and smooth, ascetic face, lined by care. He lived just a pony-ride from Castleman Hall, and almost every morning during vacations Sylvia would stop and spend a little while with him. People said that he loved her more than any of his own children.

So you can imagine what it meant when one day the girl said to him, "Uncle Basil, I have something to tell you. I've been thinking about it, and I've made up my mind that I don't believe in either heaven or hell."

Where had she got such an idea? She had certainly not learned it at the "college," for the institution was "denominational" and had no text-books of later date than 1850. Somewhere she had found a volume of Huxley's "Lay Sermons," but she had got nothing out of that, for the Major had discovered her reading page three, and had solemnly consigned the book to the flames. No, it was simply that she had been thinking for herself.

The Bishop took it well. He did not try to frighten her, he did not even show her his distress of mind. He told her that she was an angel, the very soul of purity and goodness, and that God would surely lead her to truth if only she kept herself humble. As Sylvia put it to me: "He knew that I would come back, and I knew that I would never come back."

And that was the situation between them to the very end—the bitter end. He always believed that she would learn to see things as he saw them. He died a year or so ago, the courtly old gentleman—consoled by the thought that he was now to meet his God and Sylvia face to face, and hear the former explain to the latter the difference between Divine Law and mere human ideas of Justice.

The rest of the family were not so patient as the Bishop. To have a heretic in the household was even worse than having a Methodist! Mrs. Castleman, who agreed with the Bible as she agreed with everything, was dumb with bewilderment; while the Major set to work to hunt out dusty volumes from the attic. He read every word of Paley's "Evidences" aloud to his daughter, and some of Gladstone's essays, and several other books, the very names of which she forgot. You may smile at this picture, but it was a serious matter to the Castlemans, who had based their morality upon the fear of fire and brimstone and the weeping and gnashing of teeth, and who kept Sylvia three months from school to impress such images upon her imagination.

There were several religious sects represented in the county. These were generally at war with one another, but they all made common cause in this emergency, and committees of old ladies from the "Christians," the "hard-shell Baptists," the "predestination Presbyterians," would come to condole with "Miss Margaret," and would kneel down in the parlor with Sylvia and pray for her salvation, shedding tears over the cream velour upholstery of the hand-carved mahogany sofas. A distant cousin who was "in orders," a young gentleman of charming presence and special training in dialectics, was called in to answer the arguments of this wayward young lady, and stayed for three days, probing deeply into his patient's mind—not merely her theological beliefs, but the attitude to life which underlay them. When he had finished he said to her, "My dear Sylvia, it is my opinion that you are the most dangerous person in this county." She told me the story, and added, "I hadn't the remotest idea what the man meant!" But I answered her that he had been perfectly right. In truth, he was a seer, that young clergyman!

## § 5

THERE was a general feeling that Sylvia had learned more than was good for her; and so the family made inquiries, and selected the most exclusive and expensive "finishing school" in New York, for the purpose of putting a stop to her intellectual development. And so we come to the beginning of Sylvia's wordly career, and to the visit she paid to Lady Dee—who now, at the age of ninety, felt herself failing rapidly, and wished to leave to her great-niece her treasures of worldly counsel.

Lady Dee was one of those quaint figures you meet in the South, who go to balls and parties

wnen they are old enough to be sewing the *layettes*
of their great-grandchildren.  I have seen a picture of her at the age of eighty-five, in a cerise-
colored silk ball-gown with a lace "bertha," her
white hair curled in front and done in a pile with
a coronet of diamonds.  You must imagine her
now, in an invalid's chair upon the gallery, but still
with her hair dressed as of old; telling to Sylvia
tales of her own young ladyhood—and incidentally, with such deftness that the girl never guessed
her purpose, introducing instruction in the strategy
and tactics of the sex war.

Life was short, according to Lady Dee, and the
future was uncertain.  A woman bloomed but
once, and must make the most of that.  To be
the center of events during her hour, that was
life's purpose; and to achieve it, it was necessary
to know how to hold men.  Men were sometimes
said to be strange and difficult creatures, but in
reality they were simple and easily handled.  The
trouble was that most women went blindly at
the task, instead of availing themselves of the
wisdom which their sex had been storing up for
ages, in the minds of such authorities as Lady Dee.

The old lady went on to expound the science
of coquetry.  I had read of the sex game, as it
is played in the *grand monde*, but I had never supposed that the players were as conscious and
deliberate as this veteran expert.  She even used
the language of battle: "A woman's shield, my
child, is her innocence; her sharpest weapon is
her *naïveté*.  The way to disarm a man's sus-

picions is to tell him what you're doing to him—
then you're sure he won't believe it!''

She would go into minute details of these Ama-
zonian arts: how to beguile a man, how to promise
to marry him without really promising, how to
keep him at the proper temperature by judicious
applications of jealousy. Nor was this sex war
to stop after the wedding ceremony—when most
women foolishly laid down their weapons. A
woman must sleep in her armor, according to
Lady Dee. She must never let her husband
know how much she loved him, she must make
him think of her as something rare and unattain-
able, she must keep him in a state where her
smile was the greatest thing in life to him. Said
the old lady, gravely: ''The women of our family
are famous for henpecking their husbands—they
don't even take the trouble to hide it. I've
heard your grandfather, the General, say that
it was all right for a man to be henpecked, if
only it was by the right hen.''

A training, you perceive, of a decidedly worldly
character; and yet there was nothing upon which
Sylvia's relatives laid more stress than the preserving of what they called her ''innocence.''
There were wild people in this part of the world—
high-spirited and hot-tempered, hard drinkers
and fast livers; there were deeds of violence,
and strange and terrible tales that you might
hear. But when these tales had anything to do
with sex, they were carefully kept from Sylvia's
ears. Only once had this rule been broken—an

occasion which made a great impression upon the child. The daughter of one of the neighboring families had eloped, and the dreadful rumor was whispered that she had traveled in a sleeping-car with the man, and been married at the end of the journey, instead of at the beginning.

And there was Uncle Mandeville, the youngest of the Major's brothers—half drunk, though Sylvia did not know it—pacing the veranda and discussing the offending bridegroom. "He should have been shot!" cried Mandeville. "The damned scoundrel, he should have been shot like a dog!" And suddenly he paused before the startled child. He was a giant of a man, and his voice had the power of a church-organ. He placed his hands upon Sylvia's shoulders, pronouncing in solemn tones, "Little girl, I want you to know that I will protect the honor of the women of our family with my life! Do you understand me, little girl?"

And Sylvia, awestricken, answered, "Yes, Uncle Mandeville." The worthy gentleman was so much moved by his own nobility and courage that the tears stood in his eyes; he went on, melodramatically, "With my life! With my life! And remember the boast of the Castlemans—that there was never a man in our family who broke his word, nor a woman with a stain upon her name!"

That had been in Sylvia's childhood. But now she was a young lady, about to start for the metropolis, and the family judged that the time

had come for her to be instructed in some of these
delicate matters. There had been consultations
between her mother and aunts, in which the
former had been prodded on to the performing
of one of the most difficult of all maternal duties.
Sylvia remembered the occasion vividly, for her
mother's agitation was painful to witness; she
led the girl solemnly into a darkened room, and
casting down her eyes, as if she were confessing
a crime, she said:

"My child, you will probably hear evil-minded
girls talking of things of which my little daughter
has never heard. When these things are discussed, I want you to withdraw quietly from the
company. You should remain away until vulgar
topics have been dismissed from the conversation. I want your promise to do this, my
daughter."

Her mother's sense of shame had communicated itself to Sylvia. At first she had been
staring wonderingly, but now she cast down her
own eyes. She gave the desired promise; and
that was all the education concerning sex that
she had during her girlhood. This experience
determined her attitude for many years—a min-
gling of shame and fear. The time had come for
her to face the facts of her own physical development, and she did so with agony of soul, and in
her ignorance came near to injuring her bodily
health.

Also, the talk had another consequence, over
which Mrs. Castleman would have been sorely

distressed had she known it. Though the girl
tried her best, it was impossible for her to avoid
hearing some of the "vulgar" conversation of the
very sophisticated young ladies at the "finishing
school." In spite of herself, she learned something of what sex and marriage meant—enough
to make her flesh creep and her cheeks burn with
horror and disgust. It seemed to her that she
could no longer bear to meet and talk to men.
When she came home for the Christmas holidays
and discovered that her mother was expecting a
child, the thought of what this meant filled her
with shame for both her parents; she wondered
how they could expect a pure-minded girl to love
them, when they had so degraded themselves.
So intense was this impression that it continued
over the Easter vacation, when she returned to
find the house in possession of the new heir of
all the might, majesty and dominion of the
Lysles.

## § 6

Miss Abercrombies "finishing school" was
located on Fifth Avenue, immediately opposite—
so the catalogue informed you—to the mansions
of the oldest Knickerbocker families. It was
Miss Abercrombie's boast that she had married
more than half her young ladies to millionaires,
and she took occasion to drop allusions to the
subject to all whom it might interest. She ran

her establishment upon an ingenious plan, about half her pupils being the daughters of Western buccaneers, who paid high prices, and the other half being the daughters of Southern aristocrats, accepted at reduced rates. So the young ladies from the West got the "real thing" in refinement, and the young ladies from the South made acquaintances whose brothers were "eligible."

Sylvia had always had everything that she wanted, and was under the impression that immense sums of money had been spent upon her upbringing. But among these new associates she found herself in the class of the poorest. She had never owned a dress which they would consider expensive, whereas the dresses of these girls were trimmed with real lace, and cost several hundreds of dollars each. It was a startling experience to many of them to discover that a girl who had so few jewels as Sylvia could be so haughty and self-possessed; which was, of course, just what they had come for—to acquire that superiority to their wealth which is the apex of culture in millionairedom.

So Sylvia became an uncrowned queen, and all the lumber princesses and copper duchesses and railroad countesses vied in entertaining her. They treated her to box-parties, where, duly chaperoned, they listened to possibly indecent musical comedies; and to midnight feasts where they imperiled their complexions with peanut butter and almond paste and chocolate creams and stuffed olives and anchovies and crackers and mustard pickles and fruit cake and sardines and plum pudding and sliced ham and salted almonds—and what other delicacies might come along in anybody's boxes from home. To aid in the digestion of these "goodies" Sylvia was taken out twice daily, and marched in a little private parade up Fifth Avenue, wearing a hat so large that all her attention was required to keep it on in windy weather, and so heavy that it made her head ache if the air were still; a collar so high that she could not bend her head to balance the hat; high-heeled shoes upon which she toddled with her feet crowded down upon the toes; and a corset laced so tight that her lower ribs were bent out of shape and her liver endangered. About the highest testimony that I can give to the altogether superhuman wonderfulness of Sylvia is that she stayed for two years at Miss Abercrombie's, and came home a picture of radiant health, eager, joyous—and lovely as the pearly tints of dawn.

She came home to prepare for her *début;* and what an outfit she brought! You may picture her unfolding the treasures in her big bedroom, which had been freshly done over in pink silk; her mother and aunts and cousins bending over the trays, and the negro servants hovering in the doorway, breathless with excitement, while the "yard-man" came panting up the stairs with new trunks. Such an array of hats and gowns and *lingerie*, gloves and fans, ribbons and laces, silk hose and satin slippers, beads and buckles!

The "yard-man," a negro freshly promoted from the corn-fields, went down into the kitchen with shining eyes, exclaiming, "I allus said dis house was heaven, and now I knows it, 'cause I seen dem 'golden slippers'!"

It was not a time for a girl to do much philosophizing; but Sylvia knew that these "creations" of Paris dressmakers had cost frightful sums of money, and she wondered vaguely why the family had insisted upon them. She had heard rumors of a poor crop last year, and of worries about some notes. Glad as the Major was to see her, she thought that he looked careworn and tired.

"Papa," she said, "I've been spending an awful lot of money."

"Yes, honey," he answered.

"I hope you don't think I have been extravagant, Papa."

"No, no, honey."

"I tried to economize, but you've no idea how things cost in New York, and how those girls spend money. My clothes—Mamma and Aunt Nannie *would* have me buy them——"

"It's all right, my child—you have only one springtime, you know."

Sylvia paused a moment. "I feel as if I ought to marry a very rich man, after all the money you've spent upon me."

Whereat the Major looked grave. "Sylvia," he said, "I don't want any daughter of mine to feel that she has to marry. I shall always be able to support my children, I hope."

This was noble, and Sylvia was grateful for it; but with that serene, observing mind of hers she could not help noting that if her father by any chance called her attention to some man of her acquaintance, it was invariably a "marriageable" man; and always there was added some detail as to the man's possessions. "Billy Harding's a fellow with a future before him," he would remark. "He's one of the cleverest business men I know."

Sylvia was also impressed with a comical phrase of her mother's, which seemed to indicate that that good lady classified poverty with small-pox and diphtheria. The Major had suggested inviting to supper a young medical student who was honest but penniless; and "Miss Margaret" replied, "I really cannot see what we have to gain by exposing our daughters to an undesirable marriage." Sylvia concluded that her family pinned its faith to the maxim of Tennyson's "Northern Farmer"—

"Doän't thou marry for munny, but goä wheer munny is!"

## § 7

You must have a glimpse of Castleman Hall as it was at the time of the *début*. The old house stands upon a hill, terraced on one side, and overlooking the river from a high bluff on the other. It is of red brick, originally square, with a two-storied portico and hanging balcony in front; later on there had been added two wings of white painted wood, for the library and conservatory—now nearly covered with red roses and Virginia creepers. On the afternoon of the great day there was a reception to all the married friends of the family. They came in conveyances of every kind, from family coaches to modern high-power limousines; they came in costumes varying from the latest Paris modes to the antebellum splendor of old Mrs. Tagliaferro, who hobbled cautiously over the polished hardwood floors, with the help of her gold-headed cane on one side, and her husband, the General, on the other. Once arrived, she laid her hands upon Sylvia's, and told her how pretty she was, and how she must contribute a new stone to the archway through which the Castlemans had marched to fame for so many generations. There had been many famous Castleman beauties, quavered the old gentleman, in his turn, but none more beautiful than the present one—save only, perhaps, her mother. (This last as "Miss Margaret" appeared at his elbow, clad in ample folds of gray satin and tulle.) So one by one ladies and gentlemen came up and delivered gallant speeches and grave exhortations, until Sylvia was overwhelmed with the sense of responsibility involved in being a daughter of the Castlemans.

And then came the evening, with the *début* dance for the young people. Ten years later I saw Sylvia in the gown she wore: white chiffon over white messaline, with roses and a string of

pearls. Wonderful she must have been that
night, at the age of eighteen, the climax of her
beauty; eager, glowing, a-quiver with excitement.
I picture her standing before the mirror, child-
ishly ravished by her own loveliness, her mother
and aunts, scarcely less excited, putting the final
touches to her toilette. I picture her girl friends
in the dressing-room and the hall, gossiping,
chattering, laughing; the buzz of excitement,
then the hush when she appeared, the cries of
congratulation and applause. I picture the downstairs rooms, decorated with lilies, magnolias and
white ribbons, the furniture covered with white
brocade, the chandeliers turned into great bells
of lilies, the soft light from white-shaded candles
flooding everything. I picture the swains, waiting eagerly at the foot of the staircase, each with
a bouquet for his chosen one in his hand. I can
hear the strains of the violins floating up the
staircase, and see the shimmering form of Sylvia
floating down, crowned with her dazzling glory
of golden hair. There was no one in Castleman
County who failed to realize that a belle was born
that night!

## § 8

IT was just a week after these festivities that
there occurred the death of Sylvia's great-aunt.
Nothing could have been more characteristic
than the method of her departure. She left home

and betook herself to an aristocratic boarding-house, kept by a "decayed gentlewoman" in New Orleans; she might be a long time a-dying, she said, and did not want anybody making a fuss over her. Also she did not care to have her nieces and nephews calling in to drop hints as to the disposition of her rosewood bedroom set, her miniature piano and her Queen Anne baby's crib. She left a will in which she bequeathed her property to her grand-niece, Sylvia Castle-man, to be held in trust for her until she was forty years of age. "Some man will take care of her while she is beautiful," she wrote, "but later on she may find use for my pittance." And finally the old lady put in a clause to the effect that the bequest was conditional upon her grand-niece's obeying her injunction to wear no mourning for her. "It is impossible to make a woman with brown eyes look presentable in black," she wrote. And this, you understand, in a document which had to be filed for probate! Most fortunate it was that all the editors of newspapers in the South are gentlemen, who can be relied upon not to print the news.

Sylvia obeyed the instructions of this extraor-dinary document, and felt it a solemn duty to go to entertainments, even with tears in her eyes. So now began a bewildering succession of dinners, dances and receptions, balls and suppers, house parties, hunting parties, auto parties, theatre parties. It speaks marvels for her constitution that she was able to stand the strain. When the last light had been extinguished she would drag herself upstairs to bed, a limp train hung over her limp arm, her feet aching in the tiny slippers and her back aching in the cruel stays. The Governor saw fit to appoint her as his "sponsor" at the state militia encampment; and so for ten days she would rise every morning at daybreak, ride out with an "escort" to witness guardmount, and remain in the midst of a rush of gaieties until three or four o'clock the next morning, when the nightly dance came to an end.

Sylvia always refused to give photographs of herself to men. It was part of her feeling about them that she could not endure the thought of her image being in their rooms. But her enterprising Aunt Nannie, the Bishop's wife, presented one to the editor of a metropolitan magazine, where it appeared under the heading of "A Reigning Beauty of the New South." It was taken up and reproduced in Southern papers, and after that Sylvia found that her fame had preceded her—everywhere she went new worshippers joined her train, and came to her home-town to lay siege to her.

You may perhaps know something about these Southern men. I had never dreamed of such, and I would listen spellbound for hours to Sylvia's tales of them. Men who, as Lady Dee had phrased it, had nothing to do but make love to their women! There were times when the realization of this brought me a shudder. I would see, in a sudden vision, the torment of a race of creatures who were doomed to spend their whole existence in the chase of their females; and the females devoting their energies to stinging them to fresh frenzies!

The men liked it; they liked nothing else in the world so much. "You may make me as unhappy as you please," they would tell Sylvia—"if only you will let me love you!" And Sylvia, in the course of time, became reconciled to letting them love her. She learned to play the game—to play it with constantly increasing excitement, with a love of mischief and a thirst for triumph.

She would show her latest victim twenty moods in one evening, alluring him, repelling him, stimulating him, scorning him, pitying him, bewildering him. When they met again, she would be completely absorbed in the conversation of another man. He would be reduced at last to begging for a chance to talk seriously with her; and she, pretending to be touched, might let him call, and show him her loveliest and most sympathetic self. So, before he realized it, he would be caught fast. If he happened to be especially conspicuous, or especially rich, or especially otherwise worth while, she might take the trouble to goad him to desperation. Then he would be ready to give proofs of his devotion—to go through West Point, or to be made a judge, if only she would promise to marry him. Each of these tasks she set to an unfortunate wretch, who went off and performed it—and came back and found her married!

## § 9

Such were the customs of young ladies in Sylvia's world; but I must not fail to mention that she had sometimes the courage to set her face against this "world." For instance, she had a prejudice against drunkenness. She stood fast by the bold precedent that she would never permit an intoxicated person to dance with her; and terrible humiliations she put upon two or three who outraged her dignity. They hid in their rooms in an agony of remorse, and sent deputations of their friends to plead for pardon, and went away from home and stayed for months, until Sylvia consented to take them into her favor again.

She took her place upon the icy heights of her maidenhood, and was not to be drawn therefrom. There were only two men in the world, outside of fathers and uncles and cousins, who could boast that they had ever kissed her. About both of these I shall tell you in the course of time. She was famous among other men for her reserve—they would make wagers and lay siege to her for months, but no one ever dared to claim that he had secured his kiss.

With boyish frankness they would tell her of these things; they told her all they thought about her. I have never heard of men who dealt so frankly in personalities, who would discuss a woman and her various "points" so openly to her face. "Miss Sylvia, you look like all your roses to-night."—"Miss Sylvia, I swear you've got the loveliest eyes in the world!"—"You'll be fading soon now; you'd better marry while you've got a chance!"—"I came to see if you were as pretty as they say, Miss Castleman!"

She would laugh merrily. "Are you disappointed? Don't you find me ado'able?"

So far I have made no attempt to give you an idea of Sylvia's way of speaking English. It was a drawl so charming that Miss Abercrombie had given instructions not to mar it by rash corrections. I can only mention a few of her words— which is as if I gave you single hairs out of her golden glory. She always spoke of "cannles." She could, of course, make nothing of the letter r, and said "funnichuh" and "que-ah" and "befoah mawnin'." There had been an English heiress at Miss Abercrombie's who had won the whole school over to "gel," but when Sylvia arrived, she swept the floor with "go-il." The most irresistible word of all I thought was "bug;" there is no way to indicate this by spelling—you must simply take three times as long to say it, lingering over the vowel sound, caressing it as if you thought that "bu-u-u-gs" were the most "ado'able" things in all the "wo'il."

Sylvia learned to apply with deadly effect the maxim of Lady Dee—that a woman's sharpest weapon is her *naïveté*. "Beware of me!" she would warn her helpless victims. "Haven't you heard that I'm a coquette? No, I'm not joking. It's something I'm bitterly ashamed of, but I can't help it; I'm a cold-hearted, selfish creature, a deliberate breaker of hearts." And then, of course, the victim would thrill with excitement and exclaim, "See what you can do to me, Miss Sylvia! I'll send you armfuls of roses if you can break my heart!" You may judge how these competitions ended from a chance remark which Sylvia made to me—"When I look back upon my life, it seems to me that I waded in a river of roses."

The only protection which nature has vouchsafed against these terrors is the fact that sooner or later such cold and cruel huntresses themselves get snared. In the simile of "Sterne's starling," they are lured up to a certain cage, and after much hopping about and hesitating, much advancing and retreating, much chattering and chirping, they adorn themselves in satin robes and lace veils and lilies-of-the-valley, and to the sound of sweet strains from "Lohengrin" they enter the golden cage. And then, snap! the door is shut and locked fast, and the proprietor of the cage mounts guard over it—in Sylvia's part of the world with a shotgun in his hands.

§ 10

So I come to the time when this haughty lady was humbled; that is to say, the time of her meeting with Frank Shirley. Because it was through Harriet Atkinson that she came to know him, I must first tell you in a few words about that active and pushing young lady.

Harriet Atkinson was the one weak spot in the fortifications of respectability which Sylvia's parents had built up about her. Harriet's ancestors were Yankees, of the very most odious "carpet-bag" type. Her grandfather had been a pawnbroker in Boston, so fierce rumor declared; and her father was a street-railroad president, who purchased "red-neck" legislators for use in his business. Harriet herself was a brunette beauty, so highly colored that she looked artificial, no matter how hard she tried to look natural.

But in spite of these appalling facts, Harriet Atkinson was the most intelligent girl whom Sylvia had met during her three years at the "college." She had a wit that was irresistible, and also she understood people. You might spend weeks in her company and never be bored; whereas there were persons who could prove possession of the "very best blood in the South," but who were capable of boring you most frightfully when they got you alone for half an hour.

Sylvia was never allowed to go to Harriet's home, nor was Harriet ever asked to Castleman Hall. But Sylvia refused to give up her friend, and for a year she intrigued incessantly to force Harriet upon her hostesses, and to persuade her own suitors to call at the Atkinson home. In the end she married her off to the scion of a great family—with consequences which are to be told at a later stage of my story. The point for the present is that things happened exactly as Sylvia's aunts had predicted; through her intimacy with the undesirable Harriet Atkinson she was "exposed" to the acquaintance of several undesirable men, among them Frank Shirley.

Sylvia had known about the Shirleys from earliest childhood. She had heard the topic talked about at the family dinner-table, and had seen tears in her father's eyes when the final tragedy came. For the Shirleys were among the "best people," and this was not the kind of thing which was allowed to happen to such.

About twelve years previously the legislature had appropriated money for the building of a veterans' home, and the funds had been entrusted to a committee, of which Robert Shirley was treasurer. The project had lapsed for a couple of years, and when the money was called for, Robert Shirley was unable to produce it. Rumors leaked out, and there came a demand in the legislature for an accounting.

The Major was one of a committee of friends who were asked by the Governor to make a private investigation. They found that Shirley had deposited the money to his private bank account, after the unbusinesslike methods of a Southern gentleman. Checks had been drawn upon it; but there was evidence at the bank tending to show that the checks might not have been signed by Shirley himself. He had a younger brother, a spendthrift and gambler, whom he had indulged and protected all his life. Such were the hints which Sylvia had heard at home—when suddenly Robert Shirley proceeded to the state Capitol and requested the Governor to stop the investigation, declaring that he alone was to blame.

It was a terrible thing. Shirley was besought to fly, he was told by the Governor's own authority that he might live anywhere outside the state, and the search for him would be nominal. But he stood fast; the money was gone, and some one must pay the penalty. So the world saw the unprecedented spectacle of a man of "good family" standing trial, and receiving a sentence of five years in the penitentiary.

He left a broken-hearted wife and four children. Sylvia remembered the horror with which her mother and her aunts had contemplated the fate of these latter. Two girls, soon to become young ladies, and cut off from all hope of a future! "But, Mamma," Sylvia cried, "it isn't *their* fault!" She recollected the very tone of her mother's voice, the dying away to a horrified whisper at the end: "My child, their father *wore stripes!*"

The Shirleys made no attempt to hold up their heads against the storm, but withdrew into strict seclusion on their plantation. Now, ten years later, Robert Shirley having died in prison, his widow was a pitiful shadow, his daughters were hopeless old maids, and his two sons were farmers, staying at home and acting as their own managers.

Of these, Frank Shirley was the elder. I am handicapped in setting out to tell you about him

4

by the fact that he sits in the next room, and
will have to read what I write; he is not a man
to stand for any nonsense about himself—nor yet
one whose ridicule an amateur author would
wish to face.  I will content myself with stating
simple facts, which he cannot deny; for example,
that he is a man a trifle below the average height,
but sturdily built and exceedingly powerful.  He
had in those days dark hair and eyes, and he
would not claim to have been especially bad-
looking.  He is the most reserved man I have
ever known, but his feelings are intense when they
are roused, and on these rare occasions he is
capable of being eloquent.  He is, in general,
a very solid and dependable kind of man; he
does not ask anything of anybody, but he is
willing to give, cautiously, after he has made
sure that his motive will be understood.  As I
read that over, it seems to me a judicious and
entirely unsentimental statement about him,
which he will have to pass.

He was, he tells me, a lively boy; but after
the age of eleven he always had, as the most
prominent fact in his consciousness, the knowledge
that men set him apart as something different
from themselves.  And this, of course, made
intercourse with them difficult; if they were
indifferent to him, that was insult, and if they
were cordial, then they were taking pity upon
him.  He always knew that the people who met
him, however politely they greeted him, were
repeating behind his back the inevitable whisper,

"His father wore stripes!" So naturally he found it pleasanter not to meet people.

Then, too, there were his mother and sisters; it was hard not to be bitter about them. He knew that the girls were gentle and lovely; and it rather made men seem cowardly, that it should be certain that no one in their own social world would ever ask them in marriage. There is so much asking in marriage in the South—it is really difficult for a gentlewoman to be passed over altogether. The Shirley girls could not discuss this, even in the bosom of their family; but Frank came to understand, and to brood over the thing in secret.

### § 11

So you see Frank Shirley was a difficult man to get at—as much so as if he had been an emperor or an anchorite. I have been interested in the psychology of sex, and I wondered how much this aloofness had to do with what happened to Sylvia. There were so many men, and they were all so much alike, and they were all so easy! But here was a man who was different; a man whom one could not get at without humiliating efforts; a man of mystery, about whom one could imagine things! I asked Sylvia, who thought there might be something in this; but much more in a deeper fact, which is known

to poets and tellers of love-tales, but has not
been sufficiently heeded by scientists—that intui-
tive, commanding and sometimes terrifying revelation of sexual affinity, which we smile at and
discredit under the name of "love at first sight."
The first time Sylvia met Frank she did not
know who he was; she saw at first only his back;
and yet she began at once to experience a thrill
which she had never known in her life before.
Absurd as they may sound, I will repeat her
words: "There was something about the back
of his neck that took my breath!"

It had been some years since she had heard
the Shirleys mentioned. They had quietly declined all invitations, and this made it easy for
everybody to do with decency what everybody
wanted to do—to cease sending invitations. The
Shirley plantation was remotely located, some
twenty miles away from Castleman Hall; and
so little by little the family had been forgotten.

But there was a certain Mrs. Venable, a young
widow who owned a hunting-lodge near the Shirley place; and as fate would have it, she was
one of the people whom Sylvia had persuaded to
take up Harriet Atkinson. One day, as the latter
was driving to the lodge in her automobile, she
was "mired" in the midst of a terrific thunder-
storm, when along came a gentleman on horse-
back, who politely insisted upon her taking his
waterproof, and then mounting behind him and
riding to his home up on the hill; by which
romantic method the delighted Harriet found

herself conveyed to an old and evidently aristocratic homestead, and welcomed by some altogether lovely people.

Being younger than Sylvia, and not so much on the "inside" as to local history, Harriet had been obliged to get the story from Mrs. Venable. It had heightened her interest in the Shirleys—for Harriet's great merit was that she was human and spontaneous where she should have been respectable. She went to call again on the family, and when she got home she made haste to tell Sylvia about it. "Sunny," she said—that was her way of taking liberties with Sylvia's complexion—"you ought to meet that man Frank Shirley." She went on to tell how good-looking he was, how silent and mysterious, and what a fine voice he had. "And the sweetest, lazy smile!" she declared. "I'm sure he could be a lady-killer if he did not take life so seriously!" So, you see, Sylvia had something to start her imagination going, and a reason for accepting Mrs. Venable's invitation to a hunting party.

One sunshiny morning in the late fall she was taking part in a deer-hunt, carrying a rifle and looking as picturesque as possible. They put her on a "stand" with Charlie Peyton, who ought to have been at college, but was hanging round making a nuisance of himself by sighing and gazing. After waiting a half hour or so, off in the woods they heard a dog yelping. Charlie went off to investigate, thinking it might be a bear; and so Sylvia was left to her fate.

She heard a sound in the bushes at one side, and thought it was a deer. The creature moved past her, hidden by a dense thicket, and passed a little way ahead, with a heavy trampling sound. She had half raised her gun, when suddenly the bushes parted, and with a leap over a fallen log there came into view—not a deer, but a horse with a rider upon his back.

The girl lowered her gun. The dog yelped again and the man reined up his horse and stood listening. The horse was restive; as he drew rein upon it, it turned slightly, exhibiting the rider's face. To the outward eye he was a not unusual figure, wearing the khaki shirt and knickerbockers affected by the younger generation of planters when on duty. The shirt was open, with a red bandana handkerchief tucked round at the throat.

But Sylvia was not looking with the outward eye. Sylvia had been reading romances, and had a vague idea of a lover who would some day appear, being distinguished from the ordinary admirers of salons and ball-rooms by something knightly in his aspect. And this man seemed to have that something. His face was a face of power, yet not harsh, rather with a touch of melancholy.

As a rule Sylvia was immediately observant of her own emotional states, especially where men were concerned; but this once she was too much interested to think what she was thinking. She was noting the man's deeply-shadowed eyes and shiny black hair, his statue-like figure and his mastery of the horse. She wondered if he would look in her direction, and she waited, fascinated, for the moment when his glance would rest upon her.

The moment came. He started slightly, and then quickly his hand went up to his hat. "I beg your pardon," he said, politely.

Sylvia noted his deep, full-toned voice; and with a sudden thrill she recollected Harriet's adventure. "Can this be Frank Shirley?" she thought. She caught herself together and smiled. "It is for me to beg pardon," she said. "I came near shooting at you."

"I deserved it," he answered, smiling in turn. "I was trespassing on my neighbor's land."

Sylvia had by now been "out" a full year, and it must be admitted that she was a sophisticated young lady. When she met a man, her thought was: "Could I love him? And how would it be if I married him?" Her imagination would leap ahead through a long series of scenes: the man's home, his relatives and her own, his occupations, his amusements, his ideas. She would see herself traveling with him, driving with him, presiding at dinner-parties for him—perhaps helping to get him sober the next morning. As a drowning man is said to live over his whole past in a few seconds, so Sylvia might live her whole future during a figure at a "german."

But with this man it was different. She could not imagine him in any position in her world.

He was an elemental creature, belonging in some wild place, where there was danger to be faced and deeds to be done. Sylvia had read "Paul and Virginia," and "Robinson Crusoe," and "Typee," and in her mind was a vague idea of a primitive, close-to-nature life, which one yearned for when one was tightly laced, or was sent into the parlor to entertain an old friend of the family. She imagined this strange knight springing forward and lifting her upon his saddle-bow, to bear her away to such a world. She could feel his powerful arms about her, his whispered words in her ear; she could hear the clatter of his horse's hoofs—away, away!

She had to make another effort, and remember who she was. "You are not lost, I suppose?" he was asking.

"Oh, no," she said. "I am on a 'stand.'"

"Of course," he replied; again there was a pause, and again Sylvia's brain went whirling. It was absurd how the beating of her heart kept translating itself into the clatter of horse's hoofs.

The man turned for a moment to listen to the dog; and she stole another look at him. His eyes came back and caught her glance. She absolutely had to say something—instantly, to save the situation. "I—I am not alone," she stammered. Oh, how dreadful—that she, Sylvia Castleman, should stumble over words!

"My escort has gone to look for the dog," she added. "He will be back in a moment."

"Oh," he said; and Sylvia noted a sudden

change in his expression—a set, repressed look. She saw the blood mounting slowly, until it colored his cheeks to a crimson.

"I beg your pardon," he said, coldly. "Good-morning." He turned his horse and started on his way.

He had taken her words as a dismissal. But that was the least part of the mistake. Sylvia read his mind in a flash—he was Frank Shirley, and he thought that she had recognized him, and was thinking of his father who had worn stripes! Yes, surely it must be that—for what right had he to be hurt otherwise—that she did not care to stand conversing with a strange man in a forest?

The thought sent her into a panic. She thought of nothing but the cruelty of that idea. "No, no!" she cried, the tears almost starting into her eyes. "I did not mean to send you away at all!"

He turned, startled by her vehemence. For a moment or two they stood staring at each other. The girl had this one swift thought: "How dreadful it must be to have such a thing in your mind, to have to be waiting for insults from people—or at best, for pity!"

Then, in his quiet voice, he said, "I really think I had better go." Again he turned his horse, and without another glance rode away, leaving Sylvia staring at his vanishing figure, with her hands tightly clutching her gun.

## § 12

AFTER that Sylvia felt that she had in common decency to meet Frank Shirley. She asked nothing more about her motives—she simply *had* to meet him, to remove one thought from his mind. But for two days she was at her wit's end, and went round bored to death by everything and everybody. She had a sudden whim to be let alone; and how difficult it is to be let alone at a house party! There was the everlasting Charlie Peyton, looking at her out of sickly blue eyes, and forever trying to get hold of her hand; there was Billy Aldrich, with his sybaritic silk socks, his shiny finger nails and talcum-powdered face; there was Malcolm McCallum, a dandy from Louisville, with his endless stream of impeccable suits and his caravan of trunks; there was Harvey Richards, a "steel-man" from Birmingham, who had thrown his business to the winds and settled down to the task of boring Sylvia. He was big and burly, and had become the special favorite of her family; he dandled the baby brother and made fudge with the sisters—but Sylvia declared viciously that his idea of love-making was to poke at her with his finger.

She took to getting up very early in the morning, so that she could go riding alone. As there was but one road, it was not her fault if she passed near the Shirley place. And if by any remote chance he were to be out riding too——

It was the third morning that she met him.

He came round a turn, and it all happened in a flash, before she had time to think. He gave her the stiffest greeting that was consistent with good breeding; and then he was past. Of course she could not look back. It was ten chances to one that he would not do the same, but still he might, and that would be dreadful.

She went on. She was angry with herself for her stupidity. That she should have met him thus, and had no better wit than to let him get by! Theoretically, of course, ladies cannot stop gentlemen to whom they have not been introduced; but there are always things that can happen, in cases of emergency like this. She thought of plans, and then she fell into a rage with herself for thus pursuing a man.

The next morning when she went riding, she forced herself to turn the horse's head in the other direction from the Shirley place. But her thoughts would come back to Frank, and presently she was making excuses for herself. This man was not as other men; if he avoided her, it was not because he did not want to know her, but because of his misfortune. It was wicked that a man should be tied up in such a net of misapprehension; to get him out of it would be, not unmaidenly, but heroic. When she had met him yesterday morning, she ought to have stopped her horse, and made him stay and talk with her. She was to leave in two days more!

She turned her horse and went back; and when she was near the Shirley house—here he came!

She saw him far down the road, and so had plenty of time to get her wits together. Had he, by any chance, come out in the hope of meeting her? Or would he be annoyed by her getting in his way? Suppose he were to snub her—how could she ever get over it?

She took a diamond ring from her finger, and reached back and shoved it under the saddle-cloth. It was a "marquise" ring, with sharp points, and when she threw her weight upon it, the horse gave a jump. She repeated the action, and it began to prance. "Now then!" whispered Sylvia to herself.

### § 13

HE came near; and she reined up her chafing steed. "I beg pardon," she said.

He raised his hat, and holding it, looked at her inquiringly.

"I think my horse must have a stone in his foot."

"Oh!" he said, and was off in a moment, throwing the reins of his mount over its head and handing them to her.

"Which foot?" he asked.

"I don't know."

He bent down and examined one hoof, then another, and so on for all four, without a word. Then, straightening up, he said, "I don't see anything."

He looked very serious and concerned. How "easy" he would be! "There really must be something," she said. "He's all in a lather."

"There might be something deep in," he answered, making his investigation all over again. "But I don't see any blood." (What a fine back he has! thought Sylvia.)

He stood up. "Let me see his mouth," he said. "Are you sure you've not held him too tight?"

"I am used to horses," was her reply.

"Some of them have peculiarities," he remarked. "Possibly the saddle has rubbed——"

"No, no," answered Sylvia, in haste, as he made a move to lift the cloth.

It was always hard for her to keep from laughing for long; and there was something so comical in his gravity. Then too, something desperate must be done, for presently he would mount and ride away. "There's surely no stone in his foot," he declared.

Whereat Sylvia broke into one of her radiant smiles. "Perhaps," she said, "it's in *your* horse's foot!"

He looked puzzled.

"Don't you see?" she laughed. "Something *must* be wrong—or you couldn't be here talking to me!"

But he still looked bewildered. "Dear me, what a man!" thought she.

A color was beginning to mount in his cheeks. Perhaps he was going to be offended! Clearly, with such a man one's cue was frankness. So her tone changed suddenly. "Are you Mr. Shirley?" she asked.

"Yes," he said.

"And do you know who I am?"

"Yes, Miss Castleman."

"Our families are old friends, you know."

"Yes, I know it."

"And then, tell me—" She paused. "Honestly!"

"Why—yes."

"I've been honest and told you—I'm not really worried about my horse. Now you be honest and say why you rode out this morning."

He waited before replying, studying her face—not boldly, but gravely. "I think, Miss Castleman, that it would be better if I did not."

Then it was Sylvia's turn to study. Was it a rebuke? Had he not come out on her account at all? Or was it still the ghost of his father's prison-suit?

He did not help her with another word. (I can hear Frank's laugh as he told me about this episode. "We silent fellows have such an advantage! We just wait and let people imagine things!")

Sylvia's voice fell low. "Mr. Shirley, you have me at a great disadvantage." And as she said this she gazed at him with the wonderful red-brown eyes, wide open, childlike. So far there had never been a man who could resist the spell of those eyes. Would this man be able? The busy little brain behind them was watching every sign.

"I don't understand," he replied; and she took up the words:

"It is *I* who don't understand. And I dare not ask you to explain!"

She was terrified at this temerity; and yet she must press on—there was no other way. She saw gates opening before her—gates into wonderland!

She leaned forward with a little gesture of abandonment. "Listen, Frank Shirley!" she said. (What a masterstroke was that!) "I have known about you since I was a little girl. And I understand the way things are now, because I am a friend of Miss Atkinson's. She asked you to come over and meet me, and you didn't. Now if the reason was that you have no interest in me—why then I'm annoying you, and I'm behaving outrageously, and I'm preparing humiliation for myself. But if the reason is that you think I wouldn't meet you fairly—that I wouldn't judge you as I would any other man—why, don't you see, that would be cruel, that would be wicked! If you were afraid that I wanted to—to patronize you—to do good to you——"

She stopped. Surely she had said enough!

There was a long silence, while he gazed at her—reading her very soul, she feared. "Suppose, Miss Castleman," he said, at last, "that I was afraid that you wanted to do *harm* to me?"

That was getting near to what she wanted! "Are you afraid?" she asked.

"Possibly I am," he replied. "It is easy for those who have never suffered to preach to those who have never done anything else."

Sylvia did not know quite how to meet that. It was so much more serious than she had been looking for, when she had slipped that ring under the saddle-cloth! "Oh," she cried, "what shall I say to you?"

"I will tell you exactly," he said, "and then neither of us will be taking advantage of the other. You are offering me your friendship, are you not?"

"Yes."

"Well, then, can you say to me that if I were to accept it, the shame of my family would never make any difference to you?"

She cried instantly, "That is what I've been trying to tell you! Of course it would not."

"You can say that?" he persisted. "It would make no difference whatever?"

She was about to answer again; but he stopped her. "Wait and think. You must know just what I mean. It is not a thing about which I could endure a mistake. Think of your family —your friends—your whole world! And think of everything that might arise between us!"

She stared at him, startled. He was asking if he might make love to her! She had not meant it to go so far as that—but there it was. Her own recklessness, and his forthrightness, had brought it to that point. And what could she say?

"Think!" he was saying. "And don't try to evade—don't lie to me. Answer me the truth!"

His eyes held hers. She waited—thinking, as he forced her to. At last, when she spoke, it was with a slightly trembling voice. "It would make no difference," she said.

And then she tried to continue looking at him, but she could not. She was blushing; it was a dreadful habit she had!

It was an absolutely intolerable situation, and she must do something—instantly. *He* never would—the dreadful sphinx of a man! She looked up. "Now we're friends?" she asked.

"Yes," he replied.

"Then," she said, laughing, "reach under the saddle-cloth and get out my ring. I might lose it."

Bewildered, he got the ring, and understanding at last, laughed with her. "And now," cried Sylvia, in her friendliest tone of voice, "get on your horse again and behave like a man of enterprise! Come!" She touched her mount and went galloping; she heard him pounding away behind her, and she began to sing:

> "Waken, lords and ladies gay,
> On the mountain dawns the day,
> All the jolly chase is near
> With hawk and hound and hunting-spear!"

## § 14

THEY were good comrades now; all their problems solved, and a stirrup-cup of happiness to quaff between them. Sylvia was amazed at herself—the surge of exultation which arose in her and swept her along upon its crest. Never in all her life had she been as full of verve and animation as she was throughout that ride. She laughed, she sang, she poured out a stream of fantasy; and all the while the clatter of the horses hoofs—romance blending itself with reality!

But also she was studying the man. There was something in her which must always be studying people. Thank Heaven, he was a man who could forget himself, and laugh and be good fun! It was something to have got him out of his melancholy, and set him to galloping here— admiring her, marveling at her! She felt his admiration like a storm of wind pushing her along.

At last she drew up, breathless. "Dear me," she exclaimed, "what a lot of chattering I have done! And we must be—how many miles from home?"

"Ten, I should say," he replied.

"And I've had no breakfast!" she said. "We really *must* go back."

He made no objection, and they turned. "You must come and see me at the lodge," she said. "I am going home to-morrow afternoon."

But he shook his head. "Don't ask me," he

replied. "You know I don't belong among smart people."

She started to protest; but then she thought of Billy Aldrich with his tight collars and fancy stick-pins—of Malcolm McCallum with his Japanese valet; no, there was no use pretending about such things. And besides, she did not want these people to know her secret.

"But where can we meet?" she said. (How perfectly appalling was that—without any hint from him!)

"Can't we ride again to-morrow morning?" he asked, quite simply.

And so they settled it. He left her at the place where the road turned in to the lodge. He tried to thank her for what she had taken the trouble to do; but she was frightened now— she dared not stay and listen any longer to his voice. She waved him a bright farewell, and rode off, feeling suddenly faint and bewildered.

She had half a mile or so to ride alone, and in that ride it was exactly as if he were by her side. She still heard his horse's hoofs, and felt how he would look if she were to turn. Once she thought of Lady Dee, and then she could not help laughing. What *would* Lady Dee have said! How many of the rules of coquetry had she not broken in the space of two brief hours! But after a little more thought, she consoled herself. Possibly there were moves in this game which even Lady Dee had never heard of! "I don't think I managed it so badly," she was saying to herself, as she dismounted from her horse.

And that was the view she took when she told Harriet about it. She had not meant to tell Harriet at all, but the secret would out—she had to have some one to talk to. "Oh, my dear," she exclaimed, "he's perfectly wonderful!"

"Who? What do you mean?" asked Harriet.

"Frank Shirley."

"What? You've met him?"

"Met him? I've been riding with him the whole morning, and I've almost let him propose to me!"

"Sylvia!" cried Harriet, aghast.

The other stood looking before her, grown suddenly thoughtful. "Yes, I did. And what's more, I believe that to-morrow morning I'm *going* to let him propose to me."

"Sunny," exclaimed her friend, "are you a woman, or one of Satan's imps?"

For answer Sylvia took her seat at the piano and began to sing—a song by which all her lovers set much store:

"Who is Sylvia? What is she,
    That all our swains commend her?
Holy, fair and wise is she—
    The heavens such grace did lend her
That she might adored be!"

### § 15

Sylvia did very little thinking that first day—she was too much possessed by feelings. Besides

this she had to go through all the routine of
a house party; to go to breakfast and make
apologies for her singular desire to ride alone;
to go quail-shooting and remind Charlie Peyton
to fire off his gun now and then; to curl her hair
and select a gown for dinner—and all the while
in a glow of happiness so intense as to come
close to the borderland of pain.

It was not a definite emotion, but a vague,
suffused ecstasy. She was like one who goes
about hearing exquisite music; angels singing
in the sky above her, little golden bells ringing
in every part of her body. And then always,
penetrating the mist of her feelings, was the
memory of Frank Shirley. She could see his
eyes, as they had looked up at her; she could
hear the tones of his voice—its low intensity as
he had said, "Think of everything that might
happen between us!" She would find herself
blushing crimson at the dinner-table, and would
have to chatter to hide her confusion.

When night came she went into a sleep that
was a half swoon of happiness; and awoke in
the early dawn, first bewildered, then horrified,
because of what she had done—her boldness,
her lack of dignity and reserve. She had thrown
herself at a man's head! And of course he would
be disgusted and would flee from her. She drank
her coffee and dressed a full half hour too early;
and meanwhile she was planning how she would
treat him that morning. But then, suppose he
did not come that morning?

She rode out in the light of a sunrise she did not see, amid the song of birds she did not hear. Suppose he did not come! When she saw him, far up the road, she wanted to turn and flee. Her heart pounded, her cheeks burned, there was a clashing as of cymbals in her ears. She reined up her horse and sat motionless, telling herself that she must be calm. She clenched her hands and bit a little hole in her tongue; and so, when he arrived, he found a young woman of the world awaiting him.

She saw at once that something was wrong with him. He too had been having moods and agonies, and had come full of resolutions and reservations! He greeted her politely, and had almost nothing to say as they rode away together. Sylvia's heart sank. He had come because he had promised; but he was regretting his indiscretions. Very well, she would show him that she, too, could be polite! Under the spur of her fierce pride, she could be a light-hearted child, utterly unaware of the existence of any sulking male.

So they rode on. It was such a beautiful morning, the odor of the pine-forests was so refreshing and the song of the birds so free, that Sylvia was soon all that she had set out to pretend. She forgot her cavalier for several minutes, laughing and humming. When she realized him again, she had the boldness to tease him about himself—

"Oh, what can ail thee, knight-at-arms,
Alone, and palely loitering?"

And when he had no poetry ready to reply, she grew tired of him altogether, and touched her horse and cantered quickly on. Let him follow her if he chose—what mattered it! Moreover, she rode well, and men always noticed it; she was bare-headed, and no man ever saw the golden glory of her hair in bright sunlight that his heart did not begin to quiver within him!

After a while he spurred his horse and rode at her side, and without looking, she saw that he was watching her. She gave him just a little smile, absent-minded and barely polite. Resolving to punish him still more, she asked him the time. He gravely drew out his watch and replied to her question. "I will ride as far as the spring," she said. "Then I must be going back."

But he did not make the expected protest. He was going to lose her, and he did not care! Oh, what a man!

As they drew near the spring, Sylvia began to be uneasy again. She did not want him to lose her; she wanted him to care. She stopped to breathe her horse, and to look at the moss-ringed pool of water, and at the field of golden-rod beyond. "How lovely!" she said; and repeated, "How lovely!" He never said a word—and when he might so easily have said, "Let us stay a while!"

She was growing desperate. Her horse had got its breath and had had some water—what else? "I must have some of that golden-rod!" she exclaimed, suddenly. What was the matter with him, staring into space in that fashion? Had he no manners at all? "I must have some golden-rod," she repeated; and when he still made no move, she said, "Hold my horse, please," and started to dismount.

He sprang off, and took the reins of her horse, and those of his own in the same hand, giving his other hand to her. It was the first time he had touched her, and it sent a shock through her that sent her flying in a panic—out into the field of flowers, where she could hide her cheeks and her trembling!

## § 16

HE made the horses fast to the fence, carefully and deliberately; and meantime she was gathering golden-rod. She knew that she made a picture in the midst of flowers. She was very much occupied as he came to her side.

A moment later she heard his voice: "Miss Castleman."

Panic seized her again, but she looked up, with her last flicker of courage. "Well?" she asked.

"There is something I want to tell you," he began. "I can't play this game with you—I am no match for you at all."

"Why—what do you mean?" she managed to say.

As usual, he knew just what he meant. "I

am not a man who can play with his emotions,"
he said. "You must understand this at the
very outset—the thing is real to me, and I've
got to know quickly whether or not it is real to
you."

There he was! Like a storm of wind that threatened to sweep away her pretenses, the whole pitiful
little structure of her coquetry. But she could
not let the structure go; it was her only shelter,
and she strove desperately to hold it in place.
"Why should you assume that I play with my
emotions?" she demanded.

"You play, not with your own, but with other
peoples' emotions," he replied. "I know; I've
heard about you—long ago."

She drew herself up haughtily. "You do not
approve of me, Mr. Shirley? I'm very sorry."

"You must know—" he began.

But she went on, in a rush of defensive recklessness: "You think I'm hollow—a coquette—a
trifler with hearts. Well, I am. It's all I know."
She flung her head up, looking at him defiantly.

"No, Miss Castleman," he said, "it's *not* all
you know!"

But her recklessness was driving her—that
spirit of the gambler that was in the blood of
all her race. "It *is* all I know." She bent over
and began strenuously to pluck sprays of golden-
rod.

"To break men's hearts?" he asked.

She laughed scornfully. "I had a great-aunt,
Lady Dee—perhaps you've heard of her. She

taught me—and I've found out through much experience that she was right." She gazed at him boldly, over the armful of flowers. " 'Sylvia, never let yourself be sorry for men. Let them take care of themselves. They have all the advantage in the game. They are free to come and go, they pick us up and look us over and drop us when they feel like it. So we have to learn to manage them. And, believe me, my child, they like it—it's what they're made for!' "

"And you believe such things as that?"

She laughed, a superbly cynical laugh, and began to gather more flowers. "I used to think they were cruel—when I was young. But now I know that Aunt Lady was right. What else have men to do but to make love to us? Isn't it better for them than getting drunk, or gambling, or breaking their necks hunting foxes? 'It's the thing that lifts them above the brute,' she used to say. 'Naturally, the more of them you lift, the better.' "

"Did she teach you to deceive men deliberately?"

"She told me that when she was ordering her wedding trousseau, she was engaged to a dozen; a cousin of hers was engaged to another dozen, and couldn't make up her mind which to choose, so she sent notes to them all to say that she'd marry the man who got to her first."

He smiled—his slow, quiet smile. Sylvia did not know how he was taking these things; nor did his next remark enlighten her. "Did it not surprise you to be taught that men were the centre of creation?"

"No. They taught me that God was a man."

He laughed, then became grave. "Why do you need so many men? You can't marry but one."

"Not in the South. But when I am ready to marry that one, I want it to be the one I want; and the only way to be sure is to have a great many wanting *you*. When a man sees a girl so surrounded with suitors that he can't get near her, he knows it's the one girl in the world for him. Aunt Lady had a saying about it, full of wisdom." And Sylvia looked very wise herself. " 'Men are sheep!' "

"I see," he said, somewhat grimly. "I fear, Miss Castleman, I cannot enter such a competition."

"Is it cowardice?"

"Perhaps. It has been said that discretion is the better part of valor. You see, to me love is not a game, but a reality. It could never be that to you, I fear."

Poor Sylvia! She was trying desperately hard to remember and make use of her training. But the rules she had learned were, so to speak, for fresh-water sailing; no one had ever thought that her frail craft might be blown out upon a stormy ocean like this. Picture her as a terrified navigator, striving to steer with a broken rudder, and gazing up into a mountain-wave that comes roaring down upon her!

He was a man who meant what he said. She had tried her foolish arts upon him and had only disgusted him. He was going away; and once he had left her, she would be powerless to get hold of him again!

Love could never be a reality to her, he had said. With sudden tears in her voice she exclaimed, "It could! It could!"

His whole aspect changed in a moment. A fire seemed to leap into his eyes. "You mean that?" he asked. And that was enough for her. As he moved towards her, she backed away a step or two. She thrust out the great bunch of golden-rod, filling his arms with that, and retreated farther into the yellow field.

He stood for a moment, nonplussed, looking rather comical with his unexpected load. Then he turned away without a word, and went to where his horse was fastened, and began to tie the flowers to his saddle.

She joined him before he had finished and mounted her own horse, saying casually, "It is late. We must return." He mounted and rode beside her in silence.

At last he remarked, "You are going away this afternoon?"

"Yes," she said.

"Then where can I see you?"

"You will have to come to my home."

There was a pause. "It will be a difficult experience," he observed. "You will have to help me through it."

She answered, promptly, "You must come as
any other man would come.  You must learn to
do that—you must simply not *know* what other
people are thinking."

At which he smiled sadly.  " There is nothing
in that.  When everybody in the world is thinking one thing about you, you find there's no use
pretending not to know what it is."

There he was again—simple and direct.  He
had a vision of the hostility of her relatives, the
horror of her friends; he went on to speak his
thoughts quite baldly.  Was she prepared to face
these difficulties?  She might have the courage,
she might not; but at least she must be fore-
warned, and not encounter them blindly.  She
said, "My own people will be kind, I assure you."
And when he smiled dubiously, she added,
"Leave it to me.  I promise you I'll manage
them."


## § 17


SYLVIA, as you know, had been taught to discuss the affairs of her heart in the language of
military science.  Continuing the custom, the
fortress of her coquetry had withstood an on-
slaught which had brought dismay to the garrison, who had never before known what it was to
be in real danger.  In the hope of restoring con-
fidence to the troops there was now undertaken
a raid into the territory of perfectly innocent and
defenseless neighbors.

The first victim was Charlie Peyton. He had implored one last opportunity to prove his devotion—being unable to imagine how his devotion could be of no interest to Sylvia. So the guests of the house-party were treated to the amazing spectacle of this dignified and self-conscious youth standing for two hours in the crotch of an apple-tree. Meanwhile Sylvia went off for a walk with Malcolm McCallum; and when at last Charlie's time was up, and he set out in search of her, he found his rival occupied in crawling on his knees the length of a splintery dock which ran out into the lake. Sylvia sat by, absorbed in a book, and when Charlie questioned her as to the meaning of this strange phenomenon, she replied that Mr. McCallum (known to us previously as "the Louisville dandy") was probably experimenting with the creases in his trousers.

Dressing for luncheon and the trip home, Sylvia had a consultation with her friend Harriet. "Do you suppose I'm really in love?" was her question.

"With whom?" asked Harriet.

But Sylvia paid no heed to this feeble wit. "I don't think he approves of me, Harriet. He thinks I'm shallow and vain—a trifler with hearts."

"What would you have him think?" persisted the other.

"He isn't like other men, Harriet. He makes me ashamed of myself. I think I ought to treat him differently."

Whereat her friend became suddenly serious.

"Look here, Sunny, don't you lose your nerve! You stick to your game!"

"But suppose he won't stand it?"

"*Make* him stand it! Take my advice, now, and don't go trying experiments. You've learned one way, and you're a wonder at it—don't get yourself mixed up at the critical moment."

Sylvia was gazing at herself in the mirror, wondering at the look on her own face. "I don't know what to do next!" she cried.

"The Lord takes care of children and fools," said Harriet. "I hope He's on His job!" Then the luncheon gong sounded, and they went downstairs.

There was a new man, who had arrived the night before. He was named Pendleton, and Sylvia found herself placed next to him. She suspected that he had arranged this, and was bored by the prospect, and purposely talked with Charlie Peyton on her other side. Towards the end of the meal a servant came in and whispered to the hostess, who rose suddenly with the exclamation, "Frank Shirley is here!" Amid the general silence that fell Sylvia began suddenly to eat with assiduity.

The hostess went out, and returned after a minute or so with Frank at her heels. "Do sit down," she was saying. "At least have some of this sherbet."

"I've had my luncheon," he replied; "I supposed you'd have finished." But he seated himself at the table, as requested. There was a general pause, everybody expecting some explanation; but he volunteered none.

Opposite to Sylvia was Belle Johnston, an insipid young person who had a reputation for wit, for which she made other people pay. "Did you think it looked like rain, Mr. Shirley?" she inquired. Sylvia could have destroyed her.

"The weather is very pleasant," said Frank. No one could be sure whether he was imperturbable, or had missed the jest altogether.

Harriet, seeing her friend's alarming appetite and discomfort, stepped in now to save the situation. "I hope you brought me a message from your sister," she remarked. "I am expecting one."

But Frank would have none of any such devices. "I'm sorry," he said, "but I haven't brought it."

Sylvia was furious. Had he no tact, no social sense at all—not even any common gratitude? He ought to have waited outside, where he would have been less conspicuous; instead of sitting there, dumb as an oyster, looking at her and obviously waiting for her! Sooner or later everyone must notice.

With a sudden impulse she turned to the man at her side. "I am sorry you came so late," she said.

"I am more than sorry," he replied, brightening instantly.

"I really must go home this afternoon," she said.

He was encouraged by her tone of regret. "I think I will tell you something," he said.

"Well?"

"I came here on purpose to meet you. I was visiting my friends, the Allens, at Thanksgiving, and all the men there were talking of you."

This, of course, was ancient history to Sylvia. "What were they saying?" she asked—and stole a glance at Frank.

"They said you'd never let a man go without hurting him. At least, not if you thought him worth while."

"Dear me!" she exclaimed, astonished and flattered. "I wonder that you weren't afraid to meet me!"

"I was amused," answered the other. "I thought to myself, I'd like to see her hurt me."

Sylvia lifted her delicate eyebrows and gave him a slow, quiet stare, four-fifths scorn and one-fifth challenge.

"Gad!" he exclaimed. "You are interesting for a fact! When you look like that!"

"Not otherwise?" she inquired, now wholly scornful.

"Oh, you're not the most beautiful woman I ever saw! Nor the cleverest!"

"Do not challenge me like that."

"Why not?" he laughed.

"You might regret it."

"It would be a good adventure—I'd be willing to pay the price to see the game. I admire a woman who knows her business."

6

So the banter continued; the man displaying his cleverness and Sylvia casting upon him glances of mockery, of contempt, half veiling curiosity and interest. He, of course, being secretly convinced of his own irresistibility, was noting these glances and speculating about them, thrilled by them without realizing it, persuading himself that the girl was really coming to admire him. This was a kind of encounter which had occurred, not once, but a hundred times in Sylvia's career, and usually it meant nothing in particular to her. But now it brought a reckless joy, because of the shock it was giving to that other man—the terrible man who sat across the way, his eyes boring into her very soul!

## § 18

When the luncheon was over, Sylvia made her way to Harriet Atkinson and caught her by the arm. "Harriet!" she exclaimed. "You must help me!"

"What?" whispered the other.

"I can't see him!"

"But why not?"

"He wants to lecture me, and I won't stand it! I'm going into the garden—take him somewhere else—you must!" Then, seeing Frank making toward her, she gave Harriet a vicious pinch, and fled from the room. There was a summer-house in the garden at the far end, and thither she went upon flying feet.

I was never sure how it happened—whether, as Harriet always vowed, she tried to hold Frank and could not, or whether she turned traitor to her friend. At any rate Sylvia had been there not more than a minute, and had scarcely begun to get control of herself, when she heard a step, and looking up, saw Frank Shirley coming down the path.

There was but one door to the summer-house —and he soon occupied that. "Go away!" she cried. "Go away!" (That was all that was left of her *savoir faire!*)

He stopped. "Miss Castleman," he said—and his voice was hard, "I came here to see you. But now I'm sorry I came."

The garrison rallied as to a trumpet-call. "That is too bad, Mr. Shirley," she- said, with appalling *hauteur*. "But you know you do not have to stay an instant."

He gazed at her in doubt for a moment. Her heart was pounding and the color flooding her face. "I don't believe you know what you are doing!" he exclaimed.

"Really!" she replied, witheringly. "Do you?"

"No," he went on, "I don't understand you at all. But I simply *will* find out!"

He strode towards her. She shrank into the seat, but he caught her hands. For a moment she resisted; but he held fast, and from his hands she felt a current as of fire, flowing through all her veins.

Slowly he drew her to her feet. "Sylvia!" he whispered. "Sylvia! Look at me!"

She obeyed him instinctively, and their eyes met. "You love me!" he exclaimed. She could hear his quick breathing. She felt herself sinking towards him. She felt his arms about her, his breath upon her cheek.

"I love you!" he murmured. And she closed her eyes, and he kissed her again and again. In his kisses it seemed to her that she would melt away.

She was exultant and happy. The testimony of his love was rapture to her. But then suddenly came a fear which they had inculcated in her. All the women who had ever talked to her on the problem of the male-creature—all agreed that nothing was so fatal as to allow the taking of "liberties." Also there came sudden shame. She began to struggle. "You must not kiss me! It is not right!"

"But, Sylvia!" he protested. "I love you!"

"Oh, stop!" she pleaded. "Stop!"

"You love me!" he whispered.

"Please, please stop!"

A gentle pressure would have held her, but she felt that he was releasing her—all but one hand. She sank down upon the seat, trembling. "Oh, you ought not to have done it!" she cried.

He asked, "Why not?"

"No man has ever done that to me before!" The thought of what he had done, the memory of his lips upon her cheek, sent the blood flying there in hot waves; she began to sob: "No, no! You should not have done it!"

"Sylvia!" he pleaded, surprised by her vehemence. "Don't you realize that you love me?"

"I don't know! I'm afraid! I must have time!" She was weeping convulsively now. "You will never respect me again!"

"You must not say such a thing as that! It is not true!"

"You will go away and remember it, and you will despise me!"

His voice was calm and very soothing. "Sylvia," he said, "I have told you that I love you. And I believe that you love me. If that is so, I had a perfect right to kiss you, and you had a perfect right to let me kiss you."

There he was, sensible as ever; Sylvia found the storm of her emotion dying away. She had time to recall one of the maxims of Lady Dee: "A woman should never let a man see her weeping. It makes her cheeks pale and her nose red." She resolved that she would stay in the protecting shadows of the summer-house until after he had departed.

## § 19

SHE went home; and at the dinner-table she was telling some of the adventures of the house-party. "Oh, by the way," she said, carelessly, "I met Frank Shirley."

"Really?" exclaimed Mrs. Castleman. "Those poor, unfortunate people!"

"He must be quite a man now," said Aunt Varina. "How old is he?"

"About twenty-one," said the mother. Sylvia was amazed; she had not thought definitely of his age, but he had seemed a mature man to her.

"I see him now and then," put in the Major. "He comes to town. Not a bad-looking chap."

"He asked if he might call," said Sylvia. "I told him, Yes. Was that right, Papa?"

"Why, certainly," was the reply.

"He seems a very shy, silent kind of man," she added. "He wasn't sure that he'd be welcome."

"Why, my dear," exclaimed Mrs. Castleman. "I'm sure we've never made any difference in our treatment of the Shirleys!"

"Bob Shirley's children will always be welcome to my home, so long as they behave themselves," declared the father.

And so Sylvia left the matter, content with their attitude. Frank was wrong in his estimate of her family.

Two days later there came a negro man, riding a mule and carrying a bag, with a note from Frank. He begged her to accept this present of quail, because she had lost so much of her hunting time, and Charlie Peyton's aim had been so bad. Sylvia read the note, and got from it a painful shock. The handwriting was boyish and the manner of expression crude. She was used to leisure-class stationery, with her monogram in gold at the top, and this was written upon a piece of cheap paper. Somehow it made the whole matter seem unreal and incredible to her. She found herself trying to recall how he looked.

So she went to sleep; and awakening early the next morning, waiting for the agreeable tinkle of the approaching coffee-cup—there suddenly he came to her! Just as real as he had been in the summer-house, with his breath upon her cheek! The delicious, blinding ecstasy possessed her again—and then fresh humiliation at the memory of his kisses! Oh, why did he not come to see her—instead of leaving her the prey of her fancy? She could not escape from the idea that she had lost his respect by flinging herself at his head—by permitting him to kiss her.

The next morning came the negro again, this time with a great bunch of golden-rod. "What a present!" exclaimed the whole family; but Sylvia understood and was happy. "It's because of my hair," she told the others, laughing. It must be that he loved her, despite her indiscretions!

He wrote that he was coming to see her that evening; and that because of the length of the ride, he would accept her invitation and come to dinner. So Sylvia braced herself for the ordeal.

She dressed very simply, so as not to attract attention. Uncle Mandeville was there, and two girl cousins from Louisville, visiting the family, and two of the Bishop's boys and one of Barry

Chilton's, who dropped in at the last moment to
see them.　That was the way at Castleman Hall
—there were never less than a dozen people at
any meal, and the cook allowed for twenty.　To
all this crowd Sylvia had to introduce her strange
new conquest, ignoring their glances of inquiry
and parrying their mischievous shafts.

I must let you see this family at dinner.　At
the head of the table sits the Major, with gray
hair and a gray imperial, wearing his black vest
cut so low that he can plead it is evening dress;
still adhering valiantly to the custom of his
fathers, and carving the roast for his growing
family, while the littlest girls, who come last,
follow each portion with hungry eyes and count
the number intervening.　At the foot sits Mrs.
Castleman, serving the salad and dessert, her
ample figure robed in satin.　"Miss Margaret"
is just at that stage of her life, after the birth
of the son and heir, when she has definitely
abandoned the struggle with an expanding waist-
line.　When I met her, some years later, she
weighed two hundred and eighty pounds, and
was the best-natured and most comically in-
efficient human soul I have ever encountered in
my life.

There is Aunt Varina Tuis, humble and incon-
spicuous, weary after a day of trotting up and
down stairs after the housekeeper, to see that the
embroidered napkins were counted before they
went to the laundry, that the drawing-room furniture was dusted, the dead flowers taken out of

the dining-room, the fleas in the servants' quarters kept in subjection. Mrs. Tuis' queer little voice is seldom heard at the dinner-table, unless she is appealed to in some matter of family history: whom this one married, whom that one had been engaged to, whether or not it was true that some neighbor's grandfather had kept a grocery store, as rumored.

Then there is Uncle Mandeville, home to recuperate from a spree in New Orleans; enormous in every direction, rosy-faced and prosperous, with a resounding laugh and an endless flow of fun. Beside him sits Celeste, the next daughter, presenting a curious contrast to Sylvia, with her restless black eyes, her positive manner and worldly view-point. There are the two cousins from Louisville, healthy and radiant, and the two Chilton boys, Clive and Harley, and Barry's boy, who is a giant like Uncle Mandeville, and whenever he laughs, makes the cut glass to rattle on the buffet.

All this family hunts in one pack. They know all each other's affairs, and take an interest in them, and stand together against the rest of the world. They are a noisy crew, good-humored, careless, but with hot tempers and little control of them—so that when their interests clash and they get on one another's toes, they quarrel as violently as before they loved. Their conversation is apt to be bewildering to a stranger, for they seldom talk about general questions, having a whole arcanum of family allusions not easily understood. At this meal, for example, they are merry for half an hour over the latest tales of the doings of an older brother of Clive and Harley, who has married a girl with rich parents, but is too proud to take a dollar from them, and is forcing his bride to play at decent poverty. When the provisions run out they visit the Bishop, or the Major, or Uncle Barry, as may be most convenient, and go off with an automobile-load of hams and sausage-puddings and pickles and preserves. How many jokes there are, and what gales of merriment go round the table! The Bishop's son the first kleptomaniac in the family! Barry's young giant declaring that a single smile from the bride cost his father a cow and calf! The little girls, Peggy and Maria, chiming in with their tale of how the predatory couple found a lone chicken foraging in the rose-garden, confiscated it, carried it off under Basil's coat, tied it by the leg under the piazza at the back of their house in town—and then forgot it and let it starve to death!

Sylvia sat watching this tableful of care-free, rollicking people—the men handsome, finely built, well-fed and well-groomed, the women delicate, soft-skinned and exquisitely gowned—representing the best type their civilization could produce. A pleasant scene it was, with snowy damask cloth and bouquets of roses, precious old silver and quaint hand-painted china, with a background of mahogany furniture and paneled walls. She watched Frank in the midst of it, thinking of his home as Harriet had pictured it—the people subdued and sombre, the stamp of poverty upon everything. She was glad to see that he was able to fit himself into the mood of this company, enjoying the sallies of fun and pleasing those he talked to.

The house being full of young couples who wanted to be alone, Sylvia took Frank into the library. She liked this room, with its red leather furniture and cozy fireplace, and queer old bookcases with diamond-shaped panes of glass. She liked it because the lights were on the table, and no woman looks beautiful when lighted from over her head. This may seem a small matter to you, but Sylvia had learned how much depends upon detail. She remembered one of the maxims of Lady Dee: "Get a man on your home-ground, where you can have things as you want them; and then place your chair to show the best side of your face."

These things I set down as Sylvia told them to me—a long time afterwards, when we could laugh over them. It was a fact about her all the way through, that whatever she did, good or bad, she knew why she was doing it. In this she differed from a good many other women, who are not honest, even with themselves, and who feel that things become vulgar only when they are mentioned. The study of her own person and its charms was of course the very essence of her rôle as a "belle." At every stage of her life she had been drilled and coached—how to dance, how to enter a drawing-room, how to receive a compliment, how to toy with a suitor. At Miss Abercrombie's, the young ladies had an etiquette teacher who gave them instructions in the most minute details of their deportment; not to bend your body too much, but mainly your knees, when you sat down; not to let your hands lie flat at your sides, but to turn your little fingers gracefully out; never to hesitate or think of yourself when entering a room, but to fix your thoughts upon some person, and move towards that person with decision. Sylvia had needed this last instruction especially, for in the beginning she had had a terrible time entering rooms. It should be a comfort to some would-be belles to know that Sylvia Castleman, who attained in the end to such eminence in her profession, was at the outset a terrified child with shaking knees and chattering teeth, who never would have gone anywhere of her own choice!

## § 20

Now she was ready to try out all these instructions upon Frank. The scene was set and lighted, the curtain rose—but somehow there was a hitch in the performance. Frank was moody again. He sat staring before him, frowning somberly; and she looked at him in a confusion of anxieties. He did not love her after all—she had simply seized upon him and compelled his attention, and now he was longing to extricate himself! Even if this were not true, it would soon come to that, for she could think of nothing interesting to say, and he would be bored.

She racked her wits. What could she talk about to a man who knew none of her "set," who never went to balls or dinners, who could not conceivably care about polite gossip? Why didn't *he* say something—the silent man! What manners to take into company!

"I must make him look at me," she resolved. So without saying a word, she began taking a rose from her corsage and adjusting it in her hair. The motion distracted him, and she saw that he was watching. She had him!

"Is that in right?" she asked. Of course a *la France* rose in perfectly arranged hair is always "in right," and Sylvia knew it. Her little device failed abjectly, for Frank answered simply "Yes," and began staring into space again.

She tried once more, contenting herself with the barest necessities of conversation. "Did you shoot those quail yourself?"

Then he turned. "Miss Sylvia, I have something I must say to you. I've had time to think things over." He paused.

Ah, now it was coming! He had had time to think things over—and he called her "*Miss Sylvia!*" Something cried out in her to make haste and release him before he asked it. But she could not speak—she was as if pinned by a lance.

He went on. "Miss Sylvia, I had made up my mind that love was not for me. I knew that to women of my own class I was a man with a tainted name—a convict's son; and I would rather die than marry ¨¨neath me. So I shut up my heart, and when I me. ˀ woman, I turned and went away—as I tried to do with you. But you would not have it, and I could not resist you. I've been amazed at the intensity of my own feelings; it's something I could not have dreamed of—and unless I'm mistaken, it's been the same with you."

It was a bold man who could use words such as those to Sylvia. To what merciless teasing he laid himself open! But she only drew a deep sigh of relief. He still loved her!

"I forced myself to stay away," he continued, without waiting for her to answer. "I said, 'I must not go near her again. I must run away somewhere and get over it.' And then again I said, 'I can make her happy—I will marry her.' I said that, but I'm not going to do it."

He paused. Oh, what a voice he had! Sylvia felt the blood ebbing and flowing in her cheeks, pounding in her ears. She could not hear his words very well—but he loved her!

"Sylvia," he was saying, earnestly—as if half to convince himself—"we must both of us wait. You must have time to consider what loving me would mean. You have all these people—happy people; and I have nothing like that in my life. You have this beautiful home, expensive clothes—

every luxury. But I am a poor man. I have
only a mortgaged plantation, with a mother and
a brother and two sisters to share it. I have no
career—I have not even an education. All your
uncles, your cousins, your suitors, are college
men, and I am a plain farmer. So I face what
seems to me the worst temptation a man could
have. I see you, and you are everything in the
world that is desirable; and I believe that I could
win you and carry you away from here. My
whole being cries out, 'Go and take her! She
loves you! She wants you to!' But instead, I
have to come here and say, 'Think it over. Make
sure of your feelings; that it's not simply a flush
of excitement.' You being the kind of tender-
hearted thing you are, it might so easily be a
romantic imagining about a man who's apart
from other men—one you feel sorry for and would
like to help! You see what I mean? It isn't
easy for me to say it, but I'd be a coward if I
didn't say it—and mean it—and stand by it."

There was a long pause. Sylvia was thinking.
How different it was from other men's love-
making! There was Malcolm McCallum, who
had taken her driving yesterday, and had said
what they all said: "Never mind if you don't
love me—marry me, and let me teach you to
love me." In other words, "Stake your life's
happiness upon a blind chance, at the command
of my desire." Of course they would surround
her with all the external things of life, build her
a great house and furnish it richly, deck her with

silks and jewels and supply her with servants. All the world would come to admire her, and then she would be so grateful to her generous lord that she could not but love him.

Her voice was low as she answered, "A woman does not really care about the outside things. She wants love most. She wants to be sure of her heart—but of the man's heart too."

"As to that," he said, "I will not trust myself to speak. You are the loveliest vision that has ever come to me. You are——"

"I know," she interrupted. "But that, too, is mostly surface. I am luxurious, I am artificial and shallow—a kind of butterfly." This was what she said to men when she wished to be most deadly. But now she really meant it; there was a mist of tears in her eyes.

"That is nothing," he answered. "I am not such a fool that I can't see all that. There are two people in you, as in all of us. The question is, which do you want to be?"

"How can I say?" she murmured. "It would be a question of whether you loved me——"

"Ah, Sylvia!" he cried, in a voice of pain that startled her. And suddenly he rose and began to pace the room. "I cannot talk about my feeling for you," he said. "I made up my mind before I came here that I would not woo you—not if I had to bite off my tongue to prevent it. I said, 'I will explain to her, and then I will go away and give her time.' I want to play fair. I want to *know* that I have played fair."

As he stood there, she could see the knotted tendons in his hands, she could see the agitation of his whole being. And suddenly a great current took her and bore her to him. She put her hands upon his shoulders, whispering, "Frank!"

He stood stiff and silent.

"I love you!" she said. "I love you!" She gave a little sob of happiness; and he caught her in his arms and pressed her to his bosom, crushing all her roses, and stifling her words with his kisses. And so, a few minutes later, Sylvia was lying back in her favorite chair, with the satisfaction of knowing at last that he was looking at her. A couple of hours later, when he went away, it was as her plighted lover.

## § 21

FRANK came again two days later; and then Mrs. Castleman made her first remark. "Sylvia," she said, "you mustn't flirt with that man."

"Why not, Mother?"

"Because he'd probably take it seriously. And he's had a hard time, you know. We can't treat the Shirleys quite as we do other people."

"All right," said Sylvia. "I'll be careful."

Frank wanted the engagement made known at once—at least to the family. Such was his direct way. But Sylvia had an instinct against telling; she wanted a little time to watch and study and plan.

It was hard, however; she was absolutely shining with happiness—there seemed to be a kind of soul-electricity that came from her and affected everyone she met. It gathered the men about her thicker than ever—and at the very time that she wanted to be alone with Frank and the thought of Frank!

One evening when the Young Matrons' Club gave its monthly cotillion, Frank, knowing nothing about this event, called unexpectedly. A visit meant to him forty miles on horseback; and so, to the general consternation, Sylvia refused to attend the dance. All evening the telephone rang and the protests poured in. "We won't stand for it!" the men declared; and the women asked, "Who is it?" She had been to a bridge-party that afternoon, and everyone knew she was not sick. But what man could it be, when all the men were at the cotillion?

So the gossip began; and a week later another incident gave it wings. It was a great occasion, the semi-annual ball of the Country Club, and Frank had been warned that Sylvia would not be at home. But he wanted to see her in her glory, and he galloped his twenty miles in darkness and rain, and turned up at the club-house at midnight, and stood in the doorway to watch. Sylvia, seeing him and realizing what his presence meant, was seized with a sudden impulse to acknowledge him. She stopped dancing, and sent her partner away, and stood talking to Frank. Oh, what a staring, what a wagging of tongues! Frank

Shirley! Of all people in the world, Frank Shirley!

Of course, the news came to the Hall. Early in the morning, Aunt Nannie called up, announcing a visit, and there followed a family conclave with Mrs. Castleman, Aunt Varina and Sylvia.

"Sylvia," said Mrs. Chilton, trying her best to look casual, "I understand that Frank Shirley was at the ball."

"Yes, Aunt Nannie."

There was a pause. "What was he doing there?" asked "Miss Margaret," evidently having been coached.

"Why, I'm sure, Mother, I don't know."

"Did you invite him?"

"Indeed, I did not."

"He isn't a member of the Club, is he?"

"No; but he knows lots of other people who are."

"Everybody is saying he came to see you," broke in Aunt Nannie. "They say you stopped dancing to talk with him."

"I can't help what they say, Aunt Nannie."

"Do you think," inquired the Bishop's wife, "that it was altogether wise to get your name associated with his?"

"Isn't he a gentleman?" asked Sylvia.

"That's all right, my dear, but you've got to remember that you live in the world, and must consider other people's point of view."

"Do you mean, Aunt Nannie, that Frank Shirley's to be excluded from society because of his father's misfortune?"

"Not excluded, Sylvia. There are shades to such things. The point is that a young girl— a girl conspicuous, like you——"

"But, Aunt Nannie, I asked mother and father, and they were willing to receive him. Isn't that true, Mother?"

"Why, yes, Sylvia," said "Miss Margaret," weakly, "but I didn't mean——"

"It was all right for him to come here, once or twice," interrupted Aunt Nannie. "But at a Club ball——"

"The point is, Sylvia dear," quavered Mrs. Tuis, "you will get yourself a reputation for singularity."

And the mother added, "You surely don't have to do that to attract attention!"

So there it was. All that fine sentiment about the unhappy Shirleys went like a film of mist before a single breath of the world's opinion! They would not say it brutally—"He's a convict's son, and you can't afford to know him too well." It was not the Southern fashion—at least among the older generation—to be outspoken in worldliness. They had generous ideals, and made their boast of "chivalry;" but here, when it came to a test, they were all in accord with Aunt Nannie, who was said to "talk like a cold-blooded Northern woman."

Sylvia decided at once that some one must be told; so she went back to lunch with her aunt, and afterwards sought out the Bishop in his study. The walls of this room were lined with ancient theological treatises and sermons in faded greenish-black bindings: an array which never failed to appal the soul of Sylvia, who realized that she had consigned to the scrap-heap all this mass of learning—and had not yet apologized for her temerity.

"Uncle Basil," she began, "I have something very, very important to tell you." The Bishop turned from his desk and gazed at her. "I am engaged to be married," she said.

"Why, Sylvia!" he exclaimed.

"And I—I'm very much in love."

"Who is the man, my dear?"

"It is Frank Shirley."

Sylvia was used to watching people and reading their thoughts quickly. She saw that her uncle's first emotion was one of dismay. "Frank Shirley!"

"Yes, Uncle Basil."

Then she saw him gather himself together. He was going to try to be fair—the dear soul! But she could not forget that his first emotion had been dismay. "Tell me about it, my child," he said.

"I met him at the Venable's," she replied, "only a couple of weeks ago. He's an unusual sort of man, lonely and unhappy, very reserved and hard to get at. He fell in love with me—very much in love; but he didn't want me to know it. He did tell me at last."

The Bishop was silent. "I love him," she added.

"Are you sure?"

"As I've never loved anybody—as I never dreamed I could love."

There was a pause. "Uncle Basil—he's a good man," she said. "That is why I love him."

Again there was a pause. "Have you told your father and mother?" asked the Bishop.

"Not yet."

"You must tell them at once, Sylvia."

"I know they will make objections, and I want you to meet Frank and talk with him. You see, Uncle Basil, I'm going to marry him—and I want your help."

The Bishop was silent again, weighing his next words. "Of course, my dear," he said, "from a worldly point of view it is not a good match, and I fear your parents will regard it as a calamity. But, as you know, I think of nothing but the happiness of my darling Sylvia. I won't say anything at all until I have met the man. Send him to see me, little girl, and then I will give you the best counsel I can."

## § 22

FRANK went to pay his call the next day, and then came back to Sylvia. "He's a dear old man," he said. "And he wants what is best for you."

"What does he want?" demanded Sylvia.

"He says we should not marry now—that I

ought to be better able to take care of you.
And of course he's right."

There was a pause; then suddenly Frank
exclaimed, "Sylvia, I can't be just a farmer if
I'm going to marry you."

"What can you be, Frank?"

"I'm going to go to college."

"But that would take four years!"

"No, it needn't. I could dig in and get into
the Sophomore class this winter. I've been
through a military academy, and I was going to
Harvard, where my father and my grandfather
went, but I thought it was my duty to come
home and see to the place. But now my brother
has grown up, and he has a good head for business."

"What would you do ultimately?"

"I've always wanted to study law, and I think
now I ought to. Nobody is going to be willing
for us to marry at once; and they're much less
apt to object to me if I'm seriously going to make
something of myself."

Sylvia went over the next morning to get her
uncle's blessing. The good Bishop gave it to
her—together with some exhortations which he
judged she needed. They were summed up in
one sentence which he pronounced: "There is
nothing more unhappy in this world than a
serious-minded man with a worldly-minded wife."
Poor old Uncle Basil, with his snow-white hair
and his patient, saintly face, worn with care—
how much of his own soul he put into that

utterance! Sylvia laid her head upon his shoulder, and let the tears run down upon his coat.

After a while, he remarked, "Sylvia, your aunt saw Frank come here."

"What!" exclaimed Sylvia. "You don't mean that she'll guess!"

"She's very clever at guessing, my child." So Sylvia, as she rode home, realized that she had no more time to lose. When she got to the Hall, she set to work at once to carry out her plans.

She found her Aunt Varina in her room with a headache. On her dressing-table was a picture of the late-lamented Mr. Tuis, which Sylvia picked up. By manifesting a little interest in it, she quickly got her aunt to talking on the subject of matrimony.

Mrs. Tuis was the youngest of the Major's sisters. In the face of the protests of her relatives she had married a comparatively "common" man, who was poor and had turned out to be a drunkard, and after leading Aunt Varina a dog's life, had taken chloral. So Mrs. Tuis had come back to eat the bread of charity—which, though it was liberally sweetened with affection, had also a slightly bitter taste of compassion.

Her ill-fated romance was a poor thing, perhaps—but her own. As she told it her bosom fluttered and the tears trickled down her cheeks; and when she had got to a state of complete deliquescence, her niece whispered: "Oh, Aunt Varina, I'm so glad you believe in love! Aunt

Varina, will you keep a solemn secret if I tell it to you?"

And so came the story of the amazing engagement. Mrs. Tuis listened with wide-open, startled eyes, every now and then whispering, "Sylvia! Sylvia!" Of course she was thrilled to the deeps of her soul by it; and of course, in the mood that she had been caught, she could not possibly refuse her sympathy. "You must help me with the others," said the girl. "I'm going to tell mother next."

§ 23

THE first thing that struck you about "Miss Margaret" was her appalling incompetence. But underneath it lay the most exclusively maternal soul imaginable. She had nursed her children when they were almost two years old, great healthy calves running about the place and standing up to suck; she had rocked them to sleep in her arms when they were big enough to be reading Virgil; she had shed as many tears over a broken finger as most mothers shed over a funeral. She wanted her daughters to be happy, and to this end she would give them anything that civilization provided; she would even be willing that one of them should marry a man whose father "wore stripes"—so far as she was concerned, and so long as she remained alone with the daughter. You must picture her,

clasping Sylvia in her arms and weeping from
general agitation; moved to pity by the tale of
Frank's loneliness, moved to awe by the tale of
his goodness—but then suddenly smitten as by
a thunderbolt with the thought: "What will
people say! What will your Aunt Nannie say!"

While Sylvia was bent upon having her way,
you must not imagine that she did not feel any
of these emotions. Although she was mostly
Lady Lysle, her far-off ancestress, she was also
a little of "Miss Margaret," and was almost
capsized in these gales of emotion. She remembered a hundred scenes of tenderness and devotion; she clasped the great girl-mother in her
arms, and mingled their tears and vowed that
she would never do anything to make her unhappy. It was a lachrymal lane—this pathway
of Sylvia's engagement!

With her father she took a different line. She
got the Major alone in his office and talked to
him solemnly, not about love and romance, but
about Frank Shirley's character. She knew that
the Major was disturbed by the wildness of the
young men of the world about him; she had
heard him discuss the pace at which Aunt Nannie's boys were traveling. And here was a man
who had sowed no wild oats, and had learned the
lesson of self-control.

She was surprised at the way the Major took
it. He clutched the arms of his chair and went
white when he caught the import of her discourse; but he heard her to the end, and then

sat for a long while in silence. Finally, he inquired, "Sylvia, did anybody ever tell you why
your Uncle Laurence killed himself?"

"No," she replied.

"He was engaged to a girl, and her parents
made her break off the match. I never knew
why; but it ruined the girl's life, as well as his,
and it made a terrible impression on me. So I
made a vow—and now, I suppose, is the time I
have to keep it. I said I would never interfere
in a love-affair of one of my children!"

Sylvia was deeply affected, not only by his
words, but by the intense agitation which she
saw he was repressing. "Papa, does it seem so
very dreadful to you?" she asked.

Again there was a long wait before he answered. "It is something quite different from
what I had expected," he said. "It will make
a difference in your whole life—to an extent
which I fear you cannot realize."

"But if I really love him, Papa?"

"If you really love him, my dear, then I will
not try to oppose you. But oh, Sylvia, be sure
that you love him! You must promise me to
wait until I can be sure you are not mistaken
about that."

"I expect to wait, Papa," she said. "There
will be no mistake."

They talked for half an hour or so, and then
Sylvia went to her room. Half an hour later
"Aunt Sarah," the cook, came flying to her in
great agitation. "Miss Sylvia, what's de matter
wid yo' papa?"

"What?" cried Sylvia, springing up.

"He's sittin' on a log out beyan' de garden, cryin' fo' to break his heart!"

Sylvia fled to the spot, and fell upon her knees by him and flung her arms about him, crying, "Papa, Papa!" He was still sobbing; she had never seen him exhibit such emotion in her life before, and she was terrified. "Papa, what is it?"

She felt him shudder and control himself. "Nothing, Sylvia. I can't tell you."

"Papa," she whispered, "do you object to Frank Shirley as much as that?"

"No, my dear—it isn't that. It's that the whole thing has knocked me off my feet. My little girl is going away from me—and I didn't know she was grown up yet. It made me feel so old!"

He looked at her, trying to smile and feeling a little ashamed of his tears. She looked into the dear face, and it seemed withered and wrinkled all of a sudden. She realized with a pang how much he really had aged. He was working so hard—she would see him at his accounts late at night, when she was leaving for a ball, and would feel ashamed for her joys that he had to pay for. "Oh, Papa, Papa!" she cried, "I ought to marry a rich man!"

"My child," he exclaimed, "don't let me hear you say a thing like that!"

Poor, poor Major! He said it and he meant it; he was, I think, the most *naïve* of all the

members of his family.   He was a "Southern
gentleman," not a business man; he hated money
with his whole soul—hated it, even while he spent
it and enjoyed what it brought him.   He was
like a chip of wood caught in a powerful current;
swept through rapids and over cataracts, to his
own boundless bewilderment and dismay.

## § 24

"HE is without any pride of family."   That
had been the verdict upon the Major pronounced
by his mother, who had been a grand lady in her
own day.   She would turn to her eldest daughter
and say, "Look after him, Nannie!   Make him
keep his shoes shined!"   And so now, towards
the end of their conference, Sylvia and her father
found themselves looking at each other and saying, "What will Aunt Nannie say?"   Sylvia
was laughing, but all the same she had not the
nerve to face her aunt, and 'phoned the Bishop
to ask him to break the news.

Half an hour later the energetic lady's automobile was heard at the door.   And now behold,
a grand council, with the Major and his wife,
Mrs. Chilton, Mrs. Tuis, Mr. Mandeville Castleman, Sylvia and Celeste—the last having learned
that something startling had happened, and being
determined to find out about it.

"Now," began Aunt Nannie, "what is this
that Basil has been trying to tell me?"

There was no reply.

"Mandeville," she demanded, "have you heard this news?"

"No," said Uncle Mandeville.

"That Sylvia has engaged herself to Frank Shirley!"

"Good God!" said Uncle Mandeville.

"Sylvia!" exclaimed Celeste, in horror.

"Is it true?" demanded Aunt Nannie—in a tone which said that she declined to comment until official confirmation had been received.

"It is true," said Sylvia.

"And what have you to say about it?" inquired Aunt Nannie. She looked first at the Major, then at his wife, and then at Mrs. Tuis; but no one had anything to say.

"I can't quite believe that you're in your right senses," continued the speaker. "Or that I have heard you say the words. What *can* have got into you?"

"Nannie," said the Major, clearing his throat, "Sylvia doesn't want to marry him for a long time."

"But she proposes to be engaged to him, I understand!"

"Yes," admitted the other.

"And this engagement is to be announced?"

"Why—er—I suppose——"

"Certainly," put in Sylvia.

"And when, may I ask?"

"At once."

"And is there nobody here who has thought

of the consequences? Possibly you have over-looked the fact that one of my daughters has planned to marry Ridgely Peyton next month. That is to be called off?"

"What do you mean, Aunt Nannie?"

"Can you be childish enough to imagine that the Peytons will consent to marry into a family with a convict's son in it?"

"Nannie!" protested the Major.

"I know!" replied Mrs. Chilton. "Sylvia doesn't like the words. But if she proposes to marry a convict's son, she may as well get used to them now as later. It's the thing that people will be saying about her for the balance of her days; the thing they'll be saying about all of us everywhere. Look at Celeste there—just ready to come out! How much chance she'll have—with such a start! Her sister engaged to Frank Shirley!"

Sylvia turned to Celeste, and the eyes of these two met. Celeste turned pale, and her look was eloquent of dismay.

"Nannie," put in the Major, protestingly, "Frank Shirley is a fine, straight fellow——"

"I've nothing to say against Frank Shirley," exclaimed the other. "I know nothing about him, and never expect to know anything about him. But I know the story of his family, and I know that he's no right in ours. And what's more, he knows it too—if he were a man with any conscience or self-respect, he'd not consent to ruin Sylvia's life!"

"Aunt Nannie," broke in the girl, "is one to think of nothing in marriage but worldly pride?"

"Worldly pride!" ejaculated the other. "You call it worldly pride—because you, who have been the favorite child of the Castlemans, who have been given every luxury, every privilege, are asked not to trample your sisters and cousins! To give way to a blind passion, and put a stain upon our name that will last for generations! Where do you suppose you'd have been to-day if your forefathers had acted in such fashion? Do you imagine that you'd have been the belle of Castleman Hall, the most sought-after girl in the state?"

That was the argument. For some minutes Mrs. Chilton went on to pour it forth. And angry as she was, Sylvia could not but feel the force of it, and realize the effect it was producing on the other members of the council. It was not the voice of a woman speaking; it was the voice of something greater than any of them, or than all of them together—a thing that had come from dim-distant ages, and would continue into an impenetrable future. It was the voice of the Family! No light thing it was, in truth, to be the favorite daughter of the Castlemans! Not a responsibility one could evade, an honor one could decline!

"You are where you are to-day," proclaimed the speaker, "because other women thought of you when they chose their husbands. And I have never observed in you any unwillingness to accept the advantages they have handed on to you, any contempt for admiration and success. You are only a girl, of course; you can't be expected to realize all the meaning of your marriage to your family; but your mother and father know, and they ought to have impressed it on you, instead of leaving you to run wild and be trapped by the first unprincipled man that came along!"

There was a pause. The Major and his wife sat in silence, with a guilty look upon their faces. "Worldly pride!" exclaimed Aunt Nannie, turning upon them. "Have you told her about your own marriage?"

"What do you mean?" asked the Major.

"You know very well," was the reply, "that Margaret, when she married you, was head over heels in love with a nice, respectable, poor young preacher. And that she married you, not because she was in love with you, but because she knew that you were a noble-minded gentleman, the head of the oldest and best family in the county." And then Aunt Nannie turned upon Sylvia. "Suppose," she demanded, "that your mother had been sentimental and silly, and had run away with the preacher—have you any idea where you'd be now?"

Sylvia was hardly to be blamed for having no answer to this question, which might have been too much for the most learned scientist. There was silence in the council.

"Or take Mandeville," pursued the Voice of the Family.

"Nannie!" protested Mandeville.

"You don't want it talked about, I know," said the other, "but this is a time for truth-telling. Your Uncle Mandeville was madly in love with a girl—a girl who had position, and money too; but he would not marry her because she had a sister who was 'fast,' and he would not bring such blood into the family."

There was a pause. Uncle Mandeville's head was bowed.

"And do you remember," persisted Aunt Nannie, "that when the question was being discussed, your brother here asked that his growing daughters be spared having to hear about a scandal? Do you remember that?"

"Yes," said Mandeville, "I remember that."

"And how much nobler was such conduct than that of your Uncle Tom. Think——"

One could feel a sudden thrill go through the assembly. ".Oh!" cried Miss Margaret, protestingly; and Mrs. Tuis exclaimed, "Nannie!"

"Think of what happened to Tom's wife!" the other was proceeding; but here she was stopped by a firm word from the Major. "We will not discuss that, sister!"

There was a solemn pause, during which Sylvia and Celeste stared at each other. They knew that Uncle Tom Harley, their mother's brother, was an army officer stationed in the far West; but they had never heard before that he had a wife, and were amazed and a little frightened by the revelation. It is in moments such as these, when the tempers of men and women strike sparks, that one gets glimpses of the skeletons that are hidden far back in the corners of family closets!

## § 25

THERE was a phrase which Sylvia had heard a thousand times in the discussions of her relatives; it was "bad blood." "Bad blood" was a thing which possessed and terrified the Castleman imagination. Sylvia had but the vaguest ideas of heredity. She had heard it stated that tuberculosis and insanity were transmissible, and that one must never marry into a family where these disorders appeared; but apparently, also, the family considered that poverty and obscurity were transmissible—besides the general tendency to do things of which your neighbors disapproved. And you were warned that these evils often skipped a generation and reappeared. You might pick out a most excellent young man for a husband, and then see your children return to the criminal ways of his ancestors.

That was Aunt Nannie's argument now. When Sylvia cried, "What has Frank Shirley done?" the reply was, "It's not what he did, but what his father did."

"But," cried the girl, "his father was innocent! I've heard Papa say it a hundred times!"

"Then his uncle was guilty," was Aunt Nannie's

response. "Somebody took the money and gambled it away."

"But is gambling such a terrible offence? It seems to me I've heard of some Castlemans gambling."

"If they do," was the reply, "they gamble with their own money."

At which Sylvia cried, "Nothing of the kind! They have gambled, and then come to Uncle Mandeville to get him to pay their debts!"

Now that was a body-blow; for it was Aunt Nannie's own boys who had adopted this custom, which Sylvia had heard sternly reprehended in the family councils. Aunt Nannie flushed, and Uncle Mandeville made haste to interpose— "Sylvia, you should not speak so to your aunt."

"I don't see why not," declared the girl. "I am saying nothing but what is true; and I have been attacked in the thing that is most precious in life to me."

Here the Major felt it his duty to enter the debate. "Sylvia," he said, "I don't think you quite realize your aunt's feelings. It is no selfish motive that leads her to make these objections."

"Not selfish?" asked the girl. "She's admitted it's her fear for her own daughters, Papa——"

"It's just exactly as much for your own sister, Sylvia." It was the voice of Celeste, entering the discussion for the first time. Sylvia stared at her, astonished, and saw her eyes alight, her face as set and hard as Aunt Nannie's. Sylvia realized all at once that she had an enemy in her own house.

She was trembling violently as she made reply. "Then, Celeste, I have to give up everything that means happiness in life to me, because I might frighten away rich suitors from my sister?"

"Sylvia," put in the Major, gravely, before Celeste could speak, "you must not say things like that. It is not because Frank Shirley is poor that we are objecting. The pride of the Castlemans is not simply a pride of worldly power."

"She degrades us and degrades herself when she implies it!" exclaimed Aunt Nannie.

"It is a high and great pride," continued the Major. "The pride of a race of men and women who have scorned ignoble conduct and held themselves above all dishonor. That is no weak or shallow thing, Sylvia. It is a thing which sustains and upholds us at every moment of our lives: that we are living, not merely for our individual selves, but for all the generations that are to be. It may seem a cruel thing that the sins of the fathers should be visited upon the children, but it is a law of God. It was something that Bob Shirley himself said to me, with tears in his eyes—that his children and his children's children would have to pay for what had been done."

"But, Papa!" cried Sylvia. "They don't have to pay it, except that we make them pay it!"

"You are mistaken, my child," said the Major, quietly. "It's not we alone. It was the whole of society that condemned him. We cannot possibly wipe out the blot on the Shirley escutcheon."

"We can only drag ourselves down with them!" exclaimed Aunt Nannie.

"Why, it's just as if we said that going to prison was nothing!" cried Celeste.

"You must remember how many people there are looking up to us, Sylvia," put in Uncle Mandeville, solemnly.

There they were, all in chorus; Sylvia gazed in anguish from one to another. She gazed at her mother, just at the moment that that good lady was preparing to express her opinion. For the particular thing which held the imagination of "Miss Margaret" in thrall was this vision of the Castlemans living their life as it were upon a stage, with the lower orders in the pit looking on, imbibing instruction and inspiration from the action of the lofty drama.

Sylvia had heard it all before, and she could not bear to listen to it now. The tears, which had long been in her eyes, suddenly began to roll down her cheeks; she sprang up, exclaiming passionately, "You are all against me! Everyone of you!"

"Sylvia," said her father, in distress, "that is not true!"

"We would wade through blood for you!" exclaimed Uncle Mandeville—who was always looking for a chance to shoot somebody for the honor of the Castleman name.

"We are thinking of nothing but your own future," said the Major. "You are only a child, Sylvia——"

But Sylvia cried, "I can't bear any more!
You promised to stand by me, Papa—and now
you let Aunt Nannie come here and persuade
you—Mamma too—all of you! You will break
my heart!" And so saying she fled from the
room, leaving the family council to proceed as
best it could without her.

§ 26

Sylvia shut herself in her room and had a
good, exhaustive cry. Then, with her soul atmosphere cleared, she set to work to think out her
problem.

She had to admit that the family had presented
a strong case. There was the matter of heredity,
for example. Just how much likelihood might
there be, in the event of her marrying Frank, of
her finding herself with children of evil tendencies?
Just what truth might there be in Aunt Nannie's
point of view, that he was a selfish man, seeking
to redeem his family fortunes by allying himself
with the Castlemans? The question sounded
cold-blooded, but then Sylvia always had to face
the truth.

Also there was the problem, to what extent
a girl ought to sacrifice herself to her family.
There was no denying that they had done much
for her. She had been as their right eye to them;
and what did she owe them in return? There

was no one of them whom she did not love, sincerely, intensely; there was no one over whose sorrows she had not wept, whose burdens she had not borne. And now she faced the fact that if she married Frank Shirley, she would cause them unhappiness. She might argue that they had no right to be unhappy; but that did not alter the fact—they would be unhappy. Sylvia's life so far had been a process of bringing other people joy; and now, suddenly, she found herself in a dilemma where it was necessary for her to cause pain. Upon whom ought it to fall—upon her mother and father, her uncles and aunts—or upon Frank Shirley and herself?

Of all the arguments which produced an effect upon her, the most powerful was that embodied in Aunt Nannie's phrase, "a blind passion." Sylvia had been taught to think of "passion" as something low and shameful; she did not like the vision of herself as a weak, infatuated creature, throwing away all that other people had striven to give her. Many were the phrases whereby all her life she had heard such conduct scorned; there was a phrase from the Bible that was often cited—something about "inordinate affection." Just what was the difference between ordinate and inordinate affection? And how was she to decide in which category to place her love for Frank Shirley?

For the greater part of two days and two nights Sylvia debated these problems; and then she went to her father. The color was gone from her cheeks, and she was visibly thinner; but her mind was made up.

She told the Major all the doubts that had beset her and all the arguments she had considered. She set forth his contention that the pride of the Castlemans was not a "worldly pride;" and then she announced her conclusion, which was that he was permitting himself to be carried along, against his own better judgment, by the vanity of the women of his family.

Needless to say, the Major was startled by this pronouncement, delivered with all the solemnity of a pontiff *ex cathedra*. But Sylvia was ready with her proofs. There was Aunt Nannie, scheming and plotting day and night to make great marriages for her children. Spending her husband's money in ways he disapproved, and getting—what? Was there a single one of her children that was happy? Was there a single couple—for all the rich marriages—that wasn't living beyond its income, and jealous of other people who were able to spend more? Harley, grumbling because he couldn't have a motor of his own—Clive, because he couldn't afford to marry the girl he loved! And both of them drinking and gambling, and forcing Uncle Mandeville to pay their debts.

"Sylvia, you know I have protested to your Aunt Nannie."

"Yes, Papa—but meantime you're ruining your own health and fortune to enable your daughters to run the same race. Here's Celeste, like a

hound in the leash, eager to have her chance—
just Aunt Nannie all over again! I know, Papa
—it's terrible, and I can't bear to hurt you with
it, but I have to tell you what my own decision
is. I love Frank Shirley; I think my love for
him is a true love, and I can't for a moment
think of giving it up. I'm sorry to have to
break faith with the Family; I can only plead
that I didn't understand the bargain when I
made it, and that I shall take care not to make
my debt any greater."

"What do you mean, Sylvia?"

"I mean that I want to give up the social
game. I want to stop spending fortunes on
clothes and travel and luxuries; I want to stop
being paraded round and exhibited to men I'm
not interested in. I want you to give me a little
money—just what I need to live—and let me go
to New York to study music for a year or two
more, until I am able to teach and earn my own
living."

"Earn your own living! *Sylvia!*"

"Precisely, Papa. And meantime, Frank can
go through college and law school, and when we
can take care of ourselves, we'll marry. That's
my plan, and I'm serious about it—I want you
to let me do it this year."

And there sat the poor Major, staring at her,
his face a study of unutterable emotions, whispering to himself, "My God! My God!"

When Sylvia told me about this scene I reminded her of her experience with the young

clergyman who had come to convert her from heresy. "Don't you see now," I asked, "why he called you the most dangerous woman in Castleman County?"

## § 27

THIS procedure of Sylvia's was a beautiful illustration of what the military strategists call an "offensive defence." By the simple suggestion of earning her own living, she got everything else in the world that she wanted. It was agreed that she might make known her engagement to Frank Shirley. It was agreed that she need have no more money spent upon clothes and parties. Most important of all, it was agreed that Aunt Nannie was to be informed that Sylvia's course was approved by her parents, and that Frank Shirley was to be welcomed to Castleman Hall.

But of course she was not to be allowed to earn money. Her father made it clear that the bare suggestion of this caused him more unhappiness than she could endure to inflict. When she protested, "I want to learn something useful!" the dear old Major was ready with the proposition that they learn something useful together; and forthwith unlocked the diamond-paned doors of the old mahogany book-cases, and dragged forth dust-covered sets of Grote's "History of Greece," and Hume's "History of England," and Jefferson Davis' "Rise and Fall of the Confederate

Government"—out of which ponderous volumes Sylvia read aloud to him for several hours each day thereafter.

So from now on this is to be the story of a wholly reformed and chastened huntress of hearts. No more for her the tournaments of coquetry, no more the trumpets of the ball-room peal. No longer shall we behold her, clad in armor of chiffon and real lace, with breastplate of American beauty roses and helmet of gold and pearls. No longer shall we see the arrows of her red-brown eyes flying over the stricken field, deep-dyed with the heart's blood of Masculinity. Instead of this the dusty tome and the midnight oil and the green eye-shade confront us; we behold the un- canny spectacle of the loveliest of created mortals clad in blue stockings and black-rimmed spec- tacles.—All this scintillating wit, I make haste to explain, is not mine, but something which Avery Crittenden, the town wag, dashed off in a moment of illumination, and which appeared in the Castleman County *Register* (no names, if you please!) a couple of weeks after the news of Sylvia's reformation had stunned the world.

I wish that space were less limited, so that I could tell you how Castleman County received the tidings, and some few of the comical episodes in the long war which it waged to break down her resolution of withdrawal. It was the light of their eyes going out, and they could not and would not be reconciled to it. They wrote let- ters, they sent telegrams; they would come and literally besiege the house—sit in the parlor and condole with "Miss Margaret," no longer because Sylvia refused to marry them, but merely because she refused to lead the german with them! They would come with bands of music, with negro singers to serenade her. One spring night a whole fancy-dress ball adjourned by unanimous consent, and stormed the terraces of Castleman Hall and held its revels under the windows; and so of course Sylvia had to stop trying to read about Walpole's ministry and invite them in and give them wine and cake. On the evening of one of the club dances there was an organized conspiracy; seventeen of her old sweethearts sent her roses, and when in spite of this she did not come, the next day came seventeen messengers, bearing seventeen packages, each containing a little cupid wrapped in cotton-wool—but with his wings broken!

Such was the pressure from outside; and within—there would be a new gown sent by Uncle Mandeville, who was on another spree in New Orleans; a gown that was really a dream of beauty and a crime not to wear. Or there would be talk at the table about Dolly Witherspoon, Sylvia's chief rival, and the triumph she had won at the cotillion last night; how Stanley Pendleton was "rushing" her, and how Cousin Harley had been snubbed by her. And then some one gave a ball, and Charlie Peyton rang up to say that he was getting drunk and going to the devil unless Sylvia would come and dance with him! And when this device succeeded, and the rumor of it spread—how many of the nicest boys in the county took to getting drunk and going to the devil, because Sylvia would not come and dance with them!

I mention these things in order that you may understand that, sincere as Sylvia was in her effort to withdraw from "society," she was not entirely successful. She still met "eligible" men, and she was still an object of family concern. A few days after the council, she had been surprised by a visit from Aunt Nannie, who came to apologize and make peace. "I want you to know, Sylvia dear," she declared, "that what I said to you was said with no thought of anything but your own good." There was a reconciliation, with tears in the eyes of both of them—and a renewal of the activities of Aunt Nannie. How often it happened to Sylvia, when at some dance she fell into the clutches of an undesirable man, that Aunt Nannie found a pretext for joining them—and presently, without quite realizing how, Sylvia found that the man was gone, and that she was settled for a *tête-a-tête* with a more suitable companion! Once she stopped to luncheon with the Bishop, and found herself being shown a new album of photographs. There among English cathedrals and Rhenish castles she stumbled upon a picture of the "Mansion House," the home of the wealthy Peytons. "What a lovely old place!" she exclaimed; and her aunt remarked, "Charlie will inherit that, lucky boy!"

She remembered also the case of Ned Scott, the young West Pointer who came home on furlough, setting all the girls' hearts aflutter with his gray and gold gorgeousness. "My, what a handsome fellow!" exclaimed Aunt Nannie. "It makes me happy just to watch him walk!"

"An army man always has a good social position," remarked "Miss Margaret," casually.

"And an assured income," added Aunt Varina, timidly.

"He has a mole on his nose," observed Sylvia.

## § 28

FRANK SHIRLEY had passed the midwinter examinations at Harvard, and was settled in the dormitory of his fathers; and so for a while the acute agitation subsided. It began again in the summer, however—when Sylvia proposed staying at the Hall, instead of going with the family to the summer-place in the mountains of North Carolina. It was obvious that this was in order to be near her lover; and so the whole battle had to be fought over again. Aunt Nannie was unable to understand how Sylvia could be willing to "publish her infatuation to the world."

"But I have only the summer when I can see him," the girl argued.

"But even so, my dear—to give up everything else, to change all your plans, the plans of your whole family!"

"Nobody need change, Aunt Nannie. Aunt Varina will stay with me gladly."

"Others have to stay, if it's only to hide what you are doing. It's not decent, Sylvia! Believe me, you will lose the man's own respect if you behave so. No man can permanently respect a woman who betrays her feelings so openly."

"My dear Aunt Nannie," said Sylvia, quietly, "I am quite sure that I know Frank Shirley better than you do."

"Poor, deluded child," was Mrs. Chilton's comment. "You'll find to your sorrow some day that men are all alike!"

But the girl was obdurate. The family had to proceed to desperate measures. First her mother declared that she would stay also—she must remain to protect her unfortunate child. And then, of course, the Major decided that it was his duty to remain. There came the question of Celeste, who had planned a house party, and foresaw the spoiling of her fun by the selfishness of her sister. There was also the baby—the precious, ineffable baby, the heir of all the might, majesty and dominion of the Lysles. The family physician intervened—the child must positively have the mountain air. Also the Major's liver trouble was serious, he was sleeping badly and working too hard, and was in desperate need of a change. Prompted by Aunt Nannie, the doctor said this in Sylvia's hearing—and settled the matter.

It had been Frank's idea to remain at Cambridge and study during the summer, so as to

make up some "conditions;" but when he learned
that Sylvia intended to remain at the Hall, he
decided to stand the expense of coming home.
He arrived there to find that she had suddenly
changed her mind and was going—and offering
but slight explanation of her change. Sylvia
was intensely humiliated because of the attitude
of her family, and was trying to spare Frank the
pain of knowing about it.

So came the beginning of unhappiness between
them. Frank was acutely conscious of his inferiority to her in all worldly ways. And he knew
that her relatives were trying to break down her
resolution. He could not believe that they would
succeed; and yet, there was a bitter and disillu-
sioned man within him who could not believe that
they would fail. In his soul there were always
thorns of doubt, which festered, and now and
then would cause him pangs of agony. But he
was as proud as any savage, and would have
died before he would ask for mercy. When he
learned that she was going away from him, for
no better reason than her relatives' objections,
he felt that she did not care enough for him.
And then, when he did not protest, it was Sylvia's
turn to worry. So it really did not matter to
him whether she stayed or not! It might be
that Aunt Nannie was right after all, that a man
ceased to love a woman who gave herself too
freely.

## § 29

THE matter was complicated by the episode of Beauregard Dabney, about which I have to tell.

You have heard, perhaps, of the Dabneys of Charleston; the names of three of them—Beauregard's grandfather and two great-uncles—may be read upon the memorial tablets in the stately old church which is the city's pride. In Charleston they have a real aristocracy—gentlemen so poor that they wear their cuffs all ragged, yet are received with homage in the proudest homes in the South. The Dabneys had a city mansion with front steps crumbling away, and a country house which would not keep out the rain; and yet when Beauregard, the young scion of the house, fell prey to the charm and animation of Harriet Atkinson, whose father's street railroad was equal to a mint, the family regarded it as the greatest calamity since Appomattox.

He had followed Harriet to Castleman County; and when the news got out, a detachment of uncles and aunts came flying, and captured the poor boy, and were on the point of shipping him home, when Harriet called Sylvia to the rescue. Sylvia could impress even the Dabneys; and if only she would have Beauregard and one of the aunts invited to Castleman Hall, it might yet be possible to save the situation.

Sylvia had met young Dabney once, when visiting in Charleston. She remembered him as

an effeminate-mannered youth, with what would
have been a doll-baby face but for the fact that
the nose caved in in the middle in a disturbing
way. "Tell me, Harriet," she asked, when she
met her friend—"are you in love with him?"

"I don't know," said Harriet. "I'm afraid
I'm not—at least, not very much."

"But why do you want to marry a man you
don't love?"

Harriet was driving, and she grasped the reins
tightly and gave the horse a flick with the whip.
"Sunny," she said, "you might as well face the
fact—I could never fall in love as you have.
I don't believe in it. I wouldn't want to. I'd
never let myself trust a man that much."

"But then, why marry?"

"I have to marry. What can I do? I'm tired
of being chaperoned, and I don't want to be an
old maid."

Sylvia pondered for a moment. "Suppose,"
she said, "that you should marry him, and then
meet a man you loved?"

"I've already answered that—it won't happen.
I'm too selfish." She paused, and then added,
"It's all right, Sunny. I've figured over it, and
I'm not making any mistake. He's a good fellow,
and I like him. He's a gentleman—he does not
offend me. Also, he's very much in love with
me, which is the best way; I'll always be the
boss in my own home. He's respected, and I'll
help out my poor struggling family if I marry
him. You know how it is, Sunny—I vowed I'd

never be a climber, but it's hard to pull back
when your people are eager for the heights. And
then, too, it's always a temptation to want to go
where you're told you can't go."

"Yes, I know that," said Sylvia. "But that's
a joke, and marrying's a serious matter."

"It's only that because we make it so," retorted
the other. "I find myself bored to death, and
here's something that rouses my fighting blood.
They say I shan't have him—and so I want him.
I'm going to break into that family, and then
I'm going to shake the rats out of the hair of some
of those old maid aunts of his!"

She laughed savagely and drove on for a while.
"Sunny," she resumed at last, "you're all right.
You know it, but I tell you so anyway. You
never were a snob that I know—but I'm cynical
enough to say that it's only because you are too
proud. Can you imagine how you'd feel if anybody tried to patronize you? Can you imagine
how you'd feel if everybody did it? I'm tired
of it—don't you see? And Beauregard is my way
of escape. I'm going to marry him if I possibly
can; my mind is made up to it. I've got the
whole plan of campaign laid out—your part
included."

"What's my part, Harriet?"

"It's very simple. I want you to let Beauregard fall in love with you."

"With *me!*"

"Yes. I want you to give him the worst
punishment you ever gave a man in your life."

"But what's that for?"

"He's in love with me—he wants me—and he's too much of a coward to marry me.  And I want to see him suffer for it—as only you can make him.  I want you to take him and maul him, I want you to bray him and pound him in your mortar, I want you to roll him and toss him about, to walk on him and stamp on him, to beat him to a jelly and grind him to a powder!  I want you to keep it up till he's thoroughly reduced— and then you can turn him over to me."

"And then you will heal him?" inquired Sylvia —who had not been alarmed by this bloodthirsty discourse.

"Perhaps I will and perhaps I won't," said the other.  "What is there in the maxims of Lady Dee about a broken heart?"

"The best way to catch a man," quoted Sylvia, "is on the rebound!"

## § 30

I DON'T know how this adventure will seem to you.  To me it was atrocious; but Sylvia undertook it with a child's delight.

"I had on a white hat with pink roses," she said, when she told me about it; "and I could always do anything to a man when I had pink roses on.  Beauregard was waiting for Harriet to go driving when I first saw him; she was upstairs, late on purpose.  He said something about my looking like a rose myself—he was the most obvious of human creatures. And when he asked me to get in and sit by him, I said, 'Harriet will be jealous.' Of course he was charmed at the idea of Harriet's being jealous. So he asked me to take a little drive with him, and we stayed out an hour—and by the time we got back, I had him!"

Two days later he was on his knees begging Sylvia to marry him. At which, of course, she was horrified. "Why, you're supposed to be in love with my best friend!"

He was frank about it, poor soul. "Of course, Miss Sylvia," he explained, "I was in love with Harriet; and Harriet's a fine girl, all right. It's bad about her family, but I thought we could go away where nobody knew her, and people would accept her as my wife, and they'd soon forget. She's jolly and interesting, and all that. But you understand, surely, Miss Sylvia—no man would marry Harriet Atkinson if he could get you. You—you're quite different, Miss Sylvia. You're one of us!"

He made Sylvia furious by his matter-of-fact snobbery; and so she was lovely to him. She told him that she, too, had been in love, but her family was opposed to the man, and now she was very unhappy. She told him that she was not worthy of the love of such a man as he. Poor Beauregard tried his best to reassure her, and followed her about day and night for ten days, and was a most dreadful nuisance.

Each day she would report to Harriet the stage of infatuation to which he had come; until at last Harriet's thirst for blood was satisfied. Then, dressed all in snow-white muslin and lace, Sylvia took her devoted suitor off to a seat in a distant grape-arbor, and there administered the dose she had prepared for him. "Mr. Dabney," she said, "this joke has got to be such a bore that I can't stand it."

"What joke?" asked Beauregard, innocently.

"You know that I have called myself a friend of Harriet Atkinson's. When you came to me and told me that you loved her, but wanted to marry me because my family was better than hers—did it never occur to you how it would strike her friend? Evidently not. Well, let me tell you then—I could think that it was the stupidest joke I had ever heard, or else that you were the most arrogant jack that ever walked on two legs. I said that I would punish you—and I've been doing it. You must understand that I never felt the least particle of interest in you; I never met a man who'd be less apt to attract me, and I can't see how you managed to interest Harriet. I assure you you've no reason for holding the extravagant opinion of yourself which you do."

The poor youth sat staring at her, unable to believe his ears. And so, of course, Sylvia began to feel sorry for him. "I can see," she said, "that there might be something in you to like— if only you had the courage to be yourself. But you're so terrorized by your aunts and uncles, you've let them make you into such a dreadful snob——"

She paused. "You really think I am a snob?" he cried.

"The worst I ever met. I couldn't bring myself to discuss it with you. Let me give you this one piece of advice, though; if you think you're too good to marry a girl, pray find it out before you tell her that you love her. Of course, I'm not sorry that it happened this time, for you won't break Harriet's heart, and she's a thousand times too good for you. So I'm not sorry that you've lost her."

"You—you think that I've lost her, Miss Sylvia?" gasped the other.

"Lost her?" echoed Sylvia. "Why, you don't mean——" But then she stopped. She must not make it impossible for him to think of Harriet again. "You've lost her, unless she's a great deal more generous than I'd ever be."

Beauregard took his drubbing very well. He persuaded Sylvia to discuss his snobbery with him, and confessed the offence, and got up quite a fire of indignation against his banded relatives. Also he admitted that Harriet was too good for him, and that he had treated her like a cad. His speeches grew shorter and his manner more anxious, and Sylvia could see that his main thought was to get back and find out if he'd really lost Harriet.

So she called her friend up on the 'phone and

announced, "He's coming. Get on your prettiest dress without delay!" And then Sylvia went away and had a cry—first, because she had said such cruel things, and second, because her mother and father would be unhappy when they learned that Beauregard had escaped her.

An hour later Harriet called up to say that it was all over. "Did you accept him?" asked Sylvia.

To which the other answered, "You may trust me now, Sunny! You have made him into a soft dough, and I'll knead him." And sure enough, the new Beauregard Dabney sent his aunts and uncles flying, and followed Harriet to her summer home on the Gulf, and was hardly to be induced to wait for a conventional wedding—so eager was he to prove to himself and to Sylvia Castleman that he was really not a coward and a snob!

## § 31

IT was in the midst of these adventures that Frank Shirley made his unexpected return from the North. On the day when he came to see her first, she naturally forgot about the existence of Beauregard Dabney—until Beauregard suddenly appeared and flew into a fit of jealousy. Then the imp of mischievousness got hold of Sylvia; she found herself wondering, "Would it be possible for Frank to be jealous of Beauregard? And if he was, how would he behave?"

"I knew it was dreadful then," she told me, "but I couldn't have helped it if I'd been risking my life. I had to see what Frank would do when he was jealous. I simply *had* to! It was a kind of insanity!"

So she tried it, and did not get much fun out of the experience. Frank was like an Indian in captivity; he could not be made to cry out under torture. He saw Beauregard's position, and the unconcealed delight of the family; but he set his lips together and never gave a sign. Sylvia was going away for the summer, and Beauregard was talking about following her. There would be other suitors following her, no doubt—and new ones on the ground. Frank went home, and Sylvia did not hear from him for several days.

The Beauregard episode came to its appointed end, and then, in a letter to Frank, Sylvia mentioned that she had accomplished her purpose— the youth was engaged to Harriet. She thought this was explaining things. But how could Frank imagine the complications of the art of man-catching? Was Sylvia jesting with him, or trying to blind him, or apologizing to him, or what?

Sylvia kept putting off her start to the mountains—she could not bear to go while things were in such a state between them. But, while she was still hesitating, to her consternation she received a note from him saying that he was starting for Colorado. He had received a telegram that an aunt was dead; there were business matters to be attended to—some property which for his sisters' sake could not be neglected. It was a cold, business-like note, with not a word of sorrow at parting; and Sylvia shed tears over it. Such is the irrationality of those in love, she had forgotten all about young Dabney or any other cause for doubt and unhappiness she might have given Frank. She thought that he, and he alone, had been unkind. And meantime, Frank had made up his mind that she was repenting of her engagement, and that it was his duty to make it easy for her to withdraw.

So the two spent an unhappy summer. Sylvia let herself be taken about to parties, but she grew more weary every hour of the social game. "I've smiled until I've got the lockjaw," she would say. She was losing weight and growing pale, in spite of the mountain air.

September came, and Harriet's wedding was set for the next month, and likewise Frank's return to Harvard. He came back from the West, and Sylvia wrote asking him to come and visit her for a week. But to her consternation there came in reply a polite refusal from Frank. There was so much that needed his attention on the plantation, and some studying that must be done if he was to make good. For three days Sylvia struggled with herself, the last stand of that barbarian pride of hers; then she gave way completely and sent him a telegram: "Please come at once."

She would have recalled it an hour afterwards, but it was too late; and that evening she received an answer, to the effect that he would arrive in the morning. She spent a sleepless night imagining his coming, and a score of different ways in which she would meet him. She would throw herself at his feet and beg him not to torture her; she would array herself in her newest gown and fascinate him in the good old way; she would climb once more upon the pinnacle of her pride and compel him to humble himself before her.

In the morning she drove to meet him, together with a cousin who had come on the same train. She never stood a worse social ordeal than that drive and the luncheon with the family. But at last they were alone together, and sat gazing at each other with eyes full of bewilderment and pain.

"Sylvia," said Frank, finally, "you do not look happy."

"Why should I be happy?" she asked.

There was a pause. "Listen," he said. "Can we not deal honestly with each other—openly and sincerely, for once. Surely that is the best way, Sylvia—no matter how much it hurts."

"I am ready to do it," she replied.

"You don't have to spare my feelings," he went on. "I know all you have to contend with, and I shan't blame you. The one thing I can't bear is to be played with, to be lured by false hopes, to drag on and on, tormented by uncertainty."

She was gazing at him, bewildered. "Why do you say all that, Frank?" she cried.

"Why should I not say it?" he asked; and again they stared at each other.

Suddenly she broke out, in a voice full of anguish, "Frank, this is what I want to know—answer me this! Do you love me?"

"Do I love you?" he echoed.

"Yes,"—and with greater intensity, "I want you to be honest about it!"

"Honey!" he said, his voice trembling, "it's the question of whether I'm allowed to love you. It's so terrible to me—I can't stand the uncertainty."

She cried again, "But do you *want* to love me?"

She heard his voice break, she saw the emotion that was shaking him, and with a sudden sob she was in his arms. "Oh, Frank, Frank!" she exclaimed. "What *have* we been doing to each other?"

And so at last the fog of misunderstanding was lifted. "Sweetheart," he exclaimed, "what could you have been thinking?"

"I thought you had stopped loving me because I had been too bold, because I had been unwomanly."

"Why, Sylvia, you must be mad! Have I not been hungry for your love?"

"Oh, tell me that I can love you!" she wailed. "Tell me that you won't grow tired of me if I love you!"

He clasped her in his arms and covered her lips with kisses; he soothed her like a frightened child. She was free now to sob out her grief, to tell him what she had felt throughout all these months of misery. "Oh, why didn't you come to me like this before?" she asked.

"But, Sylvia," he answered, "how could I know? I saw you letting another man make love to you——"

"But, Frank, that was only a joke!"

"But how could I know that?"

"How could you imagine anything else? That I could prefer Beauregard Dabney to you!"

"That's easy to say," he replied. "But there was your family—I knew what they'd prefer, and I saw how they were struggling to keep us apart. And what was I to think—why should you be giving him your time, unless you wanted to let me know——"

"Ah, don't say that! Don't say that!" she cried, quickly. "It's wicked that such a thing should have happened."

"We must learn to talk things out frankly," he said. "For one thing you must not let your family come between us again. You must free me from this dreadful fear that they are going to take you from me."

And suddenly Sylvia blazed up. All the misunderstanding had come from the opposition of her family, and her unwillingness to talk to Frank about it. "I never saw it so clearly before," she exclaimed. "Frank, I can never make them see things my way. And they'll always have this dreadful power over me—because I love them so!'

"What can you do then?" he asked.

"I'm going to betray them to you!" she cried. And as he looked puzzled, she went on, "I'm

going to tell you about them! I'm going to tell
you everything they've said and done, and everything they may say and do in the future!"

"And that," said Frank to me, "was the most
loving thing she ever said!" Such was the power,
in Sylvia's world, of the ideal of the Family!

# BOOK II

## *Sylvia Lingers*

10

At the railroad station in Boston, on an afternoon in May, Sylvia Castleman and Mrs. Tuis
were arriving from New York. You must picture
Sylvia in a pale gray cloak, with a pale blue
blouse; also a gray hat with broad brim and
"bluets" on top. You can imagine, perhaps,
how her colors shone from under it. She was
meeting Frank for the first time in eight months.

The host of the occasion was Cousin Harley
Chilton, now also a student at Harvard. It was
mid-afternoon, and he had borrowed a motor car
to show her something of Cambridge. Their
bags were sent to their hotel in the city, and
Frank took his place by Sylvia's side. They
had to talk about commonplaces, but he could
feel her delight and eagerness like an electric
radiance. As they flew over the long bridge,
he wrapped a robe about her. What a thrill
went through him as he touched her! "Oh, I'm
so happy! so happy!" she exclaimed, her eyes
shining into his. He had given her a new name
in his letters, and he whispered it now into her
ear: "Lady Sunshine! Lady Sunshine!"

They came to a vista of dark stone buildings,
buried in the foliage of enormous elms. "Here
are the grounds," he said; and Sylvia cried, "Oh
Harley, go slowly. I want to see them." Her

cousin complied, and Frank began pointing out the various buildings by name.

But suddenly the car drew in by the curb and stopped. Harley leaned forward, remarking, "Spark-plug loose, I think."

Now the sparking seemed to be all right, so far as Frank could judge, but he did not know very much about automobiles. In general he was a guileless nature, and did not understand that this was the beginning of Sylvia's social career at Harvard. But Sylvia, who knew about automobiles, and still more about human nature, saw two men strolling in her direction, and now about twenty yards away—upper classmen, clad in white flannel trousers, blue coats, huge straw hats like baskets, and ties knotted with that elaborately studied carelessness which means that the wearer has spent fifteen minutes before the mirror prior to emerging from his room.

Naturally Sylvia looked at them, for they were interesting figures; and naturally they looked back, for Sylvia was an interesting figure too. One could not hear, but could almost see them exclaiming: "By Jove! Who is she?" They went by—almost, but not quite. They stopped, half turned and stood hesitating.

Harley looked up from his spark-plugs, a frown of annoyance on his face. He glanced toward the two men. "Hello, Harmon," he said.

"Hello, Chilton," was the reply. "Something wrong?"

"Yes," said Harley. "Can't make it out."

The two approached, lifting their hats, the one who had spoken a trifle in advance. "Can I help?" he asked, solicitously.

"I think I can manage it," answered Harley; but the men did not move on. "Whose car?" asked the one called Harmon.

"Bert Wilson's," said Harley. "I don't know its tricks."

The other's eyes swept the car, and of course rested on Sylvia, who was in the seat nearest the curb. That made an awkward moment—as he intended it should. "Mr. Harmon," said Harley, "let me present you to my cousin, Miss Castleman."

The man brightened instantly and made a bow. "I am delighted to meet you, Miss Castleman," he said, and introduced his companion. "You have just arrived?" he inquired.

"Yes," said Sylvia.

"But you've been here before?"

"Never befo-ah," said Sylvia; whereupon he knew from what part of the world she had come. There began an animated conversation—Harley and his spark-plugs being forgotten entirely.

All this Frank watched, sitting back in his seat in silence. He knew these men to be Seniors, high and mighty swells from the "Gold Coast;" but he had never been introduced to them, and so he was technically as much a stranger to them as if he had just arrived from the far South himself. Sylvia, who was new to the social customs of Harvard, never dreamed of this situation, and so left him to watch the comedy undisturbed.

There came along a couple of Freshmen; class-mates of Harley's and members of his set. He was buried in his labors, but they were not to be put off. "What's the matter, old man?" they asked; and when he answered, "Don't know," they stood, and waited for him to find out, stealing meantime fascinated glances at the vision in the car.

Next came two street-boys; and of course street-boys always stop and stare when there is a car out of order. Then came an old gentleman, who paused, smiling benevolently, as he might have paused to survey a florist's window. So there was Sylvia, quite by accident, and in perfect innocence, holding a levee on the side-walk, with two men whose ties proclaimed them members of an ineffable and awe-inspiring "final" club doing homage to her.

"My cousin's a Freshman," she was saying. "So I'll have three years more to come here."

"Oh, but think of us!" exclaimed the basket-hats together. "We go out next month!"

"Can't you manage to fail in your exams?" she inquired. "Or is that impossible at Harvard?" She looked from one to another, and in the laugh that followed even the street-boys and the benevolent old gentleman joined.

By that time the gathering was assuming the proportions of a scandal. Men were coming from the "Yard" to see what was the matter.

"Hello, Frank Shirley," called a voice. "Anybody hurt?" And Sylvia answered in a low voice, "Yes, several." She looked straight into Harmon's eyes, and she got his answer—that she had not spoken too rashly.

The *séance* came to a sudden end, because Harley realized that he was subjecting club men to an ordeal on the street. He straightened up from his spark-plug. "I think she's all right now," he said—and to one of the street-boys, "Crank her up, there."

"Where are you stopping?" asked Harmon.

Harley named the hotel, but did not take the hint—which was presumptuous in a Freshman. "Good-bye, Miss Castleman," said the Senior, wistfully; and the crowd parted and the car went on.

After which Sylvia sank back in her seat and looked at Frank and laughed. "Isn't it wonderful," she exclaimed, "what a woman can do with her eyes!"

§ 2

THEY returned to the hotel, where there were engagements—a whole world waiting to be conquered. But Sylvia delivered an ultimatum; she would pay no attention to anyone until she had an hour alone with Frank. When Aunt Varina had meekly left her, she first flew into Frank's arms and permitted him to kiss her; and then, seated decorously in a separate chair, she proceeded to explain to him the mystery of her presence there.

She had come to New York to buy clothes for herself and the rest of the family; that much Frank had known. He had begged her to run up to Cambridge, but the family had refused permission. Celeste was going to have a house party, the baby had been having more convulsions—these were only two of a dozen reasons why she must return. Frank had been intending to go down to New York to see her—when suddenly had come a telegram, saying that she would arrive the next afternoon.

"It was my scheme," she said, "and I expect you to be proud of me when you hear it. If you scold me about it, Frank——!" She said this with the tone of voice that she used when it was necessary to disarm some one.

It was difficult for Frank to imagine himself objecting to any device which had brought her there. "Go ahead, honey," said he.

"It has to do with Harley," she explained. "Mother sent me one of his letters, telling about the terrible time he's been having here. You see, he's scared to death for fear he won't make the 'Dickey'—or that he won't be among the earlier tens. So they were all upset, and they've been scurrying round getting letters of introduction for him, moving heaven and earth to get him in with the right people. I read his letter, and then suddenly the thought flashed over me, 'There's my chance!' Don't you see?"

"No," said Frank, and shook his head—"I don't see at all."

"Sometimes," said the girl, "when I think about you, I get frightened, because—if you knew how wicked I really am—! Well, anyhow, I sat down and wrote to Harley that he was a goose, and that if he had sense enough to get me to Harvard, he'd make the 'Dickey,' and one of the 'final' clubs as well. I told him to write Aunt Nannie at once; and sure enough, just about the time they got Harley's letter, there came a telegram saying I might come!"

It was impossible for Frank not to laugh—if it were only because Sylvia was so happy. "So," he said, "you've come to be a social puller-in for Harley!"

"Now, Frank, don't be horrid! I saw it this way—and it's obvious arithmetic: If I do this, I'll see Frank part of every day for a couple of weeks; if I don't, I'll only see him for a day when he comes to New York. There's only one trouble—you must promise not to mind."

"What is it?"

"We must not tell anybody that we're engaged. If people knew that, I couldn't do much with them."

"But I've told some people."

"Whom?"

"Well, my room-mate."

"He's not a club man, so that won't matter. It doesn't really matter, if we simply don't announce it. You must promise not to mind, Frank—be good, and let me have my fun in my foolish way, and you sit by and smile, as you did in the car."

Frank's answer was that he expected to sit by and smile all his life; a statement which led to a discussion between them, for Sylvia made objection to his desire to shrink from the world, and declared that she meant to fight for him, and manage him, and make something out of him. When these discussions arose he would laugh, in his quiet, good-natured way, and picture himself as a diplomat at St. James', wearing knee-breeches and winning new empires by means of the smiles of "Lady Sunshine." "But, you forget one thing," he said—"that I came to Harvard to learn something."

"When you go out into the world," propounded Sylvia, "you'll realize that the things one knows aren't half so important as the people one knows."

Frank laughed. "That wouldn't be such a bad motto for our Alma Mater," he said; then, thinking it over, "They might put it up as an inscription, where Freshmen with social ambitions could learn it. A motto for all college climbers— 'Not the things one knows, but the people one knows!'"

Sylvia was looking at him, a trifle worried. "Frank," she said, "suppose you go through life finding fault with everything in that fashion?"

"I don't know," he replied. "But I shall always fight a wrong when I see one. Wait till you've been here a while, and you'll see about this!"

"I ought to have come before," she said; "I could have solved so many problems for you.

It's the same everywhere in life—those who are out rail at those who are in, but when you hear both sides, you see the matter differently. I've a grudge against you, Frank—you misrepresented things. You told me they had abolished the Fraternity system here, and I didn't know about the clubs, and so I permitted you to be a 'goat.' "

"They call it a 'rough-neck' here," he corrected.

"Well, a 'rough-neck.' Anyway, I let you take a back seat. And just as if you didn't have ability——"

"Ability!" Frank exclaimed. Then, checking himself, he went on gently to explain the social system he had found at Harvard. In the Southern colleges, ability and good breeding might still get a poor man recognition. But the clubs here were run by a little group of Boston and New York society men, who had been kept in a "set" from the day they were born. They went to kindergarten together, to dancing school together —their sisters had private sewing circles, instead of those at church. They had their semi-private dormitories on Auburn Street—one might come with a string of automobiles and a stud of polo ponies, but he would find that his money would not rent one of those places unless the crowd had given its O. K. They roomed apart, they ate and drank apart, and the men in their own class never even met them.

Sylvia listened in bewilderment. "Surely, Frank," she exclaimed, "there must be some friendliness——"

He smiled. "Just as I said, honey—you're judging by the South. We've snobbery enough there, God knows—but some of us are kind-hearted. You can't imagine things up here—how cold and formal people are. They have their millions of dollars and the social position this gives them; they are jealous of those who have more and suspicious of those who have less—and they've been that way for so long that every plain human feeling is dead in them. Take a man like Douglas van Tuiver, for example. You've heard of him, I suppose?"

"I've heard of the van Tuivers, of course."

"Well, Douglas is our bright particular social star just now. He's inherited from three estates already—the Lord only knows how many tens of millions in his own right. He's gone the 'Gold Coast' crowd one better—has his own private house here in Cambridge, and an apartment in Boston also, I'm told. He entered society there at the same time that he entered college; and he doesn't think much of our social life—except the little set he'd already met in Boston and New York. He's stiff and serious as a chief justice—self-conscious, condescending——"

"Do you know him?" asked Sylvia.

"I never met him, of course; but I see him all the time, because he's in some of my sections."

"In some of your sections!" cried Sylvia. "And you never met him?"

The other laughed. "You see, honey," he said, "how little you are able to imagine life at Harvard! Douglas, my dear, has been yachting with English peers; he has Scotch earls for ancestors, and an accent that he has acquired in their honor. He sets more store by them, I suppose, than he does by his old Knickerbocker ancestors, who left him several farms between Fifth and Madison Avenues."

"Is he a club man?" asked Sylvia.

"He lives to set the social standards for our clubs; a sort of *arbiter elegantiarum*. It's one of the sayings they attribute to him, that he came to Harvard because American university life was in need of 'tone.' "

"Oh, dear me!" exclaimed Sylvia; and again, in a lower voice, "Oh, dear me!" She pondered, and then with sudden interest inquired, "He'd be a good man for Harley to meet, wouldn't he?"

"None better," smiled Frank, "if he wants to make the 'Dickey.' "

"Then," said Sylvia, "he's the man I'd best go after."

The other laughed. "All right, honey. But you'll find him hard to interest, I warn you. His career has all been planned—he's to marry Dorothy Cortlandt, who'll bring him ten or twenty millions more."

And Sylvia set her lips in a dangerous expression. "He can marry Dorothy Cortlandt," she said, "but not until I've got through with him!"

## § 3

THAT evening was reserved for a performance of the "Glee Club;" and just before dinner Harley came in, bubbling over with delight, to say that Harmon had called up and invited him to bring his cousin and share his box.

And so behold Sylvia, clad in pale blue silk, with touches of gold embroidery and a gold band across one shoulder, swimming like a new planet into the ken of the watchers of these brilliantly lighted skies. There were few acquaintances of "Bob" Harmon who did not come to the door of the box to get a closer view of the phenomenon; while the delighted cousin found himself besieged. Sedate upper-classmen put their arms across his shoulders, tremendous club men got him by the coat sleeve in the lobby. "Let us in on that, Chilton!" "Now don't be a hog, old man!"— "You know me, Chilton!" Yes, Harley knew them all, and calculated to keep knowing them for some time to come.

The next morning he came early, and took Sylvia for a drive, to lay before her the whole situation, and coach her for the part she was to play; for this was the enemy's country, and there were many pitfalls to be avoided.

It ought perhaps to be explained at the outset how it happened that Aunt Nannie, whose time was spent in erecting monuments to Southern heroes, had sent one of her sons to the headquarters of those who had slain them. It had come about through the seductions of a young lady named Edith Winthrop, whose father was building a railroad through half a dozen of the Southern states. He had brought a private-train party upon an inspection trip, and the Major and Harley, happening to be at the capital, had met them at a luncheon given by the Governor. Everybody knows, of course, that the Winthrops live in Boston; and everybody in Boston knows of Mrs. Isabel Winthrop, that charming matron whose home has been as the axle of the Hub for the past twenty years. At Cambridge it was at first a scandal, and later a tradition, how the lovely lady was strolling in the "Yard" one spring evening, and a group of Seniors broke into the merry chorus of a popular musical-comedy air—

> "Isabella, Isabella,
> Is a queen of good society!
> Isabella, Isabella,
> Is the dandy queen of Spain!"

And now Harley had come to Cambridge to lay siege to the princess of this line. They had invited him to tea, where he had felt himself an obscure and humiliated Freshman. In his pride he had gone away, vowing that he would not return until he had made the "Dickey," and made it without any social aid from the lady of his adoration. But, alas, Harley had found this a task of undreamed-of difficulty. There were so many Edith Winthrops in Boston, New York,

Philadelphia and other centers of good breeding; and there were so many obscure Freshmen trying to make the "Dickey" in order to shine before them!

"You can't imagine how it is, Sylvia," he said. "They don't know us here—we're nobodies. I've met all the Southern men who amount to anything, but it's Eastern men who run the worth-while clubs. And it's almost impossible to meet them—I'd be ashamed to tell you how I've had to toady."

"Harley!" exclaimed the girl.

"I'll tell you the facts," he answered—"you'll have to face them—just as I did."

"But how could you stay?"

He laughed. "I stayed," he said, "because I wanted Edith."

He paused, then continued: "First I thought I'd try football; but you see I haven't weight enough—I only made the Freshman 'scrub.' I joined the Shooting Club—and I certainly can shoot, you know; but that hasn't seemed to help very much. I went in for the Banjo Club, and I've worked my fingers off, and I expect to make the Board, but I don't think that will be enough. You see, ability really doesn't count at all."

"That's what Frank said," remarked Sylvia, sympathetically. "What is it that counts? Learning?"

"Rot—no!' exclaimed Harley.

"Then what is it?"

"It's knowing the right people. But you can't

manage that here—it has to be done before you get to college. The crowd doesn't need you, they don't care what you think about them—and I tell you, they know how to give you the cold shoulder!"

Sylvia was indignant in spite of herself. "You, a Castleman!" she exclaimed. "Why, your ancestors were governors of this place while theirs were tavern-keepers and blacksmiths!"

"I know," said the other—"but it isn't ancestors that count here—it's being on the ground and holding on to what you've got."

"They're all rich men, I suppose?"

"Perfectly rotten! You're simply out of it from the start. I heard of a man last year who spent fifty thousand dollars trying to make the 'Dickey,' and then only got in the seventh ten! You've no idea of the lengths men go to; they pull every sort of wire, social and business and financial and political—they bring on their fathers and brothers to help them——"

"And their cousins," said Sylvia, and brought the discussion to an end with a laugh. "Now come, Harley," she said, after a pause. "Let's get down to business. You want me to meet the right men, and to make them aware of the existence of my Freshman cousin. Have you got a list of the men? Or am I to know by their ties?"

Harley named and described several she would meet. Through them she would, of course, meet others; she must feel her way step by step, being

11

guided by circumstances. There was another matter, which was delicate, but must be broached. "I don't want to seem like a cad," said he, "but you see, Frank Shirley isn't a club man—he hasn't tried to be——"

"I understand," said Sylvia, with a smile.

"Of course, the fact that you come from his home town, that's excuse enough for his knowing you. But if you make it too conspicuous—that is——"

Harley stopped. "It's all right, Harley," smiled Sylvia; "you may be sure that Frank Shirley has too much of a sense of humor to want to get in our way."

The other hesitated over the remark. It looked like deep water, and he decided not to venture in. "It's not only that," he went on— "there's Frank's crowd. They're all outsiders, and one or two of them especially are impossible."

"In what way?"

"Well, there's Jack Colton, Frank's room-mate. He's gone out of his way to make himself obnoxious to everybody. He's done it deliberately, and I suppose he has his reasons for it. I only hope he has sense enough not to want to 'queer' you."

"What's he done?"

"He's a Western chap—from Wyoming, I think. Seems to have more money than he knows how to spend decently. He insisted on smoking a pipe in his Freshman year, and when they tried to haze him, he fought. He's wild as anything, they say—goes off on a spree every month or two——"

"How does Frank come to be rooming with such a man?" asked Sylvia, in surprise.

"Met him traveling, I understand. They were in a train-wreck."

"Oh, that's the man! But Frank didn't tell me he was wild."

"Well," said the other, "Frank would naturally stand up for him. I suppose he's trying to keep him straight."

There was a silence. Then suddenly Sylvia asked, "Harley, did you ever meet Douglas van Tuiver?"

"No!" replied Harley. "Why do you ask?"

"Nothing—only I heard of him, and I was thinking perhaps he'd be a good man to help you."

"Small doubt of that," said the boy, with a laugh. "But it might be difficult to meet him."

"Why?"

"Well, he picks the people he meets. And he doesn't come to public affairs."

"Stop and think a minute. Is there nobody who might know him?"

"Why—there's Mrs. Winthrop."

"He goes there?"

"They're great chums, I understand. I could get her to invite you."

But Sylvia, after a moment's thought, shook her head. "No," she said, "I think I'll let him take me to her."

"By Jove!" laughed Harley. "That's cool!" And then he asked, curiously, "What makes you pick him out?"

"I don't know," said Sylvia. "I find myself thinking about him. You see, I meet men like Mr. Harmon and the others last night—they're all obvious. I've known them by the dozen before, and I can always tell what they'll say. But this man sounds as if he might be different."

"Humph!" said Harley. "I wish you could get a chance! But I fear you'd find him a difficult proposition. Girls must be forever throwing themselves at his head——"

"Yes," said Sylvia. "But I wouldn't make that mistake." Then, after a pause, she added, "I think it might be good for him, too. I might make a man of him!"

## § 4

THERE was a Senior named Thurlow, whom Sylvia had met at the "Glee Club" affair, and who, after judicious approach through Harley and Aunt Varina, had secured her promise to come to tea in his rooms. So she saw one of the dormitories on Auburn Street, having such modern conveniences as "buttons," a squash court, and a white marble swimming pool—with a lounging room at one end, and easy chairs from which to watch one's fellow mermen at play.

Thurlow showed her about his own apartments, equipped with that kind of simplicity that is so notoriously expensive. He showed her his tennis cups and rowing trophies, talking most interestingly about the wonderful modern art, the pulling of an oar—in which there are no less than seventy errors a man can commit in the "catch," and a hundred-and-seventy in the "stroke." Thurlow, it appeared, must have committed several in last year's race, for he had snapped his oar, and only saved the day by jumping overboard, being picked up in a state of collapse, and reported as drowned in the first newspaper extras.

There came others of his set: Jackson, the coxswain of the crew, known as "Little Billee," a wizened up and drolly cynical personage; also Bates, his room-mate, who was called "Tubby," and was hard put to it when the ladies asked him why, because he could not explain that he was "a tub of guts." The wits declared that he weighed two hundred and twenty when he was in training for the fat man's race; he had been elected the official funny man of his class, and whenever he made a joke he led off with a queer little cackle of high-pitched laughter, which never failed to carry the company with him. There came Arlow Bynner, the famous quarter-back, and Tom, his twin brother, so much like him that when he had first come to college the Sophomores had dyed his hair. There came Shackleford, millionaire man-of-fashion, who had been picked for president of the new Senior Class, and who looked so immaculate that Sylvia thought of magazine advertisements of leisure-class brands of tobacco.

There were six men in the room, and only two women—of which one was Aunt Varina, the chaperone. You can imagine that it was an ordeal for the other woman! It is easy enough for a girl to make out when she is looking at memorial inscriptions and historic elm trees, at smoking outfits and rowing sculls; but it's another matter to be cornered by six fastidious upper-classmen, their looks saying plainer than words: "We've been hearing about you, but we're from Missouri —now bring out your bag of tricks!"

Poor Sylvia—she began, as usual, by having a fright. She could think of nothing to say to all these men. She chose this moment to recollect some warnings which had been given by Harriet, before she left home, as to the exactingness and blaséness of Northern college men; also some half-ventured hints of her cousin, that possibly her arrows might be too light in the shaft for the social heavyweights of this intellectual center. She gazed from one to another in agony; she bit her tongue until she tasted blood, scolding and exhorting herself like a football coach driving a "scrub" team.

It was "Bob" Harmon whose coming saved her. The very sight of him brought her inspiration. She had managed him, had she not? Where was the man she had ever failed to manage? She recollected how she had looked at him, and what she had said to him in the auto; there came suddenly the trumpet-call in her soul, in the far deeps of her the trampling and trembling, the

fluttering of banners and murmuring of voices—
signs of the arrival of that rescuing host which
came to her always in emergencies, and constituted
the miracle of Sylvia.  Her friend Harriet Atkinson, herself no dullard in company, would sit by
and watch the phenomenon in awe.  "Sunny,"
she would say, "I can see it coming!  I can see
it beginning to bubble!  The light comes into
your eyes, and I whisper to myself, 'Now, now!
She's going to make a killing!'"

What is it—who can say?  That awakening in
the soul of man, that sense of uplift, of new
power arriving, of mastery conscious and exultant!
To some it is known as genius, and to others as
God.  To have possessed it in some great crisis
is to have made history; and most strange have
been the courses to which men have been lured
by the dream of keeping it continuously—to stand
upon a pillar and be devoured by worms, to hide
in desert caves and lash one's flesh to strips—or
to wear tight stays and high-heeled shoes, and
venture into a den of Harvard-club men!

## § 5

HALF an hour or so later, when they were
passing tea and cake, the flame of her fun burned
less brightly for a few minutes, and she had time
to remember a purpose which was stored away
in the back of her mind.  All her faculties now

became centered upon it; and those who wish may follow the winding serpent of her cunning.

She had been telling them about the negro boy who had bitten a piece out of the baby. Thurlow remarked, "Yours must be an interesting part of the world."

"We love it," she said. "But you wouldn't."

"Why not?"

"You'd miss too many things you are used to. Our college boys have no such luxury as this." She looked about her.

"You think this so very luxurious?"

"I do indeed. I'm not sure that I think it's good taste for young fellows."

"But why not?"

"It gets you out of touch with life," replied Sylvia, with charming gravity. ("Don't play too long on one string!" had been a maxim of Lady Dee.) "I think it's demoralizing. This place might be a sanatorium instead of a dormitory—if only you had elevators to take the invalids upstairs."

Somebody remarked, "We have elevators in many of the dormitories."

"Is that really so?" asked Sylvia. "I don't see how you can go beyond that—unless some of you take to having private houses."

There was a laugh. "We've come to that, too," said Bates.

"What?" cried the girl. "Surely not!"

"Douglas van Tuiver has a house," replied Bates.

"Surely you are jesting!"

"No! I'll show it to you, Miss Castleman."

"Who is Douglas van Tuiver?"

The men glanced at one another. "Haven't you ever heard of the van Tuivers?" asked one.

"Who are they?" countered Sylvia, who never lied when she could avoid it.

"They are one of our oldest families," said Shackleford—who came from New York. "Also one of the best known."

"Well," said Sylvia, duly rebuked, "you see how very provincial I am."

"He's a nephew of Mrs. Harold Cliveden," ventured Harmon.

"Cliveden?" repeated Sylvia. "I th'nk I've heard that name." She kept a straight face—though the lady was the reigning queen of Newport, and a theme of the society gossip of all American newspapers. Then, not to embarrass her friends by too great ignorance, she hurried on, "But you surely don't mean that this man has a house all to himself?"

"He has," said Thurlow.

"He has more than that," said Jackson. "He has a castle in Scotland."

"I don't mind castles so much. One can inherit them——"

"No, he bought this one."

"Well, even so—castles are romantic and interesting. One might have a dream of founding a family. But for a man to come to college and occupy a whole house—what motive could he have but ostentation?"

No one answered—though she waited for an answer. At last, with a grave face, she pronounced the judgment, "I would expect to find such a man a degenerate."

They were evidently shocked, but covered it by laughing. "Lord!" said Bates, "I'd like to have van Tuiver hear that!"

"Probably it would be good for him," replied Sylvia, coldly.

Everybody grinned. "Wish you'd tell him!" said the man.

"I'd be delighted."

"Would you really?"

"Why certainly."

"By Jove, I believe you'd do it!" declared Bates.

"But why shouldn't I do it?"

"I don't know. When people meet van Tuiver they sometimes lose their nerve."

"Is he so very terrible?"

"Well, he's rather imposing."

Then Sylvia took a new line. "Of course," she said, hesitatingly, "I wouldn't want to be irreverent——"

"May I go and bring him here?" inquired Bates, eagerly.

To which she replied, "Perhaps one owes more deference to Royalty. Shouldn't you take me to him?"

"We'll keep you on a throne of your own," said Thurlow—"at least, while you are here." (It was quite as if he had been a Southern man.)

But Bates was not to be diverted from his idea. "Won't you let me go and get him?" he inquired.

"Does he visit in dormitories?"

"Really, Miss Castleman, I'm not joking. Wouldn't you like to meet him?"

"Why should I?"

"Because—we'd all like to see what would happen."

"From what you say about him," remarked Sylvia, "he sounds to me like a bore. Or at any rate, a young man who is in need of chastening."

"Exactly!" cried Bates. "And we'd like to see you attend to it!"

The time had come, Sylvia thought, to play upon a new string. She looked about her with a slightly *distrait* air. "Don't you think," she inquired, "that we are giving him too large a portion of this charming afternoon?"

The men appreciated the compliment; but the other theme still enticed them. Said Jackson, "We can't give up the idea of the chastening, Miss Castleman."

"Of course, if you are afraid of him—" added Bates, slyly.

There was a momentary flash in Sylvia's eyes. But then she laughed—"You can't play a game like that on me!"

"We would *so* like," said Jackson, "to see van Tuiver get a drubbing!"

"Please, Miss Castleman!" added Harmon, "give him a drubbing!"

But the girl only held out her white-gloved hands. "Look at these," she said, "how pure and spotless!

Said "Tubby": "I hereby register a vow, I will never partake of food again until you two have met!"

Sylvia rose, looking bored. "I'm going to run away," she said, "if you don't find something interesting to talk about." And strolling towards a cabinet, "Mr. Thurlow, come and introduce me to this charming little Billikin!"

§ 6

SYLVIA had promised to go with Frank the next day to a luncheon in his rooms. She found herself looking forward with relief to meeting his "crowd." "Oh, Frank," she said, when they had set out together, "you've no idea how glad I am to see you. I have such a craving for something home-like. You can't understand, perhaps——"

"Perhaps I can," said Frank, smiling. "I can't say that I've been in Boston society, but I've been on the outskirts."

"Frank," she exclaimed, "you don't ever worry about me, do you? Truly, the more I see of other people, the more I love you. And all I want is to be alone with you. I'm tired of the game. Everybody expects me to be pert and saucy; and I can be it, you know——"

She stopped, and he smiled. "Yes, I know."

"But since I've met you, I get sorry, sometimes even ashamed. You see what you've done to me!"

"What in the world have you been doing?" he asked.

"Oh, some day I'll tell you—don't ask me now. It's just that I'm tired of society—I wasn't cut out for the life."

"Why, it was only a few days ago that you were talking about bringing me out!"

"I know, Frank. I try to play the game, but deep down in my soul I hate it. I'm successful now, but it's the truth that in the beginning I never took a step that I wasn't driven. When I went into a ball-room, my teeth would chatter with fright, and I'd want to hide in a corner. Aunt Nannie would get hold of me, and take me into the dressing-room, and scold me and stir me up. I can hear her now. 'You! Sylvia Castleman, my niece, a wall-flower! Have you forgotten who you are?' So then, of course, I'd have to think of my ancestors and be worthy of them. She'd pinch my cheeks until they were red, and wipe the wet corners of my eyes, and put a fresh dab of powder on my nose, and stick in a strand of hair, and twist a curl, and shift a bow of ribbon to the other shoulder—and then out I'd go to be stared at."

"You've got the job pretty well in hand by now," smiled Frank.

"Yes, I know, but I don't really like it—not

with my real self. I'm always thinking what fun it would be to be natural! I wonder what I'd turn into! And whether you'd like me!"

"I'd take my chances."

"Would you really, Frank? Just suppose I stopped dressing, for instance? Suppose I never wore high heels and stiff collars? Suppose I dispensed with my *modiste*, and you discovered that I had no figure."

"I'd take my chances," he laughed again.

"You look at me, and you like what you see. But you've no idea what a work of art I am, nor how much I cost—thousands and thousands of dollars! And so many people to watch me and scold me—so much work to be done on me, day after day! Suppose my hair wasn't curled, for instance! Or suppose my nose were shiny!"

"I don't mind shiny so much, Sylvia——"

"Ah! But if it was red! That's what they're always hammering into me—whenever I forget my veil. Or look at these lovely soft hands of mine—such beautiful nails. Do you realize that I have to keep them in glycerine gloves all night —and ugh! how clammy and nasty they are when it's cold! And the time it takes to keep the nails polished!"

"You see," she went on, after a pause, "you don't take my wickedness seriously. But you should ask Harriet Atkinson about some of the things we've done. She'll come and say, 'There's a new man coming to-night. Teach me a "spiel"!' She'll tell me all about him, where he comes from and what he likes, and I'll tell her what to say and what to pretend to be. And I've done it myself—hundreds of times."

"Did you do it for me?" asked Frank, innocently.

Sylvia paused. "I tried to," she said. "Sometimes I did, but then again I couldn't." She put her hand upon his arm, and he felt a pressure, thrilling him with a swift delight.

But they had come now to the dormitory, so her outburst had to end. She took her hand from his arm, saying, "Frank, I don't want you to kiss me any more until we're married. I'm going to stop doing everything that makes me ashamed!"

## § 7

BEHOLD now a new "Lady Sunshine," in a clean white apron which her hosts had provided for the occasion, stirring mushrooms in cream and superintending stewed chicken, while Frank washed salad in the bathroom, and Jack Colton was half way up to his elbows in mayonnaise. This was the first time that Sylvia had met Frank's room-mate, with whom she had intended to be very stern, because of his "wildness." Although she was used to wild boys, and had helped to tame a number of them, she did not approve of such qualities in a companion of her lover.

Jack, however, was a boy with what the Irish call "a way with him." He had curly brown hair and a winning countenance, and such a laugh that it was not easy to disagree with him. Moreover a halo of romance hung about him, owing to the fact that Frank had first met him after a railroad wreck, sitting in the snow and holding in his lap a baby whose mother had been killed. Jack had engaged a nurse and sent the child all the way out to his own mother in Wyoming; and how could any girl object to a friendship begun under such auspices? If his mother was indulgent and sent him more pocket money than he could decently spend, might not one regard that as the boy's misfortune rather than his fault?

There was Dennis Dulanty, a fair-haired young Irishman who wrote poems, and was Sylvia's slave from the first moment she entered the room. There was Tom Firmin, a heavily built man with a huge head made bigger by thick, black hair. Firmin was working his way through college and had no time for luncheon parties, but he had come this once to meet Sylvia. The girl listened to him with some awe, because Frank had said he had the best mind in the class. Finally there was Jack's married sister, who lived in Boston, and was chaperone.

There were four little tables with four chafing dishes, and two study tables put together and covered with a spread of linen and silver. There were strawberries which Dulanty had dropped upon the floor; there were sandwiches which

Tom Firmin had tried in vain to cut thin, and wine about which Jack Colton talked far too wisely, for one so young. Jack had been round the world, and had tasted the vintage of many countries, and told such interesting adventures that one forgot one's disapproval.

Sylvia found herself happy here, and decided that Frank's crowd was far more interesting than Thurlow's. All these men were outsiders, holding themselves aloof from the social life of the University and resentful of the conditions they had found there. After awhile it occurred to Sylvia that it would be entertaining to hear what these men would have to say upon a subject which had been occupying her mind; so, by a few deft touches, she brought the conversation to a point where some one else was moved to mention the name of Douglas van Tuiver.

Immediately she discovered that she had touched a live wire. There was Tom Firmin, frowning under his thick black eyebrows. "For my part, I have just one thing to say: a man who has any pretense at self-respect cannot even know him."

"Is he as bad as all that?" Sylvia asked.

"It's not a question of personality—it's a question of the amount of his wealth."

Sylvia would have appreciated this if it had been a jest. But apparently the speaker was serious, and so she gazed at him in perplexity. "Is a very rich man to have no friends?" she asked.

12

"Never fear," laughed Jack, "there are plenty of tuft-hunters who will keep him company."

"But why should you sentence him to the company of tuft-hunters, just because he happens to be born with a lot of money?"

"It isn't I that sentence him," said Firmin—"it's the nature of things."

"But," exclaimed the girl, "I've had millionaires for friends—and I hope I'm not the dreadful thing you say."

The other smiled for the first time. "Frank Shirley insists that there are angels upon earth," he said. "But if you don't mind, Miss Castleman, I'd prefer to illustrate this argument by every-day mortals like myself. I'm willing to admit, as a theoretical proposition, that there might be a disinterested friendship between a poor man and a multimillionaire; but only if the poor man is a Diogenes and stays in his tub. I mean, if he has no business affairs of any sort, and takes no part in social life; if he never lets the multimillionaire take him automobiling or invite him to dinner; if he has no marriageable sisters, and the multimillionaire has none either. But all these, you must admit, make a difficult collection of circumstances."

"Miss Castleman," said Jack, "you can see why we call Tom Firmin our Anarchist."

But Sylvia was not to be diverted. She had never heard such ideas as this, and she wanted to understand them. "You must think hardly of human nature!" she objected.

"As I said before, it has nothing whatever to do with personality, it's the automatic effect of a huge sum of money. Take my own case, for example—so I can talk brutally and not hurt anyone. I want to be a lawyer, but meanwhile I have to earn my living. I love a girl, but I've no hope of marrying, because I'm poor and she's poor. If I struggle along in the usual way, it'll be five years—maybe ten years—before we can marry. But here I am in college, and here's Douglas van Tuiver; if by any device of any sort I can manage to penetrate his consciousness —if I can make him think me a wit or a scholar, a boon companion or a great soul, the best half-back in college or an amusing old bull in the social china shop—why, then right away things are easier for me. You've heard what Thackeray said about walking down Piccadilly with a duke on each arm? If I can walk across the Yard with Douglas van Tuiver, then a lot of important men suddenly realize that I exist; the first thing you know I make a club, and so when I come out of college I'm the chum of some of the men who are running the country, and I have a salary of five thousand a year at the start, and ten thousand in a year or two, a hundred thousand before I'm forty, and a go at a rich marriage into the bargain. Do you think there are many would-be lawyers to whom all that would be no temptation? Let me tell you, it's the temptation which has turned many a man in this college into a boot-licker!"

"But, Mr. Firmin!" cried Sylvia, in dismay.

"What is your idea? Would you forbid rich men coming to college?"

To which the other replied, "I'd go much farther back than that, Miss Castleman—I'd forbid rich men existing."

Sylvia was genuinely shocked. She had never heard such words even in jest, and she thought Tom Firmin a terrifying person. "You see," laughed Jack, "he really *is* an Anarchist!" And Sylvia believed him, and resolved to remonstrate with Frank about having such friends. But nevertheless she went out from that breakfast party with something new to think about in connection with Douglas van Tuiver—and with her mind made up that Mr. "Tubby" Bates would have to die of starvation!

§ 8

THAT afternoon Sylvia was invited to one of the club teas. These were very exclusive affairs, and Jackson, who asked her, mentioned that among those who poured tea would be Mrs. Isabel Winthrop; also that Mrs. Winthrop had expressed a particular desire to meet her.

This would mark a new stage in Sylvia's campaign for her cousin; but quite apart from that, she was curious to meet this *belle ideal* of Auburn Street. Sylvia had listened attentively to what the denizens of the "Gold Coast" had to say about

"Queen Isabella," and had found herself rather awe-stricken. When one spoke of a favorite hostess in the South, one gave her credit for tact, for charm, perhaps even for brilliance. But apparently Mrs. Winthrop was the possessor of a much more difficult and perplexing attribute— a rare and lofty soul. She was a woman of real intellect, they said—she had written a book upon theories of æsthetics, and had taken a degree in philosophy at the older Cambridge across the seas. Such things were quite unknown in Southern society, where a girl was rather taught to hide her superfluous education, for fear of scaring the men away.

So Sylvia found herself in a state of considerable apprehension. If it had been a man, she would have taken her chances; when she had attended Commencement at her State University, there were professors who would call and talk about Assyrian bricks, and the relation between ions and corpuscles—yet by listening closely, and putting in a deft touch now and then to make them talk about themselves, Sylvia had managed to impress them as an intellectual young lady. But now she had to deal with that natural enemy of a woman—another woman. How was the ordeal to be faced?

Lady Dee had handed down the formula: "When in difficulty, look the person in the eyes, and remember who you are." This was the counsel which came to Sylvia's rescue at the moment of the dread encounter. She knew Mrs.

Winthrop as soon as she caught sight of her; she looked a woman of thirty-five—instead of forty-five, which she really was—tall and slender, undoubtedly beautiful, undoubtedly proud, and yet with a kind of *naïve* sincerity. They met in the dressing-room by accident, and the lady, recognizing Sylvia, took her hand and gazed into her face; and Sylvia gazed back, with those wide, clear eyes of hers, steadily, unflinching, without a motion or a sound. At last Mrs. Winthrop, putting her other hand upon the girl's, clasped it and whispered intensely, "We met a thousand years ago!"

Sylvia had no information as to any such event, and she had not expected at all that kind of welcome. So she continued to gaze—steadily, steadily. And the spell communicated itself to Mrs. Winthrop. "I heard that you were lovely," she murmured, in a strange, low voice, "but I really had no idea! Sylvia Castleman, you are like a snow-storm of pear blossoms! You are a Corot symphony of spring time!"

Now Sylvia had seen some of Corot's paintings, but she had not learned to mix the metaphors of the arts, and so she had no idea what Mrs. Winthrop meant. She contented herself with saying something about the pleasure she felt at this meeting.

But the other was not to be brought down to mundane speech. "Dryad!" she murmured. She had a manner and voice all her own, sybilline, oracular; you felt that she was speaking, not to you, but to some disembodied spirit. It was very disconcerting at first.

"You bring back lost youth to the world," she said. "I want to talk to you, Sylvia—to find out more about you. You aren't vain, I know. You are proud!"

"Why—I'm not sure," said Sylvia, at a loss for a moment.

"Oh, don't be vain!" said the lady. "Remember—I was like you once."

Which gave Sylvia an opportunity of the sort she understood. "I will look forward," she said, "to the prospect of being like you."

The radiant lady pressed her hand. "Very pretty, my child," she said. "Quite Southern, too! But I must take you in and give the others some of this joy."

Such was the beginning of the acquaintance so utterly different from all possible beginnings, as Sylvia had imagined them. She found in Edith Winthrop, whom she met a few minutes later, a person much nearer to what she had expected in the mother. Miss Edith had her mother's beauty and her mother's pride, but no trace of her mother's sybilline qualities. A badly spoiled young lady, was Sylvia's first verdict upon this New England *belle;* a verdict which she delivered promptly to her infatuated cousin, and which she never found occasion to revise.

The friendship thus begun progressed rapidly. Mrs. Winthrop asked if she might call, and coming the next day, discovered in Aunt Varina the perfect type of the Southern gentlewoman. So the three were soon absorbed in talking genealogy. At Miss Abercrombie's Sylvia had been surprised to learn that it was bad form to talk about one's ancestors; but apparently it was still permissible in Boston—as it assuredly was in the South.

Mrs. Winthrop invited Sylvia to a party she was giving; and when Sylvia spoke of having to leave Boston, "Oh, stay," said the great lady. "Come and stay with me—always!" Finally Sylvia said that she would come to the party.

"I'll invite your cousin for the extra man," said the other. "It is to be a new kind of party —you know how desperately one has to struggle to keep one's guests from being bored. I got this idea from a Southern man, so perhaps it's an old story to you—a 'Progressive Love' party?"

"Oh, yes, we often have them," replied Sylvia. She had not supposed that these intellectual people would condescend to such play—having pictured Boston society as occupied in translating Meredith and Henry James.

"People have to be amused the world over," said Mrs. Winthrop. And when Sylvia looked surprised to have her thought read, the other gave her a long look, and smiled a deep smile. "Sylvia," she propounded, "you and I understand each other. We are made of exactly the same material."

§ 9

¹ THERE followed after this meeting a trying time for the girl. She went to a theatre in the evening, and when she came back to the hotel she found her aunt suffering acutely, with symptoms of appendicitis. Although there was a doctor and a nurse, she spent the entire night and half the next day by her aunt's bedside. Sylvia's love for her family appeared at a time like this a sort of frenzy; she would have died a thousand deaths to save them from suffering, and there was no getting her to spare herself in any way.

Her sympathy for Aunt Varina was the greater, because this poor little lady was so patient and unselfish. Whenever there was anything the matter with her, she would make no trouble for anyone, but crawl away and endure by herself. She was one of those devoted souls, of which there is one to be found in every big family, who do not have a life of their own, but are ground up daily, as it were, to make oil to keep the great machine running smoothly. Sylvia, who had in herself the making of such a family lubricant, was irresistibly drawn to this gentle soul in distress.

All night she helped the nurse with hot "stoupes;" and even when the danger was passed she could not be persuaded to rest, but sat by the bedside, applying various kinds of smelling salts and lavender water, trying to be so cheerful that the patient would forget her pain. She smoothed the white forehead, noticing as she did so how thin the gray hairs were getting. She could look back to childhood days, when Aunt Varina had been bright and young-looking —there were even pictures of her as a girlish beauty; but now her neck was scrawny and her cheeks were wan, and most of her hair lay upon her dressing-table.

The day passed, and then Sylvia was reminded that she had promised to go to a college entertainment with Harley. She ought to have gone to bed, but she did not like to disappoint her cousin, so she drank a cup or two of strong coffee, and was ready for anything that might come along.

I used to say that I never knew a person who could *disappear* so rapidly as Sylvia; who could literally eat up the flesh off her bones by nervous excitement. After a night and a day like this she was another woman—that strange arresting creature who made men start when they saw her, and set poets to dreaming about angels and stars. She wore a soft white muslin dress and a hat with a white plume in it—not intending to be ethereal, but because an instinct always guided her hand towards the color that was right.

The entertainment being not very interesting, and the hall being close, after an hour or so she asked her cousin to take her out. It was a perfect night, and she drank in the soft breeze and strolled along, happy to watch the lights through the trees and to hear singing in the distance.

But suddenly she discovered that she had lost a medallion which she had worn about her neck. "We must find it!" she exclaimed. "It's the one with the picture of Aunt Lady!"

"Are you sure you had it?"

"I remember perfectly having it in the hall. We'll find it if we're quick. Hurry! I can't, with these heels on my shoes." So Harley started back, and Sylvia began to walk slowly, looking on the sidewalk.

Five or ten minutes passed thus; when, hearing steps behind her, she glanced up, and saw a man attired in evening dress. There was a light near by, shining into her face, and she saw that he looked at her; also, with her woman's intuition, she realized that he had been startled.

He stopped. "Have you lost something?" he asked, hesitatingly.

"Yes," she said.

"Could I be of any help?"

"Thank you," said Sylvia. "My cousin has gone back to look. He will be here soon."

That was all. Sylvia resumed her search. But the man's way was the same as hers, and he did not go as fast as before. She was really worried about her loss, and barely thought of him. His voice was that of a gentleman, so his nearness did not disturb her.

"Was it something valuable?" he asked, at last.

"It was a medallion with a picture that I prize."

She stopped at a corner, uncertain of the street by which she and Harley had come. He stopped also. "I would be very glad to help," he said, "if you would permit me."

"Thank you," she said, "but I really think that my cousin will find it. We had not come far."

Again there was a pause. As she went on, he was near her, looking diligently. After a while she began to find the silence awkward, but she did not like to send him away, and she did not like to speak again. So it was with real relief that, looking down the street, she saw Harley coming. "There's my cousin!" she said. "Oh, I *do* hope he's found it."

"He doesn't act as if he had," remarked the other; and Sylvia's heart sank, for she saw that Harley walked slowly, and with his eyes on the ground.

When he was near enough she asked, "You haven't found it?"

"No," he answered. "It's gone, I fear."

"Oh, too bad! too bad! What can we do?"

Harley had come near. Sylvia saw that he looked at the man she was with, but there was no recognition between them. Evidently they did not know each other. Then, without offering to stop, Harley passed them, saying. "I'll look back this way."

"I don't think that's worth while," said the girl. "I've searched carefully there."

"I'd better look," replied the other, who had

quickened his pace and was already some distance off.

"But wait, Harley!" she called. She wanted to explain to him how thoroughly she had searched; and, more important yet, she wanted to get decently rid of the stranger.

But Harley went on, paying no attention to her. She called him again, with some annoyance, but he did not stop, and in a moment more had turned a corner. She was perplexed and angered by his conduct—more and more so as she thought of it. How preposterous for him to brush past in that fashion, and leave her with a man she did not know! "What in the world can he mean?" she exclaimed. "There's no need to search back there any more!"

She stood, staring into the half-darkness. When after a moment he did not reappear, she repeated, helplessly, "What did he mean? What did he mean?"

She looked at her companion, and saw an amused smile upon his face. Her eyes questioned him, and he said, "I suspect he saw you were with *me.*"

For a moment Sylvia continued to stare at him. Then, realizing that here was a serious matter, she looked down at the ground—something which the search for the medallion gave her the pretext for doing.

"He saw you were with *me.*" The more she pondered the words, the more incredible they seemed to her. Taken as they had come, with

the tone and the accent and the smile, there was
only one thing they could mean. A week ago
Sylvia would have been incapable of compre-
hending that meaning; but now she had seen so
much of social climbing that she had developed
a new sensitiveness. She understood—and yet she
could not believe that she understood. This man
did not know Harley, but Harley knew him, and
knew him to be somebody of importance—of such
importance that he had deliberately gone on and
left her standing there, so that she might pick
up an acquaintance with him on the street! And
the man had watched the little comedy, and
knowing his own importance, was chuckling with
amusement.

As the realization of this forced itself upon
Sylvia, the blood mounted to the very roots of
her hair. She was seized by a perfect fury of
shame and indignation; it was all that she could
do to keep from turning upon the man and telling him what a cad and a puppy she thought him.
But then came a second thought—wasn't it true,
what he believed? What other explanation could
there be of Harley's conduct? It was her cousin
who was the puppy and the cad; she wanted to
run after him and tell him in the man's hearing.
But then again her anger turned upon the
stranger. If he had been a gentleman, would
he ever have let her know what he thought?
Would he have stood there now, grinning like a
pot-boy?

Sylvia finished her meditations, and lifted her

eyes from the ground. She was clear as to what she would do—she would punish this man, as never in her life had she punished a man before. She would punish him, even though to do it she had to walk on the proprieties with the sharp heels of her white suede slippers.

"I beg your pardon," she said, gently. "I hope I don't presume——"

"What is it?" he asked, and she looked him over. He was a tall man, with a pale, lean face, prominent features, and a large mouth which drooped at the corners with heavy lines. He was evidently a serious person, mature looking for a student.

"Are you by any chance an instructor in the University?" she asked.

"No, no," he said, surprised.

"But then—are you a public official of some sort?"

"No," he said, still more surprised. "Why should you think that?"

"Well, my cousin seemed to know you, and yet not to know you. He seemed willing to leave me with you, so I thought you might be —possibly a city detective——"

She saw him wince, and she feigned quick embarrassment. "I hope you'll excuse me!" she said. "You see, my position is difficult." Then, with one of her shining smiles, "Or have I perchance met Sir Galahad—or some other comforter of distressed damsels—St. George, or Don Quixote?"

When an outrage is offered to you by one of the loveliest beings that you have ever beheld, with the face of a higher order of angels, and a look straight into your eyes, so eloquent of simplicity and trustfulness—what more can you do than to look uncomfortable?

And Sylvia, of course, did not help him. She just continued to gaze and smile. He got his breath and stammered, "Really—I think—if you will permit me——" He paused, and then drew himself up. "I think that I had best introduce myself."

"I am willing to accept the rebuke," said Sylvia, "without putting you to that trouble."

She saw that he did not even understand. He went on—his manner that of a man laboring with a very serious purpose. "I really think that I should introduce myself."

"Are we not having a pleasant time without it?" she countered.

This, of course, was a complete blockade. He stood at a loss; and meantime Sylvia waited, with every weapon ready and every sense alert. "I beg pardon," he said, at last, "but may I ask you something? I've a feeling as if I had met you before."

"I am sure that you have not," she said, promptly.

"You are from the South, are you not? I have been in the South several times."

But still she would not give an inch; and he became desperate. "Pardon me," he said, "if I tell you my name. I am Douglas van Tuiver."

Now if there was ever a moment in her life when Sylvia needed her social training, it was then. He was looking into her face, watching for the effect of his announcement. But he never saw so much as the flicker of an eyelid. Sylvia said, quietly, "Thank you," and waited to load her batteries. She had meant harm to him before. Imagine what she meant now!

"It is an unusual name," she observed, casually. "German, I presume?"

"Dutch," said he.

"Ah, Dutch. But then—you speak English perfectly."

"My ancestors," he said, "came to this country in sixteen hundred and forty."

"Ah!" exclaimed Sylvia. "How curious! Mine came the same year. Perhaps that was where we met—in a previous incarnation." Then, after a pause, "Van Tuivel, did you say?"

She could feel his start, and she waited breathlessly to see what he would do. But there were the soft, red-brown eyes and the look of utter innocence—how *could* he gaze into them and doubt? "Van Tuiver," he said, gravely. "Douglas van Tuiver."

"Oh, I beg your pardon," Sylvia responded. "Van Tuiver. I have it now."

She waited, feeling sure that he could not bear to leave it there. And so it proved. "The name is well known in New York," he remarked.

13

"Ah," she said, "but then—there are so *many* people in New York!"

Again there was a pause, while he took thought. Sylvia remarked, helpfully, "In the South, you see, everybody knows everybody else."

"I am not at all sure," said he, stiffly, "that I should find that a desirable state of affairs."

"Neither should I," said she—"in New York."

Now perhaps you think that this kind of thing is no particular strain upon the nerves of a young girl; but Sylvia was seeking a way of escape. Where was the villain Harley, and how much longer did he mean to keep her on the rack? At this moment she saw a taxicab coming down the street, and she recognized her chance.

"Please call it!" she exclaimed.

Instinctively her companion raised his hand. Equally instinctive was his exclamation: "Are you going?"

Her answer was her action; as the vehicle drew up by the curb, she opened the door herself, and stepped in. "To Boston," she said; and the cab moved on. "Good-bye, Mr. van Tuiver," she called to her surprised companion. "Good-bye, until the next incarnation!"

## § 10

NEWS spread rapidly in Cambridge, Sylvia found. The next afternoon she received a call from Mr. "Tubby" Bates, and one glimpse of his features told her that he was moved by some compelling impulse.

"May I sit down, Miss Castleman?" he asked. "I've something to ask you about. But I'm not sure, Miss Castleman—that is—whether I've a right to talk about it. You may think that I'm gossiping——"

"Oh, but I adore gossiping," put in the girl; whereat the other stopped stammering and beamed with relief. He was more like a Southern man than anyone Sylvia had met here; she knew just how to deal with him.

"Thank you ever so much!" he exclaimed. "It's really very good of you." He drew his chair an inch or two nearer, and in a confidential voice began, "It's about Douglas van Tuiver."

"Yes, I supposed so," said Sylvia, with a smile.

"Oh, then something *did* happen!"

"Now, Mr. Bates," she laughed, "tell your story."

"This noon," he said, "van Tuiver called me on the 'phone—or at least his secretary did—and asked me if I'd lunch at the club. When we sat down, there were two other chaps, both wondering what was up. Pretty soon he got to a subject—" Bates stopped uneasily. "I'm afraid that perhaps I won't express myself in the right way, Miss Castleman—that I may say something you don't like——"

"Go on," smiled Sylvia. "I'm possessed by curiosity.

"Well, it came out that he'd had an adventure.

He was walking last evening, and he met a lady. She was tall and rather pale, he said—a Southern girl. She was dressed in white and had golden hair. 'Have any of you met such a girl?' he asked. I kept silent and let the rest do the answering. They hadn't. 'It was a lady in distress,' van Tuiver went on, 'and I offered my assistance and she accepted'——"

"Oh, I did *not!*" cried Sylvia.

"Oho!" exclaimed Bates, "I knew it! Tell me, what did you do?"

"This is your story," she laughed.

"Well, he said it was a novel rôle for him— that of Sir Galahad, or St. George, or Don Quixote. He found it embarrassing. I said, 'Was it the novelty of the rôle—or perhaps the novelty of the lady?' 'Well,' said van Tuiver, 'that's just it. She was one of the most bewildering people I ever met. She talked'—you won't mind my telling this, Miss Castleman?"

"Not a bit—go on."

"Some of it isn't very complimentary——"

"I'm wild with suspense, Mr. Bates!"

" 'Well,' he said, 'she looked like a lady, but she talked like an actress in a comedy. I never heard anybody rattle so—I never knew a girl so pert. She talked just—*amazingly.*' That was his word. I asked him just what he meant, but that was all I could get him to say. Finally he asked, 'Do you know the lady?' and of course I had to answer that I thought I did; I could be sure if he'd give me a sample of her conversation. 'She has a cousin named Harley,' he said, and I said, 'Yes—he's Chilton, a Freshman. Her name is Miss Castleman.' Then he wanted to know all about you. I said, 'I met her at a tea at Thurlow's, and about all I know of her is that she talks amazingly.' I thought that was paying him back."

"And then?" laughed Sylvia.

"Well, he wanted to know what I thought of you; and I said I thought you were the loveliest, and the cleverest, and the sweetest person that I'd ever met in my life. I really think that, you know. And then van Tuiver said—" But here Bates stopped himself suddenly. "That's all," he said.

"No, surely not, Mr. Bates!"

"But really it is. You see, we were interrupted——"

"But not until Mr. van Tuiver had said that he thought I was horrid, and he thought I was shallow, and he thought I was vain."

The other flushed slightly. Sylvia went on, "I don't mind it, because the truth is, I'd been thinking it myself. You see, I really *was* mean to him, Mr. Bates. I said things to hurt him, without his knowing I meant them; but after he went off, he must have understood. Why should we want to hurt people?"

"I don't know," said Tubby, bewildered by this unexpected new turn. He wanted Sylvia to tell him the story of what had happened that evening; but she refused. Then he went on to

a new proposition—he wished to bring van Tuiver
to call. But she refused again and begged him
not to think about the matter any further. He
pleaded with her, in semi-comic distress; he was
so anxious to see what would happen—everyone
was anxious to see what would happen! He
implored her, in the name of good society; it
was cruel, wicked of her to refuse! But Sylvia
was obdurate, and in the end he took his departure
lamenting, but vowing that he would not give up.

Just as he was leaving, Harley arrived. He
came to get his scolding for his conduct of the
previous night. But the scolding was more
serious than he had expected. To his dismay
Sylvia declared that she was sincere in her refusal
to meet van Tuiver again.

"The truth is," she said, "I've changed my
mind about the whole matter. I don't care to
have anything to do with the man."

"But why not?" asked Harley, in amazement.

"Because—I don't think that poor people like
us have any right to. We can't meet him and
keep our self-respect."

"Great God, girl! Aren't we van Tuiver's
social equals."

"We think we are, but he doesn't; and his view
prevails. When you came up here and fell in
love with a girl in his set, you found that his
view prevailed. And look what you did last
night! Don't you see the degradation—simply
to be near such a man?"

"That's all very well," objected Harley, "but
can I keep van Tuiver from coming to Harvard?"

"No, you can't; but you can help to keep him from having his way after he has got here. You can stand out against him and all that he represents."

There was a pause. Harley had nothing to say to that. Sylvia stood with her brows knitted in thought. "I've made up my mind," she said, "there's something very wrong about it all. The man has too much money. He has no right to have so much—certainly not unless he's earned it."

Whereat her cousin exclaimed, "For God's sake, Sylvia, you talk like an Anarchist!"

## § 11

A COUPLE of days later came Mrs. Winthrop's "Progressive Love" party. At this party there were twenty-four guests, twelve men and twelve women, appearing in purple silk dominoes and golden silk masks supplied by the hostess. Twelve short dances were followed by intermissions, during which the guests retired to cosy corners, and the men made ardent love to their unknown partners. "Tubby" Bates, of whom there was too much to be concealed by any domino, was appointed door-keeper, and it was his business to select the couples, so that each would have a new partner for every dance. At the end, every person voted for the most successful "lover" and also the worst, and there were prizes and "booby" prizes.

Love-making, more or less disguised, being the principal occupation of men and women in the South, Sylvia counted herself an expert at this game. She had learned to assume a different personality, disguising her voice, and doing it quite naturally—not by the crude method of putting a button under her tongue. She took her seat after the first dance, perfectly mistress of herself and pleasantly thrilled with curiosity. All of the "younger set" at home had made love to her in earnest, and their methods were an oft-told tale. But how would these strange men of Harvard play the game?

The tall domino at her side was in no hurry to begin. He sat very stiff and straight upon the velvet cushions; and finally it came to Sylvia that he was suffering from embarrassment. She leaned towards him, so as to display "a more coming-on disposition." "Sir," she whispered, "faint heart ne'er won fair lady."

The tall domino considered this in silence. "You'll have to excuse me," he said, "I never played this game before."

"It is the most wonderful game in the world!" said Sylvia, fervently.

"Perhaps," was the reply. "To me it seems a very foolish game, and I think it was poor taste on Mrs. Winthrop's part."

"Dear me!" thought the girl, "what kind of a fish have I caught here?" There was something strangely familiar about the voice, but she could not place it. She had met so many men in the last week or two.

"Sir," she said, "I fear me that you lack a little of that holiday glee which is necessary to such occasion as this. I would that I could sing a song to cheer your moping spirit—

> 'Nymphs and shepherds come away,
> For this is Flora's holiday!'

Then, leaning a little nearer yet, "Come, sir, you must make an effort."

"What shall I do?"

"You must manage to throw yourself into a state of rapture. You must tell me that you adore me. You must say that my blue eyes make dim the vault of heaven——"

"But I can hardly see your eyes."

"You should not expect to see them. Have you not been told that Love is blind?"

So she tried to drive this tall domino to play; but it was sorry frisking that he did. "You must fall down upon your knees before me," she said; but he protested that he could really not do that. And when she insisted, "You must!" he got down, with such deliberation that the girl was half convulsed with laughter.

"Sir," she chided, "that will not do. When you stop to ease each trouser-knee, how can I believe that you are overcome with the ardor of your feelings? You must get up and try again." And actually she made him get up and plump down suddenly upon his knees; and was so mischievous and so merry about it that she got even him to laughing in the end.

She was sure by this time that she had met the man before, and she found herself running over the list of her acquaintances, trying to imagine which one could be capable of making love in such a fashion. But she could not think of one. She fell to studying the domino and the mask before her, wondering what feelings could be behind them. Was it timidity and lack of imagination? Or could it be that the man was sulky and uncivil as he seemed? When the bell rang and she rose, she breathed to herself the prayer that she might be spared running into another "stick" like that.

The next partner was Harmon, as she recognized before he had said a dozen sentences. Harmon did not know her, but being in love, he knew how to behave. He poured out to Sylvia all the things which she had known for the past week he was longing to say to her; and Sylvia said in reply everything which she had no intention of saying in reality. So the episode passed pleasantly, and the girl thought somewhat better of Mrs. Winthrop's talents as a hostess.

Number Three was again a tall domino. He seated himself, and there was a long pause. "Well, sir," said Sylvia, inquiringly.

The domino delayed again. "You'll have to excuse me," he said, at last; "I never played this game before."

And Sylvia realized in a flash of dismay that it was the first man again! The same voice—even the same words! "Sir," she said, coldly, "you are mistaken. You played the same game with me not twenty minutes ago."

The tall domino expressed bewilderment. "I beg your pardon—there has been some mistake."

"There has indeed," said Sylvia. "The door-keeper has evidently got our numbers mixed." She pondered for a moment. Should she go and tell Mr. Bates?

But she realized that it was too late. The couples were all settled and the game proceeding. It was the kind of blunder that was always being made at these parties—either because the door-keeper was stupid, or was bribed by some man who wanted to make love in earnest. It spoiled the game—but then, as Sylvia had just said, Love is blind.

"What shall we do—wait?" she asked; to which the man replied, "I don't mind."

"Thank you," she said, graciously. "We'll have to make the best of it. Don't you think you can manage to do a little better than the last time?"

"I'll try," he replied. "It's beastly stupid, I think."

Sylvia considered. "No," she declared, "I believe it's the game of all games for you."

"How so?"

"Go down into the deeps of you. Haven't you something there that is real—something primitive and untamed, that chafes against propriety, and wishes it had not been born in Boston?"

"I was not born in Boston," said he.

"Perhaps not in your body," said Sylvia, "but your soul is a Boston soul. And now think of this opportunity to fling loose, to be just as bad as you want to be—and quite without danger of detection, of having your reputation damaged! Surely, sir, there could be no game more adapted to the New England conscience!"

"By Jove!" exclaimed the man; and actually there was warmth in his tone. Sylvia's heart leaped, and she caught him by the hand. "Quick! Quick!" she cried. "Gather ye rosebuds while ye may—old time is still a-flying!"

"By Jove!" exclaimed the man again; and Sylvia, kindling with mischief, pressed his hand more tightly and brought him upon his knees before her. "Make haste! You have but one life—one chance to be yourself—to vent your emotions! I've no idea who you are, I can't possibly tell on you—and so you may utter those things which you keep hidden even from yourself!"

"By Jove!" he exclaimed for the third time. "Really, if I had you to make love to——"

"But you have me! You have me! For several precious minutes—alone and undisturbed! You are not a Boston Brahmin in a domino—you are a faun in the forests of Arcady. Come, Mr. Faun!" And Sylvia began to sing in a low, caressing manner:

"Oh, come, my love, to Arcady!
    A dream path leads us, dear.
    One hour of love in Arcady
        Is worth a lifetime here!"

There was a pause. She could feel the man's hand trembling. "I am waiting!" she whispered; to which he answered, "I wish *you* would talk! You make love so much better than I!"

Sylvia broke into one of her merry laughs. "A leap-year party!" she cried.

But the other was in earnest. "I like to listen to you," he said. "Please go on!"

Sylvia was laughing so that she felt tears in her eyes, and she wanted to wipe them away under her mask. Her handkerchief was gone, and she looked for it—in her lap, beside her on the seat, and then on the floor. This led to a curious and unexpected turn in the adventure— her recognition of this New England faun. See- ing what she was doing, he said, "I beg pardon. Have you lost something?"

It was like an explosion in Sylvia's mind. Not merely the same words—but the same manner, the same accent, the same personality!

The search for the handkerchief gave her the chance to recover her breath. The Lord had delivered him into her hands again!

"Sir," she said. "I resume. You have over- whelmed me with the torrent of your ardor. I feel myself swept away in a flood which my feeble will cannot resist. You come to me like a royal

wooer—like some god out of the skies, stunning
the senses of a mere mortal maiden! Who can
this be—I ask myself. From what source can
such superhuman eloquence and fervor spring?
Can I endure it? I cry—or shall I be burned up
and destroyed, like Danaï in the legend? It is
just so that he descends upon me—like Jupiter,
in a shower of gold!"

Sylvia could feel the tall domino stiffen and
rear himself. She had meant to go on, but she
stopped, so great was her curiosity. How would
he take it?

At last came the voice from under the mask.
"I see," it said, "that you have the advantage
of me. You *do* know who I am."

Sylvia was almost transported—by a combina-
tion of amazement and amusement. "Know who
you are?" she cried. "How could I fail to
know who you are? You, my divinity! You,
to whom all the world bends the knee! Sire,
receive my homage—I bow in adoration before
the Golden Calf!"

And she sunk down upon one knee before the
tall domino!

It was putting herself into his hands. She was
fully prepared to see him rise and stalk away—
but so possessed was she that she would have
enjoyed even that! Fortunately, however, at
this moment the bell rang, saving her. She
sprang to her feet, and caught the hand of her
divinity in one quick clasp of parting. "Good-
bye, Mr. van Tuiver!" she exclaimed. "Good-
bye—until the next incarnation!"

## § 12

For the next dance Sylvia's partner was a youth whom she could not identify. He had evidently been reading the poets, for his declarations of devotion were lacking in naught but rhyme. Sylvia accepted him politely, hardly hearing his words—so busy was she with the thought of van Tuiver. Had it been accident, or a trick? She would soon know.

There came another dance—and again a tall domino. Sylvia suspected, but was not sure, until they were in their seats, when the domino sat stiff and straight, and she was certain. "Is that you?" she asked; and the answer came, "It is."

"It is evident that some one is amusing himself at our expense," said Sylvia, coldly. "I really think we shall have to stop it."

"Miss Castleman," broke in the other. "I hope you will believe me that I have had absolutely nothing to do with this."

She answered, consolingly, "I assure you, Mr. van Tuiver, your unpreparedness has been quite evident."

There was a pause, while he considered that. "What shall we do?" he asked.

"I think that you had best see Mr. Bates, and make clear to him that we have had enough."

He hesitated. "Is—is that really necessary?"

"What else can we do—spend the evening together?"

"I really wish we could, Miss Castleman!"

"What—and you making love as you have been?"

"I can do better now. I really am quite charmed with the game. I'd like to make love to you—for a long time."

"Most flattering, Mr. van Tuiver—but how about me? We've conversed a lot already, and you haven't said one interesting thing."

"Miss Castleman!"

"Not one—excepting one or two that have been insolent."

There was a pause. "Really," he pleaded, "that is a hard thing to say!"

"Do you mean," she inquired, coldly, "that you have not realized the meaning of what you said to me when we met on the street?"

"I don't know just what you refer to," he replied, "but you must admit that you had me at a great disadvantage that evening."

"What disadvantage, Mr. van Tuiver? The fact that I did not know who you were?"

She could feel him wince. She was prepared for a retort—but not so severe as the one which came. "The disadvantage," he said, "that you *pretended* not to know who I was."

"Why," she exclaimed, "what do you mean?"

He answered. "If we are going to fight, it ought to be upon a fair field. You pretended that evening that you had never heard my name. But I learned since that only a day or two before you had had a quite elaborate conversation about me."

Sylvia's first impulse was to inquire sarcastically what right he had to assume that his illustrious name would stay in her memory. But she realized that that was a poor retort; and then her sense of fair play came in. After all, he was right—the joke was on her, and she rather admired his nerve.

So she began to laugh. "Mr. van Tuiver," she said, "you have annoyed me so that I won't even take the trouble to think up new lies to tell you. Realize, if you can, the impression you managed to make upon a young girl—you and your reputation together—that she should be moved to use such weapons against you!"

He forgot his anger at this. "That's just it, Miss Castleman! I don't understand it at all! What have I done that you should take such an attitude towards me?"

Sylvia pondered. "I fear," she said, "that you would not thank me for telling you."

"You are mistaken!" he exclaimed. "I really would like to know."

"I could not bring myself to do it."

"But why not?"

"I know it could not do any good."

"But how can you say that—when I assure you I am in earnest? I have a very sincere admiration for you—truly. You are one of the most—one of the most amazing young women I ever met. I don't say that in a bad sense, you understand——"

"I understand," said Sylvia, smiling. "I have tried my best to be amazing."

"It is evident that you dislike me intensely," he went on. "I ask you to tell me why. What have I done?"

"It isn't so much what you have done—it is what you *are*."

"And what *am* I, Miss Castleman?"

"I don't know just how to put it into words. You are some sort of monstrosity; something that when I see it, fills me with a blind rage, so that I want to fly at its throat. And then I realize that even in attacking it I am putting myself upon a level with it—and so I want to turn and flee for my life—or rather for my self-respect. I want to flee from it, Mr. van Tuiver, and never see it, never hear its voice, never even know of its existence! Do you see?"

"I see," said the man, in a voice so faint as to be hardly audible; and then suddenly came the sound of the bell, and Sylvia sprang up.

"I flee!" she said.

## § 13

THERE came a new dance, the sixth, and a new partner, who was short, and was speedily discovered to be Jackson. Then came the seventh dance, and Sylvia expected that it would be her Faun again, but was disappointed. It was a man unknown, and she wondered if Bates had lost his nerve. But with Number Eight came the inevitable return.

Van Tuiver was so anxious this time that he asked before he began to dance, "Is that you?" And when Sylvia answered "Yes," she could hear his sigh of relief. All through the dance she could feel his excitement. Once or twice he tried to talk, but she whispered to him to keep the rules.

The moment they were seated he said, "Miss Castleman, you must explain to me what you mean."

"I knew I'd have to explain," she responded. "I've been thinking how I could make you understand. You see, I'm a comparative stranger to this world of yours, and things might shock me which would seem to you quite a matter of course. I suppose I'm what you'd call a country girl, and have a provincial outlook."

"Please go on," he said.

"Well, Mr. van Tuiver, you have an enormous amount of money. Twenty or thirty million dollars—forty or fifty million dollars—the authorities don't seem to agree about it. As well as I can put the matter, you have so much that it has displaced *you;* it isn't you who think, it isn't you who speak—it's your money. You seem to be a sort of quivering, uneasy consciousness of uncounted millions of dollars; and the only thing that comes back to you from your surroundings is an echo of that quivering consciousness."

"Do I really seem like that to you?"

"It's the impression you've made upon everyone who knows you."

"Oh, surely not!" he cried.

"Quite literally that," said Sylvia. "I hated you before I ever laid eyes on you—because of the way you'd impressed your friends."

There was a pause; when van Tuiver spoke again it was in a low and uncertain voice. "Miss Castleman," he said, "has it ever occurred to you to think what might be the difficulties of my situation?"

"No, I haven't had time for that."

"Well, take this one fact. You say that I have made a certain impression upon everyone who knows me. But you are the first person in my whole lifetime who's ever told me."

Sylvia gave an exclamation of incredulity.

"Don't you see?" pressed on the other, eagerly. "What is a man to do? I have a great deal of money. I can't help that. And I can't help the fact that it gives me a great deal of power. I can't help having a sense of responsibility."

"The sense of responsibility has been too much for you," said Sylvia.

This was too subtle for him. He hurried on: "Maybe it's right, maybe it's wrong—but circumstances have given me a certain position, and I have to maintain it. I have certain duties which I must fulfill, which I can't possibly get away from."

There was a pause. He seemed to feel that the situation was not satisfactory, and started again. "It's all very well for you, who don't realize my position, the responsibilities I have—it's all very well for you to talk about my consciousness of money. But how can I get away from it? People know about my money, they think about it—they expect certain things of me. They put me in a certain position, whether I will or not."

He stopped again. He was so greatly agitated that Sylvia was beginning to feel pity. "Do you have to be what people expect you to be?" she said.

"But," he argued, "I have the money, and I have to make use of it—to invest it—to protect it——"

"Ah, but all that is in the business world. What I'm talking about is in a separate sphere—your social relations."

"But, Miss Castleman, that's just it—*is* it separate? It ought to be, you'll say—but *is* it? I tell you, you simply don't know, that's all. People profess friendship for me, but they want something, and by and by I find out what it is they want. You say that's monstrous; I know, I used to think it was, myself. You say, I ought not to know it; but I can't *help* knowing it; it's forced upon me by all the circumstances of my life. Sometimes I think I've never had a disinterested friend since I was born!"

Sylvia perceived the intensity behind his words, and was silent for a minute. "But surely," she said, "here—in the democracy of college life——"

"It's exactly the same here as anywhere else. Here are clubs, social cabals, everybody pushing and intriguing, exactly as in New York society.

Take that fact you spoke of—that all the fellows dislike me, and yet not one of them has dared to tell me so!"

"*Dared?*" repeated Sylvia.

"Oh, well, perhaps they dared—the point is, they didn't. The ones who had to make their own way were busy making it; and the others, who had got in of right—well, they believe in money. They'd all shrug their shoulders and say, 'What's the use of antagonizing such a man?'"

"I see," said Sylvia, fascinated.

"Whatever the reason is, they never call me down—not a man of them. And then, as for the women——"

Sylvia had not made any sound, but somehow he felt her sudden interest. He said, with signs of agitation, "Please, Miss Castleman, don't be offended. You asked me to talk about it."

"Go on," she said. "I'm really most curious. I suppose all the women want to marry you?"

"It isn't only that. They want anything. They just want to be seen with me. Of course, when they start to make love to me—" He paused.

"You stop them, I hope," said Sylvia, modestly.

"I do when I know it. But, you see——"

He paused again; it was evidently a difficult topic. "Pray don't mind," said Sylvia, laughing. "They're subtle creatures, I know. Do many of them make love to you?"

"I know you're laughing at me, Miss Castle-

man. But believe me, it's no joke. If you'd
see some of the letters I get!"

"Oh, they write you love letters?"

"Not only love letters. I don't mind them—
but the letters from women in distress, the most
terrible stories you can imagine. Once I was
foolish enough—didn't anybody tell you the scrape
I got into?"

"No."

"That's curious—they generally like to tell it.
I was weak enough to let one woman get into
my house in Cambridge. She had a tragedy to
rehearse, and I listened to her, and finally she
wanted ten thousand dollars. I didn't know if
her story was true, and I said No, and then she
began to scream for help. The servants came
running, and she said—well, you can imagine,
how I'd insulted her, and all that. I told my
man to throw her out, but she said she'd scratch
his eyes out, she'd scream from the window,
she'd stand on the street outside and denounce
me till the police came, she'd give the newspapers the whole story of the way I'd abused her.
And so finally I had to give her all the money I
happened to have on me."

"Great Heavens!" exclaimed Sylvia, who had
not thought of anything so serious as that.

"You see how it is. For the most part I've
escaped that kind of thing, because I was taught.
My Great-uncle Douglas, who died recently—he
was my guardian, and he taught me all about
women when I was very young—not more than

ten. He had charge of my upbringing, and he wouldn't allow a woman in my household."

"Dear me," said Sylvia, "what a cynic he must have been!"

"He died a bachelor," said the other, "and left me a great deal of money. So you see— that is——"

"He'd *had* to be a cynic!" laughed the girl. And van Tuiver laughed with her—more humanly than she had ever thought possible.

She considered for a moment, and then suddenly asked, "Mr. van Tuiver, has it never occurred to you that *I* might be making love to you?"

She could not see his face, but she knew that he was staring at her in dismay. "Oh, surely not, Miss Castleman!" he exclaimed.

"But how can you be sure?" she asked. "Where is your training?"

"Miss Castleman," he said, "please take me seriously." ·

"I'm quite serious. In fact, I think I ought to tell you, I *have* been making love to you."

"Surely not!" he said.

"I mean it, quite literally. I've been doing it from the first moment I met you—doing it in spite of all my resolutions to the contrary!"

"But why?"

"Well, because I hated you, and also because I pitied you. I said, I'll get him in my power and punish him—and at the same time teach him."

"Oh!" exclaimed van Tuiver; and she thought that she detected a note of relief in the word.

"You are glad I don't mean to marry you," she said; and when he started to protest, she cut him short with, "You're not applying the wisdom of your great-uncle! I say I don't want to marry you, but most likely that's a device to disarm you, to make you want to marry *me*."

In spite of his evident distress, she was incorrigible. "You ought to be up and away," she declared—"scared out of your wits. I tell you I'm the most dangerous woman you've ever met. And I mean it literally. I'll wager that if your great-uncle had ever met my great-aunt, he would not have died a bachelor! Take my advice, and fall ill and leave this party at once."

"Why should I be afraid of you?" he demanded. "Why shouldn't I marry you if I want to?"

"What! a poor girl like me?"

"Well, I don't know. I can afford to marry a poor girl if I feel like it?"

"But—think of the ignominy of being trapped!"

He considered this. "I'm not afraid of that either," he said. "If you've had the wit to do it—and none of the others had——"

"Oh!" she laughed. "Then you're willing to be hunted!"

"Miss Castleman," he protested, "you are unkind. I've thought seriously. You really are a most beautiful woman, and at the same time a most amazingly clever woman. You would be an ornament in my life—I'd always be proud of you—"

He paused. "Mr. van Tuiver," she demanded,

"Am I to understand that this is a serious proposal?"

She could feel his quiver of fear. "Why," he stammered—"really——"

"Don't you see how dangerous it is!" she exclaimed. "You were almost caught! Make your escape, Mr. van Tuiver!"

And then came the sound of the bell. She started up. "Go and tell Mr. Bates!" she cried. "Don't let him do this again—if you do, you are lost forever!"

## § 14

THE next partner was Harley. It was a nuisance having to entertain your own cousin, but Sylvia amused herself by keeping Harley from recognizing her. And in the meantime she was wondering what her Victim would do next.

She knew his very style of dancing by now, and needed to make no inquiries of Number Ten. "You did not take my advice," she remarked, when they were seated.

"No," he said. "On the contrary, I told Bates to put us together the rest of the time."

"Oh, no!" she protested.

"I want to talk to you," he declared. "I *must* talk to you."

"But you had no right! He will tell, and everybody will be talking about it."

"I don't care if they do."

"But *I* care, Mr. van Tuiver—you should not have taken such a liberty."

"Please, Miss Castleman," he hurried on, "please listen to me. I've been thinking about it, and it interests me keenly. I believe that in you I might really have a friend—if only you would. A real friend, I mean—who'd tell me the truth—who'd be absolutely disinterested——"

The fun of it was too much for Sylvia. "Haven't I explained to you that I mightn't be disinterested?"

"I'll trust you."

"Of course," she went on, gravely. "I might give you my word of honor that I wouldn't marry you."

"Yes," he agreed, "I suppose so——"

The girl was convulsed with laughter. "Mr. van Tuiver," she remarked, "I see you are an earnest man; I really ought to stop teasing you. Don't you think I ought?"

"Yes," he replied, dubiously.. "At least—I never liked to be teased before."

"Well, I will tell you this for your comfort. There's no remotest possibility of my ever marrying you, so you can feel quite safe."

Somehow he did not seem sure whether he was pleased at this pledge. After a pause he went on: "What I mean is that I think a man in my position ought to have somebody to tell him the truth."

"Something like the court-jesters in old days," said Sylvia.

But he was not interested in mediæval customs. He was interested in his own need, and she had to promise that she would admit him to the arcanum of her friendship, and that she would always tell him exactly what she thought about him—his actions, his ideas, even his manners. In fulfilment of which promise she spent the rest of that *séance,* and the two that followed, in listening to him talk about himself and his life.

It was really most curious—an inside glimpse into a kind of life of which one heard, but with no idea of ever encountering it; just as one read of train-robbers and safe-blowers, but never expected to sit and chat with them. Douglas van Tuiver had achieved notoriety before he had cut a single tooth; his mother and father having been killed in a railroad accident when he was two months old, the courts had appointed trustees and guardians, and the newspapers had undertaken a kind of unofficial supervision. The precious infant had been brought up by a staff of tutors, with majordomos and lackeys in the background, and two private detectives and a great-uncle and Mrs. Harold Cliveden to oversee the whole. It did not need much questioning to get the details of this life—the lonely palace on Fifth Avenue, the monumental "cottage" at Newport, the "camp" in the Adirondacks, the yacht in the West Indies; the costly toys, the "blooded" pets, the gold plate, the tedious, suffocating solemnity. If Sylvia had been furious with van Tuiver before, she was ready now to go to the opposite extreme and weep over him. A child brought up wholly by employees, with no brothers and sisters to kick and scratch him into decency, no cousins, no playmates even—unless he was first togged out in an Eton suit and escorted by a tutor to the birthday party of some other little togged-out aristocrat!

Yes, assuredly this unhappy man needed someone to tell him the truth! Sylvia resolved that she would fill the rôle. She would be quite unmoved by his Royalty (the word by which she had come to sum up to herself the whole phenomenon of van Tuiverness). She would persist in regarding him as any other human being, saying to him what she felt like, pretending to him, and even to herself, that he really was not Royalty at all!

But alas, she soon found what a task she had undertaken! The last dance had been danced, and amid much merriment the guests unmasked —and still van Tuiver wanted to stay and talk to his one friend. He escorted her to supper, in spite of the fact that Mrs. Winthrop had other arrangements for him. And even if he had behaved himself, there was the tale which "Tubby" Bates had been diligently spreading. The girl realized all at once that she had achieved a new and startling kind of prominence; all the guests, men and women, were watching her, whispering about her, envying her. She felt a wicked thrill of triumph and pleasure. She, a stranger, an obscure girl from the provinces,

who would ordinarily have been an object of
suspicion and investigation—she had leaped at
one moment into supremacy! She had become
the favorite of the King!

Pretty soon came Harley, a-tremble with
delight. "Gee whiz, old girl, you sure have
scored to-night! For God's sake, how did you
manage it?" Sylvia felt herself hot with sudden
shame.

And then came Bates. She tried to scold him,
but he would simply not have it. "Now, Miss
Castleman! Now, Miss Castleman!"—that was
all he would say. What it meant was: "It is
all right for you to pretend, of course; but you
can't persuade me that you are really angry!"

"Please go away," she said at last; but he
wanted to tell her what different people said, and
would not be shaken off. While he was still
teasing, there swept past them a girl to whom
Sylvia had not been introduced—a solid-looking
young Amazon with a freckled snub nose. She
gave Sylvia what appeared to be a haughty look,
and Bates whispered, "Do you know who that
is? That's Dorothy Cortlandt!—the girl van
Tuiver is to marry."

"Really!" exclaimed Sylvia, who was cross
with all the world. "How did her nose get
broken?"

And the other answered with a grin, "You
ought to know—you did it!" And so, as
Sylvia could not help laughing, Bates counted
himself forgiven.

A little later came the encounter with Edith Winthrop. It was after supper, and the two found themselves face to face. "What a charming party it has been!" said Sylvia, and the other gave her what was meant to be a freezing stare. It was so rude that Sylvia thought she must have been misunderstood. "The party's been a success," she ventured. "Don't you think so?"

"Ideas of success differ," remarked the other, coldly, and turned her back and began an animated conversation with someone else.

"Dear me," thought Sylvia, as she moved on, "What have I done?" She saw in another part of the room her hostess talking to van Tuiver, and made up her mind at once that she would find out if the beautiful soul-friendship was shattered also. She moved over towards the two, resisting an effort on the part of Harmon to draw her into a *tête-a-tête*.

"Mrs. Winthrop," she said, "I'm so glad I stayed over."

"Queen Isabella" turned the mystical eyes upon her, one of the deep, inscrutable gazes. Sylvia waited, knowing that it might mean anything from revery to murder. "My dear Sylvia," she said at last, "you are pale to-night."

This, in the presence of van Tuiver, probably meant war. "Am I?" asked the girl.

"Yes, my dear, don't dissipate too much! Women of your type fade quickly."

"What?" laughed the other, gaily. "With my red eyes and red hair? A century could not extinguish me!"

She passed on, and discovered that van Tuiver was following her. "You aren't going, are you, Miss Castleman?" he asked; and while he was begging her to stay, Sylvia saw her hostess move across the room to Dorothy Cortlandt. These two stood conversing earnestly, and one glance was enough to tell Sylvia what they were conversing about.

All this was a sore temptation, but Sylvia was in a virtuous mood. "Mr. van Tuiver," she said, "there is something I want to say to you. I've thought it over, and made up my mind that it is impossible for me to be the friend you want."

"Why, Miss Castleman!" he exclaimed, in distress. "What is the matter?"

"I can't explain——"

"But what have I *done?*"

"It's nothing that you've done. It's simply that I couldn't stand the world you live in. Oh, I'd be a dreadful woman if I stayed very long!"

"Please, listen——" he implored.

But she cut him short. "I am sorry to give you pain, but I have made up my mind absolutely. There is no possible way I can help you. I am not willing to see you again, and you must positively not ask it." After which speech she went to look for her cousin, leaving van Tuiver such a picture of agitation that everyone in the room observed it. Could the King's nose be broken too?

## § 15

THE next morning came a note from van Tuiver. He was sure that Miss Castelman must have reconsidered her cruel decision, and he begged her to grant him one brief interview. Might he take her riding in his car that morning? The bearer would wait for an answer. Sylvia replied that her decision was unchanged and unchangeable—she was sorry to hurt his feelings, but she must ask him to give up all thought of her.

A couple of hours later came van Tuiver himself, and sent up his card and with a line scribbled on it, "What have I done to anger you?" She wrote back, "I am not angry, but I cannot see you." After which an hour more elapsed and there came a telephone-call from "Tubby" Bates, who begged the honor of a few minutes talk.

"I ought to refuse to speak to you again," said Sylvia. But in the end she gave way and told him he might call.

He had come as an emissary, of course. The young millionaire was in a dreadful state, he explained, being convinced that he had committed some unmentionable offence.

"I don't care to talk about the matter," said Sylvia.

"But," persisted Bates, "he declares that I got him into the predicament, and now I'm honor-bound to get him out."

So she had to set to work to explain her point of view. Mr. Bates, who himself owed no par-

15

ticular allegiance to Royalty, should be able to understand; he must realize that her annoyance was not personal, but was, so to speak, an affair of State. This had been her first experience at Court, she said; and the atmosphere had proven bad for her—had made her pale, and would soon turn her into a faded old woman.

Evidently "Tubby" had heard that part of the story also; first he grinned, and then in his rôle of diplomat set to work to smooth away her objections. "You surely don't mind a little thing like that," he pleaded. "Haven't you any jealous ladies down South?"

"If we are going to discuss this question, Mr. Bates, I must speak frankly. Our hostesses are polite to their guests."

The other began suddenly to laugh. "Even when the guests steal?"

"When they steal?"

"Jewels!" exclaimed the other. "Bright, particular, conspicuous jewels—crown-jewels, precious beyond replacing! Think, Miss Castleman, you trust a guest, you admit him to your castle —and suddenly you find that the great ruby of your diadem is gone!"

"Is it that Mrs. Winthrop hopes to marry van Tuiver to her daughter?" asked Sylvia, crossly.

"Oh, no," said Bates. "He is to marry Dorothy Cortlandt—that was arranged when they were babies, and Mrs. Winthrop wouldn't dream of cutting in on it."

"But then, if I haven't robbed Edith——"

"My dear Miss Castleman," said the other, "you've robbed Mrs. Winthrop herself."

"But I don't understand," said the girl.

"Please don't *mis*understand," said Bates. "It's all perfectly proper and noble, you know— and all that. I've nothing to say against Mrs. Winthrop—she's a charming woman, and has a right to be admired by everybody. But being a queen, you see, she has to have a court, with a lot of distinguished courtiers. She reads poetry to them, and they write it to her, and they sit at her feet and dream wonderful dreams, and she gazes at them. I know a dozen fellows who've been that way all through college; and I suppose it does them good—they tell me I haven't any soul and can't understand these things. What I've always said is, 'Maybe you're right, and maybe I'm a brute, but it looks to me like the same old game.'"

"The same old game," repeated Sylvia, wonderingly. She found herself thinking suddenly of one of the maxims of Lady Dee—one which she had been too young to understand, but had been made to learn nevertheless: "The young girl's deadliest enemy is the married flirt!" Could it be that Mrs. Winthrop was anything so desperate as that?

"Mr. van Tuiver is one of these poets?" she asked, finally.

"I don't think van Tuiver goes in for poetry; but he's strong on manners and things like that, and he says that Mrs. Winthrop is the only hostess in America who has the old-world charm. Of course that ravished her, and they've been great chums."

"And I came and spoiled it all!" exclaimed the girl.

"You came and spoiled it all!" said Bates.

Sylvia sat for a while in thought. "You know, Mr. Bates," she remarked, "it rather puzzles me that people consider Mr. van Tuiver as having distinguished manners. I really haven't been impressed that way."

The other laughed. "My dear Miss Castleman, don't you know that van Tuiver's in love with you!"

"No! Surely not!"

"Perfectly head over heels in love with you. He's been that way since the first moment he laid eyes on you. And the way you've treated him—you. know you are rather high-handed. Anyhow, it's rattled him so, he simply doesn't know whether he's on his head or his feet."

"Did he tell you that, Mr. Bates?"

"Not in words—but by everything about him. I never saw a man so changed. Honestly, you don't know him at all, as we've known him. You'd not believe it if I described him."

"Tell me what you mean?"

"Well, in the first place, he's always dignified—stately, even. When he speaks, it's he speaking, and his Yea is Yea and his Nay is Nay. Then he's very precise—he never does anything upon impulse, but always considers whether it's the

right thing for Douglas van Tuiver to do. You
see, he has an acute consciousness of his social
task—I mean, being a model to all the little
people in the world. You wouldn't understand
his manners unless you realized that they're
imported from England. In England—have you
ever been there?"

"No," said Sylvia.

"Well, you're walking along a country road,
and you're lost, and you see a gentleman coming
the other way. You stop and begin, 'I beg pardon'—and he goes by you with his eyes to the
front, military fashion. You see, you're not
supposed to exist."

"How perfectly dreadful!"

"I remember once I was walking in the country,
and there came a carriage with two ladies in it.
It stopped as I passed, and so I stopped. 'Can
you tell me where such and such a house is?' she
asked, and I replied that it was in such and such
a direction. And then, without even a look,
she sank back in her cushions, and the coachman
drove on. She was a lady, and she thought it
was a grand carelessness."

"Oh, but surely she must have belonged to
the '*nouveaux riches*'!" exclaimed Sylvia.

"On the contrary, she may have had the best
blood in England. You see, that's their system.
They have a ruling caste, whose rudeness is their
religion."

"We have our family pride in the South,"
said Sylvia, "but it's supposed to show itself in

a superior courtesy. In fact, if a person's rude to his inferiors, we're sure there must be plebeian blood somewhere."

"Exactly, Miss Castleman—that's what I've always been taught." There was a pause; then suddenly Bates began to laugh. "They tell such a funny story about van Tuiver," he went on. "It was a club-tea, and there were two ladies whom everybody knew to be social rivals. Van Tuiver was talking to Mrs. A. and suddenly, without any warning, he walked over and began to talk to Mrs. B. Afterwards somebody said to him, 'Why did you leave Mrs. A. and go directly to Mrs. B.? You know they hate each other— did you want to make it worse?' 'No, I never thought of it,' he said. 'The point was, there was a fireplace at my back, and I don't like a fireplace at my back.' 'But did you tell that to Mrs. A.?' asked the friend. 'No,' said van Tuiver —'I told it to Mrs. B.'"

"Oh, dear me!" cried Sylvia.

"And you must understand that he saw nothing funny in it. And the significant thing is that he gets away with that pose!"

"In other words, he has introduced the English system into America," said Sylvia.

"That's what it comes to, Miss Castleman."

"You have a king at Harvard!"

The man hesitated, and then a smile spread over his face. "Of course you realize," he said, "that it's a game we're playing."

"A game?" she repeated.

"Do you know they had a queen in New York, Miss Castleman—until she died, just recently? You came to the city, you intrigued and pulled wires, and perhaps she condescended to receive you—seated upon a regular throne of state, painted and covered with jewels like a Hindoo idol. Everybody agreed she was the queen, and nobody could go anywhere or do anything unless she said so. Only, of course, ninety-nine people out of a hundred paid no attention to her, and went ahead and lived their lives just as if she weren't queen. And it's the same way here."

"Tubby" paused for encouragement; this was unusual eloquence for him.

"As to our king," he continued, "one-eighth of the college pays him homage, and another eighth rebels against him—and the other three-quarters don't know that he's here. They're busy cramming for exams, or training for the boat-race, or having a good time spending papa's money. In other words, Miss Castleman, van Tuiver is our king when we are snobs; and some of us are snobs all the time, and others of us only when we go calling on the ladies. Do you understand?"

"I understand," said Sylvia, intensely amused. "I suspect that you are one of the rebellious subjects. You are certainly a frank ambassador, Mr. Bates!"

It was his turn to laugh. "The truth is, van Tuiver's been three years posing in a certain

rôle, and he can't turn round now and play a
different one for you. I thought it over as I was
coming here, and I said to myself, 'I'll ask her
to see him, but I'll be damned'—pardon me, but
that's what I said—'I'll be damned if I'll help
him to deceive her.' You see, Miss Castleman—
I hope I don't presume—but I know van Tuiver's
in love with you, and I thought—well—I——"

The genial "Tubby" had turned several shades
redder, and now he fell silent. "You may feel
quite at ease, Mr. Bates," smiled Sylvia. "The
danger you fear does not exist at all."

"Not by any possibility, Miss Castleman?"

"Not by any possibility, Mr. Bates.

"He—he has an enormous lot of money!"

"After all our conversation! There are surely
a few things in America which are not for sale."

"Tubby" drew a deep breath of relief. "I
was scared," he said—"honest."

"How lovely of you!" said Sylvia. She suddenly felt like a mother to this big fat boy who
was said to have no soul.

"I said to myself," he continued, "'I'll tell her
the truth about van Tuiver, even if she never
forgives me for it.' You see, Miss Castleman,
I see the real man—as you'd never be allowed
to, not in a thousand years. And you must take
my word and be careful, for van Tuiver's a man
who has never had to do without anything in
his whole lifetime. No matter what it's been
that he's wanted, he's had it—always, *always!*
I've seen one or two times when it looked as if

he mightn't get it—and I can tell you that he's
cunning, and that he persists and persists—he's
a perfect demon when he's got his mind fixed on
something he wants and hasn't got."

"Dear me!" said Sylvia. "That *is* a new view
of him!"

"Well, I said I'd warn you. I hope you don't
mind."

Sylvia smiled. "I thought you had set out
to persuade me to see him again!"

Bates watched her. "I don't know," he said,
"maybe mine was the best way to persuade you."

"Why, how charming!" she exclaimed, with a
laugh. "You are really subtle."

"We want to fight the introduction of the
English system, Miss Castleman! I don't mind
an aristocracy, because I'm one of 'em; but
I don't want any kings in America! It's a
patriotic duty to pull them off their thrones and
keep them off."

Sylvia pondered. It was a most entertaining
view. "And the queens too?" she laughed.

"Yes, and the queens too!"

There was a pause, while she thought. Then
she said, "Yes, I think you're right, Mr. Bates.
You may tell His Majesty that I'll see him—
once more!"


## § 16


SYLVIA had said that she would go motoring
with van Tuiver the following afternoon. He

came in a cab, explaining that he had been to dinner in Cambridge, and that his car had run out of fuel. "I've a chauffeur who is troubled with absent-mindedness," he remarked, with what Sylvia soon realized was enforced good-nature. For the car was longer in coming than he expected, and when at last it arrived, she was given an exhibition of his system of manners as applied to servants.

The chauffeur tried to make some explanation. There had been an accident, which he wanted to tell of; but the other would not give him a chance. "I've not the least desire to listen to you," he said. "I do not employ you to make excuses. I told you when you came to me that I required promptness from my servants. You have had your opportunity, and you are not equal to it. You may consider yourself under notice."

"Very good, sir," said the man; and Sylvia stepped into the car and sat thinking, not hearing what van Tuiver said to her.

It was not the words he had used; he had a right to give his chauffeur notice, she told herself. It was his tone which had struck her like a knife —a tone of insolence, of deliberate provocativeness. Yet he, apparently, had no idea that she would notice it; doubtless he would think it meant a lack of breeding in her to notice it.

She wished to do justice to him; and she knew that it was partly her Southern shrinking from the idea of white servants. She was used to negroes, about whose feelings one did not bother.

If Aunt Nannie discovered one of the chamber-maids trying on her mistress' ball gown, it would be, "Get out of here, you bob-tailed monkey!" Or if Uncle Mandeville's boy forgot to feed a favorite horse, the rascal would be dragged out by one ear and soundly caned—and would expect it, knowing that if it was never done the horse would never be fed. But to talk so to a white man—and not in a blaze of anger, but with cold and concentrated malevolence!

The purpose of this ride was a definite one—that van Tuiver might find out the meaning of Sylvia's change of mind at the dance. He propounded the question very soon; and the girl had to try to explain the state of mind in which she found herself. She would begin, she said, with the situation she had found at Harvard. Here were two groups of men, working for different ends, one desiring democracy in college life, and the other wishing to preserve the old spirit of caste. The conflict between them had become intense, and Sylvia's sympathies were with van Tuiver's opponents.

"Tell me," she said, "what has Harvard meant to you? What has it given you that you couldn't have got elsewhere? Here are men from all over America, but you've only met one little set. All the others—whom you're probably too refined to call 'rough-necks'—could none of them have taught you anything?"

"Perhaps they could," he answered, "but it's not easy to know them. If I met people promis-

cuously, they'd presume upon the acquaintance.
I'd have no time to myself, no privacy——"

He saw the scorn in Sylvia's face. "That's all
very well," he cried, "but you simply don't realize!
Take your own case—do *you* meet anybody who
comes along?"

"I am a girl," said Sylvia. "People seem to
think it's necessary to protect girls. But even
so, I remember experiences that you might profit
by. I went last year to our State University,
where one of my cousins was graduating. At
one of the dances I was accidentally introduced to
a man, a decent fellow, whom I liked. 'I won't
ask you to dance with me, Miss Castleman,' he
said. I asked, 'Why not?' and he said, 'I'm a
"goat".' I said, 'I'll dance with a goat, if he's
a good dancer,' and so we danced. And then
came my cousin. 'Sylvia, don't you know who
the man is you were dancing with? He's a
"goat"!' 'I like him,' I said, 'and he dances as
well as any of you. I shall dance with him.'
'But, Miss Castleman,' they all said, 'you'll
break up the fraternity system in the college.'
'What strange fraternity!' I answered. 'I think
it needs breaking up. I'll dance with him, and
if anybody doesn't like it, I won't dance with
*him*.' So I had my way."

"That's all right," said the other. "If a pretty
girl chooses to have her whim, everybody can
allow for it. But if you set to work to run a
college on that basis, you'd abolish social life
there. Men of a certain class would simply not

go where they had undesirable companionship forced upon them. Is that what you want to bring about?"

Sylvia thought for a moment, and then countered, "Is the only way you can think of to avoid undesirable companionship to have a private house?"

"A house?" replied van Tuiver. "Lots of people live in houses. Doesn't your father?"

"My father has a family," said Sylvia. "You have no one but yourself—and you don't have the house because you need it, but simply for ostentation."

He was very patient. "My dear Miss Castleman," he said, "it happens that I was raised in a house, and I'm used to it. And I happen to have the money—why shouldn't I spend it?"

"You might spend it for the good of others."

"You mean in charity? Haven't you learned that charity never does any good?"

"Sometimes I wish that I were a man, so that I could understand these things," exclaimed Sylvia. "But surely you might find some way of doing good with your money, instead of only harm, as at present."

"Only harm, Miss Castleman?"

"You are spending your money setting up false ideals in your college. You are doing all in your power to make everyone who meets you, or sees you, or even knows of you, a toady or else an Anarchist. And at the same time you are killing the best things in the college."

"What, for instance?"

"There is Memorial Hall—a building that stands for something. I can see that, even if all my people were on the other side in the war. There you find the democracy of the college, the spirit of real comradeship. But did you ever eat a meal in Memorial Hall?"

"No," said he, "I never did."

Sylvia thought for a moment. "Do ladies eat there?" she asked; and when he answered in the negative, she laughed. "Of course, that was only a 'pretty girl's whim'—as you call it. But if you, Douglas van Tuiver, would go there, as a matter of course—right along, I mean——"

"Eat at Memorial Hall!" he exclaimed. "My dear Miss Castleman, I wouldn't eat—I'd be eaten!"

"In other words," said she, coldly, "you admit that you can't take care of yourself as a man among men."

It was amusing to perceive his dismay over her idea. He came back to it, after a minute. He wanted to know if that was the sort of thing he'd have to do to win her regard; and he repeated the phrase with a sort of fascinated horror. "Eat at Memorial Hall!"

Until at last Sylvia declared with asperity, "Mr. van Tuiver, I don't care whether you eat at all, until you've found something better to do with your life."

## § 17

HE took these rages of hers very humbly. He was becoming extraordinarily tame. "I suppose you find me exasperating," he said, "but you must realize that I'm trying my best to understand you. You want me to make my life all over, and it isn't easy for me to see the necessity of it. What harm do I do here, just by keeping to myself?"

Sylvia was touched by his tone, and she tried again to explain. "It isn't that you keep to yourself," she said. "You cultivate a contempt for your classmates, and they reply with hatred and envy, and so you break up college life. It's true, isn't it, that there's a struggle going on now?"

"The class elections, you mean?"

"Yes, that's what I mean. So much bitterness and intriguing, because you keep to yourself! Why do you come to college at all? Surely you won't say it's the professors and the studies!"

"No," said he, smiling in spite of himself.

"You come, and you make yourself into a kind of idol. Excuse me, if it isn't polite, but what I said the other night is the truth—the Golden Calf! And what I say is, try the other plan a while. Stop thinking about yourself, and what they are thinking about you—above all, what they are thinking about your money. They won't all be thinking about your money."

He did not answer promptly. "Apparently," she said, "you don't feel quite sure. If you can't, I know several real men that I could introduce you to—men right in your own class."

"Who are they?"

She hesitated. She was about to say Frank Shirley, but concluded not to. "I met one the other day—he doesn't belong to a club, yet he's the most interesting person I've encountered here. He talked about you, and he wasn't complimentary; but if you sought him out in the right way, and made it clear you weren't trying to patronize him, I'm sure he'd be a friend."

"What's his name?"

"Mr. Firmin."

"Oh!" said van Tuiver, and looked annoyed.

"You know him?"

"By sight. He has a bitter tongue."

"No more bitter than you need, Mr. van Tuiver —if you are going to hear the truth about yourself."

The other hesitated. "I really do want to win your regard—" he began.

"I don't want you to do anything to win my regard! If you do these things, it must be because you want to do them. At present you're just your money, your position—your Royalty, as I've come to call it. But I'm not the least bit concerned about your Royalty; your houses and your servants and your automobiles are a bore to me —worse than that, they're wicked, for no man has a right to spend so much money on himself, to have a whole house to himself——."

"Please," he pleaded, "stop scolding about my house. I couldn't change now, for it's only a couple of weeks to Commencement."

"It would have all the more effect," she declared, "if you moved into a dormitory now. Here are the class elections, and your class split up——"

"You don't realize my position," he interrupted. "It's not merely a question of what I want. There's Ridgely Shackleford, our candidate for class president; if I deserted him and went over to the 'Yard,' they'd say I was a traitor, a coward—worse than that, they'd say I was a fool! I wouldn't have a friend left in the college."

"You really think it would be so bad?"

"It would be worse. I haven't told you half. When the story got about, I'd become a booby in society; I'd have to give up my clubs, I'd be a complete outcast. I tell you, you simply can't break down the barriers of your class."

Sylvia sat in silence, pondering his words. Suddenly she became aware that he was gazing at her eagerly. "Miss Castleman," he began, his voice trembling slightly, "what I want above all else is your friendship. I'd do anything to win it—I'd give up anything in the world. I have a regard for you—a most intense admiration. If I knew it would make me mean something to you—why then, I'd be willing to go to any extreme, to defy everybody else. But suppose I do this, and I'm left all alone——"

16

"If you did this you'd have new friends—real friends."

"But the friend I want is *you!*"

Sylvia answered, "If you did what was right because it was right, if you showed yourself willing to dare something for the sake of principle—why then, right away you'd become worth while. You'd not have to ask for my friendship."

He hesitated. "Suppose—suppose that I should find that I wanted *more* than friendship——"

She had been prepared for that—and she stopped him instantly. "Friendship comes first," she said.

"But," he pleaded, "give me some idea. Could I not expect——"

"You asked me to be a friend to you, to help you by telling you the truth. That is what we have been discussing. Pray let there be no mistake about it. Friendship comes first."

Why did Sylvia take such a course with him? You would have a false idea of her character if you did not realize that it was the first time she had ever done such a thing—and that it was a hard thing for her to do. To refuse to let a man propose to her! To forbear to draw him on, to investigate him, to see what he would reply to various baffling remarks!

It was not because she was engaged to Frank Shirley. Under the code which Lady Dee had taught her that made simply no difference whatever. Under that code it was her duty to secure every man who came into her reach; she might remain uncertain in her own mind, she might continue to explore and experiment up to the very moment when the wedding ring was slipped upon her finger. Sylvia had never forgotten Aunt Lady's vivid image: "Stand them up in a line, my child, and when you get ready, walk down the line and pick the one you want!"

She had set up a barrier before van Tuiver, and he pushed against it. The more firm she made it, the more he was moved to push. But suppose she gave way the least little bit, suppose he felt the barrier breaking—then would he not stop pushing, would he not shrink away? What fun to try him, to watch him hesitating, advancing and retreating, trembling with desire and with terror! To analyze the mixture of his longing and his caution, to add a little to the one or the other, and then see the result. Sylvia with a new man was like a chemist's assistant, mixing strange liquids in a test-tube, possessed with a craze to know whether the precipitate would be red or green or yellow—and quite undeterred by the possibility of being blown through the skylight.

But tempting as was the game, she could not play it with Douglas van Tuiver. It was as if an angel stood between them with a flaming sword. Douglas van Tuiver was no subject for joke, he was not a man as other men—he was Royalty. With Royalty one must be stern and unfaltering. "Friendship comes first," she had said; and though before that ride was over he had come again and again to the barrier, he never broke past it, nor felt any sign of its yielding to his touch.

## § 18

SYLVIA was making her plans to leave in a couple of days. It was close to Commencement, and she would have liked to stay, but there had come a disturbing letter from home—the Major was not well, and there had been an overflow, entailing serious damage to the crops and still more serious cares. At such a time the family reached out blindly to Sylvia—no matter what was going wrong, they were sure it would go right if she were present.

And besides, her work at Harvard was done. This was duly certified to by Harley, who came to see her the next morning, in such a state of bliss as is not often vouchsafed to Freshmen. "It's all right, old girl," he said, "you can go whenever you get ready. You surely are a witch, Sylvia!"

"What has happened?" she asked.

"I had a call from Douglas van Tuiver last night."

"You don't mean it, Harley!"

"Yes. Did you ask him to do it?"

"I should think I did *not!*"

"Well, whatever the reason was, he was as

nice as could be. Said he was interested in me, and that he'd back me for one of the earlier tens."

"How perfectly contemptible of him!" exclaimed Sylvia.

Needless to say, this was a turn not expected by Harley. "See here," he protested, "it seems to me you're taking a little too high a line with van Tuiver. There's really no need to go so far——"

"Now please," said Sylvia, "don't concern yourself with that. I came up here to help you, and I've done it, and that's all you can ask."

"Oh, very well," he said, and there was a sulky pause. Finally, however, the sun of his delight broke through the clouds again. "Say, Sylvia!" he exclaimed. "Do you know, the whole college is talking about what happened at that dance. Tell me, honestly—did you know anything about what they meant to do?"

"I think that's a question you'd know better than to ask, Harley."

"I was ready to knock a fellow down because he hinted it. But Bates is square—he takes it all on himself. They say Mrs. Winthrop will never forgive him."

Sylvia pondered. "Won't it make Edith angry with you?" she asked.

"I'll keep away from her for a few days," laughed Harley. "If I get my social position established, she'll get over her anger, never fear. By the way, would you like to know what Edith thinks about you?"

"Why—did she tell you?"

"No, but there's a chap in my class who knows her. He told me what she said—only of course one can't be sure."

"Tell me what it was," said Sylvia, "and I'll know if she said it."

"That you were shallow; that with the arts you used any woman could snare a man. But she would scorn to use them."

"Yes," laughed the other, "she said it."

"Are you really as bad as that?" asked Harley. "What arts does she mean?"

"This is a woman's affair, Harley. What else did she say?"

"She said her mother was disappointed in you. She thought you had a beautiful soul, but you'd let it be spoiled by flattery. She said you had no real understanding of a character like van Tuiver, or the responsibilities of his position."

Sylvia said nothing, but sat considering the matter. She had no philosophy about these affairs; she was following her instincts, and sometimes she was assailed by doubts and troubled by new points of view. She was surprised to realize how very revolutionary a standpoint she had come to take in the matter of Mrs. Winthrop's favorite. Why should she, Sylvia Castleman, a descendant of Lady Lysle, be trying to pull down the pillars of the social temple?

That was still her mood when, after Harley's departure, the telephone rang and she found herself voice to voice with "Queen Isabella." "Won't

you come and have luncheon with me, Sylvia?"
asked the latter. "I've sent Edith away, so that
we can be to ourselves. I want to have a long
talk with you." And Sylvia, in a penitent state,
answered that she would come.

## § 19

SHE chose for this visit one of her simplest
costumes—a white muslin, with pale green sprigs
in it, and a pale green toque of a most alluringly
Quakerish effect. A poet had designed it for her
—one of her victims at the State University—
and had specified that she must never wear it
without a prayer-book in her hand. In this costume she sat in Mrs. Winthrop's sombre paneled
dining-room, with generations of sombre Puritan
governors staring down from the walls at her;
while the strange white servants stole noiselessly
about on the velvet carpets, she gazed with wide,
innocent eyes, and listened to her hostess' deli-
cately-worded sermon.

Mrs. Winthrop appreciated the symbolism of
the costume, and used it in making a cautious
approach to her subject. She said that Sylvia
had wonderful gifts of beauty—not merely of
the person, but of taste and understanding.
Women so favored owed a great debt to life,
and must needs feel keenly the desire to make
recompense for their privileges. That, said Mrs.

Winthrop, was something always present in her
own thoughts. How could she pay for her
existence? It was fatally easy to fall into the
point of view of those who rebelled against social
conditions, and justified the discontent of the
poor. "You know, we have such people even in
Boston," she explained, "and they win a good
deal of sympathy. But there is a deeper and
saner view, it seems to me. Life must have its
graces, its embellishments; there must be those
who embody a higher ideal than mere animal
comfort. I think we should take our stand there
—we should justify ourselves, having the consciousness of a mission in preserving the allure-
ments and amenities of life. People talk about
the poor shop-girls, and how hard they have to
work; they seem to desire that one should give
up one's ease, one's culture, and go and join the
shop-girls. But I say, No, I am not to be seduced
by such arguments. I am something in the lives
of those shop-girls, something definite, something
vital; I am to them an uplifting vision, an ideal
of grace and dignity. When one goes among
the lower classes and sees the brutality, the sordid
animalism of their lives—oh, it is terrifying!
One flies back to the world of refinement and
serenity as to a city of refuge."

Mrs. Winthrop paused. Her beautiful eyes had
talked with her; they had gazed terrified into
social abysses, and now they came back to regions
of brooding calm. Sylvia was under their spell,
and was not conscious of any extravagance in

the lady's next utterance: "Speaking with a deep conviction, I say that I am something necessary to life, that the world could not get on without me. I say, I am Beauty, I am Art! Have you ever felt that, Sylvia?"

"I have thought a good deal about such things, Mrs. Winthrop. But as a rule, I only manage to bewilder myself and make myself unhappy. There is so much terrible suffering in the world!"

"Yes," said the other. "How many times I find myself asking, with tears in my eyes, 'How can you be happy, while all around you the world is dying? Go, bow your head with shame, because you have been happy!' " And sure enough, Mrs. Winthrop bowed her head, and two glistening, pearly tears trickled slowly from her eyes. "It is a faith I have had to fight for," she continued, "something I feel most earnestly about. For we live in times when, as it seems to me, civilization is threatened by the terrible forces of materialism—by the blind greed of the masses especially. And I think that we who have the task of keeping alive the flame of beauty ought to be aware of our mission, and to support one another."

Sylvia thought that this was the point of approach to the real subject; but she said nothing, and Mrs. Winthrop veered off again. "I have always been especially interested in University life," she said. "My father was a University professor, and I was brought up in a University town. After I was married and found that I had leisure and opportunity, I said to myself that it would be my task in life to do what I could to influence young men during their student years, by teaching them generous ideals, and above all by giving them a model of a dignified and gracious social life. It is in these years, you see, that the tastes of young men are formed; afterwards they go out to set an example to the rest of the world. More than any university, I think, Harvard is our source of culture and idealism; our crude Western colleges look to its graduates for teachers, and to its standards for their models. So you see it is really no little thing to feel that you are helping to guide and shape the social life of Harvard."

"I can understand that," said Sylvia, much impressed.

"You come from another part of our country," continued Mrs. Winthrop—"a part which has its own lovely culture. Whether you have ever realized it consciously or not, I am sure that ideas such as these must have been often impressed upon you by your family."

"Yes," said Sylvia, "my mother often talks of such things."

"I felt that, Sylvia, when I saw you. I said, 'Here is an ally.' You see, I must have help from the young people—especially from the girls, if I am to do anything with the men."

There was a solemn pause. "I hope I haven' disappointed you too much," said Sylvia at last.

Mrs. Winthrop fixed upon her one of those

intense gazes. "I've been perplexed," she said.
"You must understand, I can't help hearing
what's going on. People come to ask me for
advice, and I must give it. And I've felt that
what I've learned made it really necessary for
me to talk to you. I hope that you won't mind,
or think that I'm presuming."

"My dear Mrs. Winthrop," said Sylvia, "please
don't apologize. I am glad to have your advice."

"I will speak frankly, then. As well as I can
read the situation, you seem to have taken offense
at the social system we have at Harvard. Is
that true?"

Sylvia thought. "Yes," she said—"some parts
of it have offended me."

"Can you explain, Sylvia?"

"I don't know that I can. It's a thing that one
feels. I have had a sense of something cruel
about it."

"Something cruel? But can't one feel that
about any social system? Haven't you classes
at home? Don't your people hold themselves
above some others?"

"Yes, but I don't think they are so hard about
it—so deliberate, so matter of fact."

"Ah," said Mrs. Winthrop, "that is something
I have often talked about with Southern people.
The reason is that in the South you have a social
class which is definitely separated by color, and
which never thinks of crossing the line. But in
the North, my dear, our servants look like us,
and it's not quite so simple drawing the line."

"Oh, but I'm not talking of servants, Mrs. Winthrop. I mean here, within the boundaries of a college class. Your servants do not go to college."

The other laughed. "But they do," she said.

"Oh, surely not!"

"It costs a hundred and fifty dollars a year to go to Harvard. Any man can come, black or white, who can borrow the money. He may come, and earn his living while he's here by tending furnaces. As a matter of fact, there's a man in the class with Douglas van Tuiver whose father is a butler."

"You don't mean it!" exclaimed Sylvia.

"A man," said Mrs. Winthrop, "named Firmin."

Sylvia was aghast. "Tom Firmin!"

"Yes. Have you heard of him before?"

She answered in a faint voice, "Yes," and then was silent.

"You see, my dear," said the other, gently, "why we are conscious of our class lines in the North!"


### § 20


SYLVIA judged that it was about time for the cat to come out of the bag. And now she observed him emerging—with a grave and stately tread, as became a feline of New England traditions. Said Mrs. Winthrop: "I have just had a talk with Douglas van Tuiver. Of course, you must know, Sylvia, that he has conceived an intense admiration for you. And you must know that when a man so intensely admires a woman, she has a great influence upon him—an influence which she can use either for good or for evil."

"Yes, Mrs. Winthrop," said Sylvia.

"I gather that his admiration for you is—is not entirely reciprocated, Sylvia."

"Er—no," said the girl, "not entirely."

"He has come to me in great distress. You have criticized him, and he has felt your disapproval keenly. I won't need to repeat what he said—no doubt you understand. The point is that you have brought Douglas to a state of distraction; he wants to please you, and he doesn't know how to do it. You have put ideas into his head—really, Sylvia, you will ruin the man—you will utterly destroy him. I cannot but feel that you have acted without fully realizing the gravity of the situation—the full import of the demands you have made upon him."

"Really," protested Sylvia, "I have made no demands upon him."

"Not formally, perhaps. But you must understand, the man is beside himself, and he takes them as demands."

There was an awkward silence. "I have tried earnestly to avoid Mr. van Tuiver," said Sylvia. "I would prefer never to see him again."

"But that is not what I want. You can't help seeing him—he is determined to see *you*.

My point is that your advice to him should take
another form—you should realize the peculiar
position of a man like Douglas, the immense
responsibilities he carries, and which he cannot lay
aside.   If you could sympathize with him——"

There was again a pause.   "I hope you won't
think it obstinate of me," said the girl, "but I
know that I could never change my attitude—
that unless Mr. van Tuiver changed his way of
life, he could never be a friend of mine."

"But, Sylvia dear," remonstrated the other,
gently, "he has been a friend of *mine*."

And so the real battle was on.   There have
been defences of the Divine Right of Kings,
composed by eminent and learned men;  there
have been treatises composed upon the upbringing of statesmen and princes—from Machiavelli
and Castiglione on;  Sylvia was ignorant of their
very existence, and so she was in no way a match
for a scholarly person like Mrs. Winthrop.   But
one thing she knew, and knew it with overwhelm-
ing certainty, and repeated it with immovable
obstinacy—she did not like van Tuiver as he was,
she could not tolerate him as he was.   Mrs.
Winthrop argued and pleaded, apologized and
philosophized, interpreting most eloquently the
privileges and immunities incidental to the possession of fifty millions of dollars.   But Sylvia
did not like van Tuiver, she could not tolerate
van Tuiver.

At last Mrs. Winthrop stopped, the edges of
her temper somewhat frayed.   She gazed at

Sylvia intently. "May I ask you one thing?" she said.

"What is it?" inquired the girl.

"Has Douglas asked you to marry him?"

"No, he has not."

"Do you think that he will ask you?"

"I really don't know; but I can assure you that he will not if I can prevent it."

There was a long pause, while the other weighed this utterance. "Sylvia," she said, at last, "he has a great deal of money."

"I have heard that fact mentioned," responded the girl.

"But have you realized, my dear, how *much* money he has?"

To which Sylvia answered, "We are not taught to think so deliberately about money in the South."

Again there was a silence. She divined that Mrs. Winthrop was struggling desperately to be noble. "Do I understand you to mean, Sylvia, that you would really refuse to marry him if he asked you?"

"I most certainly mean it," was her reply— and it was given convincingly.

The other drew a breath of relief. She had found the struggle exhausting. "My dear child," she said, "I appreciate your fineness of character." She paused. "But tell me this—if you do not intend to marry Douglas, ought you to permit him to compromise himself for you?"

"Compromise himself, Mrs. Winthrop? I don't understand you."

"I mean, Sylvia, that he is exposing himself to the ridicule of his friends—he is making a spectacle of himself to the whole University. And then, after he has done this, you propose to cap the climax of his humiliation by refusing to marry him!"

Sylvia had so far been most decorous; but at this point her sense of fun was too much for her, and merriment broke out upon her countenance. "Mrs. Winthrop," she declared, "there is but one way out—you must keep Mr. van Tuiver from proposing to me!"

The other's pose became haughty and full of rebuke; but Sylvia was not to be frightened. "See the dilemma I am in!" she exclaimed. "If I refuse him, I humiliate him and compromise him. But if I marry him—what becomes of my fineness of character?" She paused for a moment, then added, "You must do this, Mrs. Winthrop; you must take the responsibility of forbidding me to see him again. You must make it so emphatic that I'll simply have to obey you."

"Queen Isabella's" feelings were approaching a state of turmoil; but the girl urged her proposition seriously, finding a quite devilish amusement in plaguing her hostess with it. The other protested that she would not, she could not, she *dared* not take the responsibility of interfering with Mr. van Tuiver's love affairs; and all without having the least idea of the abysses of malice which were hidden within the circumference of the pale green Quaker bonnet in front of her!

## § 21

Frank Shirley came to call that afternoon, and
revealed the fact that the gossip had reached
even him. "Sylvia, you witch," he exclaimed,
and pinched her ear—"what in the world have
you been doing to Douglas van Tuiver?"

She caught his hand and held it in both hers.
"What has happened, Frank?"

"A miracle, my dear—simply a miracle! Van
Tuiver has been to call on Tom Firmin!"

"Oh, how interesting!" cried Sylvia. "How
was he received?"

"Tell me first—did you suggest it to him?"

"I'm a woman—my curiosity is much less
endurable than yours. Tell me instantly."

"Oh, he came—very much subdued and ill at
ease. Said he'd realized the split in the class,
and how very unfortunate it was, and he wanted
to help mend matters."

"What did Mr. Firmin say?"

"He asked why van Tuiver had begun with
him. 'Because I'd heard you didn't like me,'
said van Tuiver, 'and I wanted to try to put
matters on a better footing. I'd like to be a
friend of yours if I might.' Tom—you know
him—said that friendship wasn't to be had for
the asking—he'd have to look van Tuiver over
and see how he panned out. First of all, they
must understand each other on one point—that
he, Tom, wouldn't be patronized, and that anybody who tried it would be ordered out." Frank

17

paused, and laughed his slow, good-natured laugh.
"Poor van Tuiver!" he said. "I feel sorry for
him. Imagine him having to say he'd be willing
to take the risk! It's about the funniest thing
I ever heard of. What I want to know is, is it
true that you did it?"

"Would you be very angry if I said 'Yes'?"

"Why, no," he answered—"only I suppose
you know you're getting a lot of publicity?"

Sylvia paused for a while. "I suppose it was
a mistake all through," she said, "but I was
ignorant when I started, and since then I've
been dragged along. Mr. van Tuiver has kept
at me to tell him why I didn't like him—and I've
told him, that's about all. I thought that your
friend Mr. Firmin was one who'd do the same."

"He's that, all right," laughed Frank.

There was a pause, then suddenly Sylvia exclaimed, "By the way, there's something I meant
to ask you. Is it true that Mr. Firmin's father
is a butler?"

"It is, Sylvia."

"And did you know that when you introduced
him to me?"

It was Frank's turn to counter. "Would you
be very angry if I said I did?"

"Why—not angry, Frank. But you must
realize that it was a new experience."

"Did you find him ill-bred?"

"Why, no—not that; but——

"I thought you might as well see all sides of
college life. I knew you'd meet the club-men.

And there's a particular reason why you'll have to be nice to Tom—he wants to make me president of the class just now."

"President of the class!"

"Yes. Politics, you see!"

"But," she exclaimed, "why haven't you told me about it?"

"I didn't know until yesterday. Things have been shaping themselves. You see, the feeling in the 'Yard' has grown more bitter, and yesterday a committee came to me and asked if I'd stand against Shackleford, who's been picked by the Auburn Street crowd, and was expected to go in without opposition. I said I'd have to think it over. I might accept the position if I was elected, but of course, I wouldn't do any wire-pulling—wouldn't seek any man's vote. They said that was all they wanted. But I don't know; it's a difficult question for me."

"But why?"

"Well, you see, they'll rake up the story of my father."

Sylvia gave a cry of horror. "Frank!"

"If there's a contest, it'll be war and no quarter."

"But would they do such a thing as that?"

"They would do it," said Frank, grimly. "So my first impulse was to refuse. But I rather thought you'd want me to run. For you see, I'll have that old scandal all my life, whatever I try to do; and I suppose you won't let me keep out of everything."

"But, Frank, how will they know about your father?"

"Lord, Sylvia, don't you suppose with all the social climbing there is in this place, they've had that morsel long ago? There are fellows here from the South—your cousin, for one. It doesn't matter, as long as I'm a nobody; but if I set out to beat the 'Gold Coast crowd'—then you'd see!"

It was amusing to Frank to see how her eyes blazed. "Oh, I ought to stay to help you!" she exclaimed. "If it only weren't for father!"

"Don't worry, Sylvia. I wouldn't let you stay for anything. I don't want you mixed up in such affairs."

"But, Frank, think what it would mean! What a blow to the system you hate! And I could pull you through—you needn't laugh, I really could! There are so many men I could manage!"

But Frank went on laughing. "Honey," he said, "you've done quite enough—too much—already. How are you going to pay van Tuiver for what he's done?"

"Pay him, Frank?"

"Of course. Do you imagine, dear, that van Tuiver's a man to do anything without being paid? He'll hand in his bill for services rendered, and he'll put a high value on his services! And what will you do?"

She sat, deep in thought. "Frank," she exclaimed, "you've been so good—not to worry about me and that man!"

He smiled. "Don't I know what a proud lady you are?"

"What's that got to do with it?"

"Honey, if I had been afraid about van Tuiver, do you suppose I'd have dared let you know it?"

She looked at him, her eyes shining. "How nicely you put it!" she said. "You're the dearest fellow in the world, a regular haven of refuge to fly to!" Then suddenly her mood became grave, and she said, "Let me tell you the truth; I'm glad I'm going away from the man and his money! It isn't that it's a temptation—I don't know how to say it, but it's a nightmare, a load on my mind. I think, 'Oh, how much good I could do with that money!' I think, 'So much power, and he hasn't an idea how to use it!' It's monstrous that a man should have so much, and no ideas to go with it. It's all very well to turn your back on it, to say that you despise it—but still it's there, it's working all the time, day and night —and working for evil! Isn't that true?"

He was watching her with a quizzical smile. "You're talking just like Tom!" he said. "They'll call *you* an Anarchist at home!"

She was interested in the idea of being an Anarchist, and would have got Frank started upon a lecture on economics. But there came an interruption in the form of a knock on the door and a boy with a card. Sylvia glanced at it, and then, without a word, passed it to Frank. He read it and they looked at each other.

"Well?" he asked. "Are you going to see him?"

"I don't know," she said. "What do you say?"

"I can stand it if you can," laughed Frank; and so Sylvia ordered Mr. van Tuiver shown up.


### § 22


HE stood in the doorway, clad in his faultless afternoon attire. Somehow he had recovered the hard brilliance, the look of the man of the world, which Sylvia had noticed the first evening. He gazed at Frank, not hiding very well his annoyance at finding a third party.

"Mr. van Tuiver, Mr. Shirley," said Sylvia. "You do not know each other, I believe."

"I know Mr. Shirley by sight," said van Tuiver, graciously. He seated himself on a spindle-legged Louis Quinze chair—so stiffly that Sylvia thought of a purple domino. She beamed from one to the other, and then remarked, "What a curious commentary on the Harvard system! Two men studying side by side for three years, and not knowing each other!"

She was aware that this remark was not of the most tactful order. She made it on purpose, thinking to force the two into a discussion. But van Tuiver was not minded that way. "Er—yes," he said, and relapsed into silence.

"Miss Castleman's notions of courtesy are derived from a pastoral civilization," said Frank, by way of filling in the breach. "You don't realize the size of Harvard classes, Sylvia."

The girl was watching the other man, and she saw that he had instantly noted Frank's form of address. He looked sharply, first at his rival, and then at her. "Mr. Shirley is also from the South?" he asked.

"Yes," said Sylvia, "we are near neighbors."

"Oh, I see," said van Tuiver. "Old friends, then, I presume."

"Quite," said Sylvia, and again there was a pause. She was willing to let the two men worry through without help, finding it fascinating to watch them and study them. What a curious contrast they made! She found herself wondering how far van Tuiver would have got in college life if he had had the handicaps of her lover!

Frank was talking about the prospects of the baseball team. He was pleasant and friendly, and of course quite unmoved by the presence of Royalty. He seemed to be wholly unaware of the tension in the air, the restlessness and impatience of the man he was talking to. But Sylvia knew and was thrilled.

It was a moment full of possibilities of drama. She asked some question of Frank, and he answered, casually, "Of course, honey." He went on, unconcerned and unperceiving; but Sylvia saw the other man wince as if he had been touched by something red hot. He looked at her, but found that she was looking away. She stole a glance at him again, and saw that he was watching his rival with strained attention. his countenance several shades paler in hue.

That was the end of conversation, so far as van Tuiver was concerned. He answered in monosyllables, and his eyes went from Frank to Sylvia like those of a hunted animal in a corner. The girl got a new and sharp realization of his condition. She had gone into this affair as a joke, but now, for a moment, she was frightened. The man was terrible; every minute, as he watched Frank, his brow grew darker, he was like a thunder-cloud in the room. And this the *arbiter* of Harvard's best society!

At last, she took pity on him. It was really preposterous of Frank to go on gossiping about the prospects of a truce with the Princeton "tiger," and the resumption of football contests. So, smiling cheerfully at him, she remarked, "You'll be missing the lecture, won't you?" And Frank, realizing that he was a third party, made his excuses and withdrew.

Van Tuiver barely waited until Frank had closed the door. Then, with a poor effort at nonchalance, he remarked, "You know Mr. Shirley quite intimately."

"Oh, yes," said Sylvia.

"You—you like him very much, Miss Castleman?"

"He's a splendid fellow," she replied. "He's one of the men you ought to have been cultivating."

But the other would not be diverted for a moment. "I—I wish—pardon me, Miss Castleman, but I want you to tell me—what is your relation to him?"

"Why, really, Mr. van Tuiver——"

"I know I've no right—but I'm desperate!"

"But—suppose I don't care to discuss the matter?" She was decided in her tone, for she saw that stern measures were necessary if he was to be checked.

But nothing could stop him—he was beyond mere convention. "Miss Castleman," he rushed on, "I must tell you—I've tried my best, but I can't help it! I love you—as I've never dreamed that a man could love. I want to marry you!"

He stopped, breathing hard; and Sylvia, off her guard, exclaimed, "No!"

"I mean it!" he declared. "I'm in earnest— I want to marry you!"

She caught herself together. She had not meant this to happen. She answered, with a tone of *hauteur*, "Mr. van Tuiver, you have no right to say that to me."

"But why not? I am making you an offer of marriage. You must understand. I mean it."

"I am able to believe that you mean it; but that is not the point. You have no right to ask me to marry you, when I have refused you my friendship."

There was a pause. He sat staring at her in pitiful bewilderment. "I thought," he said, "this was more serious." And then he stopped, reading in her face that something was wrong. "Isn't an offer of marriage more serious than one of friendship?" he inquired.

"More serious?" repeated Sylvia. "More important, you mean?"

"Exactly."

"More attractive, that is?" she suggested.

"Why—yes."

"In other words, Mr. van Tuiver, you thought that a man with so much money might be accepted as a husband when he'd been rejected as a friend?"

"Why—not exactly that, Miss Castleman——"

But Sylvia hardly heard his denial. A wave of annoyance, of disgust, had swept over her. She rose to her feet. "You have justified my worst opinion of you!" she exclaimed.

"What have I done?" he cried, miserably.

"It isn't what you've done, as I've told you before—it's what you are, Mr. van Tuiver. You are utterly, utterly impossible, and I'm furious with myself for having heard what you have just said to me."

"Miss Castleman! I beseech you——"

But she would not hear him further. She could not endure his presence. "There is no use saying another word," she declared. "I will not talk to you. I will not know you!"

The madness of love was upon him; he held out his hands imploringly. But she repelled him with blazing eyes. "You must go!" she said. "Go at once! I will not see you again—I positively forbid you to come near me."

He tried twice to speak, but each time she stopped him, crying, "Go, Mr. van Tuiver!" And so at last he went, almost crying with humiliation and distress, in his agitation forgetting his hat and gloves. So furious was Sylvia that she shut the door, and fell on the sofa weeping.

When she came to look back on it, she was
amazed by her vehemence. It could not have
been the manner of the proposal, for he had been
insufferable many times before, and she had
managed to take a humorous view of it. Had
it perhaps been seeing him in opposition to Frank
which had fired the powder mine of her rage?
Was it that jealousy of his power, of which she
had spoken? Or was it the protective instinct
with which Nature had endowed her maidenhood—that she could jest with him while he was
seeking her friendship, but was convulsed with
anger when he spoke to her of love?

## § 23

THAT evening there was an entertainment of
the "Hasty Pudding" Club, and the next afternoon Sylvia was to take her departure. All the
morning she held an informal levee of those who
came to bid her good-bye, and to make their
comments on the amazing events which were
transpiring. For one thing, the candidacy of
Frank Shirley for class-president was formally
announced; and for another, Douglas van Tuiver
had declared his intention to move from his
house into one of the cheaper dormitories, and to
take his seat at the common dining-tables in
Memorial Hall.

Earliest of all came Harley, in a terrible state.

"What can have got into you? You've ruined everything—you've undone all the good you did for me!"

"As bad as that, Harley?" she asked. She was gentle with him, realizing suddenly how completely she had overlooked him and his interests in the last few crowded days.

"What does it all mean?" he went on. "What has made you want to smash things like this?"

She knew, of course, that there was no use trying to explain to him. She contented herself with saying that things could not be as bad as he thought.

"They couldn't be worse!" he exclaimed. "Van Tuiver's gone over to the 'Yard,' bag and baggage, and the club-men are simply furious. They're denouncing you, because you made him do it, and when they can't get at you, they'll take it out on me. Sooner or later they are bound to learn that you're engaged to Frank Shirley; and then they'll say you did it all to help him—that you fooled van Tuiver and made a cat's paw of him for the sake of Frank."

That was a new aspect of the matter, and a serious one; but Sylvia realized that there was no remedying it now. She was glad when other callers arrived, so that she might send her cousin away.

There came Thurlow, who, as a chum of Shackleford, wished to protest to Sylvia against the harm she was doing to the latter's candidacy, and to all that was best in Harvard's social life. There came Jackson, who, as van Tuiver's best friend, painted a distressful picture of the collapse of his prestige. There came Harmon, also pledged to plead the cause of "Auburn Street," but proving a poor ambassador on account of his selfish weakness. He spoke of van Tuiver's pitiful state, but a very little contriving on Sylvia's part sufficed to bring him to his knees, beseeching her to make him the happiest man in the world.

Sylvia rather liked Harmon; she was grateful to him for having been the first man at Harvard to fall in love with her, thus helping her over a time of great self-distrust. He made his offer with more eloquence than one would have expected from a reserved upper-class club-man; and Sylvia gently parried his advances, and wiped away one or two tears of genuine sympathy, and promised to be a sister to him in the most orthodox old Southern style.

And then came "Tubby" Bates. "Tubby" did not ask her to marry him, but he made her several speeches which were even more pleasant to hear. She had finished her packing, and had on her gray traveling dress when he called. He stood in the middle of the floor, gazing at her approvingly, his round face beaming and his eyes twinkling with fun. "Oh, what a stir in the frog-pond we've made!" he exclaimed. "And now you're running off and leaving me to face the racket alone!"

"What in the world have *you* to do with it?" she asked.

"Me? Doesn't everybody know that it was I who set you on van Tuiver? Didn't I bring you together at that fatal dance? And now all the big guns in the college are aiming murder at me!"

The other laughed. "Surely, Mr. Bates, your social position can stand a strain!"

He laughed in return, but suddenly became serious. He said: "I wouldn't care anyhow. Honest to God, Miss Castleman! There's something I wanted to say to you—I have to thank you for teaching me a lesson."

"A lesson?"

"You know, we don't live in such a lovely world—and I'm afraid I've got to be cynical. But you've made me ashamed of myself, and I want to tell you. It's something I shall never forget; it may sound melodramatic—but I shall always think better of women for what you've done."

She looked at him and grew serious. "Tell me, just what have I done that seems so extraordinary to you? I haven't felt a bit heroic."

"I'll answer you straight. You turned down van Tuiver and his money!"

"And does that really surprise you so?" she asked.

"I can only tell you that I didn't believe there was a woman in America who'd do it. I can tell you also that van Tuiver didn't believe it!"

Sylvia could not help laughing. "But, really, Mr. Bates, how could you expect so badly of me —that I'd sell my soul for luxury?"

"It isn't luxury, Miss Castleman. That's nothing. You can buy a whole lot of luxury with no more money than I've got. But with van Tuiver it would be something else—something that not one woman in a million has offered to her. It's power, its supremacy—it's really what you called Royalty."

"And you thought that would buy me?"

He sat watching her intently; he did not answer.

"Tell me truly," she said. "I won't mind."

"No," he said, "there's something beyond that. I've read you, Miss Castleman, and I thought he'd get you this way—you'd think of all that could be done with his money. How many people you knew that you could help! How much good you could do in the world! You'd think of starving children to be fed, of sick children to be healed. You'd say, 'I could make him do good with that money, and nobody else in the world could!' That's the way he'd get you, Miss Castleman!"

Sylvia was gazing at him, fascinated. He saw a strange look in her eyes, and he felt, rather than saw, that she drew a long breath. "You see!" he said. "You *did* have to be heroic!"

So, when "Tubby" Bates took his departure, he held her hand longer than any of her other callers had been permitted to. "Dear Miss Castleman," he said, "I'll never forget you; and if you need a friend, count on me!"

He went away, and Sylvia sat in her chair, gazing before her, deep in thought. There came a knock, and a note was brought in. She frowned before she looked at it—she had come to know where these notes came from.

"My dear Miss Castleman," it read, "I have just learned that you are going away. I implore you to give me one word. I stand ready to do all that you have asked me, and I throw myself on your mercy. I must see you once again."

For a moment Sylvia was frightened, wondering if she had a madman to deal with. Then she crumpled the paper in her hand, and going to the desk, seized a pen and wrote, with the swiftness of one enraged:

"Mr. van Tuiver, I have asked you to do nothing. I wish you to do nothing. All you can accomplish is to inflict disagreeable notoriety upon me. I demand that you give up all thought of me. I am engaged to marry another man, and I will under no circumstances consent to see you again."

This note she sent down by the boy, and when Frank came for her with a motor-car, she kept him in the room and sent Aunt Varina down into the lobby to make sure that van Tuiver was not waiting there. Some instinct made her feel that she must not let the two men meet again.

Also this gave her a little interval with Frank. She put her hands in his, exclaiming, "I'm so glad I've got you, Frank! Hurry up—get through with this place and come home!"

"You didn't like it here?" he smiled.

"I'm glad I came," she answered. "It'll be good for me—I'll be happier at home with you!"

He took her gently in his arms, and she let him kiss her. "You really do love me!" he whispered. "I can't understand it, but you really do!"

And she looked at him with her shining eyes. "I love you," she said—"even more than I did when I came. The happiest moment of my life will be when I can walk out of the church with you, and have nothing more to do with the world!"

"Good-bye, Lady Sunshine!" he said. "Good-bye, Lady Sunshine!"

BOOK III

*Sylvia Loses*

## § 1

Sylvia returned to New York, where she had some shopping to attend to, and where also Celeste was waiting for her, expecting to be taken to theatres, and treated to a new hat and some false curls and boxes of candy. Celeste had heard all about van Tuiver, it appeared, and was "thrilled to death"—her own phrase. There was no repressing her questions—"Is he nice, Sylvia?"—"What does he look like?"—and so on. Nor was there any concealing her surprise at Sylvia's reticence and lack of interest in this subject.

The elder sister got a sudden realization of the extent to which she had changed during this last couple of weeks. "They will call you an Anarchist at home," Frank had predicted; and now how worldly and hard seemed Celeste to her—how shameful and cruel her absorption in all the snobbery of Miss Abercrombie's! Could it be that she, Sylvia, had ever been so "thrilled to death" over millionaire beaux and millionairess' millinery? Her sister had grown so in the few months that Sylvia hardly knew her; she had grown, not merely in body but in mind. So serene she was, so self-possessed, so perfectly certain about herself and her life! Such energy she had, such determination—how her sharp, black eyes sparkled with delight in the glories of this world! Sylvia found herself stealing glances at her during the matinee, and wondering if this could be "Little Sister"?

Sylvia had dismissed her multi-millionaire from her mind; but she was not to get rid of him as easily as that. ("He persists and persists," Bates had said.) One afternoon, feeling tired, she sent her aunt forth to attend to some of the family commissions; when to her amazement there was sent up a note, written upon the hotel stationery, in the familiar square English hand-writing.

"My dear Miss Castleman," it ran. "I know that you will be angry when you see I have followed you to New York. I can only plead with you to have pity upon me. You have put upon me a burden of contempt which I can simply not bear; if I cannot somehow manage to win your respect, I cannot live. I ask only for your respect, and will promise never to ask for anything else, nor to think of anything else. However bad I may be, surely you cannot deny me the hope of becoming better!"

You see, it would have been hard for Sylvia to refuse the request. He struck the right chord when he asked for her pity, for she pitied all things that suffered—whether they deserved it or not.

She pitied him when she saw him, for his face was drawn and his look haunted. He, the man of fashion, the exemplar of good taste, stood before her like a whipped schoolboy, afraid to lift his eyes to hers.

He began, in a low voice, "It is kind of you to see me. There is something I wish to try to explain to you. I want you to know that I have thought over what you have said to me. I have hardly thought of anything else. I have tried to see things from your point of view, Miss Castleman. I know I have seemed to you monstrously egotistical—selfish, and all that. I have felt your scorn of me, like something burning me. I can't bear it. I simply must show you that I am really not as bad as I have seemed. I want you to realize my side of it—I mean, how much I've had against me, how hard it was for me to be anything but what I am."

He paused. He had his hat in his hands, and Sylvia observed to her dismay that he was twisting it, for all the world like a nervous schoolboy.

"I want to be understood," he said, "but I don't know if you are willing—if I bore you——"

"Pray go on, Mr. van Tuiver," she said, in a gentler tone of voice than she had ever used to him before.

"This is the point!" he burst out. "You simply can't know what it's meant to be brought up as I was! I've come to realize why you hate me; but you must know that you're the first who ever showed me any other viewpoint than that of money. There have been some who seemed to have other viewpoints, but they were only pretending, they always came round to the

money viewpoint, they gave the money reaction.
If you try things by a certain measure, and they
fit it, you come to think that's the measure they
were made by. And that's been my experience;
since I was a little child, as far back as I can
remember—men and women and even children,
everybody I met was the same—until I met you."

He stopped, waiting for her to give some sign.
Her eyes caught his and held them. "How was
I able to convince you?" she asked.

"You—" he said—and then hesitated. "You'll
be angry with me."

"No," she said, "go on. Let us talk frankly."

"You refused to marry me, Miss Castleman."

"That was the supreme test?" He shrank,
but she pursued him. "You hadn't thought
that any woman would really refuse to marry
you?"

He replied in a low voice: "I hadn't."

Sylvia sat, absorbed in thought. "What a
world!" she whispered, half to herself; and then
to him: "Tell me—is Mrs. Winthrop like that?"

Again he hesitated. "I—I don't know," he
replied. "I never thought about her in that
way. She already has her money."

"If she still had to get it, then you don't know
what she'd be?"

She saw a quick look of fear. "You're angry
with me again?" he questioned. By things such
as this she realized how thoroughly she had him
cowed.

"No " she said, gently, "I'm really interested.

I do see your side better. I have blamed you for being what you are, but you're really only part of a world, and it's this world that I hate."

"Yes," he exclaimed, with a sudden light of hope in his eyes. "Yes, that's it exactly! And I want you to help me get out of that world— to be something better, so that you won't have to despise me. I only ask you to be interested in me, to help me and advise me. I won't even ask you to be my friend—you can decide that for yourself. I know I'm not worthy of you. Truly, I blush with shame when I think that I asked you to marry me!"

"You shouldn't say that," she smiled. "It was only so that you really came to trust me!"

But he would not jest. He had come there in one last forlorn effort, and he poured himself out in self-abasement, so that it hurt Sylvia merely to listen to him. She made haste to tell him that his boon was granted—she would think of him in a kindlier way, and would let him write to her of his struggles and his hopes. Some day, perhaps, she might even see him again and be his friend.

While they were still talking there came an interruption—a bell-boy with a telegram addressed to Sylvia. She glanced at it, tore it open and read it; and then van Tuiver saw her go white. "Oh!" she cried, as if in sudden pain. "Oh!"

She started to her feet, and the man did the same. "What is it?" he asked; but she did not seem to hear him. She stood with her hands clenched, staring before her, whispering, "Papa! Papa!"

She looked about her, distracted. "Aunt Varina's gone!" she cried. "And I don't know where she is! We'll be delayed for hours!" She began to wring her hands with grief and distress.

Van Tuiver asked again, more urgently, "What is it?"

She put the telegram into his hands, and he read the message: "Come home at once. Take first train. Let nothing delay. Father."

"He's ill!" she cried. "I know he's ill—maybe dead, and I'll never see him again! Oh, Papa!" So she went on, quite oblivious to the presence of the man.

"But listen!" he protested. "I don't understand. This telegram is signed by your father."

"I know!" she cried. "But they'd do that—they'd sign his name, even if he were dead, so that I wouldn't know. They'd want me home to break the news to me!"

"But," he asked, "have you reason to think——"

"He was ill. I didn't know just how ill, but that's why I was going home. He must be dying, or they'd never telegraph me like that." She gazed about her, wildly. "And don't you see? Aunt Varina's out. I'm helpless!"

"We'll have to find her, Miss Castleman."

"But I've no idea where she's gone—she just said she would be shopping. So we'll miss the four o'clock train, and then there's none till eight, and that delays us nearly a whole day, because we have to lie over. Oh, God—I must do something. I can't wait all that time!"

She sank on a chair by the table and buried her face in her hands, sobbing like one distracted. The man by her side was frightened, never having seen such grief.

"Miss Castleman," he pleaded, "pray control yourself—surely it can't be so bad. There are so many reasons why they might have telegraphed you."

"No!" she exclaimed, "no, you don't understand them. They'd never send me such a message unless something terrible had happened! And now I'll miss the train."

"Listen," he said, quickly, "don't think anything more about that—let me solve that problem for you. You can have a special, that will start the moment you are ready and will take you home directly."

"A special?" she repeated.

"A private car. I'd put my own at your disposal, but it would have to be sent around by ferry, and that would take too long. I can order another in a few minutes, though."

"But Mr. van Tuiver, I can't let you——"

"Pray, don't say that! Surely in an emergency like this one need not stand on ceremony. The cost will be nothing to speak of, and it will give me the greatest pleasure."

He took her bewildered silence for consent, and stepped to the 'phone. While he was communicating with the railroad and giving the necessary orders, she sat, choking back her sobs, and trying to think. What could the message mean? Could it mean anything but death?

She came back to the man; she realized vaguely that he was a great help, cool, efficient and decisive. He phoned for a messenger, and wrote a check and an order for the train and sent it off. He had a couple of maids sent up by the hotel to do the packing. "Now," he said, "do not give another thought to these matters—the moment your aunt comes you can step into a taxi, and the train will take you."

"Thank you, thank you!" she said. She had a moment of wonder at his masterfulness; a special train was a luxury of which she would never have thought. She realized another of the practical aspects of Royalty—he would of course use a private car.

But then she began to pace the room again, her features working with distress. "Oh, Papa! Papa!" she kept crying.

"You really ought not to suffer like this, when it may be only a mistake," he pleaded. "Give me the address and I will telegraph for further particulars. You can get the answer on your train, you know. And meantime I'll try, and see if we can get your home on the long-distance 'phone."

"Can we talk at this distance?" she asked.

"I don't know, but at least we can relay a message." So again she let him manage her affairs, grateful for his prompt decisiveness, which set all the machinery of civilization at work in her behalf.

"Now try to be calm," he said, "until we can get some more definite information. People are sometimes ill without dying."

"I've always known that I was going to lose my father suddenly!" she broke out. "I don't know why—he has tragedy in his very face. If you could only see it—his dear, dear face! I love him so, I can't tell you. I wake up in the night, sometimes, and the thought comes to me: 'Papa has to die! Some day I'll have to part from him.' And then the most dreadful terror seizes me—I don't know how I can bear it! Papa, oh, Papa!"

She began to sob again; in his sympathy he came and stood by her. "Please, please," he murmured.

"I've no right to inflict this upon you," she exclaimed.

"Don't think of that. If I could only help you—if I could suggest anything."

"It's one of those cases," she said, "where nothing can be done. Whatever it is, I'll have to endure it, somehow. If he'll only live until I get there, so that I can see him, speak with him again, hear his voice. I've never really been able to tell him how much I love him. All that he's done for me—you see, I've been his favorite child, we've been like two playmates. I've tended him when he was ill, I've read to him—

everything.  So he always thinks about me.  He
wants me to be happy, and so he hides his troubles
from me.  He hides them from everybody; and
you know how it is—that makes people lean on
him and take advantage of him.  He's a kind of
family drudge—everybody comes to him, his
brothers and sisters, his nephews and nieces—
anybody that needs help or advice or money.
He's so generous—too generous, and so he gets
into difficulties.  I've seen his light burning till
two or three o'clock in the morning, when he was
working over his accounts; and then he looks
pale and haggard, and still he smiles and won't
let me know.  But I always know, because he
stays close to me, like a child.  And now there's
been an overflow, and maybe this year's whole
crop is ruined, and that's a terrible misfortune,
and he's been worrying about it——"

Suddenly she stopped.  This was Douglas van
Tuiver she was talking to—telling him her family
affairs!  She had a sudden thrill of fear about
it—she ought not to have let him know that her
father was in difficulties as to money!

It was only for a moment, however; she could
not think very long of anything but her father.
What floods of memories came sweeping over her!
"He was always so proud of me," she continued.
"When I came out, two years ago—dear old
Daddy, he wore his wedding-suit, that he'd had
put away in a cedar chest in the attic.  He stood
beside mother, under the lilies and the bright
lights, and both of them would look at me and
beam."

She had risen to her feet, and was pacing the room, talking brokenly, but eagerly, as if it were important to make her listener realize how very lovable her father was. "Just think!" she said. "He had an old purse in his hand—one that my mother had given him on their wedding journey. In it was an orange-blossom from their bridal-bouquet, and some rose leaves that she had bitten off and let fall at his feet, once when he was courting her. He had treasured them for twenty years; and now some one brushed against his hand and knocked the dead leaves to the floor, and they broke and went all to dust, and he got down on his knees and searched for them with tears in his eyes. I remember how mother scolded him for making a spectacle of himself, and he got up and went off by himself, to grieve because his bridal-flowers had turned to dust."

Van Tuiver had listened in silence. When he spoke, his voice held a strange note. "Never mind," he said, "you will make it up to him. You will give him flowers from your bridal wreath."

Again Sylvia found herself uncomfortable. But they were interrupted by the telephone—the connections with her home had been established. She flew to the booth downstairs, but she could hear nothing but a buzzing noise, and so there were some torturing minutes while her questions were relayed—she talking with "Washington," and "Washington" with "Atlanta," and so on. What she finally got was this: No one was ill or dead, but she must come at once—nothing must delay her. They could not explain until she arrived. And of course that availed her simply nothing. She was convinced that they were hiding the truth until she was home.

When she went back to her room, she found that Aunt Varina had come. Their trunks were ready, and so they set off for the station, van Tuiver with them. He saw them settled in their car, and the girl perceived that at so much as a word from her he would have taken the long journey with her. She shook hands with him and thanked him—so gratefully that he was quite transported. As the car started and he hurried to the door and leaped off, he was a happier-looking van Tuiver than Sylvia had ever expected to see.

## § 2

By the time that Sylvia's train reached home, she had gotten herself together. Although still anxious, she no longer showed it. Whatever the tragedy might be, she was ready to face it, not asking for help, but giving help to others. It was surely for that that they had summoned her.

She was on the car platform as the train slowed up; and there before her eyes stood her father. He was haggard, and gray, and old-looking—but alive, thank God!

She flew to his arms. "Papa! What's the matter?"

"Nothing, my child," he answered.

"But who is ill?"

"Nobody is ill, Sylvia."

"Tell me the truth!"

"No one," he insisted.

"But then, why did you send for me?"

"We wanted you home."

"But, Papa! In this fashion—surely you wouldn't—" She stopped, and the Major turned to greet his sister.

Sylvia got into the motor, and they started. "Is Mamma well?" she asked.

"Yes," he replied.

"And the baby?"

"Everybody is well."

"And you, Papa?"

"I have not been so very fine, but I am better now." Sylvia suspected he had got up from his sick-bed to come and meet her, and so her sense of dread increased. But she put no more questions—she knew she would have to wait. The Major had begun to talk about the state of the crops.

The car reached home; and there on the steps were her mother, and the baby shouting a lusty welcome, and Peggy and Maria dancing with glee —to say nothing of troops of servants, inside the house and out, grinning and waiting to be noticed. There was noise and excitement, so much that for several minutes Sylvia forgot her anxiety. Then everybody wanted to know if she had brought them presents; she had to stop and think what

19

she had purchased, and what she had delayed to purchase, and what she had left behind in the rush of departure. Aunt Varina said something about the special train, and there were questions about that, and about Douglas van Tuiver, who had provided it. And still not a word about the mystery.

"But, Mamma," cried Sylvia, at last, "why did you bring me home like this?" .

"Hush, dear," said "Miss Margaret." "Not now."

And so more delay. Aunt Nannie was expected shortly—she had said she would run over to greet the returning voyagers. Sylvia scented trouble in this, and would no longer be put off, but took her mother aside. "Mamma," she pleaded, "please tell me what's the matter!"

The other colored. "It isn't time now, my child." .

"But why *not*, Mamma?"

"Wait, Sylvia, please. It is nothing——"

"But, Mamma, did you send me such a telegram for nothing? Don't you realize that I have been almost beside myself? I was sure that somebody was dead."

"Sylvia, dear," pleaded "Miss Margaret," "please wait—I will tell you by and by. There are people here now——"

"But there'll always be people here. Come into the library with me."

"I beg you to calm yourself——"

"But, Mamma, I want to *know!* Why should

I be tormented with delay? Can't I see by the manner of all of you that something is wrong? What is it?" She dragged her mother off to the library, and shut the door. "Now, Mamma, tell me!"

The other looked towards the door, as if she wished to make her escape. Something about her attitude reminded Sylvia of that "talk" she had had before her departure for school. "My dear Sylvia," began the mother, "it is something— it is very difficult——"

"For heaven's sake, go on!"

"My child, you are going to be dreadfully distressed, I fear. I wish that I could help you —oh, Sylvia, dear, I'd rather die than have to tell you this!"

Sylvia clutched her hands to her bosom in sudden fear. Her mother stretched out her arms to her. "Oh, my child," she exclaimed, "you must believe that we love you, and you must let our love help! We tried to save you from this—from this——"

"Tell me!" cried the girl. "Tell me!"

"Oh, my poor child!" wailed "Miss Margaret" again, "Why did you have to love him? We were sure he would turn out to be bad! We——"

Sylvia sprang towards her and shook her by the arm.

"Mamma, answer me! What is it?"

"Miss Margaret" began searching in the bosom of her dress. She drew out a crumpled piece of paper—a telegram. Sylvia took it with trembling fingers, and spreading it out, read these words:

"Frank Shirley arrested in disorderly house in Boston, held to await result of assault on another student. Possibly fatal. Get Sylvia home at once. Harley."

She stood perfectly rigid, staring at her mother. She could not realize the words, they swam before her in a maze. The paper fluttered from her fingers. "It's false!" she cried. "Do you expect me to believe that? It's a plot! It's some trick they've played on Frank!"

Her mother, frightened by the pallor of her face, put her arms around her. "My daughter—" she began.

"What have you done about this? I mean— to find out if it is true?"

"We telegraphed Harley to write us full particulars."

"Oh, why did you send for me?" the girl exclaimed, passionately. "If Frank is arrested, I ought to be there!"

"Sylvia!" cried her mother, aghast. "Have you read the message? Don't you see *where* he was arrested?"

Yes, Sylvia had read, but what could she make of it? In her mind was a medley of emotions: horror at what Frank had done, disbelief that he had done it, shame of a subject of which she had been taught not to think, anxiety for her lover in trouble—all these contended within her.

"The wretch!" exclaimed "Miss Margaret." "To drag my child's name in the mire!"

"Hush!" cried Sylvia, between her teeth. "It

is not true! It's somebody trying to ruin him! It's a horrible, horrible lie!"

"But, Sylvia! The telegram came from your cousin!"

"I don't care! It's some tale they've told to Harley!"

"But—he says Frank is arrested!"

"Oh, I ought to go to him! I ought to find out the truth! Frank is not that kind of man!"

"My child," ventured "Miss Margaret," "how much do you know about men?"

Sylvia stared at her mother. Vague questions trembled on her lips; but she saw there was no help in that quarter. "I have always kept my daughter innocent!" the other was saying. "He ought to be killed for coming into our home and dragging you into such shame!"

Sylvia stood silent, utterly bewildered. She knew that there were dreadful things in the world, of which she had gathered only the vaguest hints. "A disorderly house!" She had heard the name —she had heard other such names; she knew that these were unmentionable places, where wicked women lived and vile things were done; also she knew that men went there—but surely not the men she knew, surely not gentlemen, not those who ventured to ask for her love!

But why should she torment herself with such thoughts now? This charge against Frank could not be true! "How long will it be," she demanded, "before we can have the letter from Harley?"

"At least another day, your father says."

"And there is nothing else we can do?" She tried to think. "We might telephone to Harley."

"Your Aunt Nannie suggested that, but your father would not have such a matter talked about over the 'phone."

Sylvia racked her brains, but there was no other plan she could suggest. She saw that she had at least one day of torment and suspense before her. "Very well, Mamma," she said. "Let me go to my room now. I'll try to be calm. But don't let anybody come, please—I want to be alone."

She could hardly endure to go out into the hall, because of her shame, and the fear of meeting some member of the family. But there was no need of that—they all knew what was happening, and went about on tiptoe, as in a house of mourning. Everyone kept out of her way, and she went up to her room and shut herself in and locked the door. There passed twenty-four hours of agony, during which she by turns paced the floor, or lay upon the bed and wept, or sat in a chair, staring into space with unseeing eyes. They brought her food, but she would not touch it; they tempted her with wine, with coffee, but for nothing would she open the door. "Bring me Harley's letter when it comes," was all she would say.

## § 3

ON the morning of the next day her mother came to her. "Has the letter come?" asked Sylvia.

The mother hesitated, and so Sylvia knew that it had come. "Give it to me!" she cried.

"It was addressed to your father, Sylvia——"

"Where is Papa?"

She started to the door. But "Miss Margaret" stood in her way. "Your father, my child, has asked your Uncle Basil to come over." And then, as Sylvia persisted, "Sylvia, you can't talk of such things to your father. He thinks it is a matter which your Uncle Basil ought to attend to. Please spare your father, Sylvia—he has been ill, and this has been such a dreadful blow to him!"

"But for God's sake, Mamma, what is in the letter?"

"It justifies our worst fears, my child. But you must be patient—it is not a thing that a young girl can deal with. Where is your modesty, Sylvia? Your father will lose respect for you if you do not calm yourself. You ought to be hating the man who has so disgraced you—who cares no more for you—"

"Hush!" cried Sylvia. "You must not say it! You don't know that it is true!"

"But it is true! You will see that it is true. And you ought to be ashamed of yourself, to cling to a man who has been willing to—to—oh, what a shameful thing it is! Sylvia, get yourself together, I implore you—do not let your father and your uncle see you in such a state about a man—an unworthy man!"

So there was another hour of distracted waiting, until the Bishop came up, his gentle face a picture of grief. "Miss Margaret" fled, and Sylvia shut and locked the door, and turned upon her uncle. "Now, Uncle Basil, let me see the letter."

He put it into her hands without a word. There was also a newspaper-clipping, and she glanced first at that, and went sick with horror. There was Frank's picture, and that of another man, with the label: "Harvard student who may die as a result of injuries received in a brawl." Sylvia's eyes sped over the reading matter which went with the pictures; it was from one of the sensational papers, the kind which revel in personal details, and so she had the whole story. Frank had got into a fight with a man in a "resort," and had knocked him down; in falling, the man had struck his head against a piece of furniture, and the doctors had not yet determined whether his skull was fractured. In the meantime, Frank was held in three thousand dollars bail. The account went on to say that the arrested man had been prominently mentioned as candidate for class-president, on behalf of the "Yard" against the "Gold Coast;" also that he was the son of Robert Shirley, who had died in State's prison under sentence for embezzlement.

It seemed hardly necessary to read any more;

but Sylvia turned to Harley's letter, which gave various additional details, and some comments. There was one point in particular which etched itself upon her mind: "There need be no doubt as to the character of the place. It is one of the two or three high-class houses of prostitution in Boston which are especially patronized by college men. This is not mentioned in the newspaper accounts, of course, but I know a man who was present and saw the row, so there can be no question as to that part of the matter."

Sylvia let the letter fall, and sinking down upon the bed, buried her face in her arms. The Bishop could see her form racked and shuddering. He came and sat by her, and put his hand upon her shoulder, waiting in silence. "My poor child!" he began in a whisper, at last. "My poor, poor child!"

He dared not let her suffer too long without trying to help her. "My dear," he pleaded, "let me talk to you. Make an effort, hear me. Sylvia, you have to bear it. My heart bleeds for you, but there's no help—it has to be borne. Won't you listen to the advice of an old man, who's had to endure terrible grief, and shame— agony almost as great as yours?"

"Well?" she demanded, suddenly. Her voice sounded strange and hard to him.

"Sylvia, dear, I tried to prove God's words to you by logic, and I could not. God was never proved by logic, my child—men don't believe in Him for that reason. They believe because at some awful moment they could not face life alone—because suffering and grief had broken their hearts, and they were forced to pray. Sylvia, there is only one way of help for you—and that is through prayer."

He waited to know what effect his words were having. Suddenly he heard the strange, hard voice again. "Uncle Basil."

"Well, my child."

"I want you to tell me one thing. I have to understand this, but I can't—I can't ask anybody."

"What is it, Sylvia?"

"I want to know—do men do such things?"

The Bishop answered, in a low tone, "Yes, my child, I am sorry to say—many of them do."

"Oh, I hate them!" she cried, with sudden fierceness. "I hate them! I hate life! It's a shameful, hideous world, and I wish that I could die!"

"Ah, don't say that, my child!" he pleaded. "I beg you not to take it that way. If we let affliction harden us, instead of chastening and humbling us, then we miss all the purpose for which it is sent. Who knows, Sylvia—perhaps this is a punishment which God in His wisdom has adjudged you?"

"Punishment, Uncle Basil? What have *I* done?"

"You have denied His word, my child. You have presumed to set your own feeble mind against His will and doctrine. And now——"

"Oh, Uncle Basil, stop!" she exclaimed. "Your words have no meaning to me whatever!" She buried her face in the pillow, and terrible sobbing shook her, burst after burst of it, as a tempest shakes a tree. "Oh, I loved him so! I loved him so!"

The old man had tried speaking as a Bishop; now he thought that the time had come for him to speak as a Castleman. His voice became suddenly stern. "Sylvia," he said, "the man was not worthy of your affection, and you must manage to put him from your thoughts. You are the child of a proud race, Sylvia—the daughter of pure women! You must bear this trouble with character, and with the consciousness of your purity."

"Uncle Basil," she answered, "please go. I can't bear to talk to anyone now. I must be alone for a while."

He rose and stood hesitating. "There's no way I can help you?" he asked.

"Nobody can help me," she answered "Thank you, Uncle Basil, but please go."

## § 4

AND so began the second stage of Sylvia's ordeal. For days she roamed the house like a guilt-haunted ghost. She could hardly be got to speak to any one—she avoided even people's eyes, so great was her shame. She would not eat, and she could not sleep—at least, not until she had managed to bring herself to the point of utter exhaustion. Knowing this, she would pace the room until she sank upon the bed almost fainting. In their terror they sent for the doctors, but these could do nothing for her. The Major came several times a day, and made timid efforts to talk to her about her roses and the new plants he had got for her. But she could think about nothing but Frank, and sent him away. Once after midnight he crept to her room and found that she was gone, and discovered her in the rose-garden, pacing back and forth distractedly, bare-footed and clad only in her nightgown. He led her in, and found that her feet were cut and full of gravel and thorns; but she did not mind this, she said—the pain was good, it was the only way to distract her mind.

What made the thing so cruel to her was that element of obscenity in it, which was like an extinguisher clapped down upon her mind, making it impossible for her to talk of it, even to think of it. Sylvia had never discussed such things, and now she hated Frank for having forced them upon her. She felt herself degraded—made vile to the whole world, and to her own soul. She knew that everybody she met was thinking one dreadful thing; she felt that she could never face the world again, could never lift up her head again. She had given her heart to a man to keep, and he had taken it to a "high-class house of prostitution!"

On the third day the Major came to her room and knocked. He had a painful duty to perform, he explained. (He did not add that there had been a family-council for nearly an hour past, and that he had been assigned to execute the collective decision.) There had come a letter— a letter addressed to Sylvia from Frank Shirley.

The girl sprang to her feet. "Give it to me!"

"My daughter!" exclaimed the Major, with a shocked face.

She waited, looking at him with wondering eyes. "What do you mean, Papa?"

He took the missive from his pocket, and held it in his hand as he spoke. "Do you think," he asked, "that it would be consistent with my daughter's dignity to read such a letter? My child, this man has dragged your name in the mire; do you think that you ought to continue in any sort of relationship with him? Is he to be able to boast that he had you so under his thumb, that even after such an outrage as he had inflicted upon you——"

The Major stopped, words failing him. "Papa," pleaded Sylvia, "might there not be some explanation?"

"Explanation!" cried the other. "What explanation—that my daughter could read?" His voice fell low. "That is the point—I do not wish my daughter's mind to be soiled with explanations of this subject. Sylvia, you cannot know about it!"

There was a silence. "What do you want me to do, Papa?"

"There is but one thing a proud woman can do, Sylvia. Send back this letter, with a note saying that you cannot receive communications from Mr. Shirley."

There was a long silence. Sylvia sank down upon the bed, and he heard her sobbing softly to herself. "Sylvia!" he exclaimed, "this man had your affection—he kissed your pure young lips!" He saw her wince, and followed up his advantage —"He kissed you when you were in Boston, did he not?"

She could hardly bring herself to answer. "Yes, Papa."

"And do you realize that two or three days later he had gone to this—this place?" He paused, while the words sank into her soul. "My daughter," he cried, "where is your pride?"

There was something commanding in his voice. She looked up at him; his face was white, his eyes blazing. "Sylvia," he exclaimed, "you are a Castleman! You have wept enough! Rise up, my daughter!"

She rose, like one under a spell. Yes, it was something to be a Castleman. It meant to be capable of bearing any torture for the sake of pride, of facing any danger for the sake of honor. How many tales she had heard of that Castleman honor! Had not the man who stood before her, the captain of a regiment when only a half-grown youth, marched and fought with a broken shoulder-blade, and slept in mud and rain without shelter or even a blanket, living for weeks upon an allowance of six grains of corn a day?

She drew herself up, and her face became cold
and set. "Very well, Papa," she said, "he
deserves my scorn."

"Then write as I say." And he stood by her
desk and dictated:

"Mr. Shirley: I have received the enclosed
letter, but do not care to read it. All relationship between us is at an end. Sylvia Castleman."

And to such a height of resolution had she
been lifted by her Castleman pride, that she
addressed an envelope, and took Frank's letter,
and folded it and put it inside, and sealed and
stamped the envelope, and gave it to her father.
Nor did she give a sign of pain or grief until
after she had dismissed him, and closed and
locked the door.


### § 5


IN the days that followed, Sylvia's longing for
her sweetheart overcame her pride many times;
she paced her room, tearing at the neck of her
gown like one suffocating, flinging out her arms
in abandonment of grief, crying under her breath
(for she must not let others know that she was
suffering), "Oh, Frank, Frank! How *could* you?"
Anger would come; she hated him—she hated
all men! But again the memory of his slow smile,
his straight-forward gaze, his voice of sincerity.
She would find herself whispering, incoherently,
"My love! My love!"

For the sake of her family, she labored to repress her feelings. But she would have nightmares, and would toss and moan in her sleep, sometimes screaming aloud. Once she awakened, bathed in tears, and hearing faint sobbing, put out her hand, and found her mother, crouching in the darkness, watching, weeping.

They besought her to let her mind be diverted by others. For many days there was a regular watch kept, with family consultations daily, and some one always deputed to be with her—or at least to be near her door. Little by little, as she yielded to their persuasions, Sylvia got the views of the various members of her family upon what had occurred.

Aunt Varina put her arms about her and wept with her. "Oh, it is horrible, Sylvia," she said— "but think how much better that you should find it out before it's too late! Oh, dear girl, it is so awful to find it out when it's too late." Thus the voice of Aunt Varina's wasted life!

Aunt Nannie came later, as tactful as could have been expected. She did not say, "I told you so," but she managed to leave with Sylvia the idea that the outcome was within the limits of human understanding. It was a matter of "bad blood;" and "bad blood" was like murder—it would always out. Also Aunt Nannie ventured to hint that it might be that Sylvia had allowed Frank Shirley to "take liberties" with her; and this, of course, made its impression upon the girl, who persuaded herself that she must be partly to blame for her own disgrace.

She became bitter against men; she did not see how she could ever tolerate the presence of one. Her mother, discussing the subject, remarked, "The reason I married your father was that he was the one good man I knew."

"How did you know that he was good?" demanded the girl.

"Sylvia!" exclaimed her mother, in horror.

"But how? Because he told you so?"

"Miss Margaret" answered hesitatingly, choosing her words for a difficult subject. "I had heard things. Your Aunt Lady told me—how the young men in your father's set had tried to get him to—to live the wicked life they lived. They made fun of him—called him 'Miss Nancy'—". She broke off suddenly. "I cannot talk about such things to my daughter!"

Even from "Aunt Mandy," the old "black mammy" who had been the first person to hold Sylvia in her arms, the girl now received counsel. "Aunt Mandy" served the coffee in the early morning, and stood in the bedrooms and grinned while the ladies of the family gossiped; she often took part in the conversation, having gathered stores of family wisdom in her sixty-odd years. "Honey, I'se had my cross to bear," she said to Sylvia, and went on to discuss the depravity of the male animal. "I'se had to beat my old man wid a flatiron, when I ketched him lookin' roun' too much—an' even dat didn't help much, honey. Now I got dem boys o' mine, what's allus up in cou't, makin' de Major come to pay jail-fines.

20

But how kin I be cross wid 'em, when I knows it's my own fault?"

"Your fault, Mammy?" said Sylvia. "Why, you are as good a mother——"

"I know, honey, I'se tried to be good; I'se prayed to de Lord—yes, I'se took dem boys to de foot o' de cross. But de Lord done tole me it's my fault. 'Mandy,' he says, 'Mandy—look at de daddy you give dem niggers!' Oh, honey, take dis from yo' ole mammy, ef you'se gwine ter bring any chillun into de worl'—be careful what kind of a daddy you gives 'em!"

The family had gathered in a solid phalanx about Sylvia. Uncle Barry, whose plantation was a hundred miles away, and who was a most hard-working and domestic giant, left his overseers and his family and came to beg her to let him give her a hunting-party. Uncle Mandeville came from New Orleans to urge her to go to a house-party he would give her. Uncle Mandeville it was who had assured Sylvia as a little girl that he would protect her honor with his life; and now he caused it to be known throughout Castleman County that if ever Frank Shirley returned and attempted to see his niece, he, Frank Shirley, would be "shot like a dog." And this was not merely because Uncle Mandeville was drunk, but was something that he soberly meant, and that everybody who heard him understood and approved.

Just how tight was the cordon around her, Sylvia learned when Harriet Atkinson arrived, fresh from a honeymoon-voyage to the Mediterranean and the Nile.

"Why, Sunny, what's this?" she demanded. "Why wouldn't you see me?"

"See you?" echoed Sylvia. "What do you mean. I haven't refused to see you." It transpired that Harriet had been writing and 'phoning and calling for a week, being put off in a fashion which would have discouraged anyone but the daughter of a self-made Yankee. "I suppose," she said, "they thought maybe I'd come from Frank Shirley."

Sylvia's face clouded, but Harriet went on— "My dear, you look like a perfect ghost! Really, this is horrible!" So she set to work to console her friend and drag her out of her depression. "You take it too seriously, Sunny. Beauregard says you make a lot more fuss about the thing than it deserves. If you knew men better——"

"Oh don't, Harriet!" cried the other. "I can't listen to such things!"

"I know," said Harriet, "there you are—the thing I've always scolded you for! You'll never be happy, Sunny, while you persist in demanding more than life will give. You say what you want men to be—and paying no attention at all to what they really are."

"Are you happy?" asked Sylvia, trying to change the subject.

"About as I expected to be," said the other. "I knew what I was marrying. The only trouble is that I haven't been very well. I suppose it's too much rambling about. I'll be glad to settle down in my home." She was going to Charleston to live in the old Dabney Mansion, she explained; at present she was paying a flying visit to her people.

"Well, Sunny," she remarked, "you are going to give him up?"

"How can I do otherwise, Harriet?"

"I suppose you couldn't—with that adamantine pride of yours. And of course it *was* awkward that he had to get into the papers. But Beau says these things blow over sooner than one would expect. Nobody thinks it's half as bad as they all pretend to think it." (Harriet, you must understand, felt rather sorry for Frank, and thought that she was pleading his cause. She did not understand that her few words would do more to damn him than all that the family had been able to say.)

But she perceived that Sylvia did not want to talk about the subject. "Well, Sunny," she said, after a pause, "I see you've got a substitute ready."

"How do you mean?" asked Sylvia, dully.

"I mean your Dutch friend."

"My Dutch friend? Oh—you are talking about Mr. van Tuiver?"

"You are most penetrating, Sylvia!"

"You've heard about him?" said the other, without heeding her friend's humor.

"Heard about him! For heaven's sake, what else can one hear about in Castleman County just now?"

' Sylvia said nothing for a while. "I suppose," she remarked, at last, "it's because I came in a special train."

"My dear," said the other, "it's because *he* came in a special train."

"*He* came?" repeated Sylvia, puzzled.

And her friend stared at her. "Good Lord," she said, "I believe you really don't know that Mr. van Tuiver's in town!"

Sylvia started as if she had been struck. "Mr. van Tuiver *in town!*" she gasped.

"Why, surely, honey—he's been here three or four days. How they must be taking care of you!"

Sylvia sprang to her feet. "How perfectly outrageous!" she cried.

"What, Sunny? That you haven't seen him?"

"Harriet, stop joking with me!"

"But I'm not joking with you," said Harriet, bewildered. "What in the world is the matter?"

Sylvia's face was pale with anger. "I won't see him! I won't see him! He has no right to come here!"

"But Sunny—what's the matter? What's the man done?"

"He wants to marry me, Harriet, and he's come here—oh, how shameful! how insulting! At such a time as this!"

"But I should think this was just the time for him to come!" said Harriet, laughing in spite of herself. "Surely, Sylvia, if you haven't gone formally into mourning——"

"I won't see him!" cried the other, passionately. "He must be made to understand it at once— he'll gain nothing by coming here!"

"But, Sunny," suggested her friend, "hadn't you better wait until he *tries* to see you?"

"Where is he, Harriet?"

"He's staying with Mrs. Chilton."

"With Aunt Nannie!" Sylvia stood, staring at Harriet with sudden fear in her face. She saw now why van Tuiver had made no attempt to see her, why nothing had been said to her as yet! She clenched her hands tightly and exclaimed, "I won't marry him! They sha'n't sell me to him—they sha'n't, they sha'n't!"

Her friend was gazing at her in wonder, not unmixed with alarm. "Good God, Sunny," she exclaimed, "can he be so bad that you'd refuse to marry him?"

## § 6

ALL this while, you must understand, there was Sylvia's "world" outside, looking on at the drama—pitying, wondering, gossiping, speculating. Frank arrested, Frank out on bail! Frank let off with a fine, because the man did not die! Frank leaving college and coming back to his plantation! Would he try to see Sylvia, and what would Sylvia do about it? Would Mandeville Castleman carry out his threat to shoot him? How was Sylvia taking it, anyway? Would she

be seen at the next club-dance? And then—
interest piled upon interest—Douglas van Tuiver
had come! Was it true that the Yankee Crœsus
wanted to marry Sylvia? Was it true that he
had already asked her? Could it be that she had
actually refused to see him? And what would
the family do about that?—All this, you understand, most decorously, most discreetly—and yet
with such thrills, such sensations!

When the audience is stirred, the actors know
it; and people so sensitive and proud as the
Castlemans could not fail to be aware that the
world's attention was focussed upon them. So
Sylvia was not left for long to indulge her grief.
As soon as her relatives had made sure of her
breach with Frank, they turned their energies
to persuading her to present a smiling front to
"society." "You must not let people see that
you are eating your heart out over a man!"—
such was their cry. There were few things worse
that could happen to a woman than to have it
known that she was grieving about a man. Just
as a savage laughs at his enemies while they are
torturing him, so must a woman wear a smile
upon her face while her heart was breaking.

From the first moment, of course, her old suitors
rallied to protect her—a kind of outer phalanx,
auxiliary to the family. They wrote to her,
they sent flowers, they called and lingered in
the hope that she might see them. When the
time for the club-dance came, the siege of the
suitors became a general assault. A dozen times

a day came her mother or Aunt Varina to plead with her, to scold her. "I don't want to dance—I couldn't dance!" she wailed; but it would be, "Here's Charlie Peyton on the 'phone—he begs you to speak to him just a moment. Go, Sylvia, please—*don't* let people think you are so weak!"

At last she told one man that he might call. Malcolm McCallum it was—the same who had crawled upon his knees to prove his devotion to her. She had long ago convinced him that his suit was hopeless, so now he was able to plead with her without offense. Her friends wanted so to help her—would she not give them a chance? They were indignant because of the way a scoundrel had treated her; they wanted somehow to show her their loyalty, their devotion. If only she would come—such a tribute as she would receive! And surely she was not going to give up her whole life, because of one such fellow! She had so many true friends—would she punish them all for the act of one? No, they would not have it! No, not if they had to raid the house and carry her away! The belle of Castleman Hall should not wither up and be an old maid!

Sylvia promised to think it over; and then came Aunt Nannie, to protest in the name of all her cousins against her inflicting further notoriety upon the family. For Sylvia to be exhibiting such unseemly grief over Frank Shirley was almost as bad as to be engaged to him. She must positively take up her normal life again; she must go to this dance!

Sylvia, perceiving that it would be necessary to have the matter out sooner or later, inquired, "Is Mr. van Tuiver to be there?"

She was surprised at the answer, "He is not."

"Where is he?" she asked; and learned that the visitor had gone with two of the boys on a fishing-trip. Sylvia and her aunt exchanged looks—as two swordsmen might, while their weapons are being measured and the ground laid out for their duel. The girl could imagine what had happened, almost as well as if she had been present. Van Tuiver, with his usual crude egotism, had come post-haste to Castleman Hall; it was Aunt Nannie who had persuaded him to wait, and let her handle the affair with tact. Sylvia must first be drawn out into social life, and then it would be less easy for her to avoid van Tuiver. But although Sylvia felt sure of this, she could not say so. When she hinted the charge, her aunt had a shrewd retort ready: "I have daughters of my own—and may I not have plans of my own for so eligible a young man as Douglas van Tuiver?"

## § 7

SYLVIA said that she would go to the dance; and great was the excitement, both at home and abroad. All day long, between fits of weeping, she labored to steel herself to the ordeal. When night came, she let herself be arrayed in rosy chiffon, and then went all to pieces, and fell upon the bed in a paroxysm, declaring that she could not, could not go. One by one came "Miss Margaret," Aunt Varina, and Celeste, scolding her, beseeching her—but all in vain; until at last they sent for the Major, who, wiser than all of them, arrayed himself in his own evening finery, and put a white rosebud in his button-hole, and then went with cheerful face and breaking heart to Sylvia's room.

"Come, little girl," he said. "Daddy's all ready."

Sylvia sat up and stared at him through her tears. "You!" she exclaimed.

"Why, of course, honey," he smiled. "Didn't you know your old Papa was going with you?"

Sylvia had not known it, nor had anybody else known it up to a few minutes before. Her surprise (for the Major almost never went to dances) was sufficiently great to check her tears; and then came "Miss Margaret" with a glassful of steaming "hot toddy." "My child," she said, "drink this. You've had no nourishment—that's why you go to pieces."

So they washed her face again, and powdered it up; they straightened her hair and smoothed out the wrinkles in her dress, and got her bows and ribbons in order, and took her down stairs to where Aunt Nannie was waiting, grim and resolute—a double force of chaperones for this emergency!

You can imagine, perhaps, the excitement when they reached the club-house; how the whisper went round, and the swains crowded in the doorway to wait for her. The younger ones cheered when she entered—"Hi, yi! Whoop la! Miss Sylvia." They came jumping and capering across the ball-room floor—one of them tearing a great palmetto-leaf from the decorations on the wall, and performing a wonderful, sprawling salaam before her. "I'm the King of the Cannibal Islands!" he proclaimed. "Will you be my Queen, Miss Sylvia?" Several others locked arms and executed a cake-walk, by way of manifesting their delight. The dance of the country-club was turned into a reception in her honor. They worshipped her for having come—it took nerve, by George, and nerve was the thing they admired. And then how lovely she was—how perfectly, unutterably lovely! Just a little more suffering like this, and she would be ready to be carried up in a chariot of fire and set among the seraphim!

Of course, in the face of such a welcome, it was unthinkable that she should not carry the thing through triumphantly. In the refreshment-room were egg-nogg and champagne-punch, and she drank enough to keep her in a glow, to carry her along upon wings of excitement. One by one her old sweethearts came to claim a dance with her, and one by one they caused her to understand that hope was springing eternal in their breasts. She found herself so busy keeping them in order that life seemed quite as it had always been in Castleman County.

Save for one important circumstance. There had come a new element into its atmosphere—something marvellously stimulating, transcending and overshadowing all that had been before. Sylvia found out about it little by little; the first hint coming from old Mrs. Tagliaferro—the General's wife, you may remember. She had come to Sylvia's *début* party, hobbling with a gold-headed cane; but now, the General having died, she had thrown away her cane, and chaperoned her great-grandchildren at dances, because otherwise people would think she was getting old. She shook a sprightly finger at the belle of the evening, and demanded, "What's this I hear, my child, about your latest conquest? I always knew you'd be satisfied with nothing less than a duke!" Sylvia's face clouded, and the other went on her way with a knowing cackle. "Oh, you can't fool me with your haughty looks!"

And then came Mabel Taylor, a girl who had been a hopeless wallflower in her early days, and had been saved because Sylvia took pity upon her, and compelled men to ask her to dance. Now she was Sylvia's jealous rival; and greeting her in the dressing-room she whispered, "Sylvia, is he really in love with you?"

When Sylvia asked, "Who?" the other replied, "Oh, it's a secret, is it!"

The girl perceived that she must take some line at once. "Are you really going to marry him?" asked Charlie Peyton, with despair in his voice. "We can't stand that sort of competition!" protested Harvey Richards. "We shall have to have a protective tariff, Miss Sylvia!" (Harvey, as you may recall, was a steel manufacturer.)

The thing had got upon Sylvia's nerves. "Are you so completely awed by that man?" she demanded, in a voice of intense irritation.

"Awed by him?" echoed Harvey.

"Why don't you at least mention his name? You are the fourth person who's talked to me about him to-night and hasn't dared to utter his name. I believe it's not customary for Kings to use their family names, but they have Christian names, at least."

"Why, Miss Sylvia!" exclaimed the other.

"Let us give him a title," she pursued, savagely. "King Douglas the First, let us say!" And imagine the seven pairs of swift wings which that saying took unto itself! She called him a King! King Douglas the First! She referred to him as Royalty—she made fun of him as openly and recklessly as that! "What sublimity!" exclaimed her admirers. "What a pose!" retorted her rivals.

But even so, they could not but envy her the pose, and the consistency with which she adhered to it. She could not be brought to discuss the King—whether he was in love with her, whether he had asked her to marry him, whether he had come South on her account; nor did she show

any particular signs of being impressed by him—
as if she really did not consider him imposing, or
especially elegant, or in any way unusual. Oh,
but they were a haughty lot, those Castlemans—
and Sylvia was the haughtiest of them all! The
country-club began to revise its estimates of
Knickerbocker culture, and to remember that,
after all, the only real blood in America was in
the South.

## § 8

THE next afternoon came Harriet Atkinson, to
bid Sylvia farewell, and incidentally to congratu-
late her upon her triumph. After they had
chatted for a while, she put her hand upon her
friend's, and remarked in a serious tone, "Sunny,
I've had a letter from Frank Shirley."

She felt the hand quiver in hers, and she pressed
it more firmly. "He wanted to explain things
to me," she said.

"What did he say?" asked Sylvia, in a faint
voice.

But Harriet did not answer. "I wrote to him,"
she continued, "that I declined to have anything to do with the matter." Seeing her friend's
lip beginning to tremble, she added, "Sunny, I
did it for your own good—believe me. I don't
want you to open up things with that man again."

"Why not, Harriet?"

"After what's happened, you ought to know

that your people would never stand for it—
there'd surely be some kind of a shooting-scrape.
And even supposing that you got away with
him—what sort of an existence would you have?
Frank Shirley is no money-maker, and somehow
I don't seem to feel that you were cut out for
cottage-life."

She stopped and fixed her gaze upon her friend.
"Sunny," she said, "I want you to marry the
other man." Then, as Sylvia started—"Don't
ask me what other man. I'm no Mabel Taylor."

Sylvia perceived that her words were being
cherished these days. "Harriet," she exclaimed
in an agitated voice, "I can't endure Douglas
van Tuiver."

"Now, Sunny, I want you to listen to me.
This may be the last chance I'll have to talk to
you—I'm going off to-morrow, to settle down to
domestic virtue. I want to give it to you straight
—to take the place of your Aunt Lady in this
crisis. You fall in love at first sight, and it
brings you wonderful thrills, and you marry on
the strength of it—and then in a year or two the
thrills are gone, and where are you? Take my
advice, Sunny, there's a whole lot more in life
than this young-love business. Try to look
ahead a little and realize the truth about yourself. If ever there was a creature born to be
a sky-lark, it's you; and here's a man who could
take you out and give you a chance to spread
your wings. For God's sake, Sunny, don't throw
the chance away, and settle down to be a barn-
yard fowl here in Castleman County."

"Harriet!" cried Sylvia, frantically, "I tell you I can't endure the man!"

"I know, Sunny—but that's just nonsense. You're in love with one man, and of course it sets you wild to think of another. But women can get used to things; and one doesn't have to be too intimate with one's husband. The man is dead in love with you, and so you'd always be able to manage him. I told you that about Beau—and I can assure you I've found it a convenient arrangement. From what I can make out, Mr. van Tuiver isn't a bad sort at all—he seems to have charmed everybody down here. He's not bad looking, and he certainly has wonderful manners. He can go anywhere in the world, and if he had you to manage him and do things with him—really, Sunny, I can't see what more you could want! Certainly it's what your family wants—and after all, you'll find it's nice to be able to please your people when you marry. I know how you despise money, and all that— but, Sylvia, there aren't many fortunes made out of cotton planting these days, and if you could hear poor Beau tell about what his folks have been through, you'd understand that family pride without cash is like mustard without meat!"

So Harriet went on. She was a sprightly young lady, and generally able to hold her audience; but after several minutes of this exhortation, she stopped and asked, "Sunny, what are you thinking about?"

And Sylvia, her face grown suddenly old with

grief, caught her by the hand. "Oh, Harriet," she whispered, "tell me the truth—do you think I ought to hear his explanation?"

## § 9

THERE were more dances and entertainments; and each time, of course, it was harder for Sylvia to escape. She had been to one, and so people would expect her at the next. There was always somebody who would be hurt if she refused, and there was always that dreadful phenomenon called "people"—it would say that the task had been too much for her, that she was still under the spell of the man who had flaunted her. So evening after evening Sylvia would choke back her tears, and drink more coffee, and go forth and pretend to be happy.

It was at the third of these entertainments that she met Douglas van Tuiver. No one had told her of his return—she had no warning until she saw him enter the room. She had to get herself together and choose her course of action, with the eyes of the whole company upon her. For this was the meeting about which Castleman County had been gossiping and speculating for weeks—the rising of the curtain upon the second act of the thrilling drama!

He was his usual precise and formal self; unimpeachably correct, and yet set apart by a

something—a reserve, a dignity. This extended
even to his costume, which tolerated no casual
wrinkle, no presumptuous speck. There was
always just a slight difference between van
Tuiver's attire and that of other men—and somehow you knew that this was the difference between
the best and the average.

It seemed strange to Sylvia to see him here,
in her old environment; strange to compare him
with her own people. She realized that she would
have to treat him differently now, for he was a
stranger, a guest. She discovered also a difference in him. He may have been touched by the
change he saw in her; at any rate he was very
gentle, and very cautious. He asked for a dance,
and promised that he would not ask for more.
To her great surprise he kept the promise.

"Miss Sylvia," he said, when they strolled out
after the dance, "may I call you Miss Sylvia,
as they all seem to here? I want to explain something, if you will let me. I'm afraid that my
being here will seem to you an impertinence.
I hope you will accept my apology. When I got
back to Cambridge I learned from your cousin
what—what the news would mean to you; and
I came because I thought perhaps I might help.
It was absurd, I suppose—but I didn't know.
Then, when I got here, I did not dare to ask to
see you. I don't know now if you will send me
away——"

He stopped. "I am sure, Mr. van Tuiver,"
she said, quietly, "you have a perfect right to
stay here if you wish."

"No right, Miss Sylvia, but the right you give me!" he exclaimed. "I won't take refuge in quibbles. I thought that if I promised not to bother you, and really kept the promise—if I never asked to see you unless you desired it——"

It was not easy to send him away upon those terms. She did not see what good it would do him to stay, but she refrained from asking the question. He paused—perhaps to make sure that she would not ask. "Miss Sylvia," he continued, finally, "I am afraid you will laugh at me—but I want to be near you, I don't want to be anywhere else. I want to see the world you belong in; I want to know your relatives and your friends—your home, the places you go to— everything. I want to hear people talk about you. And at the same time I'm uncomfortable, because I know you dislike me, and I'm afraid I'll anger you, just by being here. But if you send me away—you see, I don't know where to go——"

He stopped, and there was a long silence. "You are missing your examinations," she said, at last.

"I don't care anything about Harvard," he replied. "I've lost all interest—I shall never go back."

"But how about the reforms you were going to work for? Have you lost interest in them?"

He hesitated. "They've all—don't you see?" He stopped, embarrassed. "The movement's gone to pieces."

"Oh!" said Sylvia, and felt a slow fire of shame mounting in her cheeks. It had not occurred to her to think of the plight of the would-be revolutionists of the "Yard" after their candidate had landed himself in jail.

They turned to go in, and van Tuiver asked, timidly, "You won't send me away, Miss Sylvia?"

"I wish," she answered, "that you would not put the burden of any such decision upon me." And so the matter rested, van Tuiver apparently content with what he had gained. Sylvia's next partner claimed her, and she did not see "King Douglas the First" again; a circumstance which, needless to say, was duly noted by Castleman County, to its great mystification. Could it be that rumor was mistaken—that he was not really after Sylvia at all? Could it be that her flouting of "Royalty" was a common case of "sour grapes"?

## § 10

SYLVIA would not be content to drift and suffer indefinitely. It was not her nature to give up and acknowledge failure, but to make the best of things. Her thoughts turned to those in her own home, and how she could help them.

All through the tragedy she had been aware of her father, moving about the house like a ghost, silent, wrung with grief; her heart bled for the suffering she had caused him. Her chief thought was to make it up to him, to be cheerful and busy for his sake—to put him into the place in her heart which Frank Shirley had left empty. After all, he was the one man she could really trust—the one who was good and true and generous.

She sought him out one night, while the light was burning in his office. She drew up a chair and sat close to him, so that she could look into his eyes. "Papa," she said, "I've been thinking hard—and I want to tell you, I'm going to try to be good."

"You are always good, my child," he declared.

"I have been selfish and heedless. But now I'm going to think about other people—about you most of all. I want to do the things I used to be happy doing with you. Let us begin to-morrow and take care of our roses, and have beautiful flowers again. Won't that be nice, Daddy?"

There were tears in his eyes. "Yes, dear," he said.

"And then I must begin and read to you. I know you are using your eyes too much, and mine are young. And Papa—this is the principal thing—I want you to let me help you with the accounts, to learn to be of some use to you in business ways. No, you must not put me off, because I know—truly I know."

"What do you know, dear?" he asked, smiling.

"I know you work too hard, and that you have things to worry you, and that you try to

hide them from me. I know how many bills
there are, and how everybody wastes money,
and never thinks of you. I've done it myself,
and now it's Celeste's turn—she must have
everything, and be spared every care, and write
checks whenever she pleases. Papa, if it's true
that this year's crop is ruined, you'll have to
borrow money—"

"My child!" he began, protestingly.

"I know—you don't want me to ask. But
see, Papa—if I married, I'd have to know about
my husband's affairs, and help him, wouldn't I?
And now that I shall never marry—yes, I mean
that, Papa. I want you not to try to marry
me off any more, but to let me stay at home
and be a help to you and Mamma."

The other was shrewd enough to humor her.
They would get to work at the roses in the
morning, and they would take up Alexander H.
Stephens' Confederate History without delay;
also Sylvia might take the bills as they came
in each month, and find out who had ordered
what, and prevent the tradesmen from charging
for the same thing twice over. But of course,
he did not tell her any of his real worries, nor
let her see his bank-books and accounts; nor
could he quite see his way to promise that Aunt
Nannie should let her alone while she settled into
old-maidenhood.

Aunt Nannie came round the next morning,
as it happened. Sylvia did not see her, being
up to the wrists in black loam in the rose-garden;

but she learned the purpose of the visit at lunch-time. "Sylvia," said her mother, "do you think it's decent for us to go much longer without inviting Mr. van Tuiver over here?"

"Do you think he wants to come?" asked Sylvia, with a touch of her old mischief.

"Your Aunt Nannie seems to think so," was the reply—given quite naïvely. "I wrote to ask him to dinner. I hope you won't mind."

Sylvia said that she would find some way to make the occasion tolerable. And she found a quite unique way. It was one of her times for bitterness, when she hated the world, and especially the male animals upon it, and herself for a fool for not having known about them. It chanced to be the same day of the week that she had prepared for Frank's coming, and had introduced him to the family with so many tremblings and agonies of soul. So now, when she came to dress, she picked out the gown she had worn that evening, and had them bring her a bunch of the same kind of roses: which seemed to her a perfectly diabolical piece of cynicism— like to the celebrating of a "black mass"!

She descended, radiant and lovely, in a mood of somewhat terrible gaiety. She laughed and all but sang at the dinner-table; she joked with van Tuiver, and flouted him outrageously—and in the next breath charmed and delighted him, to the bewilderment of the family, who knew nothing about her adventures with Royalty, and the various strange moods to which its presence drove her.

In the course of that meal she told him a story—one of the wildest and most wonderful of her stories. So at least it seemed to me, who for years have been longing for a poet to take it up and make a ballad of it—a real American ballad! It is curious, but I can hear the very rhyme and rhythm of that ballad, which I cannot write. I wonder if I may not awaken in some gray dawn, and find it all complete, singing itself in my mind!

The story of the burning of "Rose Briar," it was. "Rose Briar" was the old home of one of the Peytons, which had stood for three generations on a high bluff on the river-bank a mile or so from Sylvia's home. It had the largest and most beautiful ball-room in the county, and was a centre of continuous hospitality. One night had come a telephone-message to the effect that it was on fire, and the neighbors gathered from miles around; on a wild night, with a gale blowing and the whole roof and upper part of the house in flames, they saw that the place was doomed.

And there was the splendid ball-room, in which they and their fathers and their grandfathers had celebrated so many festivities! "One last dance!" cried the young folks, and in they trooped. The servants were trying to get the piano out, but the master of the house himself stopped them— what was a piano in comparison to a romantic thrill? So one played, and the rest danced— danced while the fire roared deafeningly in the stories above them, and creeping veils of smoke gathered about their heads. They danced like mad creatures, laughing, singing in chorus. Eddying gusts of flame poured in at the windows, and still they sang—

"When you hear dem bells go ting-a-ling-a-ling,
All join hands and sweetly we will sing—
There'll be a hot time in the old town to-night!"

And so on, until there came a crashing of rafters above them, and showers of cinders and burning wood through the windows. Then they fled, and gathered in a group upon the lawn, and watched the roof of their pleasure-house fall in, sending a burst of flame and sparks to the sky.

And here, thought Sylvia, was the roof of her pleasure-house falling in! There was something terrifying in the symbol; the house of civilization was falling in, and people were dancing, dancing! "Don't you feel that, Mr. van Tuiver?" she asked. "It seems to me sometimes that I can see the world going to destruction before my eyes, and people don't know about it, they don't care about it. They are dancing, drunk with dancing! On with the dance!"

She laughed, a trifle hysterically, for her nerves were near the breaking point. Then she happened to look towards her sister Celeste, and caught a strange look in her eyes. She took in the meaning of it in an instant—Celeste was conscious of the presence of Royalty, and shocked by this display of levity upon a solemn occasion! "Sister,

how *dare* you?" the look seemed to say; and the
message gave a new fillip to the mad steeds of
Sylvia's fancy. "Never mind, Chicken!" she
laughed. ("Chicken" was a childhood nickname,
which, needless to say, was infuriating to a young
lady soon to make her *début*.) "Never mind,
Chicken! The roof will last till you've had your
dance!"

And then, the meal at an end, Sylvia took her
guest into the library. She put him in the
same chair that Frank had occupied, and turned
on the same lights upon her loveliness; she took
her seat, and looked at him once, and smiled
alluringly—and then suddenly looked away, and
bit her lip until it bled, and sprang up and fled
from the room, and rushed upstairs and flung
herself upon her bed, sobbing, choking with her
grief.

§ 11

THERE were ups and downs like this. The
next day, of course, Sylvia was ashamed of her
behavior; she had promised to be happy, and
not to distress her people—and this was the
way she kept her promise. She began to make
new resolutions, and to think of ways of atoning.
She took her father out into the garden, and
pretended deep interest in the new cinnamon-
roses. She spent a couple of hours going over
his old check-stubs and receipted bills, and with

evidence thus discovered went into town and made a row with a tradesman, and saved her father a couple of hundred dollars.

Then, after lunch, she took him for a drive behind the new pony which Uncle Mandeville had given her. She got him out into the country, and then opened up on him in unexpected fashion. "Papa, it isn't possible for people like us to economize, is it?"

"Not very much, my child," he answered smiling. "Why?"

"I've been thinking," she said. "It's all wrong—but I don't know what to do about it. You spent so much money on me; I didn't want it, but I didn't realize it till it was too late. And now comes Celeste's turn, and you have to spend as much on her, or she'll be jealous and angry. And Peggy and Maria will see what Celeste gets, and they will demand their turn. And the Baby—he's smashing his toys now, and in a few years he'll be smashing windows, and in a few more he'll be gambling like Clive and Harley. And you can't do anything about any of it!"

"My child," he said, "I don't want you to worry about such things——"

"No, you want to do all the worrying yourself. But, Papa, I have to make my life of some use. Since I can't earn money, I've been thinking that perhaps the most sensible thing would be for me to marry some rich man, and then help all my family and friends."

"Sylvia," protested the Major, "I don't like

one of my daughters to have such thoughts in her mind. I don't want a child of mine to marry for money—there is no need of it, there never will be!"

"Not while you can sit up all night and worry over accounts. But some day you won't be able to, Papa. I can see that you're under a strain, and yet I can't get you to let me help you. If you make sacrifices for me, why shouldn't I make them for you?"

"Not that kind of a sacrifice, my child. It's a terrible thing for a woman to marry for money."

"Do you really think so, Papa? So many women do it. Are they all bad, and are they all unhappy?"

Thus Sylvia—trying to do her duty, and keep her mind occupied. They got back home, and she found new diversions—Castleman Lysle had been feeding himself in the kitchen, and had been picked up black in the face with convulsions. This, you understand, was one of the features of life at Castleman Hall; one baby had been lost that way, since which time "Miss Margaret" always fainted when it occurred. As poor Aunt Varina had not the physical strength for such emergencies, Sylvia had to get a tub of hot water, and hold the child in it—while some one else held a spoon in his mouth, in order that he might not chew his tongue to pieces!

Thus the afternoon passed busily, and in the evening was the spring dance of the Young

Matrons' Cotillion Club. Sylvia absolutely had to go to that, in order to dance with Douglas van Tuiver and atone for her rudeness. She had promised it by way of pacifying Aunt Nannie; and also her father had made plans to accompany her again.

So she put on a new "cloth of silver" gown which she had bought in New York, and drank a "toddy" of the Major's mixing, and sallied forth upon his arm. There were lights and music, happy faces, cheery greetings—so she was uplifted, dreaming of happiness again. And then came the most dreadful collapse of all.

She had strolled out upon the veranda with Stanley Pendleton. Feeling chilly, she sent her partner in for a wrap; and then suddenly came a voice—*his* voice!

If it had been his ghost, Sylvia could not have been more startled. She whirled about and stared, and saw him—standing in the semi-darkness of the garden, close to the railing of the veranda. It had rained that day, and the roads were deep in mire, and he had ridden far. His clothing was splashed and his hair in disarray; as for his face—never had Sylvia seen such grief on a human countenance.

"Sylvia!" he whispered. "Sylvia!" She could only gaze at him, dumb. "Sylvia, give me one minute! I have come here to tell you——"

He stopped, his voice breaking with intensity of feeling. "Oh!" she gasped. "You ought not to be here!"

"I had to see you!" he exclaimed. "There was no other way——"

But he got no farther. There was a step behind Sylvia, and she turned, and at the same moment heard the terrible voice of her father—"What does this mean?"

She sprang to him with a quick cry. "Papa!" She caught his arm with her hands, trying to stop what she feared he might do. "No, Papa, no!" For one moment the Major stood staring at the apparition in the darkness.

She could feel him trembling with fury. "Sir, how dare you approach my daughter?"

"Papa, no!" exclaimed Sylvia, again.

"Sir, do you wish to make it necessary for me to shoot you?"

Then Frank answered, his voice low and vibrant with pain. "Major Castleman, I would be grateful to you."

The other glared at him for a moment; then he said, "If you wish to die, sir, choose some way that will not drag my daughter to disgrace."

Frank's gaze had turned to the girl. "Sylvia," he exclaimed, "I tell you that I went to that place——"

"Stop!" almost shouted the Major.

"Major Castleman," said Frank, "Allow me to speak to your daughter. It has been——"

Sylvia was clutching her father in terror. She knew that he had a weapon, and was on the point of using it; she knew also that she had not the physical force to prevent him. She cried hysterically, "Go! Go away!"

And Frank looked at her—a last look, that she never forgot all the days of her life.  "You mean it, Sylvia?" he asked, his voice breaking.

"I mean it!" she answered.

"Forever?"

For the smallest part of a second she hesitated. "Forever!" commanded her father;  and she echoed, "Forever!"  Frank turned, without another word, and was gone in the darkness;  and Sylvia fell into her father's arms, convulsed with an agony that shook her frame.


## § 12

THEY got her home, where her first action, in spite of her exhaustion, was to insist upon seeing her Uncle Mandeville.  So determined, so vehement she was, that it was necessary to rout the worthy gentleman out from a poker-game at two o'clock in the morning.  There had been other witnesses of what Frank had done, and Sylvia knew that her uncle must hear;  so she told him herself, with her arms about him, clinging to him in frenzy, and beseeching him to give her his word of honor that he would not carry out his threat against Frank Shirley.

It was not an easy word to get;  she would probably have failed, had it not been for the Major.  He could see the force in her argument that a shooting-affair would only serve to publish the matter to the world, and make it seem more serious. After all, from the family's point of view, the one thing to be desired was to make certain that there would be no further communication between the two. And Sylvia was willing to assure them of that, she declared. She rushed to her desk, and with trembling fingers wrote a note to "Mr. Frank Shirley," informing him that the scene which had just occurred had been intolerable to her, and requesting him to perform her one last service—to write a note to her father to the effect that he would make no further attempt to communicate with her. The Major, after some discussion, decided that he would accept this as a settlement; and he being the elder brother, his word was law with Mandeville —at least so long as Mandeville was sober.

I remember Sylvia's account of the state of exhaustion in which she found herself after this ordeal; how for two days she had the sensation that her mind was breaking up. Yet—a circumstance worth noting—at no time did she blame those who had put her through this ordeal. She could not blame the men of her family; if any one were at fault, it was herself, for being at the mercy of her emotions, and capable of a secret longing to have parleyings with a man who had dragged her name in the mire. You see, Sylvia believed in her heritage. She was proud of the Castlemans—and apparently you could not have rare, aristocratic virtues without also having terrifying vices. If one's men-folk got drunk and

shot people, one's consolation was that at least
they did it in a bold and striking and "high-
spirited" way.

You will perhaps find yourself impatient with
the girl at this stage of her story. I recall my
own frantic protests while I listened. What a
cruel, needless tragedy! I cried out for the evidence of some gleam of sense on the part of any
one person concerned. Surely Sylvia, knowing
Frank, must have come to doubt that he could
have been unfaithful to her! Surely, with the
hints she got at that meeting, she must have
realized that there was something more to be
said! Surely he, on his part, would have found
some way of getting an interview with her, or
at least of sending an explanation by some friend!
Surely he would never have given up until he
had done that!

I have claimed for Sylvia the possession of clear-
sightedness. She displayed it when it was a question of revising her religion, she displayed it when
it was a question of managing her family, and
obtaining permission to be engaged to a convict's
son. But, if you look to see her display anything
of that sort in the present emergency, you will
look in vain. Sylvia could be bold in a matter
of theology, she could be bold in a matter of
love, but she could not possibly be bold in a matter of a house of prostitution. If I were to give
you illustrations of| the completeness of her igno-
rance upon the subject of sex, you would simply
not be able to believe what I told; and not only

22

was she ignorant, she could not conceive that it was possible for her to be other than ignorant. She could not conceive that it was possible for a pure-minded girl to talk about such a subject with any human being, man or woman.

I doubt very much, if it had come to an actual test, whether Sylvia would have been capable of marrying against her family's will. She had opposed them vehemently, but this was because she knew that she was right, and that they, in their inmost hearts, knew it also. The Major and "Miss Margaret" were good and generous-hearted people, and they could not sincerely condemn Frank Shirley for his father's offense. But how different it was now! In the present matter she faced the phalanx of the family, not on an open field where she could manœuvre and outwit them—but in a place of darkness and terror, where she dared not stir a foot alone.

And let me tell you also that you mistake Frank Shirley if you count upon the mere physical fact that he could have got an explanation to Sylvia. It was not easy for him to explain about such matters to the woman he loved; and if you think it was easy, you are a modern, matter-of-fact person, not understanding the notions of an old-fashioned Southerner. The simple fact was that when Frank wrote to Harriet Atkinson, to ask her to hear his plea, he felt that he was doing something desperate and unprecedented; and when Harriet wrote, coldly refusing to have anything to do with the matter, he felt that she had rebuked him for his boldness. As for the last effort he had made to see Sylvia, it was the act of a man driven frantic by love—a man willing to sacrifice his life, and even his self-respect. I have portrayed Frank poorly if I have not made you realize that from the first hour he approached Sylvia with a sense of inferiority and of guilt; that he had remained her lover against the incessant protests of his pride. People are making money rapidly these days in the South, and so becoming like us "Yankees"; yet it will be a long time, I think, before a Southerner without money will make love to a rich woman without feeling in his heart that he is acting the knave.

## § 13

THERE came another long struggle for Sylvia, another climb out of the pit. For the sake of her father, she could not delay; as soon as she was able to move about, she was out among her roses again, and reading Alexander Stephens in the evenings. Within a week she had been to a card-party and a picnic, and also had received a call from Douglas van Tuiver.

Never before had Sylvia worn such an ethereal aspect; he was gentle, even reverent, in his manner to her. He had a particular reason for calling to see her, he said. He owned a yacht, considered quite a beautiful vessel; it was now

in commission, but idle, and he had taken the
liberty of ordering it to the Southern coast, and
wished to beg her to use it to bring the color
back into her cheeks. She might take her Aunt
Varina, her sister—a whole party, if she chose—
and cruise up the coast, to Maine and the St.
Lawrence, or over in the North Sea—wherever
her fancy suggested. He would go with her and
take charge, if she would permit—or he would
stay behind, and be happy in the knowledge that
she was recovering her health.

Of course, Sylvia could not accept such a favor;
she insisted that it was impossible, in spite of all
his arguments and urgings. She thanked him so
cordially, however, that he went away quite
happy.

Then came Mrs. Chilton, and there was a conclave of the ladies. Why should she not accept
the offer? It was the very thing she needed to
divert her mind, and get her out of this disgraceful
state.

"Aunt Nannie," cried the girl, "how can you
think of wanting me to accept such a gift from
a comparative stranger? It must cost hundreds
of dollars a month to run such a yacht!"

"About five thousand dollars a month, my
dear," said the other, quietly.

Sylvia was aghast; once in a while even a fiery
revolutionist like herself was awestricken by the
actuality of Royalty. "I don't want things like
that," she said, at last. "I want to stay quietly
at home and help Papa."

"You need a change," declared the other. "So long as you are here you are never safe from that evil man; and anyway you are surrounded by reminders of him. A yachting-trip would force you to put your mind on other things. The sea-air would do you good; and if you took Celeste with you—think what a treat for her!"

"Oh, Sylvia, please do!" cried Celeste.

Sylvia looked at her sister. "You'd like to go?"

"Oh, how can you ask?" she replied. "It would be heaven!"

Sylvia said that she would think it over. But in reality she wanted to think about something else. She waited until they left her alone with her sister, and then she said, "You like Mr. van Tuiver, don't you?"

"How could I fail to like him?" asked Celeste.

The other tried to draw her out. Why did she like him? He had such beautiful manners, such dignity—there were no loose ends about him. He had been everywhere, met everybody of consequence; compared with him the men at home seemed like country-fellows. It was that indescribable thing called elegance, said Celeste, gravely. She could not understand her sister's attitude at all; she thought Sylvia treated van Tuiver outrageously, and her eyes flashed a danger-signal as she said it. It was a woman's right to reject a man's advances if she chose to; but she ought not to humiliate him, when his only offense was admiring her to excess.

"I only wish it was you he admired," said Sylvia, who was in a gentle mood.

"No chance of that," remarked the other, with a touch of bitterness in her voice. "He has no eyes or ears for anybody else when you are about."

"I'm going to try to lend him eyes and ears," responded Sylvia. For that was the idea that had occurred to her—van Tuiver must be persuaded to transfer his interest to Celeste! Celeste would marry him; she would marry him without the least hesitation or distress; and then the elder sister might settle down with her family and her rose-gardens and her Confederate History!

## § 14

SYLVIA became quite excited over this scheme. When van Tuiver asked permission to call again, she was glad to say yes; but she kept Celeste with her, guiding the conversation so as to show off her best qualities. But alas, "Little Sister" had no qualities to be shown off when van Tuiver was about! She was so much impressed by him that she trembled with stage fright. Usually a bright and vivacious girl, although somewhat hard and shallow, she was now dumb, abject, a booby! Sylvia raged at her inwardly, and when van Tuiver had taken his departure, she said, "Celeste, how can you expect to impress a man if you let him see you are afraid to breathe in his presence?"

Tears of humiliation came into her sister's
eyes. "What's the use of talking about my
impressing him? Can't you see that he pays no
more attention to me than if I were a doll?"

"*Make* him pay attention to you!" cried the
other. "Shock him, hurt him, make him angry
—do anything but put yourself under his feet!"
She went on to give a lecture on that awe-inspiring
phenomenon, the Harvard manner; trying to
prove to her sister that it was an idol with feet
of clay, which would topple if one attacked it
resolutely. She told the story of her own meeting with King Douglas the First, and how she
had been able to subdue him with cheap effront-
ery. But she soon discovered that her arguments
were thrown away upon Celeste, who was simply
shocked by her story, and had no more the desire
than she had the power to subdue van Tuiver.
At first Sylvia had thought it was mere awe of
his millions, but gradually she realized that it
was something far more serious—something quite
tragic. Celeste had fallen in love with Royalty!

But still Sylvia could not give up the struggle.
It would have been such a marvelous solution of
her problem! She let van Tuiver call as often
as he wanted to; but she became, all at once, a
phenomenon of sisterly affection. She took
Celeste horse-back riding with them—and Celeste
rode well. If van Tuiver asked to go automobiling,
she found shrewd excuses for having Celeste go
also. But in the end she had to give up—because
of the "English system." Van Tuiver did not

want Celeste, and was so brutally unaware of
her existence that Celeste came home with tears
of humiliation in her eyes.   Sylvia went off by
herself and shed tears also; she hated van Tuiver
and his damnable manners!

She realized suddenly to what extent he was
boring her.   He came the next day, and spent
the better part of an hour talking to her about
his experiences among the elect in various parts
of the world.   He had been shooting last fall
upon the estates of the Duke of Something in
Scotland.   You went out in an automobile, and
took a seat in an arm-chair, and had several score
"beaters" drive tame pheasants towards you;
you had two men to load your guns, and you shot
the birds as they rose; but you could not shoot
more than so many hundred of a morning, because the recoil of the gun gave you a headache.
The Duke had a couple of guns which were something special—he valued them at a thousand
guineas the pair.

"Mr. van Tuiver," said the girl, suddenly,
"there is something I want to say to you.   I
have been meaning to say it for some time.
I think you ought not to stay here any longer."

His face lost suddenly its expression of com-
placency.   "Why, Miss Sylvia!" he exclaimed.

"I want to deal with you frankly.   If you are
here for any reason not connected with me, why
all right; but if you are here on my account,
I ought not to leave you under any misapprehension."

He tried hard to recover his poise. "I had begun to hope"—he began. "You—are you sure it is true?"

"I am sure. You realize of course—it's been obvious from the outset that my Aunt Nannie has entered into a sort of partnership with you, to help you persuade me to marry you. And of course there are others of my friends—even members of my family, perhaps—who would be glad to have me do it. Also, you must know that I've been trying to persuade myself." Sylvia lowered her eyes; she could not look at him as she said this. "I thought perhaps it was my duty—the only useful thing I could do with my life—to marry a rich man, and use his money to help the people I love. So I tried to persuade myself. But it's impossible—I could not, *could* not do it!"

She paused. "Miss Sylvia," he ventured, "can you be sure—perhaps if you married me, you might——"

"No!" she cried. "Please don't say any more. I know you ought not to stay! I could never marry you, and you are throwing away your time here. You ought to go!"

There was a silence. "Miss Sylvia," he began, finally, "this is like a death-sentence to me."

"I know," she said, "and I'm sorry. But there's no help for it. Putting off only makes it worse for you."

"Don't think about me," he said. "I've no place to go, and nothing better I can be doing.

If you'll let me stay, and try to be of some
service"—

"No," she declared, "you can be of no service.
I want to be alone, with my father and the people
I love; and it is only distressing to me to see you."

He rose, and stood looking at her, crestfallen.
"That is all you have to say to me, Miss Sylvia?"

"That is all. If you wish to show your regard
for me, you will go away and never think of me
again."

## § 15

VAN TUIVER went away; but within a week he
was back, writing Sylvia notes to say that he must
see her, that he only sought her friendship. And
then came Aunt Nannie, and there was a family
conference—ending not altogether to Sylvia's
advantage. Aunt Nannie took the same view
as Mrs. Winthrop, that one had no right to
humiliate a man who carried such vast responsibilities upon his shoulders. Sylvia recurred to
her old phrase "Royalty"—and was taken aback
when her aunt wanted to know just what were
her objections to Royalty. Had she not often
heard her Uncle Mandeville say that there ought
to be a king in America to counteract the influence
of Yankee demagogs? That rather took the wind
out of Sylvia's sails; for she had a great respect
for the political wisdom of her uncles, and really
could give no reason why a king might not be

a beneficent phenomenon. All she could reply
was that she did not like this particular king, and
would not see him. When Aunt Nannie insisted
that van Tuiver had been a guest under her roof,
and that Sylvia's action had been an unheard of
discourtesy, the girl said that she was willing to
apologize, either to her aunt or to van Tuiver—
but that nothing could induce her to let him call
again.

King Douglas went off to Newport, where the
family of Dorothy Cortlandt had its granite cottage; and so for two months Sylvia enjoyed peace.
She read to her father, and played cards with
him, and took him driving, exercising her social
graces to keep him from drinking too many
toddies. I could wish there were space to recite
some of the comical little dramas that were played
round the good Major's efforts to cheat himself
and his daughter, and exceed the number of
toddies which his physician allowed to him!

Aunt Nannie being away at the coast, it was
easier for the girl to avoid social engagements,
especially with the excuse that her father's health
was poor, and his plantation duties engrossing.
There had been an overflow in the early spring,
just at planting-time, and so there was no cotton
that year. Fences had been swept away, cattle
drowned, and negro-cabins borne off to parts
unknown. The Major had three large plantations, whose negroes must be kept over the year,
just as if they were working. Also there were
small farms, rented to negro tenants who had

lost everything; they had to be taken care of—
one must "hold on to one's niggers." "Why
don't you let them raise corn?" van Tuiver had
inquired; to which the Major answered, "My
negroes could no more raise corn than they could
raise ostriches."

So there was much money to be borrowed, and
money was "tight." Everybody wanted it from
the local banks, and as this was the second bad
year, the local banks were in an ungenerous mood.
Worse than that, there were troubles vaguely
rumored from "Wall Street." What this meant
to Sylvia was that her father sat up at night and
worried over his books, and could not be got to
talk of his affairs.

But what distressed her most was that there
was no sign of any effort to curtail the family's
expenditure. Aunt Varina and the children were
at the summer-home in the mountains, and so
there were two establishments to be kept going.
Also Celeste was giving house-parties, and ordering new things from New York, in spite of the
fact that she had come home from school with
several trunkloads of splendor. The Major's
family all signed his name to checks, and all
these checks were like chickens which came home
to roost in the pigeon-holes in the office-desk.

In the fall the Major's health weakened under
the strain, and the doctor insisted that he must
go away at all hazards. Uncle Mandeville had
taken a place at one of the Gulf Coast resorts,
and Sylvia and her father were urged to come

there—just in time for the yachting regatta, wrote the host. They came; and about two weeks later a great ocean-going yacht steamed majestically into the harbor, and the dismayed Sylvia read in the next morning's paper that Mr. Douglas van Tuiver, who had been cruising in the Gulf with a party of friends, had come to attend the races!

"I won't see him!" she declared; and Uncle Mandeville, who was in command here, backed her up, and offered to shoot the fellow if he molested her. This, of course, was in fun, but Uncle Mandeville was serious in his support of his niece, maintaining that the Castlemans needed no Yankee princeling to buttress their fortunes.

She fully meant not to see him. But he had brought allies to make sure of her. That afternoon an automobile drew up at the door, and Sylvia, who was on the gallery, saw a lady descending, waving a hand to her. She stared, dumb-founded. It was Mrs. Winthrop!

Mrs. Winthrop—clad in spotless white from hat to shoetips, looking sunburned and picturesque, and surprisingly festive. No one was in sight but Sylvia, and so she had a free field for her wizardry. She came slowly up the gallery-steps, and took the outstretched hands in hers, and gazed. How much she read in the pale, thin face—and what deeps of feeling welled up in her!

"Oh, let me help you!" she murmured. And nothing more.

"Thank you!" said Sylvia at last.

"My dryad!" Quick tears of sympathy started in the great lady's eyes, and came running down her sunburned cheeks, and had to be brushed away with a tiny Irish lace handkerchief.

"Believe me, Sylvia, I too have known grief!" she began, after a minute. Sylvia was deeply touched; for what grief could be more fascinating than that which lurked in the dream-laden eyes before her? She found herself suddenly recalling an irreverent phrase of "Tubby" Bates': "The beautiful unhappy wife of a railroad-builder!"

They sat down. "Sylvia," said Mrs. Winthrop, "you need diversion. Come out on the yacht!"

"No," she replied, "I don't want to meet Mr. van Tuiver again."

"I appreciate your motives," said the other. "But you may surely trust to my discretion, Sylvia. Mr. van Tuiver has recovered himself, and there is no longer any need for you to avoid him."

He was a much changed man, went on "Queen Isabella"; so chastened that his best friends hardly knew him. He had become a most fascinating figure, a sort of superior Werther; his melancholy became him. He had been really admirable in his behavior, and Sylvia owed it to him to give him a chance to show her that he could control himself, to show his friends that she had not dismissed him with contempt. There was a charming party on board the yacht; it included van Tuiver's aunt, Mrs. Harold Cliveden, of whom Sylvia had surely heard; also her niece, Miss Vaillant, and Lord Howard Annersley, who was engaged to her. Sylvia had probably not seen the accounts of this affair, but it was most romantic. The girl pleaded that her father was ill and needed her. But he might come too, said Mrs. Winthrop; the diversion would benefit him. So at last Sylvia consented to go to lunch.

## § 16

VAN TUIVER came to fetch them on the following day. He looked his new rôle of a leisure-class Werther, and acted up to it quite touchingly. He was perfect in his attitude toward his guests, carefully omitting all reference to personal matters, and confining his conversation to the yachting-trip and the party on board—especially to Lord Howard. Sylvia said that she had never met a Lord before, and it would seem like a fairy-story to her. The other was careful to explain that Lord Howard was not a fortune-hunter, but a friend of his. So Sylvia furbished up her weapons—but put most of them away when she got on board, and found out what a very commonplace young man his lordship was.

It was necessary to extend a return invitation, so Uncle Mandeville took the party automobiling along the coast, and spread a sumptuous picnic-luncheon. Then the next day Sylvia let herself be inveigled on a moonlight sailing-trip; and so it came about that she was cornered in the bow of the boat, with van Tuiver at her side, declaring in trembling accents that he had tried to forget her, that he could not live without her, that if she did not give him some hope he would take his life.

She was intensely annoyed, and answered him in monosyllables, and took refuge with Lord Howard, who showed signs of forgetting that he was already in the midst of a romance. She vowed that she would accept no more invitations, and that van Tuiver would never deceive her in that way again. This last with angry emphasis to Mrs. Winthrop, who, perceiving that something had gone wrong, took her aside as the party was breaking up.

"Queen Isabella's" lovely face showed intense distress. "Oh, these men!" she cried. "Sylvia, what can we do with them?" And when Sylvia, taken aback by this appeal, was silent, the other continued, pleadingly, "You must be loyal to your sex, and help me! We all have to manage men!"

"But what do you want me to do?" asked the girl. "Marry him?"

She meant this for the extreme of sarcasm; and great was her surprise when Mrs. Winthrop caught her hand and exclaimed, "My dear, I want you to do just that!"

"But then—what becomes of my fineness of

spirit?" cried Sylvia, with still more withering
sarcasm.

Said "Queen Isabella," "The man loves you."

"I know—but I don't love him."

"He loves you deeply, Sylvia. I think you will
really have to marry him."

"In spite of the fact that I don't love him in
the least?"

The other smiled her gentlest smile. "I want
you to let me come and talk to you about these
matters."

"But, Mrs. Winthrop, I don't want to be talked
to about marrying Mr. van Tuiver!"

"I want to explain things to you, Sylvia.
You must grant me that favor—please!" In the
hurry of departure, Sylvia gave no reply, and
the other took silence for consent.

By what device van Tuiver could have reconciled Mrs. Winthrop, Sylvia could not imagine;
but when the great lady called, the next afternoon, she was as ardent on the one side as she
had formerly been on the other. She painted
glowing pictures of the splendors which awaited
the future Mrs. Douglas van Tuiver. The
courts of Europe would be open to her, her life
would be one triumphal pageant. Also, taking
a leaf out of "Tubby" Bates' note-book, "Queen
Isabella" discoursed upon the good that Sylvia
would be able to do with her husband's wealth.

This interview with Mrs. Winthrop was important for another reason; it was the means of
setting at rest what doubts were lurking in

Sylvia's mind as to her treatment of Frank Shirley. The other evidently had the matter in mind, for Sylvia needed only to allude to it, whereupon Mrs. Winthrop proceeded, with the utmost tact and understanding, to give her exactly the information she was craving. The dreadful story was surely true—everybody at Harvard knew it. All that one heard in defense was that it was a shame the story had been spread abroad; for there were men, said Mrs. Winthrop, who did these shameful things in secret, and had no remorse save when they were found out. Without saying it in plain words, she caused Sylvia to have the impression that such evils were to be found among men of low origin and ignominious destinies: a suggestion which started in Sylvia a brand-new train of thought. Could it be that *this* was the basis of social discrimination—the secret reason why her parents were so careful what men she met? It threw quite a new light upon the question of college snobbery, if one pictured the club-men as selected and set apart because of their chaste lives. It made quite a difference in one's attitude towards the "exclusiveness" of van Tuiver—if one might think of him, as Mrs. Winthrop apparently did think of him, as having been guarded from contamination, from the kind of commonness to which Frank Shirley had permitted himself to stoop.

## § 17

VAN TUIVER of course wrote letters of apology; but Sylvia would not answer them nor see him. As the yacht still lingered in the harbor, she became restless, and was glad when the Major decided to return home to the rose-gardens and Alexander Stephens. Soon afterwards she learned that the yachting-party had returned to New York; but in a couple of weeks "King Douglas" was at Aunt Nannie's again, annoying her with his letters and his importunities.

By this time everybody in Castleman County knew the situation; it had become a sort of State romance—or perhaps it would be better to say a State scandal. Sylvia became aware of a new force, vaguer, but more compelling even than that of the family—the power of public opinion. It was all very well for a girl to have whims and to indulge them; to be coquettish and wayward—naturally. But to keep it up for so long a time, to carry the joke so far— well, it was unusual, and in somewhat questionable taste. It was a fact that every person in Castleman County shone by the reflected glory of Sylvia's great opportunity; and everybody felt himself—or more especially herself—cheated of this glory by the girl's eccentricity. You may take this for a joke, but let me tell you that public opinion is a terrible agent, which has driven mighty princes to madness, and captains of predatory finance to suicide.

All this time Sylvia was thinking—thinking. Wherever she went, whatever she did, she was debating one problem in her soul. As I don't want anyone to misunderstand her or despise her, I must try to tell, briefly and simply, what were her thoughts.

She had come to hate life. Everything that had ever been sweet to her seemed to have turned to ashes in her mouth. The social game, for which she had been trained with so much care and at so great expense, upon which she had entered with such zest three years before—the game had become a sordid mockery to her. It was a chase after men, an elaboration of devices to gain and hold their attention. To be decked out and sent forth to perform tricks—no, it was an utterly intolerable thing.

Her whole being was one cry to stay at home with the people she loved. Here were her true friends, who would always stand by her, who would be a bulwark against the ugliness of life. A wonderful thing it was, after all, the family; a kind of army of mutual defense against a hostile, predatory world. "Life is a case of dog eat dog," had been the words of Uncle Mandeville. "You have to eat or be eaten." And Uncle Mandeville had seen so much of life!

So the one high duty that Sylvia could see was to stand by and maintain the family. And there were increasing signs that this family was in peril. More and more plainly was worry to be read in the face of the Major; there were even signs that his worry had infected others. Curious, incredible as it might seem, "Miss Margaret" was trying to economize! She wandered over her exquisite velvet carpets in a faded last year's gown, and a pair of rusty last year's slippers; nor could she be persuaded to purchase new—until the Major himself sent off an order to her costumer in New Orleans!

Also Aunt Varina had taken to fretting over the housekeeping extravagances. So many idle negroes eating their heads off in the kitchen! Such grocery and laundry bills, beyond all reason and sense! The echoes of her protest reached even to the tradesmen in the town, who heard with dismay that at Castleman Hall they were counting the supplies, and going over the bills, and refusing to pay for goods which had not been sent, or had been stolen by the negroes employed to deliver them!

"Aunt Mandy," the black cook, had once been heard to declare that Castleman Hall was not a home, but "a free hotel." A hotel with great airy rooms, huge four-poster beds, and quaint old "dressers" and "armours" of hand-carved mahogany! No wonder the guests came trooping! "We ought to move into one of the smaller houses on the plantation!" declared Aunt Varina; and what a horror to have such an idea mentioned in the family. Fear assailed "Miss Margaret"— what if the neighbors were to hear of it? Everybody knew that there had been droughts and floods, and somebody might suspect that these had touched the Castlemans! Mrs. Castleman decided forthwith that it would be necessary to give a big reception; and the moment this was announced came a cry from Celeste—why, if her mother could give a reception, could she not have the little "electric" for which she had begged all summer?

Celeste was going back to Miss Abercrombie's in a week or two. Going back to Fifth Avenue and its shops—to open accounts at any of them she chose, and sign her father's name to checks, just as Sylvia had done. It would have been a painful matter to curtail this privilege, for Sylvia was the favorite daughter, and Celeste knew it, and was bitterly resentful of every sign of favoritism. And yet the privilege was more dangerous in the case of Celeste, who was careless to the point of wickedness. You might see her step out of an expensive ball-gown at night, and leave it a crumpled ring upon the floor until the maid hung it up in the morning; you might see her kick off her tight, high-heeled slippers, and walk about the room for hours in her stockinged feet—thus wearing out a pair of new silk hose that had cost five dollars, and kicking them to one side to be carried off by the negroes. Celeste would permit nothing but silk upon her exquisite person, and was given to lounging about in oriental luxuriance, while Peggy and Maria gazed at her awe-stricken, as at some princess in a fairy-story book. Sylvia saw with bewilderment that everywhere about her it was the evil example which seemed to be prevailing.

## § 18

SYLVIA could not plan to stay at home and share in this plundering of her father. She must marry; yet when it came to the question of marrying, the one positive fact in her consciousness was that she could never love any man. No matter how long she might wait, no matter how much energy she might expend in hesitating and agonizing, sooner or later she would give herself in marriage to some man whom she did not love. And after all, there was very little choice among them, so far as she could see. Some were more entertaining than others; but it was true of everyone that if he touched her hand in token of desire, she shrunk from him with repugnance.

The time came when to her cool reason this shrinking wore the aspect of a weakness. When so much happiness for all those she loved depended upon the conquering of it, what folly not to conquer it! Here was the obverse of that distrust of "blind passion" which they had taught her. Whether it was an emotion towards or away from a man, was it a thing which should dominate a woman's life? Was it not rather a thing for her to beat into whatever shape her good sense directed?

Seated one day in her mother's room, Sylvia asked, quite casually, "Mamma, how often do women marry the men they love?"

"Why, what makes you ask that?" inquired the other.

"I don't know, Mamma. I was just thinking."

"Miss Margaret" considered. "Not often, my child; certainly not, if you mean their first love." Then, after a pause, she added, "I think perhaps it's well they don't. Most all those I know who married their first love are unhappy now."

"Why is that, Mamma?"

"They don't seem able to judge wisely when they're young and blinded by passion." "Miss Margaret" drifted into reminiscences—beginning with the case of Aunt Varina, who was in the next room.

"It seems such a terrible thing," said Sylvia. "Love is—well, it makes you want to trust it."

"Something generally happens," replied the other. "A woman has to wait, and in the end she marries for quite other reasons."

"And yet they manage to make out!" said the girl, half to herself.

"Children come, dear. Children take their time, and they forget. I remember so well your Uncle Barry's wife—she visited us in her courtship days, and she used to wake up in the middle of the night, and whisper to me in a trembling voice, 'Margaret, tell me—*shall* I marry him?' I think she went to the altar without really having her mind made up; and yet, you see, she's one of the happiest women I know—they are perfectly devoted to each other."

Sylvia went away to ponder these things. The next day Aunt Varina happened to talk about her life-tragedy, and told Sylvia of the death of her young love; and later on came Uncle Barry's wife, traveling a hundred miles for the sake of a casual conversation upon the state of happiness vouchsafed to those who chose their husbands in accordance with reason. All of which was managed with such delicacy and tact that no one but an utterly depraved person like Sylvia would ever have suspected that it was planned.

There was one person from whom the girl hoped for an unworldly opinion; that was the Bishop. She went to see him one day, and casually brought up the subject of van Tuiver— a thing which was easy enough to do, since the man was a guest in the house.

"Sylvia," said her uncle, at once, "why don't you marry him?"

The girl was astounded. "Why, Uncle Basil!" she exclaimed. "Would you advise me to?"

"Nothing would make me happier than the news that you had so decided."

Sylvia was at a loss for words. She had thought that here was one person who would surely not be influenced by Royalty. "Tell me why," she said.

"Because, my child," the Bishop answered, "he's a Christian gentleman."

"Oh! So it's that!"

"Yes, Sylvia. You don't know how often I have prayed that you might have a religious man for a husband."

Sylvia said no more. Her thoughts flew back to Boston, to an incident which had caused her amusement at the time. She had told "Tubby" Bates that she would go motoring with van Tuiver on a Sunday morning; and the answer was that on Sunday mornings van Tuiver passed the collection-plate in a Very High Church. Bates went on to explain—in his irreverent fashion—that van Tuiver's great-uncle had been of the opinion that the only hope for a young man with so much money was to turn him over to the Lord; so for his grand-nephew's head-tutor he had engaged a clergyman recommended by an English bishop. And now here was another bishop recommending van Tuiver as an instrument for the converting of his wayward niece!

Sylvia went away, and spent more time in doubting and fearing. But there was a limit to the time she could take, because the man was practically in her home, moving heaven and earth to get a chance to see her, to urge his suit, to implore her for mercy, if for nothing more. And truly he was a pitiable object; if a woman wanted a husband whom she could twist round her finger, of whom she could be absolute mistress all her days, here surely was the husband at hand! The voice of old Lady Dee called out to her from the land of ghosts that her victory and her crown were here.

The end came suddenly, being due to a far-off cause. There was a panic in "Wall Street"; an event of which Sylvia heard vaguely, but without paying heed, not dreaming that so remote an event could concern her. One can consult the financial year-books, and learn how many business-men went into bankruptcy as a result of that panic, what properties had to be sold as a result of it; but it has apparently not occurred to any compiler of statistics to record the number of daughters—daughters of poor men and daughters of rich men—who had· to be sold as a result of it.

The Major came home one afternoon and shut himself in his study, and did not come to dinner. Sylvia knew, by that subtle sixth sense whereby things are known in families, that something serious had happened. But she was not allowed to see her father that day or night; and when she finally did see him, she was dumb with horror. He looked so yellow and ill—his hands trembled as if palsied, and she knew by the cigar-stumps scattered about the office, and the decanter of brandy on top of the desk, that he had been up the entire night at his books.

He would not tell her what was the matter; he insisted, as usual, that it was "nothing." But evidently he had told his wife, for the poor lady's eyes were red with weeping. Later on in the day Sylvia, chancing to answer the telephone, received a message from Uncle Mandeville in New Orleans, to the effect that he was "short," and powerless to help. Then she took her mother aside and dragged the story from her. The local bank was in trouble, and had called some of the Major's loans. The blow had almost killed him, and they were in terror as to what he might do to himself.

Mrs. Castleman saw her daughter go white, and added, "Oh, if only you were not under the spell of that dreadful man!"

"But what in the world has that to do with it?" demanded the girl.

"I curse the day that you met him!" wailed the other; and then, as Sylvia repeated her question—"What else is it that keeps you from loving a good man, and being a help to your father in this dreadful crisis?"

"Mamma!" exclaimed Sylvia. She had never expected to hear anything like this from the gentle "Miss Margaret." "Mamma, I couldn't stop the panic!"

"You could stop it so far as your father is concerned," was the answer.

Sylvia said no more at this time. But later on, when Aunt Nannie came over, she heard the remark that there were a few fortunate persons who were not affected by panics; it had been the maxim of van Tuiver's ancestors to invest in nothing but New York City real estate, and to live upon their incomes. It was possible to do this, even in New York, declared Mrs. Chilton, if one's income was several millions a year.

"Aunt Nannie," said the girl, gravely, "if I promised to marry Mr. van Tuiver, could I ask him to lend Papa money?"

Whereat the other laughed. "My dear niece, I assure you that to be the father of the future Mrs. Douglas van Tuiver would be an asset in the money market—an asset quite as good as a plantation."

## § 19

Sylvia made up her mind that day; and as usual, she was both clear-sighted and honest about it. She would not deceive herself, and she would not deceive van Tuiver. She sent for the young millionaire, and taking him into another room than the library, shut the door. "Mr. van Tuiver," she began, in a voice she tried hard to keep firm, "you have been begging me to marry you. You must know that I have been trying to make up my mind."

"Yes, Miss Sylvia?" he said, eagerly.

"I loved Frank Shirley," she continued. "Now I can never love again. But I know I shall have to marry. My people would be unhappy if I didn't—so unhappy that I know I couldn't bear it. You see, the person I really love is my father."

She hesitated again. "Yes, Miss Sylvia," he repeated. She saw that his hands were trembling, and that he was gazing at her with feverish excitement.

"I would do anything to make my father happy," she said. "And now—he's in trouble—money-trouble. Of course I know that if I married you, I could help him. I've tried to bring myself to do it. To-day I said, 'I will!' But then, there is your side to be thought of."

"My side, Miss Sylvia?"

"I have to be honest with you. I can't pretend to be what I am not, or to feel what I don't feel. If I were to marry you, I should try to do my duty as a wife; I should do everything in my power, honestly and sincerely. But I don't love you, and I don't see how I ever could love you."

"But—Miss Sylvia—" he exclaimed, hardly able to speak for his agitation. "You mean that you would marry me?"

"I didn't know if you would want to marry, me—when I had told you that."

He was leaning forward, clenching and unclenching his hands nervously. "I wouldn't mind—really!" he said.

"Even if you knew—" she began.

"Miss Sylvia," he cried, "I love you! Don't you understand how I love you?"

"Yes, but—if I couldn't—if I didn't love you?"

"I would take what you could give me! I love you so much, nothing would matter. I believe that you would come to love me! If you would only give me a chance, Miss Sylvia——"

"But suppose!" she protested. "Suppose you found that I never did! Suppose——"

But he was in no mood for troublesome suppositions. Any way would do, he said. He began stammering out his happiness, he fell upon his knees before her and caught her hand, and sought to kiss it. At first she made a move to withdraw it; but then, with an inward effort, she let him have it, and sat staring before her, a mantle of scarlet stealing over her throat and cheeks and forehead.

His hands were hot and moist, and quite horrible to her. Once she looked at him, and an image of him was stamped upon her mind indelibly. It was an image quite different from his ordinary rigid and sober mask; it was the face of the man who had always got everything he wanted. Sylvia did not formulate to herself just what it was that frightened her so—except for one phrase. She said it seemed to her that he licked his lips!

He could hardly believe that the long siege was ended, that the guerdon of victory was his. She had to tell him several times that she would marry him—that she was serious about it—that would give him her word and would not take it back. And then she had to prove it to him. He was not content to clasp her hand, but sought to embrace her; and when she found that she could not stand it, she had to plead that it was not the Southern custom. "You must give me a little time to get used to the idea. I only made up my mind to-day."

"But you will change your mind!" he exclaimed.

"No, no, I won't do that. That would be wicked of me. I've decided what is right, and I mean to do it. But you must be patient with me at the beginning."

"When will you marry me?" he asked—evidently none too confident in her resolution,

"I don't know. It ought to be soon. I must talk with my parents about it."

"And where will it be?"

"That's something I meant to speak of. It can't be here." She hesitated. "I must tell you

the truth. There would be too much to remind
me. I couldn't endure it. This may seem sentimental to you, but I'm quite determined. But
I'll have a hard time persuading my people—for
you see, they're proud, and they'll say the world
would expect you to marry me here. You must
stand by me in this."

"Very well," he said. "I will urge them to
have the wedding in New York."

There was a pause, then Sylvia added: "Another thing, you must not breathe a word to
anyone of what I've told you—about the state
of my feelings—my reasons for deciding——"

He smiled. "I'd hardly boast about that!"

"No, but I mean you mustn't tell your dearest
friend—not Aunt Nannie, not Mrs. Winthrop.
You see, I have to make my people believe that
I'm quite sure of my own mind. If my father
had any idea that I was thinking of him, then
he'd surely forbid it. If he ever found out afterwards, he'd be wretched—and I'd have failed in
what I tried to do."

"I understand," said van Tuiver, humbly.

"It's not going to be easy for me," she added.
"I shall have to make everybody think I'm happy.
You must sympathize with me and help me—and
not mind if I seem unreasonable and full of
whims."

He said again that he understood, and would
do his best. He took her hand, very gently, and
held it in his; he started to kiss it, but when he
saw that she had no pleasure in the ceremony

he released it, parting from her with a formal
little speech of thanks.  And such was the manner
of Sylvia's second betrothal.

§ 20

THE engagement was announced at once, the
wedding to take place six weeks later in New
York.   Just as Sylvia had anticipated, the
family made a great to-do over the place of the
ceremony;  but finding that both she and van
Tuiver were immovable, they cast about for
some pretext to make a New York wedding seem
plausible to a suspicious world.   They bethought
themselves of an almost forgotten relative of
the family, a step-sister of Lady Dee's, who had
lived in haughty poverty for half a century in
the metropolis, and was now discovered in a
boarding-house in Harlem, and transported to
a suite of apartments in the Palace Hotel, to
become responsible for Sylvia's desertion of
Castleman County.  She had nothing to do but
be the hostess of her "dear niece"—since Mrs.
Harold Cliveden had kindly offered to see to the
practical details of the ceremonial.

The thrilling news of the betrothal spread,
quite literally with the speed of lightning; the
next day all America read of the romance.  Since
the story of van Tuiver's infatuation, his treason
to the "Gold Coast" and his forsaking of college,

24

has been the gossip of New York and Boston clubs for months, there was a delightful story for the "yellows," of which they did not fail to make use. Of course there was nothing of that kind in the Southern papers, but they had their own way of responding to the general excitement, of gratifying the general curiosity.

Sylvia was really startled by the furore she had raised; she was as if caught up and whirled away by a hurricane. Such floods of congratulations as poured in! So many letters, from people whose names she could barely remember! Was there a single person in the county who had a right to call, who did not call to wish her joy? Even Celeste wrote from Miss Abercrombie's—a letter which brought the tears to her sister's eyes.

Through all these events Sylvia played her rôle; she played it day and night—not even in the presence of her negro maid did she lay it aside! The rôle of the blushing bride-to-be, the ten-times-over happy heroine of a romance in high-life! She must be smiling, radiant with animation decorously repressed; she must go about with the lucky bridegroom-to-be, and receive the congratulations of those she knew, and be unaware—yet not ungraciously unaware —of the interest and the stares of those she did not know. More difficult yet, she had to look the Major in the eyes, and say to him that she had come to realize that she was fond of "Mr. van Tuiver," and that she honestly believed she

would be happy with him. Since her mother
and Aunt Varina were dear sentimental Southern
ladies, incapable of taking a cold-blooded look
at a fact, she had to pretend even to them that
she was cradled in bliss.

At first van Tuiver was with her all the time,
pouring out the torrents of his happiness and
gratitude. But Aunt Nannie soon came to the
rescue here; Sylvia must not have the incon-
veniences of matrimony until the knot had
actually been tied. Van Tuiver was ordered off
to New York, until Sylvia should come for the
buying of her wedding-trousseau.

The dear old Major had suspected nothing
when his friend, the president of the bank, had
suddenly discovered that he could "carry" the
troublesome notes. So now he was completely
free from care, and his daughter had a week of
bliss in his company. She read history to him,
and drove with him, and tended his flowers in
the conservatory, and was hardly apart from
him an hour in the day.

Sylvia had set out some months ago at the
task of democratizing van Tuiver; even in
becoming engaged she had kept some lingering
hope of accomplishing this. But alas, how
quickly the idea vanished before the reality of
her situation! She remembered with a smile
how glibly she had advised the young millionaire
to step away from his shadow; and how he had
labored to make plain to her that he could not
help being a King. Now suddenly she found

that she could sympathize with him—she who was about to be a Queen!

There were a thousand little ways in which she felt the difference. Even the manner of her friends was changed. She could not go anywhere that she was not conscious of people staring at her. It was found necessary to appoint a negro to guard the grounds, because of the number of strangers who came in the hope of getting a glimpse of her. Her mail became suddenly a flood: letters from inventors who wished to make her another fortune; letters from distressed women who implored her to save them; letters from convicts languishing in prison for crimes of which they were innocent; letters from poets with immortal, unrecognized blank-verse dramas; letters from lonely farmers' wives who thrilled over her romance, and poured out their souls in ill-spelled blessings; letters from prophets of the class-war who frightened her with warnings of the wrath to come!

On the second day after the engagement was announced, Sylvia went out, all unsuspecting, for a horseback-ride, and had hardly mounted when a man with a black box stepped from behind a tree, and proceeded calmly to snap-shot the fair equestrienne. Sylvia cried out in indignation, and springing from the horse, rushed in to tell the Major what had happened; whereupon the Major sallied out with a cane, and there was a cross-country gallop after the intruder, ending in a violent collision between the camera and the cane. The funniest part of the matter was that the photographer spent the better part of a day trying to get a warrant for his assailant —imagining that it was possible to arrest a Castleman in Castleman County! By way of revenge he telegraphed the story to New York, where it appeared, duly worked up—with the old photograph of the "reigning beauty of the New South," in place of the one which had died in the camera!

## § 21

Sylvia came up to New York in due course; and by the time that she had been there one day, she was able to understand the fondness of the great for traveling "incog." She was "snapped" when she descended from the train— and this time there was no one to assault the photographer. Coming out of her hotel with van Tuiver she found a battery of cameras waiting; and being ungracious enough to put up her hand before her face, she beheld her picture the next morning with the hand held up, and beside it the "reigning beauty" picture—with the caption, "What is behind the hand!"

Van Tuiver was of course known in all the places which were patronized by the people of his sort; and Sylvia had but to be seen with him once in order to be equally known. Thereafter when she passed through a hotel-lobby, or into a tea-room, she would become aware of a sudden hush, and would know that every eye was following her. Needless to say, she could count upon the attention of all the "buttons" who caught sight of her; she lived with a vague consciousness of swarms of blue-uniformed gnomes with constantly-changing faces, who flitted about her, all but falling over one another in their zeal, and making her least action, such as sitting in a chair or passing through a doorway, into a ceremonial observance.

The most curious thing of all was to go shopping; she simply dared not order anything sent home. There would be the clerk, with pad and poised pencil—"Name, please?" She would say, "Miss Sylvia Castleman," and the pencil would begin to write mechanically—and then stop, struck with a sudden paralysis. She would see the fingers trembling, she would be aware of a swift, wonder-stricken glance. Sometimes she would pretend to be unconscious, and the business would go on—"Palace Hotel. To be delivered this afternoon. Yes, certainly, Miss Castleman." But sometimes human feeling would break through all routine. A young soul, hungry for life, for beauty—and confronting suddenly the greatest moment of its whole existence, touching the hem of the star-sewn garment of Romance! A young girl—possibly even a man—flushing scarlet, trembling, stammering, "Oh—why—!" Once or twice Sylvia read in the face before her something so pitiful that she was moved to put her hand upon that of her devotee; and if you are learned in the lore of ancient times, you know what miracles are wrought by the touch of Royalty!

What attitude was she to take to this new power of hers? It was impossible to pretend to be unaware of it—she had too keen a sense of humor. But was she to spend her whole life in shrinking, and feeling shame for other people's folly? Or should she learn somehow to accept the homage as her due? She saw that the latter was what van Tuiver expected. He had chosen her among millions because she was the one supremely fitted to go through life at his side; and if she kept her promise and tried to be a faithful wife to him, she would have to take her rôle seriously, and learn to enjoy the performances.

Meantime, you ask, What of her soul? She was trying her best to forget it—in excitements and distractions, in meeting new people, going to new places, buying thousands of dollars worth of new costumes. She would stay late at dances and supper-parties, trying to get weary enough to sleep; but then she would have nightmares, and would waken moaning and sobbing. Always her dream was one thing, in a thousand forms; she was somewhere in captivity, and some person or creature was telling her that she could not escape, that it was forever, forever, forever. Her room had been made into a bower of roses, but she had to send them away, because one horrible night when she got up and walked about, they made her think of the gardens at home, and the pacing back and forth in her nightgown, and the thorns and gravel in her feet.

As a child Sylvia had read a story of a circus-clown, who had played his part when ill and almost dying, because of his wife and child at home. Always thereafter a circus-clown had been to her the symbol of the irony of human life. But now she knew another figure, equally tragic, equally terrible to be—the heroine of a State romance. To be photographed and written about, to see people staring at you, to have to smile and look like one hearing celestial music— and all the while to have a breaking heart!

## § 22

SYLVIA fought long battles with herself. "Oh, I can't do it!" she would cry. "I can't do it!" And then "You've promised to do it!" she would say to herself. And every day she spent more money, and met more of van Tuiver's friends, and read more articles about her Romance.

Then one morning came a hall-boy with a card. She looked at it, and had a painful start. "Tubby" Bates!

He came in, cheerful, jolly, reminding her of so many things—such happy things! She had had a bad night, and now she simply could not talk; her words choked her, and she sat staring at him, her eyes suddenly filling with tears.

"Why, Miss Castleman!" he exclaimed—and saw such a look upon that lovely face that his voice died away to a whisper—"You aren't happy!"

Still for a while she could not answer. He asked her what was the matter; and then, again, in greater distress, "Why did you do it?" She responded, in a faint voice, "I did it on my father's account."

There was a long silence. Then with sudden energy she began, "Mr. Bates, there is something I want to talk to you about. It's something difficult—almost impossible for me to speak of. And yet—I seem to get more and more desperate about it. I can never be happy in my life until I've talked to some one about it."

"What is it, Miss Castleman?"

"It's about Frank Shirley."

"Oh!" he said, in surprise.

"You know that I was engaged to him, Mr. Bates?"

"Yes, I was told that."

"And you can guess, perhaps, how I have suffered. I know only what the newspapers printed—nothing more. And now—you are a man, and you were at Harvard—you must know. Is it true that Frank—that he did something that would make it wrong for me ever to see him again?"

The blood had pressed into Sylvia's face, but

still she did not lower her eyes. She was gazing intensely at her friend. She must know the truth! The whole truth!

He considered, and then said, gravely, "No, Miss Castleman, I don't think he did that."

There was a pause. "But—it was a place—" she could go no further.

"I know," he said. "But you see, Shirley had a room-mate—Jack Colton. And he was always trying to help him—to keep him out of trouble and get him home sober——"

"Oh, then *that* was it!" The words came in a tone that frightened Bates by their burden of anguish.

"Yes, Miss Castleman," he said. "And as to the row—Shirley saw a woman mistreated, and he interfered, and knocked a man down. I know the man, and he's the sort one has to knock down. The only trouble was that he hit his head as he fell."

"I see!" whispered Sylvia.

"But even so, there wouldn't have been any publicity, except that some of the 'Auburn Street crowd' were there. They saw their chance to put the candidate of the 'Yard' out of the running; and they did it. It was a rotten shame, because everybody knew that Frank Shirley was not that kind of man——"

Bates stopped again. He could not bear the look he saw on Sylvia's face. She bowed her head in her arms, and silent sobbing shook her. Then she got up and began to pace back and forth distractedly. He knew very well what was going on in her thoughts.

Suddenly she turned upon him. "Mr. Bates," she exclaimed, "you must help me! You must stay here and help me!"

"Certainly, Miss Castleman. What can I do?"

"In the first place, you must not breathe a word of this to anyone. You understand?"

"Of course."

"Have you any idea where Frank Shirley is?"

"I heard that he had gone out to Wyoming with Jack Colton."

"Then you must telegraph to Mr. Colton; and also you must telegraph to Frank Shirley's home. You must say that Frank is to come to you in New York at once. He mustn't lose an hour, you understand; my father will be here next week. Then, too, Frank will have heard of my engagement, and you can't tell what he might do."

Bates stared at her. "Do you know what you are doing, Miss Castleman?" he asked.

"I do," she answered.

"Very well, then," he said, "I will do what you ask."

"Go, do it now," she cried, and he went— carrying with him for the rest of his life the memory of her face of agony. He sent the telegrams, and in due course received replies—which he did not dare to bring to Sylvia himself, but sent by messenger. The first, from Frank's home, was to the effect that his whereabouts were unknown; and the second, from Jack Colton, was to the effect that Frank had gone away a couple of weeks before, saying that he would never return.

## § 23

SYLVIA wrestled this problem out with her own soul. The only person who ever knew about it was Aunt Varina, and she knew only because she happened to awaken in the small hours of the morning and hear signs of a fit of hysteria which the girl was trying to repress. She went into Sylvia's room and found her huddled upon the bed; when she asked what was the matter, the other sobbed without lifting her face—"Oh, I can't marry him! I can't marry him!"

Mrs. Tuis stared at her in consternation. "Why, Sylvia!" she gasped.

"Oh, Aunt Varina," moaned Sylvia, "I'm so unhappy! It's so horrible!"

"But, my child! You are out of your senses! What has happened?"

"I've come to realize the mistake I've made! I'd rather die than do it!"

Poor Aunt Varina was dumb with dismay. Sylvia had played her part so well that no one had had a suspicion. Now, between her bursts of weeping, she stammered out what she had learned. Frank was innocent. He had gone away forever—perhaps he had killed himself.

At any rate, his life was ruined, and Sylvia had done it.

"But, my child," protested the other, "you couldn't help it. How could you know?"

"I should have found out! I should have trusted Frank; I should have known that he could not do what they accused him of. I have been faithless to him—faithless to our love. And now what will become of him?"

Aunt Varina sat gazing at her, tears of sympathy running down her cheeks. "Sylvia," she whispered, "what will you do?"

"Oh, I love Frank Shirley!" moaned the girl. "I never loved anybody else—I never will love anybody else! And I know—what I didn't know at first—that it's wicked, wicked to marry without love!"

"But what will you do?" repeated the other, who was dazed with horror.

For a long time there was no sound but Sylvia's weeping. "Sylvia dear," began Aunt Varina, at last, "you must control yourself. You must not let these thoughts get possession of you. You will destroy yourself if you do."

"I can't marry him!" sobbed the girl.

"I can't let you go on talking that way!" exclaimed the other, wildly. "Do you realize what you are saying? Look at me, child, look at me!"

Sylvia looked. at her, wondering a little—for never had she seen such vehemence exhibited by this gentle and submissive "poor relation."

"Listen!" Mrs. Tuis rushed on. "How can you know that what you have heard is true? You say that Frank was innocent—but your Cousin Harley investigated, and he declared he was guilty. Mrs. Winthrop told you the same—she said everybody knew. And yet you take the word of one man! And you told me at Harvard that Mr. Bates was distressed at the idea of your marrying Mr. van Tuiver. You told me he warned you against him! Isn't that so, Sylvia?"

"Yes, Aunt Varina, but——"

"He does not like Mr. van Tuiver, and he comes here at a time like this, and puts such ideas into your thoughts. Don't you see that was not an honorable thing to do—when you were on the verge of being married and couldn't get out of it! When you know that your father would be utterly ruined—that your whole family would be wrecked by it!"

"Surely it can't be so bad, Aunt Varina!"

"Think how your father has gone into debt on your account! All the clothes you have bought—the bills at this hotel—the expenses of the wedding! Thousands and thousands of dollars!"

"Oh, I didn't want all that!" wailed Sylvia.

"But you did! You insisted on coming here to New York, where a wedding would cost several times as much as at home! You have come out before all the world as Mr. van Tuiver's fiancée—and think of the scandal and the disgrace, if you were to break it off! And poor Mr. van Tuiver

—what a figure he'd cut! And when he loves you so!"

Sylvia's sobbing had ceased during this outburst. When she spoke again, her voice was hard. "He does not love me," she said.

"Why, what in the world do you mean by that?"

"I mean just what I say. He doesn't love me—not as Frank loves me. He isn't capable of it."

"But then—why—for what other reason should he be marrying you?"

"I'm beautiful, and he wants me. But it's mainly because I offended his vanity—yes, just that! I turned him down, I ridiculed him and insulted him. I was something he couldn't get; and the more he couldn't get me, the more the thought of me rankled in his mind."

"Sylvia! How *can* you be so cynical!"

"I'm not cynical at all. I just won't gild things over, as other women do. I won't make pretences, I won't cover myself and my whole life with a cloak of shams. I know right now that I'm being sold, just as much as if I were led out to an auction-block with chains about my ankles! I'm being sold to a man—and I was meant to be sold to a man from the very beginning of my life!"

There was a silence; for Aunt Varina was paralyzed by these amazing words. She had never heard such an utterance in her life before. "Sylvia!" she cried. "What do you mean? *Who* is driving you?"

"I don't know!  But something is!"

"How can you say it?  Can you imagine that your good, kind parents—"

"Oh, no!" interrupted Sylvia, passionately. "At least—they don't know it!"

Mrs. Tuis sat dumfounded.  "Sylvia," she quavered, at last, "let me implore you to get yourself together before your father arrives in New York.  If he should hear what you have said to me to-night, he would never get over it—truly, it would kill him!"

## § 24

AN event to which Sylvia looked forward with considerable interest was a meeting with Mrs. Beauregard Dabney, who was coming to New York for a visit.  Harriet, as her letters showed, was not unappreciative of the glory which had descended upon her friend, and would enjoy having some of it reflected upon herself.  Thus Sylvia might be shown what emotions she ought to be feeling; possibly she might even be made to feel some of them.  At any rate, she knew that Harriet would help to keep her courage screwed up.

But Sylvia's pleasure in the visit was marred by a peculiar circumstance, which she had failed to prepare for, in spite of warnings duly given. "You must not be surprised when you see me,"

Harriet wrote. "I have been ill, and I'm terribly changed." Her reason for coming North, it appeared, was to consult specialists about a mysterious ailment which had baffled the doctors at home.

Sylvia was quite horrified when she saw her friend. Never could she have imagined such a change in anyone in six months' time. Harriet lifted her veil, and there was an old woman with wrinkled, yellow skin. "Why, Harriet!" gasped Sylvia, unable to control herself.

"I know, Sunny," said the other. "Isn't it dreadful?"

"But for heaven's sake, what is the matter?"

"That's what I've come to find out. Nobody knows."

"Why, I never heard of such a thing!" Sylvia exclaimed. "What are you doing?"

"I'm having all sorts of things done. The doctors give me medicine, but nothing seems to do any good. I'm really in despair about myself."

"How did it begin, Harriet?"

"I don't really know. There were so many things, and I didn't put them together. I began having headaches a great deal; and then pains that the doctors called neuralgia. I had a bad sore throat over in Europe; I thought the climate disagreed with me, but I've had it again at home. And now eruptions break out; the doctors treat them with things, and they go away, but then they come back. All my hair is falling out, and I've got to wear a wig."

25

"Why, how perfectly horrible!" cried Sylvia.

She started to embrace her friend, but was repelled. "I mustn't kiss anyone," said Harriet. "You see, it might be contagious—one can't be sure."

"But what are you going to do, Harriet?"

"I've almost given up hoping. I haven't really cared so much, since the doctors told me I can never have another baby. You know, Sunny, it's curious—I never cared about children, I thought they were nuisances. But when mine came, I cared—oh, so horribly! I wanted to have a real one."

"A real one?" echoed Sylvia.

"Yes. I didn't write you about it, and perhaps I oughtn't to tell you just at this time. But you know, Sunny, he didn't seem like a human being at all; he was a little gray mummy."

"Harriet!"

"Just like that—a regular skeleton, his skin all lose, so that you could lift it up in folds. He was a kind of earthy color, and had no hair, and no finger-nails——"

Sylvia broke out with a cry of horror, and her friend stopped. "I haven't talked to anyone about it," she said— "I guess I oughtn't to, even to you."

"How long did he live?"

"About six weeks. Nobody knew what he died of—he just seemed to fade away. You can't imagine it, perhaps—but, Sunny, I wanted him to stay—even him! He was all I could ever have, and it seemed so cruel!" Suddenly the girl hid her face in her hands and began to sob— the first time that Sylvia had ever seen her do it in all her life.

So it was not the cheering visit that Sylvia had anticipated. It left her with much to think about, and to talk about with other people. Later on, speaking to Aunt Varina, she happened to mention something that van Tuiver had said about the matter; whereupon her aunt exclaimed, "You didn't talk about it with Mr. van Tuiver!"

"But why not, Auntie?"

"You mustn't do that, dear! You can't tell."

"Can't tell what?"

"I mean, dear, that Harriet might have some disease that you oughtn't to talk to Mr. van Tuiver about." Aunt Varina hesitated, then added, in a whisper, "Some 'bad disease'."

Wherat Sylvia stared in sudden dismay. So *that* was it! A "bad disease"!

You must understand how it happened that Sylvia had ideas on this subject. There was a foreign writer of plays, whose name she had heard. She had never seen his books, and would not have opened one, upon peril of her soul; but once, in a magazine picked up in a train, she had read a casual reference to an Ibsen play, which dealt with a nameless and dreadful malady. From the context it was made clear that this malady was a price men paid for evil living—and a price which was often collected from their innocent wives and children. Now and then the women of Sylvia's family spoke in awe-stricken whispers of this mysterious taint, using the phrase "a bad disease." Now, apparently, she was beholding the horror before her eyes!

## § 25

THE problem occupied Sylvia's mind for several days, to the exclusion of everything else. It lent a new dread to the thought of marriage. How could a woman be safe from such a thing? Beauregard Dabney was not the most perfect specimen of manhood that one could have selected, but there was nothing especial the matter with him that could be observed. Yet see what had happened to his wife and child!

Harriet came again, and this time her husband was with her. He was just as much in love with her as ever—in fact, Sylvia thought that she noted a new and pathetic clinging on his part. They had been to see a great specialist, and still there was nothing definite to be learned about the malady; the doctor, hearing that the couple had journeyed up the Nile, suggested that possibly it might be an African fever, and promised to look up the mysterious symptoms in his books. Wasn't it extraordinary, exclaimed Harriet; but Sylvia, who could not be deceived for very long, noticed that Beauregard was not so much excited about the African theory as his wife. Suddenly the thought came to her, Could it be that the doctors really knew what the disease was, and would not tell Harriet? Could it be that Beauregard knew, and was helping in the deception? Then—horror of horrors—could it be that he had known all along, and had upon his conscience the crime of having brought the woman he loved into this state?

Sylvia's relentless mind, once having got hold of this problem, clung to it like a bull-dog to the throat of an enemy. Of course such a disease was a loathsome thing; a woman could not very well ask questions about it—yet, what was she to do? Apparently she was dependent upon the man's honor; and could it be that a man's notion if honor permitted him, when he was desperately in love, to take such chances with a woman's life? Sylvia remembered suddenly that Beauregard had made love to *her*. More than once she had actually permitted him to hold and fondle her hand. The mere thought made her shrink with horror.

And then came another idea. (How quickly she was putting things together!) Men got this disease by evil living. Then Beauregard must have done the sort of thing that Frank Shirley had been accused of doing! Also Jack Colton had done the same! Also—had not Bates said that there were some of the "Auburn Street crowd" in that place? Club-men, gentlemen, the aristocracy of Harvard! There came back to her the phrase from Harley's letter: "one of the two

or three high-class houses of prostitution which
are especially frequented by college men!" How
much Sylvia knew about this forbidden subject,
when she came to put her mind to it! More,
apparently, than her own parents—for had they
not shown themselves willing for her to fall in
love with Beauregard Dabney? More, also,
than Mrs. Winthrop—for had not that lady
implied that it was only low and obscure men
who permitted themselves such baseness?

As you may believe, it was not long before
Sylvia's thoughts came to her own intended
husband. What had been *his* life? What
might be the chances of her being brought to
such a fate as Harriet's? Apparently nobody
had any thought about it. They had been quick
to avail themselves of the appearance of evil
on the part of Frank Shirley; but what had they
done to make sure that van Tuiver had been any
better?

For three days Sylvia debated this problem;
and then her mind was made up—she would do
something about it. She would talk to someone.
But to whom?

She began with her faithful chaperone, men-
tioning the African fever theory, and so bringing
up the subject of "bad diseases." Just how
much did Aunt Varina know about these diseases? Not very much, it appeared. Was
there any way to find out about them? There
was no way that Aunt Varina could conceive—
it was not a subject concerning which a young
girl ought to inquire.

"But," protested Sylvia, "a girl has to marry. And think of taking such chances! Suppose, for instance, that Mr. van Tuiver——"

"Ssh!" Aunt Varina almost leaped at her niece in her access of horror. "Sylvia! how can you suggest such a thing?"

"But, Auntie, how can I be sure?"

"You surely know that the man to whom you have given your heart is a gentleman!"

"Yes, Auntie, but then I knew that Beauregard Dabney was a gentleman—and so did you. And see what has happened!"

"But, Sylvia dear! You don't know that it's *that!*"

"I very nearly know it. And if Beauregard was willing to marry when he——"

"But *he* may not have known it, Sylvia!"

"Well, don't you see, Aunt Varina? That makes it all the more serious! If Mr. van Tuiver himself can be ignorant, how can I feel safe?"

"But, Sylvia, what could you do?"

"Why, I should think he ought to go to some one who knows—a doctor—and make sure."

The poor old lady was almost speechless with horror. What was the world coming to? "How can you say such a thing?" she exclaimed. "You, a pure girl! Who could suggest such a thing to Mr. van Tuiver?"

"Couldn't Papa do it?"

"And pray, who is to suggest it to your father? Surely *you* couldn't!"

"Why no," said Sylvia, "perhaps not. But couldn't Mamma?"

"Your mother would *die* first!" And Sylvia, remembering her "talk" with "Miss Margaret," had to admit that this was probably true.

But still she could not give up her idea that something ought to be done. She took a couple of days more to think, and then made up her mind to write to her Uncle Basil. The family had sent him to talk with her about Frank's misconduct, thus apparently indicating him as her proper adviser in delicate matters.

So she wrote, at some length—using most carefully veiled language, and tearing up many pages which contained words she could not endure seeing on paper. But she made her meaning clear—that she thought someone should approach her future husband on the subject.

Sylvia waited the necessary period for the Bishop's reply, and read it with trembling fingers and flaming cheeks—although its language was even more carefully veiled than her own. The substance of it was that van Tuiver was a Christian gentleman, and this must be Sylvia's guarantee that he would not bring any harm to the woman he so deeply revered. Surely, if Sylvia respected him enough to marry him, she could trust him in a matter like this! To approach him upon it would be to offer him a deadly insult.

Whereupon Sylvia took several days more to worry and wonder. She was not satisfied at all, and finally summoned her courage and wrote to the Bishop again. It was not merely a question of honor; if that were true, she would have to say that Beauregard Dabney was a scoundrel, and she did not believe that. Might it not possibly be *knowledge* that was lacking? She begged her uncle to do her the favor of his life by writing to van Tuiver; and she intimated further that if he would not do it, she would have to put the matter before her father.

So there was another wait, and then came a letter from the Bishop, saying that he was writing as requested. Then, after a third wait, a letter with van Tuiver's reply. He had taken the inquiry very magnanimously; he could understand, he said, how Sylvia had been upset by the sight of her friend's illness. As to her own case, she might rest assured that there could be no such possibility. And so at last Sylvia's fears were allayed, and she was free to be unhappy about other matters.

## § 26

You must not imagine that Sylvia was spending these days in moping; all her thinking had to be done in the odd moments of a strenuous career. Day and night she had to meet new people, and new people were always an irresistible stimulus to her curiosity. Not all of them were hall-boys and shop-clerks, falling instant victims to her charms; on the contrary, they were Knickerbocker "society"—people not infrequently as wealthy as her future husband, and having an equally great notion of their own importance. The tidings that Douglas van Tuiver had picked up a country-girl had not thrilled them with sympathetic emotions. The details of the newspaper romance inspired them only with contempt. There had to be many a flash of Sylvia's rapier-wit, and many a flash of Sylvia's red-brown eyes, before these patrician plutocrats had been brought to acknowledge her an equal.

A few of these acquaintances were kindly people, whom she could imagine making into friends, if only there had been time. But she wondered how anybody ever found time for friendship in this restless and expensive and highly ornamental life. Such a whirl of dinner-parties and supper-parties, dances and luncheons and teas! Such august and imposing splendor, such dignified and even sombre dissipation! The Major had provided abundant credit for this last splurge; and van Tuiver's aunt was also on hand, conspiring with her nephew to smother Sylvia under loads of gifts. The girl wondered sometimes, was it that van Tuiver had suspicions of her wavering, and sought to bind her by forcing these luxuries upon her? Or would she be expected always to live this kind of Arabian Nights' existence?

There came old friends, to bask in the sunlight of her success. Miss Abercrombie came, effulgent with delight, assured of a lifetime's prosperity by this demonstration of her system. With her came Celeste, playing her difficult part with bitter pride. Harley Chilton ran down from Boston, bringing the tidings that he had made the "Dickey" and saw his way clear to the top of the Harvard pyramid. Last of all, two or three days before the wedding came "Queen Isabella," distributing her largess of blessings to all concerned.

First she met "Miss Margaret" and the Major, and addressed them with such mystical eloquence that the agitated pair had not a dry eye between them. After which she sought the prospective bride and bridegroom; and not even the most reverend millionaire bishop who was to perform the ceremony could have been more pontifical and impressive than our great lady in this solemn hour. We live in a cynical world, which affords but poor soil for the nurture of the finer flowers of the spirit. But Mrs. Winthrop was one really capable of experiencing the more exalted emotions, and of giving them ungrudging utterance. She was thrilled now by the vistas which she saw unfolding; not since the day of her espousal of the celebrated railroad-builder had the wings of the seraphim rustled so loudly about her head. She might have been compared to a creative artist who labors for long in solitude, and who at last, when he reveals his masterpiece, is startled by the clamor of the world's applause.

"Sylvia," she said, and put both her hands upon the girl's—"Sylvia, you have before you a great career, a career of service. You will be happy—I know you must be happy, dear, when once you have come to realize what an inspiration you are to others. Such fortune as yours falls but rarely to a woman, but you will be worthy of it—I believe you will be worthy of everything that has come to you."

"I hope so, Mrs. Winthrop," answered Sylvia, humbly.

And then, as van Tuiver discreetly moved away, the other went on, in a low and deeply-moved voice: "Don't imagine, dear girl, that I fail to realize all your doubts and perplexities. I know just how you feel, for I had to go through with it myself. Every woman does—but believe me, such tremors are as nothing compared to all the rest of one's life. We learn to subordinate our personal feelings, our personal preferences. That is one of the duties of those who have greatness as their lot—who have to live what one might call public lives."

Now, Sylvia might have her doubts as to the soundness of this doctrine, but she had none as to the genuineness of the speaker's feelings; so she was a trifle shocked when Mrs. Winthrop went away, and she discovered that her future husband was laughing.

"What is it?" she asked.

"Nothing," he said, "it's all right—only when you are Mrs. Douglas van Tuiver, you will receive Isabella's ecstasies with a trifle more reserve. You will realize that she has her own axes to grind."

"Axes—what do you mean?"

"Social axes. You'll understand my world bye-and-bye, Sylvia. Isabella's trying to make an impression beyond her income, and she's seeking alliances. What you must remember is that the need is on her side."

There was a pause, while Sylvia sat thinking. "Tell me," she said, at last, "why did Mrs. Winthrop change so suddenly, and begin urging me to marry you?"

"It's the same thing," he answered. "She couldn't afford to displease me. When she found that I was determined to have my way, she tried to make it seem her work. Naturally, she'd want as much of the prestige of this wedding as she could get."

Again Sylvia pondered. "Hasn't Mrs. Winthrop's husband enough money?" she asked.

"He has enough, but he won't spend it. The tragedy of Isabella's life is that her husband is really interested in railroads."

"But I thought he adored her!" Sylvia remembered a pathetic stout gentleman she had seen wandering about on the outskirts of a throng of the great lady's admirers.

"Oh, yes," replied van Tuiver, with laughter. "I never saw a woman who had a man more completely bluffed. But the trouble is that he offers himself, and what she wants is his money."

There followed a long silence. Van Tuiver had pleasant things to meditate upon; but suddenly he chanced to look at Sylvia, and exclaimed, "Why, what's the matter?"

"Nothing," she said, and turned away her head to conceal the tears she had failed to repress.

"But what is it?" he demanded, not without a touch of annoyance.

"There's no use talking about it," was Sylvia's reply. "It's just that you promised you would try not to think so much about money. Sometimes I can't help being frightened, when I realize that you don't ever believe in people—but only in money."

She saw the old worried look come back to his face. "You know that I believe in *you!*" he exclaimed.

"You told me," she answered, "that the only way I was able to make an impression upon you was by refusing to marry you. And now I have given up that prestige—so aren't you afraid that you may come to feel about me as you do about Mrs. Winthrop?"

## § 27

MAJOR and Mrs. Castleman arrived next morning, and after that there were busy times for Sylvia. There was the wedding-gown to be shown, and the trousseau and the presents; there were plans for the future to be told of, and many blessings to be received. "Miss Margaret" was in a "state" most of the time—tears of joy and tears of sorrow pursuing each other down her generous cheeks. "Sylvia," she exclaimed, in one breath, "I *know* you will be happy!" And then, in the next breath, "Sylvia, I *hope* you will be happy!" And then, in a third breath, "Sylvia, how will we ever get on without you? Who will dare to spank the baby?"

It was with her father that she had the really trying ordeal; her father took her into a room alone, and held her hands in his and tried to read her soul. "Tell me, my child, are you going to be happy?"

"I think so, Papa," she answered; and had to make herself look into his eyes.

"I want you to understand me, dear Sylvia— even now, at this last hour, don't take the step unless you believe with your best judgment that you will be happy."

There was a moment of madness, when she had the impulse to fling herself into his arms and cry, "I love Frank Shirley!" But instead of that she hurried on, "I believe he loves me deeply, Papa."

Said the Major, in a trembling voice, "There is no more solemn moment in a father's life than when he sees his dearly loved daughter taking this irrevocable step. I want you to know, my darling, that I have prayed earnestly, I have done my best to judge what is right for you."

"Yes, Papa," she said, "I know that."

"I want you to know that if ever I have seemed to be stern, it has been because I believed my daughter's welfare required it."

"Yes, Papa," she said, again.

"I am sure, this man loves you, Sylvia; and I believe he's a good man—he ought to make you happy. But I want you to know that if by any chance my prayers are denied—if you find that you are not happy—then your father's home will always be open to you, his arms will always be stretched wide to clasp you."

"Dear old Daddy!" whispered the girl. She felt the arms about her now, and she began to sob softly, with a mixture of emotions. Oh, if only she might stay for the balance of her life in the shelter of those arms, that were so strong and so dependable! If only there were not the dreadful thing called marriage—which drove her out into another pair of arms, from which she shrunk with such unconquerable aversion!

This was the heart of her difficulty — her inability to conquer her physical shrinking from the man to whom she was betrothed. Here she was, upon the very eve of her wedding, and she had made no progress whatever. Mentally and spiritually she had probed him, and felt that she knew him intimately; but physically he was still an utter stranger to her—as much so as any man she might have met upon the street. She would sit talking with him, trying to forget herself and her fears for a while; and gradually she would be conscious of his gaze upon her, his eyes traveling over her form, devouring her in thought, longing for her. Then she would go almost beside herself—she would have to spring up and break the chain of his thoughts. It seemed to her that she was like the prey of some wild beast—or a beast that was just tame enough to wait patiently, knowing that at a certain time the prey would be in its grasp.

On the evening before the wedding van Tuiver was to attend a "stag-dinner" with his friends; but he called in to see her for a few minutes, and the family discreetly left them alone. In a sudden access of longing, he clasped her in his arms, and she forced herself to submit. Then he began to kiss her, to press passionate kisses upon her cheek and throat. His breath was hot, and utterly horrible to her; she could not endure it, and cried out to him to stop, and struggled and pushed him away. Still holding her, and gazing at her with desire blazing in his eyes, he whispered, "Not yet?"

"Oh, how could you?" she cried.

"Is it not time you were beginning to learn?" he demanded; and then, wholly beside himself, "Sylvia, how much longer am I to endure this? Can't you understand what you make me suffer? I love you—I love you to distraction, and I get nothing from you—nothing! I dare not even tell you that I love you!"

The passion in his voice made her shudder; and yet, too, she pitied him. She was ashamed of herself for the way she treated him. "What can I do?" she cried. "I can't help it—as God is my witness, I can't control my feelings. I ask myself, ought I to marry you so?"

26

"'It seems to me it's rather late to bring up that question," he responded.

"I know, I know! I have nothing to say for myself—except that I didn't know, I couldn't realize. It's something I must tell you—how I have come to feel—that I ought not to marry you, that you ought not to want me to marry you, while things are like this. You must know this, so that if I marry you, the responsibility will be yours!"

"And you think that is fair of you?" he demanded, his voice grown suddenly hard.

He meant to rebuke her, and she felt that he had a right to rebuke her; but the wave of emotion which swept her along was not to be controlled by her reason. "Oh, you are going to be angry about it!" she cried. "How horrible of you!"

He exclaimed, "Sylvia! Can you expect me not to be hurt?"

"I told you that I couldn't help it! I told you in the very beginning that you would have to take me as I was, and be satisfied if I did my best! I told you that again and again—that I loved another man, that I love him still——"

She stopped. A spasm of pain crossed his face—followed by a look of fear. He hesitated, and then, his voice low and trembling, he began, "Sylvia, forgive me. I know that you are right—that you are trying to do your best. I will be patient. You must be patient with me also."

She stood, her head bowed, ashamed of what

she had said. Yet—she felt that he ought to have heard it. "I hate to seem unfair," she whispered, her voice almost breaking. "I don't want to give you pain, but I can't help these feelings, and I know it's my duty to tell you of them. I don't see how you can go on—I should think you would be afraid to marry me!"

For answer he caught her hands, exclaiming, "I will take my chances! I love you, and I will never rest until you love me!"

## § 28

So far I have put together this story from the memories of Sylvia and Frank Shirley. But now I have come to the point where you may watch the events through my own eyes. I will take a paragraph or two to give you an idea of the quality of these eyes, and then proceed without further delay.

Mary Abbott, the teller of this tale, was at the age of forty a crude farmer's wife upon a lonely pioneer homestead in Manitoba. In winter in that part of the world it begins to grow dark at three o'clock in the afternoon, and it is not fully light until nine o'clock in the morning. We were a mile from the nearest neighbor, and had often three feet of snow upon the ground, with fifty degrees below zero and a sweeping wind. I had a husband whom I feared and despised, and for whom I cooked and washed and sewed, whether I was well or ill. Under these circumstances I had raised three children to maturity. I had moved to town and seen them through high-school; and now, the girl being married, and the two boys in college, I found myself suddenly free to see the world.

You must not think of me as altogether ignorant. I had fought desperately for books, and had grown up with my children. Discovering in the town the perpetual miracle of a circulating library, I had read wildly, acquiring a strange assortment of new ideas. But that, I am ashamed to say, made very little difference when I reached the East. It is one thing to read up in the theory of Socialism, and say that you have freed yourself from *bourgeois* ideals; it is quite another to come from a raw pioneer community, and be suddenly hit between the eyes by all the marvels of the great New Nineveh!

I forgot my principles; I wandered about, breathless with excitement. Everything that I had ever read about, in Sunday supplements and cheap magazines—here it was before my eyes! I got myself a hall-room in a "Greenwich Village" boarding-house, and for days I went, thrusting my inquisitive country face into everything that was cheap enough. The huge shops with their amazing treasures of silks and jewels; the great hotels with their gold and stucco splendors; the dizzy, tower-like office-buildings; the newspaper offices with their whirling presses; the theatres, the museums, the parks; the Brooklyn Bridge and the Statue of Liberty, Grant's Tomb and the Bowery—I was the very soul of that thing which the New Yorker derisively calls the "rubber-neck wagon!" I took my place in one of these moving grand-stands, and listened to all that came out of the megaphone. Here was the home of the steel-king, which had cost three millions of dollars! Here was the home where a fifty thousand dollar chef was employed! Here was the old van Tuiver mansion, where the millionaire-baby had been brought up! Here was the Palace Hotel, where Miss Sylvia Castleman was staying!

It was the day before the wedding; and I, like all the rest of the city, was thrilling over the Romance, knowing more about the preparations than the bride herself. I had read all the papers —morning papers and afternoon papers; I had read descriptions of the wedding-gown, the trousseau, the rooms full of gift-treasures with detectives on guard. I had stared at the outside of the church, and imagined the inside. Last of all, I had wandered up to the Palace Hotel and peered about in the lobby, amusing myself by imagining that each gorgeous female creature who floated by and disappeared into a motor-car might possibly be the Princess herself!

At the boarding-house we discussed the possibility of seeing the wedding-cortege, and everybody said that I could not come within a block of the church. "I'll fight my way," I declared; to which the reply was that I would find out something about New York policemen that would cure me of my fighting impulses. The result of the discussion was that I set out immediately after breakfast, fired with the spirit of the discoverers of Pike's Peak.

I must get at least a glimpse, I told myself. What a tale to be able to tell at the Women's Club receptions at home! To say: "I saw her! She was the loveliest thing! And oh, her dress! It was cream-white satin, with four graduated flounces of exquisite point-lace!" Of course I could have got all that from the newspapers; but I wanted to be able to say it truly.

The wedding-hour was noon, but at nine there was already a respectable crowd. I established myself upon the steps of a nearby house, with a newspaper to sit on and a pair of borrowed opera-glasses in my hand-bag. In the meantime I entertained myself talking with the other watchers, who were a new type to me; well-dressed women, kept in luxury, whether legal or otherwise, who fed their empty minds upon fashion sheets and "society notes," and had no idea in the world beyond the decking of their persons and the playing of their little part in the great game of Splurge. We talked about the van Tuiver family, its history and its present status; we talked with awe about the bride; we talked about the presents, the decorations, the costumes—there was so much to talk about!

Shortly after ten o'clock a calamity befell us—the police began to clear the steps, driving the

crowd far back from the church-entrance. What
agonies, what expostulations! How outrageous
—when we had waited there an hour already!
Sometimes the steps were our own steps, sometimes they were the steps of friends; but even
that made no difference. "I'm sorry, lady, the
orders are to clear everything." They were as
gentle about it as they could be, but that was
none too gentle; we had the butt-ends of clubs,
pressing into our stomachs, and back we went,
arguing, scolding, threatening, sometimes weeping
or fainting.

I was tremendously disappointed. To have
to go back to the boarding-house, and admit
defeat to the milliner's assistant who sat next
to me at meals! To hear "I told you so" from
the "floor-walker" who sat across the way!
"I won't do it!" I said to myself.

And then suddenly came my chance. Behind
me there was a commotion, angry protests—
"Officer, let us through here! We have cards!"
Cards—how our souls thrilled as we heard the
word! Here, right close to us, were some of the
chosen ones! Let us see them at least—a bit of
Royalty at second hand!

They pushed their way through—three women
and two men. As they neared me, I saw the
engraved invitations in their hands, and it flashed
over me that in my hand-bag was a milliner's
advertisement of nearly the same size and shape.
I dived in, and fished it out with trembling fingers,
and fell in behind the party, and pushed through

the crowd past the line of police.  There before
me was the open space in front of the church!

I had acted on impulse, with no idea what to
do next.  I could scarcely hope to get in to the
wedding on a milliner's card.  But fortunately
my problem solved itself, for there were always
the guests pushing into the entrance, and everybody was perfectly willing to push ahead of me.
All I had to do was to "mark time," and I was
free to stay, inhaling delicious perfumes and
feasting my ears upon scraps of the conversation
of the *élite*.  I foresaw that the banner of the
great Northwest would wave triumphantly in
"Greenwich Village" that night!


### § 29


I WILL not stop to detail the separate thrills of
this adventure.  Carriage after carriage, motor
after motor drew up, and released new revelations
of grace and elegance.  The time for the ceremony drew near, and from the stir in the throng
about me I knew that the guests from the wedding-
breakfast were passing.  How I longed to talk to
someone—to ask who was this and that and the
other one!  Then I might have been able to tell
you how "Miss Margaret" wept, and how Aunt
Varina trembled, and what "Queen Isabella" was
wearing!  But the only persons I could be sure
of were the five lovely bridesmaids, and the bride,

leaning upon the arm of a stately old white-haired gentleman. How we craned our necks, and what rapture transported us! We heard the thunder of the organ and the orchestra within, and it corresponded to the state of our souls.

There was still quite a throng at either side of the entrance—newspaper reporters, people who had come out of houses nearby, people who, like myself, had got by the police-lines upon one pretext or another. Down the street we could see a solid line of bluecoats, and behind them people crowded upon steps, leaning out of windows, clinging to railings and lamp-posts. We were in fear lest at any time we might be ordered to join this throng, so we stayed silent and very decorous, careful not to crowd or to make ourselves conspicuous.

You might have expected, perhaps, that when all the protagonists of the drama had entered the church, the crowd would have dispersed; but not a soul went. We stood, listening to the faint music, and imagining the glories that were hid from our eyes. We pictured the procession up the aisle, with the guests standing on the seats in order to get a glimpse of it. We pictured the sacred ceremony. (There were some who had prayer-books in their hands, the better to aid their imaginations.) We pictured the bride, kneeling upon a white silk cushion embroidered with gold, receiving the blessings of the million-aire bishop. We heard the wild burst of chimes which told us that the two were made one, and our pulses leaped with excitement.

All this took perhaps half an hour; and I think
that about half that time had passed when I
first noticed Claire. I never knew how she got
there; but fate, or providence, or what you will,
had set her next to me, and that strange intuition
which sometimes comes to me, and puts me
inside the soul of another person in less time
than it takes for my eye to look them over, gave
me the warning of danger from her presence.

She was a tall and striking woman, beautifully
gowned, with high color and bold black eyes—
a woman you would have noticed in any gathering. You would have thought at once that she
was a foreigner, but you might have been puzzled
as to her country, for she had none of the characteristic French traits, and her English was
quite perfect. I glanced at her once, and thereafter I forgot everything else—the crowd, the
ceremony, all. What was the matter with this
woman?

What first made me turn was a quick motion,
as of a nervous spasm. Then I saw that her hands
were clenched tightly, and drawn up in front of
her as if she were struggling with someone.
Her lips were moving, yet I heard no sound; she
was staring in front of her fixedly, but at nothing.

I must explain that it did not occur to me
that she had been drinking. My country
imagination was not equal to that flight. To
be sure, since my arrival I had learned that the
women of the New Nineveh did drink; I had
peered into the "orange room," and the "palm

room," and several other strange rooms, and had seen gorgeous peacock-creatures with little glasses of highly-colored liquids before them. But I had not got so far as to imagine any consequences; I had never thought of connecting the high color in women's cheeks, the sparkle in women's eyes, the animation of women's chatter with the little glasses of highly-colored liquids. They had so many other reasons for being animated, these fortunate, victorious ones!

No, I only knew that this woman was excited; and I began forthwith to imagine most desperate and romantic things. You must remember what I said when I was first telling about Sylvia—that my ideas of the *grand monde* had been derived from cheap fiction in "Farm" and "Home" and "Fireside" publications. You all know the old story of the beautiful heroine who marries the dissolute duke; how the duke's cast-off mistress attends the wedding, and does something melodramatic and thrilling—perhaps shoots at the duke, perhaps throws vitriol at the bride, perhaps hands her a letter which is worse than vitriol to her innocent young soul. I smile when I think how instantly I understood this situation, and with what desperate seriousness I made ready to play my part—watching the woman like a cat, ready to spring and seize her at the first hostile move. And yet, after all, it was no joke, for Claire was really quite capable of a murderous impulse when she was in her present condition.

Other people had begun to notice her peculiar

behavior; I saw one or two women edging away from her, but I stayed all the closer. The time came when we heard the music of the Mendelssohn March, and the excitement in the crowd told us what was coming. Suddenly the doors of the church swung open—and there, in her radiant loveliness—the bride!

Her veil was thrown back, but her eyes were cast down, and she clung to the arm of her husband. Oh, what a vision she was, and what a thrill went about! For myself, however, I scarcely saw her. My eyes were on the strange woman.

She looked like a mad creature; quivering in every nerve, her fingers twisting and untwisting themselves like writhing snakes. She had crouched, as if ready to spring; and I had my hands within a foot of hers, ready to stop her. The procession moved through the passage kept clear by the police, and I literally held my breath while they passed—held it until the bride had stepped into a limousine, and the bridegroom had followed, and the door had slammed. Then suddenly the strange woman drew herself up and turned upon me, her face glaring into mine. I saw her wild eyes—and also I got a whiff of her breath. She laughed, a hysterical, hateful laugh, and muttered: "She'll pay for what she gets!"

I whispered "Hush!" But the woman cried again, so that several people heard her: "She'll pay for everything she gets from him!" She added a phrase in French, the meaning and im-

port of which I learned to understand long afterwards—"*Le cadeau de noce que la maîtresse
laisse dans la corbeille de la jeune fille!*" Then
suddenly I saw her sway, and I caught her and
steadied her, as I know how to steady people
with my big strong arms.

And that, reader, was the strange way of my
coming into the life of Sylvia Castleman!